three screenplays

by
Tom Bradley

Published by
Dog Horn Publishing
45 Monk Ings, Birstall, Batley WF17 9HU
United Kingdom
doghornpublishing.com

Cover art and author portrait by
David Aronson
AlchemicalWedding.com

Typesetting by
Jonathan Penton

UK Distribution: Central Books
99 Wallis Road, London, E9 5LN, United Kingdom
orders@centralbooks.com
Phone:+44 (0) 845 458 9911
Fax: +44 (0) 845 458 9912

Overseas Distribution: Printondemand-worldwide.com
9 Culley Court
Orton Southgate
Peterborough
PE2 6XD
Telephone: 01733 237867
Facsimile: 01733 234309
Email: info@printondemand-worldwide.com

three screenplays

tom bradley

VITAL FLUID

Dedicated to **JOHN-IVAN PALMER**
Hypnotist on the stage
Mesmerist on the page

Then Philip went and preached unto them...
But there was a certain man, called Simon,
which beforetime in the same city used sorcery,
and bewitched the people...
—Acts 8:5-9

The pointed finger of the stage hypnotist is
the same finger used by ancient healers in
the Temple of Sleep.
—John-Ivan Palmer

FADE IN

EXT. KANSAS RODEO CORRAL--SUNSET

A scratchy old record of "Great Balls of Fire" plays full-blast on tin speakers.

A crowd of small-town FOLKS sits in the stands, spellbound.

In the middle of the corral, where bulls and steers normally stomp around, is a husky farm-boy named BIFF.

He does a Jerry Lee Lewis impression to the music, lip-synching the verses of the song, using an upturned water trough as a piano. At first, it's hard to tell how this behavior could hold the Folks' attention so firmly.

But a closer look reveals something strange and amazing about Biff.

His performance is uncanny. His lips match the words perfectly, and his fingers make the exact motions of Jerry Lee's piano riffs. The expression on his face, the wiggling of his butt--everything he does is inspired. Biff is almost better than the original.

Weirdest of all, his eyes are shut the whole time. He seems unaware of his own presence in the corral.

Standing off to one side is a man dressed in an electric-blue tux with a plum satin cummerbund. His hair is done in the big way of professional stage entertainers, and his face is made up accordingly.

This is PHIL DEACON, "the World's Greatest Stage Hypnotist," according to a glittery placard propped nearby.

He's thirty-five years old, tallish, slim, and kindly. Phil has a good baritone speaking voice that he tones down, making it somewhat flat and nasal, to avoid intimidating his audience.

He switches off the music.

PHIL

(into a microphone)

Okay, well done. When I snap my fingers

you will no longer be Jerry Lee Lewis. You'll go back to being Biff. You'll feel calm and relaxed...

He snaps his fingers.

Poor Biff nearly dies when he sees the whole town staring at him in amazement. When they burst into applause, all he can do is clamber over the corral and skedaddle across an alfalfa field.

Biff heads west, toward the setting sun and Main Street, which stretches along two blocks at the far edge of the field.

After the gas station, the town's most conspicuous building is The Bijou, a little movie theater straight from the forties. Through deepening sunset shadows, the MANAGER can be seen unlocking the front door and dragging in a big plastic bag of popping corn.

But Phil's not looking across the field at Main Street. He stares at his audience instead.

He listens to their cheers, and realizes for the first time what a great show it's been. He was so bored, he didn't notice.

PHIL

(eagerly)

Wasn't that fantastic, ladies and gentlemen? Biff's a splendid lad, but you know as well as I that he couldn't have given us such a stellar performance without a little help. And where did that help come from? I'll tell you where. Inside his own head. In the same place where every human being has limitless stores of talent and energy, which most of us are never aware of, and...

The Folks have stopped listening. They're vacating the stands.

PHIL
(into the microphone)
...and you're abandoning me faster than most sod-busters do. Must be time to change the filters in your backyard meth labs.

Nobody heard that, and Phil's not surprised. But he is puzzled at the speediness of this particular mass exit.

Then he turns and sees that The Bijou has switched on its lights for the evening. According to the marquee, tonight's feature is--

MeL gIBbSUns pASiON OfF ChRIzt

PHIL
Stiff competition.

He watches the Folks make their pilgrimage through the alfalfa stubble to The Bijou.

Only one person remains.

Hulking by the beer concession is a very large middle-aged woman with strange vacuum-eyes. She wears a black bra under a loose tank top. A faded tattoo between her deflated breasts makes her cleavage look like a seismic crack in a granite wall. Her whole big body is flexed, like a single anguished muscle. She stares at Phil with a mindless kind of appetite.

This is the BIG WEIRD WOMAN. Phil knows her all too well, and averts his eyes.

EXT. INTERSTATE HIGHWAY--NEXT DAY

Phil's car speeds along the ruler-straight road, cutting across the prairie, toward the eastern slope of the Rocky Mountains. He's trying to make it to his next gig on time.

INT. PHIL'S CAR

He reaches into the back seat and grabs a well-worn old book: "The Life and Times of LaFontaine the Mesmerizer."

Steering with his right hand, he holds the book in his left

and begins to read. Moving his eyes back and forth from the page to the road, Phil gradually starts spending more time reading than driving.

The needle on his speedometer climbs ever closer to the eighty mark.

INT. PARIS OPERA HOUSE--EVENING

It's 1874, and LAFONTAINE is having one of his usual triumphs.

Huge and perfect, a demigod with a mountain of shining black curls on his head, he stands on the stage of the freshly built Paris Opera House.

The place is a marvel of neo-baroque opulence, with marble statues, jewel-studded arches, crystal chandeliers and gold-leafed pillars gleaming everywhere.

The vast dome overhead features a fresco of God in his Heaven, being serenaded by hundreds of plump, rosy angels.

Several PRINCES are in the audience, along with MARQUISES, DUCHESSES, and various other continental glitterati of the time, each dressed more beautifully than the next.

It's a capacity crowd, and they're all on their feet, loudly expressing their amazement, and their love, for Monsieur LaFontaine, the greatest of all mesmerizers.

INT. PHIL'S CAR--DAY

Doing eighty now, Phil has dropped the book and removed his hand from the steering wheel.

He has mentally traveled across the Atlantic and back in time, and now shares the soul of LaFontaine.

Phil does the same thing with LaFontaine that Biff did with Jerry Lee Lewis: synching his eloquent lips, mirroring his facial expressions, mimicking his grand gestures to perfection.

Phil's eyes are shut just as tightly as Biff's were, as the car speeds along.

INT. PARIS OPERA HOUSE--EVENING

LaFontaine bows gracefully as a ballet dancer, as red roses rain down on him. He waves massive, white-gloved hands through the air like a magician or a priest.

Stretched out before him is a lovely young NOBLEWOMAN, completely under his power. She looks like an angel in a white satin gown. Her body is suspended between two intricately carved rosewood chairs, which touch only the back of her neck and her ankles.

LAFONTAINE
(his voice is magnificent)
You hear only my voice...

EXT. PRAIRIE INTERSTATE--DAY

The flat-lands lurch into the foothills of the Rockies.

LAFONTAINE (VO)
Your will is not your own, but has merged with the vital fluid that emanates from my mind...

Phil's heading straight for an outcrop of granite.

INT. PHIL'S CAR

LAFONTAINE (VO)
(Phil lip-synchs)
Universal forces hold your astral body in suspension, like a pearl dissolved in ocean water...

With grace worthy of LaFontaine, he regains control just in time, and penetrates the canyons of Colorado.

EXT. SUBURBAN DENVER HIGH SCHOOL--SAME DAY

High-country right-wing FUNDAMENTALISTS are picketing Phil's appearance at a student assembly. They carry signs equating him with Satan, Bin Laden, and Bill Clinton.

A local TV NEWS CREW is on the scene. The reporter is CANDY, a happy-talker in her early twenties.

CANDY
Speak of the devil, here, um, he is...
(fumbling with her notes)
Phil Dinkum, the World's Greatest Magician! Welcome to the Denver area, Mr. Dingus!

She gets hit with an egg intended for Phil.

PHIL
I didn't know sawing ladies in half could be so controversial.

He pauses to consider whether it's worthwhile dealing further with Candy. The decision is made for him when the demonstrators surge forward and knock her CAMERAMAN on his ass.

At the front of the mob, doing most of the pushing, is SIMON MAGUS.

He's in show-biz, too, like Phil, but sleazy and sinister. His sharp, envious eyes notice everything.

Today Simon has camouflaged his big-city flashiness under Intermountain Western attire and manners. He's got the natural-fiber, earth-tone shirt, but his gaudy gold neck chains glint between the buttons.

Phil is just trying to get into the venue without being burnt at the stake. But he stops long enough to face Simon Magus.

PHIL
Since when do these people need the services of an outside agitator?

When Simon replies, he disguises his evil-sounding New York accent under a bland Far-Western twang.

SIMON
(trying not to snicker)
Go to Eye-rack and feed on A-rab children instead of ours!

PHIL
I guess this is the only way you can

get near a high school nowadays, eh, Simon?

SIMON
(angry now, shouting)
Beelzebub! Moloch!

The Fundamentalists take up the cry and turn it into a chant.

The loudest chanter is the Big Weird Woman. She has beaten Phil here, all the way from Kansas.

In her loose tank top, black bra and tattoo, she doesn't fit in with the crowd at all, but it seems not to bother her. In fact, nothing bothers her. She has all the emotions of a zombie.

The Big Weird Woman has eyes only for Phil--which is strange, because she has linked arms with Simon Magus, and is clearly associated with him in some bent way.

Among the Fundamentalists are two HOUSEWIVES, one plump, the other skinny. They are deeply offended by the idea of stage hypnosis, and by Phil himself. Their faces are red-hot and their bodies pulsate with strong emotions.

When Phil elbows through, brushing them with the electric-blue tails of his tux, these two Housewives nearly faint in righteous mortification.

Their HUSBANDS, a couple of suburban wimps, blush and simper apologetically at Phil.

INT. HIGH SCHOOL--AT THE SAME TIME

A beefy RENT-A-COP encourages a German shepherd to gnash and claw at students' lockers. The dog's snarls are drowned out by the beeps of metal detectors that occupy several doorways.

Outside the nurse's office, REGULAR BOYS wait to be chemically castrated for the day. The SCHOOL NURSE, who's built like an Olympic hammer thrower, hands out pills like candy.

A couple of TROUBLED TEENS, made up like Marilyn Manson,

try to sneak past her. But she detains them.

NURSE
Very funny. Bratty kids.

Using half a packet of Wet-Wipes and a quantity of grandmotherly saliva, the Nurse soon has their pimples makeup-free. She fusses over them and sends them on their way with a couple love-pats on their butts.

NURSE
Now, you rascals behave yourselves today.

INT. HIGH SCHOOL AUDITORIUM--A BIT LATER

The Fundamentalists' chanting can be heard outside, muffled through the barred windows.

FUNDAMENTALISTS (OS)
Beelzebub! Moloch! Beelzebub! Moloch!...

In the back of the auditorium some BAD KIDS aren't paying attention. They're entranced by ear-plugged electronic radios and pocket video games.

A TEACHER, stuck with patrol duty, cowers nearby. He suffers from all the tics of terminal nervous exhaustion. Someone snaps bubblegum and he ducks.

The Bad Kids don't even bother to laugh at him. That's how jaded they are.

On the stage, Phil has put a half-dozen NICE KIDS under hypnosis.

A sweet little PUNK GIRL is up there, all black leather and pink lace, with a flashing tongue stud and turquoise-spiked hair. She's faking it, but Phil doesn't mind in her case.

The Nice Kids currently think they're on the moon.

PHIL
Time for you astronauts to put on your space suits, so we can leave the landing module and stretch our legs.

The COOPERATIVE BOYS are good at this. They give their imaginary helmets that half-twist, which every sci-fi fan knows is required to lock the apparatus on your shoulders.

PHIL
Don't forget your gravity boots.

Leaving her classmates to struggle with nine-pound footwear, the Punk Girl exits the spacecraft, blissfully unshod.

EXT. THE MOON--DAY

She dances ten feet over the lunar surface.

Phil stands in a crater below, observing her with fatherly affection.

PHIL
(quietly, into the mike)
Watch out for meteors, dear.

The planet Earth rises over the pearly-white horizon, bathing everything in bright blue light, including Phil's face.

With a couple waves of his hands, he brings down Jupiter and Saturn, and stretches out the Punk Girl between them, just like LaFontaine's lovely Noblewoman.

PHIL
Stay up there, honey. It's much safer.

We hear the cheers and "bravos" of the Princes, Marquises and Duchesses at the Paris Opera House.

INT. HIGH SCHOOL AUDITORIUM--AT THAT MOMENT

Phil's taking a deep bow, with all the grand flourishes of LaFontaine.

The few STUDENTS who are paying attention start laughing at him, and he snaps out of it.

INT. HIGH SCHOOL MAIN ENTRANCE--A BIT LATER

Simon Magus infiltrates the building, walking through the

metal detector and right past the check-point without being subjected to the routine cavity search.

The Rent-a-Cop doesn't notice Simon. Even the German shepherd stalks by without snapping at him.

He slinks down the corridor.

INT. AUDITORIUM--A FEW MOMENTS LATER

Simon comes in and loiters at the back among the Bad Kids.

He eyes the Punk Girl lasciviously as she wriggles and slides around the stage.

PHIL
(glaring at Simon)
I know there's at least one wanna-be hypnotist out there, and I'd rather my secrets not get stolen. So, pay no attention to this.

He points at Simon and snaps his fingers--to no apparent effect.

The two Troubled Teens slither onto the stage and follow the Punk Girl around, mocking her dance movements in a mean teen way.

Phil tries to put them under with a couple light bops on the forehead. They fake it, stumbling all over the place, thinking themselves quite clever. He's not fooled.

PHIL
Thanks so much, guys.
(off-mike)
You can go away now.

They put their faces right up against his in a challenging manner, and lift their tee shirts just enough to reveal what appears to be a couple of nine-millimeter semi-automatic handguns tucked under their belts.

Phil looks straight into their faces, one after the other.

PHIL
You kiddies should pull up those darn

britches. Everybody can see your thingies.

The Troubled Teens have been put further under than they know. They cover themselves and leave the stage, rapidly as five-year-olds who need to go potty.

PHIL
(winking at the Punk Girl)
The Ritalin must have kicked in.

Simon hasn't missed a thing that just happened.

He quietly claps his hands, applauding Phil's handling of the situation, pretending to be merely amused.

But Simon is, in fact, impressed by Phil's skill. His face contorts with a flash of agonized envy. He considers Phil a professional rival.

The Punk Girl looks at Simon in fascination, until Phil sends her and her classmates on another errand.

PHIL
Let's play a little B-ball at the bottom of a sea of kiwi marmalade.

The Cooperative Boys dribble and slam dunk more realistically, but the Punk Girl has the marmalade down pat.

PHIL
The darn ball sure is buoyant. Don't let it get away from you!

As he works, Phil keeps one anxious eye on Simon's doings at the back.

By some invisible means, Simon has attracted several of the Bad Kids to his side. He chats them up, no doubt implanting all manner of anti-social post-hypnotic suggestions into their already addled minds.

Simon discreetly purchases a baggie of Ecstasy from them, and passes some to the Big Weird Woman, who has materialized in the shadows behind him.

She gobbles the poison obediently.

He hands her some more, and she gobbles that.

The Bad Kids are amazed when Simon repeats the process yet again. This time he adds a theatrical flourish of the hands, causing the Big Weird Woman to stiffen like a board, her arms out in the crucified position.

The Bad Kids are the only ones doing any applauding today.

EXT. CHEAP DENVER MOTEL PARKING LOT--THAT NIGHT

The two Housewives from the demonstration come looming out of the darkness, their faces and bodies stained lurid red by a big VACANCY sign.

They seem to be lying in wait for someone.

INT. SUV--AT THAT MOMENT

Their wimpy husbands have been told to wait in the SUV.

The FIRST HUSBAND cowers behind the wheel, the SECOND HUSBAND cringes in the death seat. Both are looking out the windows self-consciously.

FIRST HUSBAND
Can I share feelings?

SECOND HUSBAND
You know I'm here.

FIRST HUSBAND
(earnestly searching for words)
Well...
(chokes up)

SECOND HUSBAND
(whispering)
It's okay. It's okay.

FIRST HUSBAND
Sometimes I really feel that it can be kind of, um, emasculating, in a way, to be married to someone who's so... well, so darn brim-full of the Holy Spirit.

The Second Husband is feeling too emotional right now to reply.

EXT. CHEAP DENVER MOTEL PARKING LOT--A MINUTE LATER

Phil just wants to get into his squalid room, but the Housewives bar his way.

PLUMP HOUSEWIFE
(breathlessly)
He used enchantments, and used witchcraft...

SKINNY HOUSEWIFE
...and dealt with a familiar spirit, and with wizards.

PLUMP HOUSEWIFE
And he wrought much evil in the sight of the Lord, to provoke him to anger!

SKINNY HOUSEWIFE
Chronicles Two, chapter thirty-three--

PHIL
Verse six. You don't say.

The Housewives are deeply affected to discover this evil man's familiarity with the Word of God. They begin to close in on him.

PLUMP HOUSEWIFE
The Lord God caused a deep sleep to fall upon the man.

SKINNY HOUSEWIFE
(waving her fingers hypnotically)
A deep, de-e-e-ep sleep.

PLUMP HOUSEWIFE
(eyeing the door of Phil's room)
And while he slept...

SKINNY HOUSEWIFE
... took one of his ribs and closed up its place with f-f-f-flesh.
(almost fainting at the F-word)

PLUMP HOUSEWIFE
And with the rib, he made woman...

She hikes up her skirt to display a scarlet thong.

Phil is not surprised.

PLUMP HOUSEWIFE
...and brought her to him!

She also hikes up her skirt, to display an identical scarlet thong. Hers is barely visible under rolls of cellulite.

PHIL
Genesis, chapter two, verse...whatever. Christ almighty.

He's already opened his LaFontaine book and found his place before shutting the door on the Housewives' squeals and grunts.

INT. PHIL'S SQUALID MOTEL ROOM--NIGHT

Phil kicks off his shoes, undoes his plum satin cummerbund, tosses it over the television, and stands in the middle of the room.

Holding his book up high, like an opera singer with a libretto, he begins to read some more about LaFontaine the Mesmerizer.

INT. PARIS SALON--EVENING

LaFontaine stands majestically in the middle of the floor in an opulent parlor, furnished in the most elaborate style of the day.

It's a soiree of late nineteenth-century Europe's most brilliant intelligentsia, including a POET, a few ARTISTS, a couple PHILOSOPHERS, and their aristocratic HANGERS-ON.

The HOST is a fabulously wealthy nouveau riche from the world of international finance, who knows just enough to keep his mouth shut.

Also present, of course, are several of the world's most

BEAUTIFUL WOMEN. They stare at LaFontaine, enrapt, flushed with spiritual aspirations.

Remaining aloof is BARON DUPOTET. He is plump and swarthy, with a cruelly sensual mouth and serpent's eyes. He simmers with envy.

PHILOSOPHER
Monsieur LaFontaine! I heard you were languishing in a southern prison.

LAFONTAINE
And so I was. The king of Naples allowed me to roll the stone from the sepulcher and come forth.

PAINTER
Surely you mesmerized his Neapolitan Majesty to gain such clemency.

LAFONTAINE
He did set one condition.

HANGER-ON
Which was?

LAFONTAINE
That I cease restoring sight to the blind and hearing to the deaf.

POET
But, Monsieur LaFontaine, why would the king have you behave so uncharitably toward the wretches of this world?

LAFONTAINE
A small matter of the all-too-faithful imitation of Christ.

Everyone titters at this near-blasphemous remark, except Baron Dupotet.

BARON DUPOTET
You imitate Christ, LaFontaine? Bah! Mesmerism's pretensions toward healing were pooh-poohed a hundred years ago by no less a personage than Doctor

Guillotine--

BEAUTIFUL WOMAN

--who deserved to be consulted on the topic of staying healthy. Right up till the moment of death.

More titters are heard.

LaFontaine looks at the Beautiful Woman with chaste appreciation. She nearly melts under his eyes.

He turns to deal with the Baron.

LAFONTAINE

It's a matter, my dear Dupotet, of psychologizing--or "animal-magnetizing," as you would inaccurately say--the astral body, which is poised intermediate between the spiritual and physical--

BARON DUPOTET

I don't require schooling on the rudiments of our art.

LAFONTAINE

But I'm afraid you do. I wouldn't call it "our" art, in any case.

Baron Dupotet swells with anger.

The Poet looks as though he'll expire like a delicate flower if this conflict escalates any further.

He withdraws from the inner circle and approaches a purple couch situated in the corner among exotic potted ferns.

Sitting upon this couch is a seven-foot-tall Punjabi HINDU.

Curled up next to him is a Roman Catholic CARDINAL, capped and robed in red satin, an envoy from the Vatican. He's almost as tall as the Hindu, and is obviously his lover--for tonight, at any rate.

The Hindu wears a vast white turban with a fist-sized ruby pinned at the helm. Wrapped in the serpentine hose of an exquisite jade hookah, he shares slow sips of soup-thick narcotic smoke with the Cardinal.

The two of them listen to LaFontaine with a pleased look in their eyes.

The Poet tries to appropriate some opiated hashish from an alabaster box which the Hindu holds in the palm of one gigantic hand.

HINDU
That's Soma. Or something near enough. It's not intended for profane consumption. Aryans only.

POET
But those two megalomaniacs are going to draw stilettos any moment. It's so unpleasant to have corpses bleeding underfoot at soirees this time of year.

CARDINAL
I'm enjoying their contretemps.

HINDU
LaFontaine is quite good.

POET
The Baron needs mollification.

The Poet and the Hindu have a friendly mock battle over the narcotic morsel, slapping one another's hands away. The Poet prevails, and comes away in triumph with the prize.

CARDINAL
(calling after him)
Don't mollify our two wonder-workers too much. His Eminence, the Holy Father in Rome, has a very important job for both of them.

The Poet lays the hashish on the green marble mantelpiece and proceeds to knead it together with some potent-looking herbs from his waistcoat pocket.

The resulting concoction is nestled in golden spoons and passed around on a silver tray.

Baron Dupotet gobbles two helpings, then three. His eyes grow red and aggressive with intoxication.

BARON DUPOTET
So, LaFontaine, do you have your way with those lovely young subjects of yours?

LAFONTAINE
(glancing at Dupotet's plump belly)
I'm not quite so comfortably confined in my coat of flesh as you are in yours, Monsieur le Baron.

Dupotet is enraged by that remark. He snatches a golden spoon of the hashish mixture and brandishes it in LaFontaine's face like a poisoned dagger.

The great mesmerist turns aside in revulsion.

INT. PHIL'S SQUALID MOTEL ROOM--DAWN

At the bathroom mirror, Phil turns aside in identical revulsion from his own foaming toothbrush.

LAFONTAINE (VO)
(Phil lip-synchs)
Unlike yours, Dupotet, my body plays host to no demons that demand nourishment.

Through the corner of one eye, Phil observes the image of himself in the mirror. He practices arching his eyebrows and lowering his eyelids with haughty disdain.

But he doesn't disdain his toothbrush for long, because sunlight is already seeping through the hideous motel drapes.

He's got a long drive to his next gig.

EXT. SOUTHERN UTAH DESERT--LATER THAT DAY

A native-American Indian named MILTON, wearing plaid Bermuda shorts and a loud Hawaiian shirt, squats and smokes a cigarette at the edge of a high sandstone cliff.

He appears to be standing guard, in a very relaxed manner, over a nearby cavern, whose entrance has been fitted with a sturdy aluminum grate and a padlock.

Milton looks out into the bright distance and sees a small cloud of dust moving slowly along the unpaved road, far below.

It's being raised by Phil's car.

Milton smiles and takes a drag on his cigarette. He blows the smoke in the direction Phil's traveling.

EXT. INDIAN RESERVATION GATE--A FEW MOMENTS LATER

This is the terminus of the unpaved road.

The GATEKEEPER, an old Indian woman, sits on an upturned Royal Crown Cola crate, holding a battery-operated cassette tape player to her ear.

She scats toothlessly along with Thelonious Monk's "Epistrophe."

GATEKEEPER
(eyes closed, deep in the groove)
Sha-boopadee-yop a-gloopadee pow-pow-wow...

For no apparent reason, she looks up and smiles.

She climbs slowly to her arthritic feet and starts to untie the lasso that holds the gate shut.

EXT. DIRT ROAD--SAME DAY

Phil's car, with him at the wheel, eases through the sand and rocks.

He sticks his head out the window now and then, watching for chuck-holes.

PHIL
(trying to hypnotize his car)
Let's not break an axle today.

On the left, a T-intersection appears.

Leading off at ninety degrees is an asphalt road--a strange enough sight for these parts. The freshly painted yellow stripe down the middle is almost blinding in the desert sunlight.

It stretches into the waterless distance, toward something that, in the wobbling heat waves, resembles a small state penitentiary, or a military installation.

A sign reads--

SAMARIA, UTAH
INCORPORATED MUNICIPALITY
POPULATION 140

A billboard stands nearby. It features a white woman who would look right at home in the big city, busting mighty men's balls at the helm of a major corporation.

It reads--

RE-ELECT JEZ AHAB, COUNTY ATTORNEY

INT. PHIL'S CAR

Shuddering, he tries not to look at her.

He continues driving straight down the dirt road, toward the Indian reservation, a little faster than before.

A helicopter is heard crossing his path overhead.

EXT. HELICOPTER--AT THAT MOMENT

It's a scarlet Huey, trimmed in black, bearing a severe-looking stylized letter A.

INT. HELICOPTER

At the controls sits an eighteen-year-old, red-haired, blue-eyed PILOT, dressed in a brown uniform resembling those worn by military cadets.

Simon Magus is strapped in a passenger seat, grinning down

at Phil's car and its little cloud of dust.

Simon straightens up a bit when, up front, through the cockpit window, his destination heaves into view--

EXT. SAMARIA, UTAH--SAME DAY

It's an anti-oasis of concrete and asphalt, seeming deader and drier than the surrounding desert.

Several simple, low-slung, but solid buildings are arranged in an orderly compound, secure behind the sort of razor wire and electrified chain-link that brings correctional institutions to mind.

The gate is heavy and motorized, and bears the same letter-A logo as the helicopter.

There's no sign of life, other than the SENTRY, another red-haired, blue-eyed lad, who stands at attention in a uniform identical to the Pilot's.

Though barely more than a child, this Sentry is far too disciplined to look up at the approaching chopper.

EXT. "BIG HEAP O' WAMPUM"--SAME DAY

This is a casino which the Indians maintain on their reservation.

Despite their attempts to trot out every stale redskin stereotype that might appeal to ignorant Caucasians--teepees, totem poles, etc.--it's a sadly languishing concern.

A few white ranchers from the vicinity wander in and out, by no means high rollers.

Three sunburned JAPANESE TOURISTS in dusty hiking clothes stand on the casino's front stoop, looking puzzled.

FIRST JAPANESE
(in Japanese)
Ask somebody where the arches are.

Most alien of all is a MIDDLE-AGED COUPLE FROM BACK EAST.

FEMALE BACK-EASTERNER
(a very thick accent)
Oh, look, Lenny. Papooses.

She's referring to several dozen Indian YOUNGSTERS, boys and girls, toddlers, teens and everything in between, who move past in a quietly cheerful mass.

They steer clear of the visitors, politely declining to pose for photos, and proceed around to the back of the casino.

EXT. BEHIND THE CASINO--DAY

The Youngsters approach the tribal meeting ground, an open-air enclosure, the periphery of which is marked with a circle of interestingly shaped sandstone boulders.

Propped against one of these rocks is a life-size cardboard cut-out of Phil. He's in his electric-blue tux and plum satin cummerbund, and he's got hypnotic eyes and hands.

Glittery letters read--

PHIL DEACON, WORLD'S GREATEST STAGE HYPNOTIST

An old fellow leans against this cut-out, his gnarled brown hand resting on Phil's shoulder.

His fine turquoise beads, along with the white eagle feather stuck in the band of his cowboy hat, reveal him to be the tribal MEDICINE MAN.

He does a Phil-impression for some OLDER BOYS, who grin back at him, and pass into the enclosure.

An amazingly beautiful Indian MAIDEN of about fourteen walks by. She trusts the Medicine Man enough to try out what promises, someday, to be a formidable set of flirtatious skills. She eyes him sidelong and makes tentative little motions with her slender hips.

The Medicine Man tilts his head and sighs, as if overwhelmed with adoration. His knees start to wobble comically and he grabs his chest.

She breaks into girlish giggles and scampers off.

A tiny TYKE comes to a halt before the cut-out. Sucking an index finger, he looks up at Phil's plum satin cummerbund, unsure if it's safe to go any further.

MEDICINE MAN

You're gonna love this guy. He's a riot.

The Youngsters move into the tribal meeting ground and sit on wooden benches, creating an easy, natural order of their own accord, needing no authority figure to tell them how to go about it.

INTERCUT BEWTWEEN INDIAN RESERVATION AND SAMARIA

INT. SAMARIA BOYS' ACADEMY

Male CADETS, ages six through eighteen, silent and unsmiling, buttoned tightly into uniforms like the Pilot's and the Sentry's, march in lockstep down harshly fluorescent-lit corridors.

EXT. TRIBAL MEETING GROUND

In open air and sunshine, the Indian Youngsters rearrange the benches as they please, without making a big deal of it.

A general circular configuration is more or less preserved, with loose adjustments here and there to make sure everyone gets a good view of the upcoming show.

INT. SAMARIA BOYS' ACADEMY 3RD-GRADE CLASSROOM

LITTLE CADETS, perfectly disciplined, file in and occupy desks bolted in rows on the glaring linoleum floor.

In unison, they take out spotless copies of their textbook: a facsimile edition of a very stern-looking nineteenth-century primer.

EXT. TRIBAL MEETING GROUND

A BIG BOY has taken the scared Tyke by the hand. He leads him to a good seat and sits next to him.

BIG BOY
(with mock solemnity)
Don't worry. I'll protect you from the weird white guy.

The Tyke looks up and starts to laugh.

INT. SAMARIA BOYS' ACADEMY MARTIAL ARTS ROOM

NINTH-GRADE CADETS are learning to defend themselves against broken bottles and flung chairs.

EXT. TRIBAL MEETING GROUND

A GRANDPA and GRANDMA show up. The Grandpa's carrying a big thermos and a stack of paper cups.

GRANDMA
We want to be entranced. Can we come, too?

Lots of Youngsters scoot over for them.

GRANDPA
I brought lemonade.

GRANDMA
(holding up a big plastic bag)
And trail mix.

The Tyke makes an icky face at the Big Boy.

BIG BOY
(whispering, in order not to hurt the Grandma's feelings)
So pick out the pine nuts and feed them to my gerbil after the show. If you can stay awake.

Delighted at that prospect, the Tyke opens his eyes wide and fixes himself firmly to the bench. He is determined not to fall asleep.

INT. SAMARIA BOYS' ACADEMY 11TH-GRADE CLASSROOM

On the walls are schematic diagrams exposing the guts of machine guns, surface-to-air missiles, tanks, Bradley Urban

Assault Vehicles, and various types of obnoxious-looking helicopters.

TEEN CADETS file in, even more militaristically than the third-graders, and take their bolted-down seats.

Only now do we begin to notice something strange about the student body of this institution, even stranger than their fascist dress and behavior...

INT. SAMARIA BOYS' ACADEMY CORRIDOR--SAME DAY

Glimpses through windows in a succession of classroom doors reveal that most of Cadets, grade-schoolers as well as upperclassmen, have red hair, like the Pilot and Sentry.

Even the few blonds and brunettes bear a very eerie resemblance to their carrot-topped classmates. If they don't have similar blue eyes, their chins or noses match.

Only blood brothers could mirror each other so closely.

There's something odd about the faculty as well: they also bear a resemblance to one another. But it's not genetic.

They're all CLASSY WOMEN of the same intimidating type as County Attorney Jez.

INT. SAMARIA BOYS' ACADEMY 12TH-GRADE CLASSROOM--SAME DAY

The SENIOR CADETS begin to pore, in unison, over the pages of the ANARCHIST'S COOKBOOK. But they don't snicker with naughty delight, as most red-blooded American boys do when reading this classic. None of them cracks a smile.

Their teacher is yet another Classy Woman.

12th-GRADE TEACHER
(sharp, assertive tones
of an educated Back-Easterner)
Turn to the chapter on phosgene.

In this scene of almost perfect order, there's one slightly jarring element. One of the students, a black-haired youth, has a hint of individual personality, well hidden, but conspicuous under these circumstances.

This is ELIJAH. He turns to the chapter on phosgene and digs in with more enthusiasm, and more comprehension, than his brothers.

INT. SAMARIA TEXTILE FACTORY--SAME DAY

Only pre-Industrial Revolution technology is used here.

Forty or so female VIRGINS, of all juvenile ages, but only one physical type, sit at spinning wheels and looms. They're dressed in uniform mid-length denim skirts and plain white blouses.

These girls are obviously the biological sisters of the Cadets in the academy.

AHAB stands before them. He's an old polygamist patriarch, tall, with a very powerful back. His pony tail was once red as most of his children's, but has faded.

He is the source of Samaria's under-age population. His huge, luminescent sky-blue eyes, long nose and powerful chin are the originals from which the Cadets' and the Virgins' features are derived.

AHAB
My daughters. I've come to acknowledge, on the advice of certain of your mothers...

He glances at his Number-One Plural Wife, none other than County Attorney JEZ, who's hovering at his elbow. Her smug expression makes it obvious that she's been henpecking him in feministic ways.

AHAB
...that certain tensions will build up inside the modern young woman's heart while working under these apparently stultifying conditions.

He waves his hand at the ceiling fans and looks exasperated and puzzled, as if to say, "What do you want? Air conditioning?"

AHAB
The result, I am told, can be acts of

personal excess, so to speak, once the modern young woman is out from under the yoke of paternal authority. She's like a shaken pop bottle.

That's Jez's cue to hold up a copy of today's Salt Lake City Tribune for all the Virgins to see.

On the front page, a red-haired, blue-eyed, long-nosed, powerful-chinned female American soldier mocks an Iraqi's penis.

Ahab cringes. He can't help running a quick defensive hand over his own genitalia. Jez nudges him before he can forget his lines.

AHAB

So, against my better judgment, I have been prevailed upon to allow--for the first time in Samarian history--those of you Virgins who have been behaving yourselves to participate with your brethren in the yearly Casting Out.

None of Ahab's daughters makes a sound or a motion in response. But it's clear, from the sudden change in the color of their faces, that a few of the preadolescent Virgins are terrified.

Many of the teenaged Virgins, on the other hand, are excited by this news, in particular a pair of strapping IDENTICAL TWINS seated at adjacent looms toward the rear.

Continuing to face forward, as all young Samarians do when being addressed by their patriarch, these Identical Twins glance at each other sidelong with gleeful anticipation.

AHAB

You are now dismissed early from work--another first in Samarian history--to prepare yourselves. Consult your respective mothers on the proper hygienic procedures.

As the Virgins file out, the helicopter is heard approaching.

AHAB
(to Jez)
Simon, the Magus, descends upon Samaria. The Master of Ceremonies has arrived.

INT. HELICOPTER--SEVERAL MINUTES LATER

As the chopper hovers down into the polygamists' world, Simon gazes thoughtfully at the person strapped into the seat across from him--who happens to be the Big Weird Woman.

She stares dumbly back.

EXT. NEW YORK CITY SLUM--NIGHT (FLASHBACK)

Deep in a dark, dripping neighborhood wobbles a building that looks as though it should have been condemned and abandoned ten years ago.

Strange sounds from within rattle the paint-blackened windows, frightening droves of rats into the street. We hear hoots, screams, maniacal laughter, and a slurring saxophone.

INT. "SMOLDERING GEHENNA" NIGHTCLUB--NIGHT

It's more of a purgatory than a place of social resort.

The patrons are, without exception, scary. They embody every nightmare that heartland folks have about the wormy bits of the Big Apple.

Simon Magus moves among his people, doing his act--and it couldn't contrast more hideously with what we've seen of Phil's wholesome brand of Midwestern and Intermountain Western family entertainment.

Since all of Simon's subjects have been spawned and bred in sunless urban canyons, not a square inch of healthy tan skin can be seen. With their eyes closed in hypnosis, they look like--

UNDERWATER SHOT

--those eyeless albino creatures that float sluggishly

around volcanic vents in ocean trenches.

Simon's got any number of wretches deeply hypnotized, all going in different directions at once.

He's got at least three AMBIGUOUS CREATURES from Times Square displaying unassignable body parts. He's got a MIDDLE-CLASS JUNKY from Long Island finding veins in places where he didn't know he had places. He's made a GUTTER CRIPPLE blind, and a WALL STREET MISER is buying invisible drinks for everyone.

SIMON
(screaming over the ruckus)
And remember, ladies and gentlemen, it's impossible to hypnotize people to do anything they wouldn't do otherwise.

WORKING-CLASS STIFF
(wandered into the wrong dive)
So why bother?

In a dark corner, a competition appears to be going on.

Using unidentifiable pigments, a decadent BIG-CITY PAINTER, eyes closed, puts incomprehensible images on the wall, while a troupe of SOPHISTICATED PERFORMANCE ARTISTS do inexplicable things with food items.

A female GYPSY CABDRIVER stands by, watching them, her head turned critically to one side.

SIMON
You guys will have to do better than that if you want the grant--
(to the Gypsy Cabdriver)
Right, Mrs. Guggenheim?

GYPSY CABDRIVER
I'd sooner throw money at a good bowel movement.

Meanwhile, in the background, a shirtless SAXOPHONIST, who could be Bela Lugosi's body-double, makes depraved love to an invisible horn.

Simon is screaming out for more volunteers just as the Big

Weird Woman stumbles in off the street, black bra, loose tank top, seismic-crack tattoo and all.

At first sight he's fascinated with her.

SIMON
(leering)
Ladies and gentlemen, we have someone with rare talents here, I think.
(to himself)
A once-in-several-lifetimes opportunity, if I'm not mistaken...

EXT. SAMARIA HELIPAD--DAY

Ahab, patriarch of Samaria, stands with eyes raised to the heavens in joyful anticipation.

He is escorted by an HONOR GUARD composed of seven of his favorite teenaged sons. Their uniforms are resplendent with gold epaulets and white silken shoulder braids. They have been selected for stature as well as especially red hair, blue eyes, long noses and powerful chins--seven chips off the old block.

At the head of the escort stands the most splendid lad of all. He is the proud CAPTAIN of the Honor Guard, a full eighteen years of age, every bit as tall and gleaming and impressive as the old man.

The chopper lands, blasting sand into the Captain's unflinching eyes.

Simon alights and is greeted warmly by Ahab.

AHAB
Simon, the Magus. Welcome, welcome, my good friend. Has it been a year already?

SIMON
(very respectfully)
It has, sir.

AHAB
And are you ready to help my spawn release a little hellacious steam?

SIMON
It will be an honor, as always, sir, for me to do my best.

AHAB
Excellent. I have a surprise for you. This year my daughters will attend the Casting Out.

SIMON
No fucking shit?
(grabbing hold of himself)
I mean, er, that's an interesting idea, sir...
(suppressing a wicked smile)
I'll see what I can accomplish with them.

AHAB
(ignoring these vicissitudes)
Another surprise. This time you'll be performing under a roof, for what I trust is a welcome change.

SIMON
Really? I'm honored! Thank you so much, sir!

AHAB
As there is no space in Samaria to erect a permanent venue for such infrequent frivolities, we have rented an excellent room for you, with colorful lights and a wicked Dolby sound system. Everything an artist requires to work his magic.

SIMON
(simpering)
Not magic, sir. Hypnosis.

AHAB
Of course, of course. Shall we go? The convoy awaits.
(glancing toward the helipad)
Don't forget your, shall we say, stage prop.

The Big Weird Woman has wandered off the chopper, and stands under the whirling blades. She's too weird to bother ducking, and big enough to make it extra-dangerous not to.

A sudden shift in the desert breeze nearly results in the removal of the top of her head. She loses some hair but doesn't notice.

INT. "SMOLDERING GEHENNA" NIGHTCLUB (FLASHBACK)

It's the wee hours. This dive has no closing time, and most of the scary patrons are still there, slumped in exhausted stupors on the floor. The place is silent as a morgue.

Simon Magus is working on the Big Weird Woman. He has spent all night pushing her deeper and deeper into the bottomless pit of her psyche. In fact, she's flat on her back on the floor.

The expression on her face belongs on a corpse.

EXT. VICTORIAN LONDON GRAVEYARD--NIGHT

At the bottom of a hole in the ground lies a DEAD WOMAN with that very facial expression.

She is being rousted from her eternal repose by a couple of Cockney RESURRECTIONISTS, whose illegal job is to supply the Royal College of Surgeons with bodies to dissect.

FIRST RESURRECTIONIST

Right, Jasper. Be so pleasant as to grab that trotter. Heave-ho.

INT. "SMOLDERING GEHENNA" NIGHTCLUB--NIGHT

Simon waves his hand over the Big Weird Woman, and she rises to her feet.

SECOND RESURRECTIONIST (VO)

Gin and pies tonight, as they say at Buckingham Palace.

The leer has left Simon's face, and now he is concentrating in an unemotional, even clinical way, on his craft.

INTERCUT BETWEEN NEW YORK CITY AND VICTORIAN LONDON

The two Resurrectionists carry the Dead Woman through the darkness, discreetly stuffed in a burlap bag.

Simon and the Big Weird Woman exit the night club and venture down the sidewalks of New York.

EXT. ROYAL COLLEGE OF SURGEONS--NIGHT

The Resurrectionists approach the back door and knock softly.

A white-coated SURGEON peeks out. He looks warily at a paid-off BOBBIE who stands nearby, very obviously paying no attention.

EXT. NEW YORK STREET--NIGHT

Simon and the Big Weird Woman turn down the sort of shadowy alley that even God would shrink from.

EXT. ROYAL COLLEGE OF SURGEONS--NIGHT

The Surgeon admits the Resurrectionists with their load.

SURGEON
Make haste, make haste, you two--er, three.

A dark, plump figure suddenly slides out of the shadows, and slips into the college on the Resurrectionists' heels. Nobody seems to notice.

Before the door can close, he glances back over his shoulder, revealing himself to be Baron Dupotet.

INT. DISSECTION ROOM--SAME NIGHT

A PROFESSOR goes to work, soberly and respectfully, on the Dead Woman.

His INTERNS gather around, paying close, clinical attention. Almost nobody ogles her bosom.

Baron Dupotet can be seen creeping past the door.

INTERCUT BETWEEN DUPOTET AND SIMON

Dupotet moves down the brown wooden corridor of the Royal College of Surgeons. The place is softly gas-lit and quiet as a temple. He passes a series of lecture halls where serious medical studies are being pursued.

Simon walks the Big Weird Woman down the horrible alley, presenting her to a succession of stuporous BUMS and catatonic MADMEN. He gives her time to ponder each one.

INT. ROYAL COLLEGE OF SURGEONS LECTURE HALL--SAME NIGHT

Baron Dupotet sneaks in, unseen, and leans against the back wall. He has come to heckle his rival, LaFontaine, who stands at the podium, delivering a formal lecture.

The great mesmerizer has dressed himself a bit more soberly for this occasion than he does for his public performances and soirees. His manner and voice are modulated for the academic circumstances. But he is no less impressive for that.

The lecture hall is full of frowzy old PHYSICIANS of various specialties.

With their outdated frock coats, pinchy wire-rim spectacles and bushy gray beards down to their watch-chains, these codgers look as though they wouldn't crack a smile if LaFontaine were to levitate the whole building, or cause elves to materialize.

They listen to him very carefully, anyway. It's clear, from the skeptical look in their eyes and the sardonic way they stroke their whiskers, that they want only to dissect his ideas and expose them as unscientific.

But LaFontaine seems to be getting through to a number of their YOUNGER COLLEAGUES, who stand at the back, apparently unaware of the Baron's presence among them.

LAFONTAINE

Gentlemen, please know that mesmerism is the conscious or, indeed, unconscious projection of the vital fluid. Certain deluded amateurs insist on describing this as "animal-magnetism."

He glances at Dupotet, who swells with anger.

BARON DUPOTET
(screaming)
We'll see who's deluded!

Nobody but LaFontaine heard that.

LAFONTAINE
(as if nothing has happened)
The quality of the vital fluid's power is determined by the moral or spiritual status of the mesmerist...

EXT. NEW YORK STREET--NIGHT

The Big Weird Woman stands over a BUM sleeping between two garbage cans.

When Simon's hand reaches out of the darkness, touching her shoulder, she gets down in the filth, next to the Bum.

She begins to imitate his posture, in a tentative way, starting with an arm, then a leg.

All the while, the Big Weird Woman keeps silent, and her face remains expressionless.

INT. LECTURE HALL--NIGHT

LAFONTAINE
Herein lies the danger of the practice. For if the mesmerist is corrupt, foul-minded and of a debased moral character...

Once again he glances at Dupotet, who bows deeply, as if acknowledging a compliment and accepting applause.

EXT. NEW YORK STREET--NIGHT

Simon stands on a gutter curb, bowing graciously as STREET CREEPS applaud the behaviors he elicits from the Big Weird Woman.

LAFONTAINE (VO)
...the vital fluid which he projects to the patient will be morally tainted...

Continuing down the alley, Simon puts her through further stages of development.

At first she imitates sleeping DERELICTS' postures, then their facial expressions, and then, with ever increasing skill, their snores, coughs, even sleep-talk.

The Big Weird Woman comes to a MANIAC with Tourette Syndrome, palsied, babbling, grimacing all at once. She does him handily, without Simon having to tap her forehead or snap his fingers.

Even Simon is surprised at this performance. Perhaps he's even getting a bit scared.

INT. LECTURE HALL--NIGHT

As he speaks, LaFontaine glances again toward the back of the room, and is distressed to see that the Baron is gone.

LAFONTAINE
Under the influence of such tainted vital fluid, the patient can become morally and spiritually weakened...

EXT. NEW YORK STREET--NIGHT

The Maniac storms down the middle of the street, causing several accidents as the traffic dodges him. He screams and waves his hands.

The Big Weird Woman is right behind, mirroring his every move, echoing his every sound, suffering his every agony.

EXT. SAMARIA HELIPAD--DAY

LAFONTAINE (VO)
And this will constitute a grave danger to the patient's life...

She goes into convulsions, rolling on the ground and foaming at the mouth.

The chopper blades, still whirling overhead, suck and swirl a lacerating tornado of sand all around her.

Simon runs to squat at her side. He lays his left hand on her forehead.

SIMON
(pleading, yearning, tender, almost like a small boy)
Stay with me. Please don't go away...

Using his handkerchief to dab most of the foam away from the Big Weird Woman's quaking mouth, Simon looks abashedly back at Ahab, who waits unperturbed among his seven sons.

SIMON
(shouting over the chopper)
Won't take a minute, sir. Long trip.

AHAB
Of course, of course. I've got three or four of my own, just like her.

SIMON
(quietly)
No, you don't, asshole.

AHAB
Start her on Sanka decaffeinated as soon as she can hold down liquids. Does the trick every time.

EXT. T-INTERSECTION--LATER THAT DAY

A silver Mercedes Benz approaches, leading a convoy of yellow school buses down the asphalt road. All the vehicles bear the letter-A logo.

This procession passes County Attorney Jez's billboard, and turns left onto the dirt road which Phil earlier negotiated, on the way to the Indian Reservation.

The members of Ahab's family are neatly packed in the buses.

INT. OLDEST SONS' BUS--SAME DAY

The DRIVER is the sort of barefoot and pregnant drudge you'd normally expect to find in a desert polygamist's harem. The only thing lower than her intelligence is her self-esteem. She couldn't be more unlike her co-wives, the Classy Women on the Boys' Academy faculty.

The Cadets she's transporting all sit ramrod straight, affectless, in full dress uniform. Ahab's Honor Guard occupies the front seats.

Simon Magus lounges among this elite seven. With his usual perversity, he has set himself the impossible task of trying to chat these robots up.

SIMON
(to the Captain)
So, Admiral. A couple of those little textile workers are pretty hot.
(reaching out to fiddle with a gold tassel on the Captain's epaulet)
They're only your half sisters, right? Are you allowed to, sort of, mess around with them?

No response is forthcoming.

Never before in the history of show biz has there been a more unpromising audience. But Simon doesn't appear to be worried. He relaxes back into his seat.

Casually, he looks over his shoulder and appraises the other passengers, with the sharp eye of a stage hypnotist scoping out his marks.

Unlike the other Cadets, Elijah looks right back at Simon, and smiles.

INT. LITTLEST DAUGHTERS' BUS--SAME DAY

At the wheel is yet another barefoot and pregnant DRUDGE.

While driving, she suckles a TWO-YEAR-OLD in a cute miniature cadet uniform. He stands by the dashboard and fiddles with knobs as he slurps and burps.

He makes the doors open, and his mommy slaps his hand away, without interrupting his meal.

As this bus is the last in line and eats all the dust, it contains the lowest-ranking Samarians, namely the youngest females, not much older than the thirsty Toddler.

The small Virgins are dressed for the occasion in matching calico aprons and gingham gowns, straight out of "Little House on the Prairie."

They don't move or make a peep. But from the contorted expressions on their little faces, it is clear that they're out of their minds with fear, because the Big Weird Woman rides with them.

Having recovered from her convulsions, but retaining a few flecks of dried foam about the chin, she mutters a frantic song in nonsense language, punctuating the choruses with clipped bursts of hysterical, but silent weeping.

A little BROWN-HAIRED GIRL has been assigned the seat next to the Big Weird Woman.

A typical Samarian child, she's too disciplined to show her mortal terror, except by a certain palsy of the eyeballs, which grows worse every time the Big Weird Woman suffers a spasm and rams an elbow into the side of her little head.

EXT. INDIAN RESERVATION GATE--A LITTLE LATER

The convoy arrives.

Ahab gets out of his silver Mercedes and personally greets the old Gatekeeper, who's seated on her upturned Royal Crown Cola crate, still scatting to Thelonious Monk. This time the tune is "Manganese."

The patriarch looms up before her, exerting all the charm that has drawn so many women to his bed.

The Gatekeeper doesn't acknowledge his existence on the planet. Neither does she pay a lot of attention to the fleet of vehicles idling in her face.

Slowly, as if for personal reasons that aren't especially urgent, she climbs to her old feet and starts to fiddle with the lasso that fastens the gate.

This is going to take a while, because she only uses one hand. The other holds her cassette player up to her ear.

GATEKEEPER
Shab-wabba-gloop. I'd sooner make babies with a Hanta-virus rodent. Ooh-bop a-yiddle, wham.

INT. "BIG HEAP O' WAMPUM" GAMING ROOM--LATER THAT AFTERNOON

The casino is almost deserted.

Three or four DRUGSTORE COWBOYS, from some no-doubt horrible little town nearby, languidly play the one-armed bandits and neglect their cans of beer.

It's dead-quiet, and boring to the point of time stopping altogether. Even the payoffs come in sluggish trickles, eliciting no response at all. The Drugstore Cowboys don't even reach down to collect their dribbles of nickels.

Then, all at once, the doors bang open, and about two dozen LACTATING DRUDGES barge in with their yowling NURSLINGS, ages a few hours to nearly four years.

These Samarian intruders dispose themselves among the slot machines, setting up nests on clattering metal folding chairs, which they have toted in themselves, along with several bales of cloth diapers.

The Drudge who drove the littlest daughters' bus plops down next to a slot machine that supposedly pays off in silver dollars.

Her Two-Year-Old dogs her steps and soon resumes his feeding schedule.

FIRST DRUGSTORE COWBOY
(wincing at the sight)
Jesus Mahogany Christ.

He and his pardners leave quickly

They brush past the Medicine Man, who stands by the door, gaping at the nursery, or perhaps dairy, which Ahab's pregnant Drudges and their suckling offspring have turned the place into.

MEDICINE MAN
(to the fleeing Drugstore Cowboys)
They'll be gone by first light. With any luck.

Jez approaches.

MEDICINE MAN
Are you gonna wean them by the time they're old enough to start paying for some beers around here?

Bothering neither to respond, nor even look at him, Jez forks over a Samaria Corporation check, which he takes like an inoculation.

She turns her back and walks off.

MEDICINE MAN
(to nobody in particular)
Of course, for all that, she don't forget to wiggle her ass.

INT. "BIG HEAP O' WAMPUM" CORRIDOR--A FEW SECONDS LATER

This passageway features wallpaper with canoes, pine-trees and Hiawathas. The utter corniness is lost on County Attorney Jez.

All business, she takes her position as Number-One Plural Wife quite seriously, and has no time to master the subtleties of interior decoration.

Jez approaches a triangular door which is apparently supposed to resemble a tent-flap. It's labeled, "TOM-TOM ROOM."

A piece of construction paper scotch-taped to the wall nearby reads--

RESERVED FOR "CASTING OUT"
SAMARIA CORP.

INT. "TOM-TOM ROOM"--A MOMENT LATER

This is the party venue reserved for white folks. It's tarted up to look like Gene Autry's idea of a redskin camp, even cornier than the corridor.

Moccasin-shaped ashtrays dominate the cocktail tables. The swizzle-sticks look like tomahawks. Cardboard quivers full of rubber arrows hang everywhere, by way of decor.

Cellophane feathers of unnatural colors have been stapled to every stationary surface. The wallpaper depicts buffaloes whose big asses bristle with spears.

Jez enters, and goes to take her appointed place among the family.

Starting at the rear of the room, she first passes among Ahab's multitude of daughters, from the youngest to the oldest. The Virgins are seated in folding chairs at the periphery of the party, just as they occupied the last buses in the convoy.

All dressed up in matching calico aprons and gingham gowns, they behave no less perfectly than their brothers.

The Cadets have been assigned lounge chairs around tom-tom-shaped tables. They're not as nervous as their sisters, because the Casting Out has been a yearly event for them all their lives. Nevertheless, their backs and necks are stiff and straight.

The only hint of an organic shape among the Cadets' right angles is Elijah, who sits in a relaxed posture.

An armchair has been placed up front and center, reserved for the patriarch, who has not made his entrance yet. He will enjoy the show surrounded by his harem.

To the right of Ahab's throne sit the Classy Women, including the Twelfth-Grade Teacher who was teaching Elijah and his classmates about phosgene.

To the left are the NON-LACTATING DRUDGES, including the Driver of the oldest sons' bus. She and her fellow BUS DRIVERS are bored already, with no heavy machinery to operate.

The Non-Lactating Drudges are holding, at the ready, many mops and buckets, plus rolls of white adhesive tape and big bales of cotton batting, to accommodate the puke and blood that will be spilled.

The entire population of the incorporated municipality of Samaria, Utah, patiently await the advent of their ruler.

The sound of marching is heard.

INT. "BIG HEAP O' WAMPUM" CORRIDOR--AT THAT MOMENT

At the head of his Honor Guard, Ahab strides briskly down the corny corridor.

The seven splendid lads move crisply and briskly as grown professional soldiers who've been charged with guarding one of the world's most significant men.

INT. THE VATICAN, PAPAL RESIDENCE--1882

Seven huge, blond, blue-eyed SWISS GUARDS, in elaborate ceremonial armor and helmets, shouldering lethal-looking halberds, march down a hallway far more splendiferous than the Indian casino's.

The ceilings are gold-leafed, the walls are covered with frescoes of magnificent saints. Polished bronze statues stand in niches every few yards.

We can't see him very well because he's so short and stooped, but an old man hobbles along in the Swiss Guards' midst. Wearing a full-length white satin robe and skull-cap, it's none other than His Eminence, POPE PIUS IX.

INT. "BIG HEAP O' WAMPUM" DRESSING ROOM--AT THAT MOMENT

Phil and Simon, wearing big paper bibs around their necks, are both trying to put on their makeup at the same time. They jostle for position in front of a light bulb-surrounded mirror.

PHIL

(elbowing Simon)

So, they let you come indoors this year. Did you remember to wipe your feet?

SIMON
(elbowing back)
You're the expert at showdowns at the OK Corral.

PHIL
You're better off behind closed doors, where you won't scare the livestock.

SIMON
How do you do the old lit-match-under-the-nose trick in the middle of a dust devil, pardner?

INT. "BIG HEAP O' WAMPUM" CORRIDOR

Ahab and his Honor Guard are approaching the door, marked "Dressing Room," behind which our two hypnotists can be heard bickering.

PHIL (OS)
Why does the Grand Stud-Bull have you back every year?

SIMON (OS)
I'm dorking a few dozen of his plural wives for him.

PHIL (OS)
As ridiculous as that sounds--

INT. "BIG HEAP O' WAMPUM" DRESSING ROOM

A well-timed nudge causes Simon to smear his lipstick.

PHIL
--it's the most likely explanation. Your stage presence can't have anything to do with it.

SIMON
I just know you're going to say "Fuck off, Simon," but--

INT. THE VATICAN, PAPAL RESIDENCE

Pope Pius IX has moved to the front of the procession, so

we can get a better look at him.

His Grace is an obese old lecher, with puffy lips and swollen lower eyelids, heavily made up. There's an expression perpetually fixed on his face which makes him look as though he just had an orgasm or two.

SIMON (VO)
--can I borrow some of that aquamarine mascara you wore in Colorado?

The Pope and his mighty Swiss Guards are approaching, at the end of the fabulous hallway, a huge pair of cast-bronze doors which depict grandiose and grotesque scenes from Dante.

Two more colossal Swiss Guards stand sentry to the left and right.

INT. "BIG HEAP O' WAMPUM" DRESSING ROOM

PHIL
(handing the mascara over)
I can't believe the Medicine Man would let your employer past the gate.

SIMON
The two of them have been on buddy-buddy terms for quite a while, ever since Ahab started arming up for the "End Time," as he calls it.

Phil stops shoving and stares at Simon via the mirror.

SIMON
Yeah. In return for an immodest financial consideration, the old savage lets Ahab hide his arsenal in a secret cavern somewhere around here.

PHIL
Sure, Simon. You bet. As if the most peaceful and least greedy human being in existence would do that.

Phil resumes his primp-job, not interested in listening to any more of this nonsense.

SIMON

The feds can't some anywhere near an Injun reservation. The Medicine Man could stick an H-bomb among the totem poles in front of this casino, if he felt like it. The words "Bureau of Alcohol, Tobacco and Firearms" get hoots from the stoniest-faced old squaw.

PHIL

(getting uneasy)

Until I hear you make a squaw hoot, I won't believe you.

SIMON

Where do you think the money came from to pay the thieving white contractors who built this place so shoddily? Didn't you smell the phosgene leaks when you pulled in?

PHIL

I thought it was your aftershave.

INT. VATICAN, PAPAL RESIDENCE

Pope Pius IX arrives at the big bronze doors, and the Guards swing them open to reveal--

INT. PAPAL AUDIENCE CHAMBER

--a splendid room, straight from the glory days of Michelangelo. It's full of marble statuary and boasts a gold-leaf ceiling with a vast chandelier.

On an alabaster table is a selection of five different kinds of beautiful wine in crystal carafes.

Standing at that table is Baron Dupotet.

Seeing the Pope, he quickly puts down a glass of gravy-thick burgundy that he's been swilling without permission. He falls to his knees and begins to cross himself with great fervency.

Standing nearby, mildly amused, is LaFontaine.

PHIL (VO)
Leave me just enough of that mascara to see me through the rest of the year, why don't you?

INT. "BIG HEAP O' WAMPUM" CORRIDOR

Ahab arrives at the dressing room. The Captain opens the door for him, revealing--

INT. "BIG HEAP O' WAMPUM" DRESSING ROOM

--Phil and Simon having a tug-o'-war over the mascara brush.

Ahab clears his throat, then enters, followed by the Honor Guard, who stand at attention against the walls. The room's pretty crowded at this point.

Simon, who has the business end of the mascara brush, quickly lets go. He wipes his hands on his makeup bib, turning it aquamarine.

To Phil's surprise and amusement, Simon prostrates himself before the patriarch and submits to a pre-show blessing.

AHAB
(squatting and laying hands on Simon's head)
By the potency vested in me through the Samarian priesthood, I make potency flow into you.

HONOR GUARDSMEN
(in unison)
Amen.

Simon responds in a soft voice, hoping Phil won't hear.

SIMON
Amen.

Ahab approaches Phil, hands outstretched, offering the same service.

PHIL
No, thanks. I'm a devout god-scoffer.

AHAB
(coming close, towering over him)
What did you say to me?

Phil doesn't answer, but just stares back at him.

Simon, and the Honor Guard as well, are flabbergasted by Phil's guts, or maybe just his foolhardiness. They wince in anticipation of the patriarch's wrath.

But nothing happens for the longest while. This is a stare-down, a war of wills. Phil's not even trying to use hypnosis.

When Ahab turns to leave as if nothing has happened, Phil wins the war.

Once Simon stops being astonished, he gets another, all-too-familiar look about him. Again, as in the Colorado high school auditorium, his face contorts with a flash of agonized envy. He recovers quickly, before Phil can notice.

The two hypnotists see the eight Samarians off--

INT. "BIG HEAP O' WAMPUM" CORRIDOR

--and watch them march importantly away between the pine trees, canoes and Hiawathas.

A bit further down the corridor, Ahab and the Honor Guard disappear behind the triangular "Tom-Tom Room" door.

SIMON
Family man.

PHIL
Do you think that prick's ever alone?

SIMON
(pretending to suddenly get a brilliant idea)
Hey, Phil. Know what?

PHIL
What?

SIMON

My polygamist brats aren't allowed to know what a TV is. Your Mohawks get almost no reception at all. Unlike everyone else in this lousy country, our audiences tonight aren't already crammed to the gills with post-hypnotic suggestions. It's almost like laboratory conditions out here, like a power outage has shut down all the screens. We both should be able to work wonders. A perfect battleground for a duel.

PHIL

How are we going to decide the winner?

Simon produces a matched brace of battery-operated Sony-brand decibel meters.

PHIL

Just happened to be carrying those around, eh? This tribe communicates mostly by telepathy. You'll win if you get your splinter-Mormons breathing hard.

SIMON

You have the advantage of coyotes and crickets.

Simon hands one over.

SIMON

I plan to use mine.

INT. "TOM-TOM ROOM"--AT THAT MOMENT

The Honor Guard march in formation to the front and form a semicircle behind the patriarch's armchair.

This is their post, where they are to remain, standing at full parade attention, for the duration of the Casting Out. Top-ranking Cadets contain no hellacious steam that needs release.

One of them deliberately slams a knee into Elijah in

passing, as if to drive home that black-haired boy's disqualification for this high honor.

Elijah absorbs the blow. It only serves to broaden his un-Samarian smile. Like many bullied teens, he seems to be biding his time.

Ahab moves to the front, holding up high a venerable book entitled, "The Apocryphal Acts of Peter."

AHAB
My sons--er, children. Today's reading, as always on this day each year, is from the fourth chapter of--

Jez's cell-phone goes off.

JEZ
Hello? What? No. The answer is no. Forget it. The patriarch does not agree to that price. That's his decision, as of right now.

She doesn't bother to glance in the patriarch's direction.

AHAB
(pretending not to notice)
--is from the fourth chapter of the Apocryphal Acts of--

Jez's voice is very loud, because she's getting angry at whoever's on the other end of the line. She drowns out her husband.

JEZ
Yes, Samaria Corporation is going public, and, no, that initial offer is not acceptable to the Board of Directors. What? Would you care to repeat that? Why you--

Rather than expose the children's delicate ears to her next few words, she exits via the fake tent flap.

She can be heard screaming in the corridor.

JEZ

You miserable smegma-gulping whelp of a greasy cunting--

AHAB

(raising his voice, reading aloud)

Now there was a great commotion in the midst of Samaria, for some said that they had seen wonderful works done by a certain man, whose name was--

The Cadets take the liberty of saying the name along with their father--

CADETS

--Simon!

AHAB

(gratified)

Simon, yes!

(warming to the task)

And Simon spoke to the people with a great voice, saying, "Tomorrow about the seventh hour ye shall see me fly over the gate."

The level of enthusiasm rises, not just among the Cadets, but some of the older Virgins as well.

AHAB

(voice swelling to greatness)

And when it was the seventh hour, behold! Suddenly a roaring cloud of dust was seen in the sky afar off, like smoke, shining with hot rays that stretched both far and wide!

By this point, the Cadets are reciting along. They know the words by heart. Some of them are shouting.

The room heats up, and Ahab's daughters blush. The older, bolder Virgins tentatively applaud, and even begin to cheer.

Though the Big Weird Woman is nowhere to be seen, the little Brown-Haired Girl is still out of her mind with horror. But now she's starting to show it. She seems to have developed an unusually vocal case of the hiccoughs.

Elijah is the only person in the room laughing, and he's laughing hard.

AHAB AND CADETS

And Simon, the Magus, arrived in his flying chariot!

That's Simon's cue. The room blackens, as in a power outage.

EXT. TRIBAL MEETING GROUND--A BIT LATER THAT EVENING

Not-quite identifiable, but definitely ugly sounds filter through the back wall of the casino, between crumbling cinder-brick and cheap particle-board. (Simon was telling the truth about thieving white contractors.) The racket is not too loud, yet.

The Medicine Man tosses some sagebrush to simmer slowly like incense in a tidy campfire pit at the center of the tribal meeting ground.

MEDICINE MAN

Okay. So, like always, let's start with our tribal hymn to the Coyote goddess. Tell her thanks for all the good stuff in our life, and for bringing good old Phil back.

Everyone stands in a circle holding hands, and sings. Some of the MOMS and DADS are there, too.

The sun is beginning to set, the shadows to lengthen. The circle of Indians is lit softly by the sweet sagebrush embers.

In the orange and lavender shadows that gather behind their backs as they sing, we see Phil moving quietly.

He selects certain Youngsters and ADULTS, tapping their right shoulders and whispering into their right ears. Each person smiles at what he says.

When the hymn is over, everyone sits, and Phil occupies the center, at the edge of the fire. They applaud quietly but warmly.

PHIL
(typical show biz manner)
Thank you, thank you very much, ladies and gentlemen. Good evening. I'm so glad to be back here on the reservation with you tonight. You're obviously going to be a great audience.

Noticing that some of the children are wincing at his brassy tone, he softens for them.

PHIL
I see that some of you brought your friends along.

The selected Indians have ravens nestled in their laps or perched on their forearms, which only they, and we, can see. These are gorgeous, enormous, black and shiny, as though carved from volcanic glass.

They're well-behaved, too, submitting to strokes and pets like cats, arching their necks to meet the Indians' hands, and making soft sounds that sound almost like purrs.

As the sun sinks a bit further into the western desert, turning the sky purple and pink, Phil proceeds around the circle, chatting up the proud owners of the birds.

PHIL
I've never seen such creatures.
(to a child)
Ravens can be pretty tough. Is yours a nice one or a mean one?

CHILD
A nice one. Her name is Cynthia.

PHIL
(to the Big Boy)
My goodness, that's an especially big fellow.

BIG BOY
(arm straining a bit)
He's real heavy.

PHIL
(to the Grandpa)
Can yours talk?

GRANDPA
Of course.

PHIL
What's he saying?

GRANDPA
He wants to know if anybody's got a Marlboro they're not gonna be using for the next few minutes.

Everyone laughs. Somebody passes one along, and the Grandpa lights up, taking a big drag.

GRANDPA
I have to get it going for him. He's got no hands. This ain't no cartoon raven.

Thumping is heard on the other side of the casino wall.

MEDICINE MAN
Here it comes.

INT. "TOM-TOM ROOM"--AT THAT MOMENT

The place is unwholesomely dark. A few sickly green and red spotlights have been switched on, with a bit of black light oozing here and there.

An elementary-school Cadet, armed with a ceramic moccasin-shaped ashtray, is hacking maniacally away at a the spear-bristling ass of one particular buffalo on the wallpaper.

This is the BANGING BOY. Phil has informed him that, henceforth, he has no other function in the universe than to kill that buffalo and reduce its carcass to single atoms.

Little Virgins shriek by in a hunting party, clambering and crawling under the Banging Boy's legs, having ripped off some of the decor and decked themselves out.

Their little bodies bristle with cellophane feathers. Cardboard quivers full of rubber arrows are strapped to their backs. They have transformed themselves, at Simon's post-hypnotic suggestion, into savages.

The head of this hunting party is the Brown-Haired Girl, who still has the hiccoughs, but churns them out now in the form of clipped, convulsive shrieks.

Simon, on the stage, hisses into the ear of the twelve-year-old GRIMACING BOY.

SIMON
Guess what? This is a one-man show, starring you. Get to work. Your father needs entertaining.

Simon leaves him standing alone at the front of the stage.

After a moment's thought, the Grimacing Boy starts to pull a rapid series of every ugly contortion the human face can produce without the aid of fingers. He'd be wrenching and straining any number of muscles right now if he weren't under hypnosis.

Ahab sits in his armchair, front and center, surrounded by his many spouses. He seems pleased enough with how things are going.

His Honor Guard remain fixed in their semi-circle behind him, like seven statues. They are unaffected by their siblings' various transformations, so far.

EXT. TRIBAL MEETING GROUND--NIGHT

The poor casino wall is holding back the splinter-Mormon racket well enough so that Phil only needs to raise his voice a bit to get above it.

The air out here is clear and pure, the vastness of the heavenly vault incomprehensible. On Phil's cue, the stars come out, in the impossible numbers that only inland desert dwellers, far from the big city, get to see.

PHIL
Look. Some new constellations have formed up there tonight, just for us.

GRANDPA
Is that a Pontiac up there?

PHIL
And here comes a meteor shower.

TYKE
I saw a silver meteor.

BIG BOY
It looked like a needle stitchin' black cloth.

GRANDMA
(slightly afraid)
I see a blood-red one.

INT. PAPAL AUDIENCE CHAMBER--DAY

A fat, gore-colored ruby weighs down the flounder-pale forefinger of Pope Pius IX.

Baron Dupotet is on his knees, fellating it.

Soon it's LaFontaine's turn.

Choosing not to kneel, but only to bend slightly at the waist, LaFontaine brings his lips correctly close to the tasteless bauble, but no closer.

POPE PIUS IX
Gentlemen, let us wish and hope that, for the good of humanity, animal-magnetism may soon be generally employed for the benefit of--

LAFONTAINE
I prefer the term "mesmerism."

Baron Dupotet, still on his knees, pretends to be shocked at his rival's rudeness.

POPE PIUS IX
(choosing to ignore the interruption)
I encourage you, my sons, to continue your magnificent work, in the

confidence that it will enhance the spiritual well-being of all Christendom... The blessings of Our Lord and Savior, Jesus Christ, be with you.

BARON DUPOTET

Amen.

The Pope pauses for LaFontaine to say, "Amen."

It going to be quite a wait, if the look on the latter's face is any indication.

INT. "TOM-TOM ROOM"--A BIT LATER

Some ELEMENTARY SCHOOL CADETS have joined the Banging Boy in hacking at that one spot in the wall, using chairs now. They seem to have formed the collective determination to do major structural damage to this building.

They've blasted the wallpaper away, and the sheetrock under that, and are chipping at the particle-board beneath.

A reinforcing rod pops through.

Meanwhile, on the stage, four ADOLESCENT CADETS have shoved the Grimacing Boy to one side, and have formed a heavy metal band. Abusing air-guitars and air-drums, they writhe like victims of Vlad the Impaler, and have about as much fun.

Some little Virgins stand before these rock stars, fixed to the spot, unable to flee, holding their ears and crying at the destruction of their ability to hear. The girls see blood gushing from the sides of each others' heads.

Ahab, knowing it's all make-believe, winks at the pertinent mothers.

AHAB

Plenty more tiny eardrums where those came from.

As if his point has not been made clearly enough, he cups his scrotum through his pants and chuckles fondly.

A Drudge who sees the girls' blood is told to mop it up.

EXT. TRIBAL MEETING GROUND--SAME TIME

The polygamists' sick noise is getting more audible out here, but at least it's an invisible pollution. The night canopy remains clear.

The Grandma and the Grandpa are not hypnotized, exactly, but have decided to use the occasion to do some really slow swing-era dancing in the cool desert breeze.

The Indian Children now have more than ravens to play with. It looks as though they've got some foxes and an easy-going bear, plus a stream full of leaping trout.

MEDICINE MAN
(to Phil)
They're remembering when we lived in Idaho. Before there was a Idaho.

Some TEEN BRAVES do an aboriginal dance around the fire, with great dignity and atavistic pride. Their chests swell out at least as far as the Honor Guards'.

In spite of the thumping that comes from the casino, perhaps even lulled by the monotony of it, the Tyke is getting sleepy on the bench.

Phil watches him sink into the side of the Big Boy, who would like to rise up and dance with his brothers, but does not move, or even breathe much, so as not to disturb the little fellow's rest.

PHIL
(to the Medicine Man)
I can never tell when your people are faking it.

MEDICINE MAN
Neither can they. It's not important.

PHIL
You're right. I'll just stand here and do what all stage hypnotists fear to do: relinquish control.

The Medicine Man is very pleased to hear that. It's as if Phil has achieved an insight that qualifies him for a signal honor.

The Medicine Man removes a string of uncut turquoise nuggets from his neck. They are beautiful, with veins of gold.

MEDICINE MAN
(placing them around Phil's neck)
Phil, the people love your shows.

PHIL
(overwhelmed)
Really, I can't take--

MEDICINE MAN
You're not taking. You're wearing.

INT. PAPAL AUDIENCE CHAMBER, VATICAN--DAY

Pope Pius IX fondles a sapphire and emerald rosary that would make Marie Antoinette want to use the bidet. He's still waiting for his "Amen."

He looks into LaFontaine's eyes.

LaFontaine looks into his--not hypnotically, not even in defiance, but with disdain.

The "Amen" doesn't seem to be forthcoming.

INT. "TOM-TOM ROOM"--A BIT LATER

County Attorney Jez and her fellow Classy Women watch with satisfaction the behavior of certain Older Virgins.

Particularly pleasing are the strapping Identical Twins, who have somehow persuaded a couple of the Honor Guards to abandon their post.

While their five comrades remain standing at attention behind Ahab, these boys are allowing themselves to be ridden like donkeys.

Ahab is not happy about this development.

Simon, on the other hand, can barely contain his glee.

SIMON
(whispering to the Twins)
I know they're only donkeys. But if you kick their balls hard enough, they just might win this Kentucky Derby.

He grabs a rubber arrow from a cardboard quiver strapped to the back of a Little Virgin who happens to be shrieking by, and he hands it to the FIRST TWIN.

She applies it without mercy, like a riding crop, to her half-brother's buttocks. An especially stern donkey mistress, she nearly dislocates his spine by squinching up her thigh muscles.

EXT. TRIBAL MEETING GROUND--SAME TIME

The beautiful fourteen-year-old Indian Maiden stands, straight and still, bathing herself in moonlight and starlight. The top few buttons of her shirt have come undone, and she's enjoying the unpolluted desert breeze on the skin of her chest.

She's lovely, nubile, and completely self-absorbed.

Nobody gropes her or gawks at her; they let her have her experience. She is given respect and space, while she tries on Nature's powers and starts to become a woman, in the deepest and fullest sense of the word.

Her eyes are closed, and she aims her face to the sky in unutterable bliss.

INT. "TOM-TOM ROOM"--A BIT LATER

In growing anguish, Ahab watches four more members of his so-called Honor Guard being ridden and whipped like donkeys through the imaginary redskin camp.

The splendid Captain is the only one who has not forsaken his post, but still stands, like saint cast in bronze, behind Ahab's chair. He is the old patriarch's sole consolation in this world.

EXT. TRIBAL MEETING GROUND--A FEW MOMENTS LATER

Phil and the Medicine Man stand off to one side, admiring the Maiden. Phil regards her with the same fatherly affection he felt for the Punk Girl back in Colorado, but with more than a touch of awe.

Then comes a huge cracking sound, and the casino wall suddenly sags.

INT. "TOM-TOM ROOM"--AT THAT MOMENT

The Banging Boy and his comrades have worked their way deep into the cinder-bricks, and have managed to loosen a structural member, almost bringing down this whole section of the building.

EXT. TRIBAL MEETING GROUND--AT THAT MOMENT

The noise has disrupted the mood, frightening the Tyke, who wakes up and starts to cry.

The Teen Braves snap out of their aboriginal dance and look ashamed of themselves.

The Maiden is jolted out of her trance. She covers her chest and withdraws to cower on a bench.

The Medicine Man is almost shaken off his feet. He looks in anger at the casino.

MEDICINE MAN
(to Phil)
Never again. We don't need this aggravation. I say we close the damn place tomorrow and go back to hawking trinkets on the soft shoulder...
(glancing at the weeping Tyke)
...Churned out by babies in Indonesian sweatshops.

The Medicine Man stares out across the desert. He, and we, see the high sandstone cliff where Milton stands sentry over a padlocked cavern.

MEDICINE MAN
(complete despair)
To hell with everything.

He walks off.

INT. "TOM-TOM ROOM"--AT THAT MOMENT

Simon is examining his decibel meter, which has just been blown out by collapsing masonry. He laughs and tosses the dead appliance into the Banging Boy's pile of rubble.

SIMON
Phil lost this battle, at least.

He approaches the damaged wall, and sees, between some shattered cinder-bricks, a small segment of sky. A few unimportant and ugly little stars are dimly visible through the cloud of asbestos raised by the wanton destruction.

At that moment Simon, the so-called Magus, achieves a state of grace--or at least the closest thing available to scoundrels like him. His eyes fill with perverse religious ecstasy.

Elijah moves near, looking at him in expectation.

Simon considers the dark lad awhile.

SIMON
(dreamily)
Seems like only last year you were no bigger than them.

Simon points to five KINDERGARTEN CADETS who have pulled down their little khaki trousers and are having a pissing contest against the destroyed part of the wall.

INT. PAPAL AUDIENCE CHAMBER, VATICAN--DAY

The same number of delicious ALTAR BOYS, all golden curls, sapphire eyes and pudgy pink dimples, suck with pouting lips on almonds and grapes.

They lounge languidly on purple velvet cushions strewn about the pearl-encrusted taffeta slippers of Pope Pius IX.

The Holy Father has seated himself upon a throne that would make Nero feel like the Whore of Babylon.

Before this throne stand Baron Dupotet and LaFontaine, the former ogling the Altar Boys, the latter fastidiously averting his gaze.

His Holiness observes LaFontaine's eyes alighting upon one child who sits apart from the rest.

POPE PIUS IX
Can either of you wonder-workers magnetize, or mesmerize, or whatever, a smile onto that gloomy little wretch? As you have probably guessed, he's the reason I summoned you.

A dark, severe boy is sitting straight and motionless as a Samaria Cadet before the Casting Out. He shrinks from contact with the corrupted Altar Boys, preferring the hard marble floor to a velvet cushion in their scented midst.

Perhaps a tad frail, but handsome, even at his tender age he is revolted by the decadence that surrounds him. This is the little JEWISH BOY.

POPE PIUS IX
As you can see, he's a Jew from the countryside. Son of a bailiff. A Christian servant girl baptized him in secret. But she left him otherwise untouched.

BARON DUPOTET
Wasteful girl.

The Pope snickers. LaFontaine does not respond.

POPE PIUS IX
The baptism was performed in a Papal state, so, according to Church Law, he must be raised a Catholic. I've taken him under my wing, so to speak.

The Altar Boys giggle.

FIRST ALTAR BOY
That's a funny thing to call it.

SECOND ALTAR BOY
I've heard you call it many names, Your Holiness, but never a "wing."

POPE PIUS IX
Silence! In the knotted bowels of Christ, I adjure you to hold those pink tongues!

He flings a massive, bejeweled, solid-gold chalice at the smart alecks, braining one of them in a splash of purple wine.

This strikes the Baron as quite funny. He suppresses laughter. His plump belly jiggles, and he holds one hand over his mouth.

The other Altar Boys watch Dupotet's belly, and giggle some more.

POPE PIUS IX
(to the Altar Boys)
You think this is humorous? I'll cause my Colossal Guard to skewer all of you at once on his halberd! He'll flick you down to Hell like so many flies--though I know Satan will be angry with me for cluttering up his abode with such pallid trash!

The FIRST ALTAR BOY eyes the COLOSSAL GUARD, who happens to be standing at attention against the wall.

FIRST ALTAR BOY
Oh, Daddy wouldn't do that...

LaFontaine looks up in surprise, and is appalled to see this giant has precisely the same blue eyes, golden hair and ample pale flesh as the Altar Boys. It's obvious he's fathered at least three of them.

With pouting lips, on hands and knees like an infant, the First Altar Boy starts sidling up to his daddy.

INT. "TOM-TOM ROOM"--NIGHT

One of the five Kindergartener Cadets has lost the pissing contest, but has not pulled his little uniform trousers back up. He has decided, instead, with semi-conscious oedipal intentions, to slither on his belly up between Ahab's and Jez's chairs.

Jez just observes his creeping approach without any emotion whatsoever. He's only a male, after all.

But Ahab shies back from this particularly depraved son of his. He freezes in terror, as if a pit viper were down there on the floor, about to sink its needle-fangs into his instep.

INT. PAPAL AUDIENCE CHAMBER, VATICAN--DAY

The Colossal Guard's sanctified job is to stand like a statue and never move except to shield the Pope from assassination or abduction.

Now he has broken into a sweat under his nine-pound helmet. He wears an agonized look on his table-sized face, and tries, with frantic eye movements, to tell his creeping brat to shut the fuck up and back off.

FIRST ALTAR BOY
(caressing Daddy's big boot)
You wouldn't be so mean as to poke me with your big pokey thing...

INT. "TOM-TOM ROOM"

Sweating, too, and wearing a similarly agonized look on his own broad, fair face, the Captain of the Honor Guard remains standing at attention behind his father, while his half-sister, the First Identical Twin, leans on his golden epauletted shoulder and licks his earlobe.

FIRST ALTAR BOY (VO)
...would you, Da-a-a-addy?

The Captain is too steadfast to move a muscle from the neck down, but his big blue eyes can't help filling with tears of humiliation. He looks down at his father and tries to apologize with those sopping orbs.

FIRST IDENTICAL TWIN
(whispering)
Bark like a dog... Bark like a dog.

Ahab sits there, turned around in his armchair, looking up at his two linked children.

He winces at each "woof" that's torn from inside the boy's chest like a chunk of someone's heart.

INT. PAPAL AUDIENCE CHAMBER, VATICAN--DAY

The First Altar Boy is leering at his own reflection in his daddy's standard Vatican-issue shin-bone armor.

He slowly gets up on his pudgy little haunches and starts to fondle the poor man's steel knee-spike.

Dupotet can contain himself no longer. Pointing first at the knee-spike, then to the brat who licks and tickles it, he explodes in belly laughs.

BARON DUPOTET
The little... The filthy... Oh, Mother Mary hemorrhaging on a close stool!

POPE PIUS IX
(icily)
You are dismissed, Monsieur le Baron.

INT. "TOM-TOM ROOM"

When the Casting Out has reached the precise fever pitch Jez desires, she opens her purse and makes out a Samaria Corporation check. She hands it to the Classy Woman who teaches the Anarchist's Cookbook to Elijah and the other Twelfth-Grade Cadets.

Jez nods in the direction of Simon, who stands on the stage in a state of excitation, well pleased at how the show's proceeding.

When she approaches, Simon recognizes in the Classy Woman a fellow Back-Easterner, another sophisticate from the Big Apple.

SIMON
(coming on to her)
Am I casting them far enough out for you, baby?

She looks at him as if to say, "Do you exist?"

CLASSY WOMAN
(handing him the check)
Dismissed.

Simon watches her classy ass wiggle back to be replaced in its appointed seat at her husband's right hand.

He turns to Elijah, who's standing close by.

SIMON
Tell me that one's not your mom.

ELIJAH
Who knows? Could be my sister. Or both...
(getting a naughty look)
Not to change the subject, but would you like to see some of my father's toys, Mr. Magus, sir?

Surprised, Simon looks at the Cadet for a moment. He's appalled, and thrilled, at the extraordinary amounts of mischief contained in Elijah's dark eyes.

SIMON
(willing to be tempted)
Toys are good... Especially those belonging to Daddy.

Elijah slips his arm around Simon's waist, and the pair of them seep into the shadows.

Ahab, morally exhausted and heartbroken at his Honor Guards' craven acquiescence, somehow persuades himself to get up and try to deliver the Closing Benediction, even though he's almost unable to raise his hands.

AHAB
(hoarsely)
The Casting Out has achieved its

fullness. Go in peace.

Nobody pays any attention.

Jez gets up and grabs a mike.

JEZ
That's enough.

The place comes to order just as her cell-phone goes off again.

EXT. PARKING LOT--A FEW MINUTES LATER

The polygamist spawn file into the buses, their uniforms and calico aprons back in place, as far as possible.

The last residue of human expression is just draining from the Virgins' faces, with a certain hint of smugness remaining on the Identical Twins'.

As for the Cadets, they're looking slouchy and softened around the edges.

EXT. TRIBAL MEETING GROUND--SAME TIME

The splinter-Mormons gone, Phil's friends have some silence in which to wind their own annual proceedings down.

They close the same way they opened, with a hymn to the beneficent Coyote Goddess.

In spite of himself, Phil cops a glance at the decibel meter which Simon forced on him earlier. He frowns, raps the dial on his knee, and checks the batteries.

While they sing, the Indians form, slowly and naturally, back into the original circle. Phil goes around and, one by one, gives them soft taps on the forehead, removing all post-hypnotic suggestions.

Everyone is calm and relaxed, and themselves.

EXT. CASINO PARKING LOT--A BIT LATER

Ahab stands by the Oldest Sons' bus and watches them climb the steps in a haggard way, as if their knees were sore from playing the ass all night.

He retreats toward the consolation of his silver Mercedes Benz.

A Non-Lactating Drudge CHAUFFEUR opens the door for him, revealing Jez, who is perched in the death seat, looking pointedly at her watch.

Her cell-phone goes off.

JEZ
Hello? You again? Listen, you rancid clit-twirling glop of pig pecker-snot--

AHAB
I'll walk.

He heads off, alone, into the black desert.

INT. PAPAL AUDIENCE CHAMBER, VATICAN--DAY

No longer laughing, but quite unhappy, Baron is escorted out by a couple of Swiss Guards.

LaFontaine has a brief moment to ponder the little Jewish Boy. He is charmed by the lad, in a chaste, fatherly way.

POPE PIUS IX
Your incontinent colleague--who will remain nameless throughout Christendom till the Day of Reckoning, if I have anything to say about it--once told me that young children are especially easy to, shall we say, put under one's "animal-magnetic" power. Malleable little souls, and so forth... Can you do anything with this small son of Abraham, Isaac and Jacob? I'll make it worth your while, Monsieur LaFontaine.

What little reverence there might have been in LaFontaine's eyes is gone now. With infinite tenderness, and without permission, he gathers up the little Jewish Boy from the cold marble floor.

EXT. TRIBAL MEETING GROUND--NIGHT

Lulled by the ancient hymn, the Tyke has fallen back to sleep.

It's time to go home, but his MOM has his two even younger SIBLINGS to carry, so Phil offers to help.

As he lifts the Tyke in his arms, Phil notices a parallel movement in the shadows just outside the campfire glow.

He's chilled, but not surprised, to see the Big Weird Woman standing in the sand.

Staring at him with her vacuum-eyes, precisely mimicking his posture, she cradles an invisible child to the seismic crack tattooed between her deflated breasts.

Keeping an eye on her, he pats the Tyke on the back.

She does the same to her absent child.

The little Indian wakes up just enough to notice the Medicine Man's turquoise necklace strung around Phil's neck. He fiddles with it drowsily.

Just before drifting back to sleep, the Tyke reverts to an earlier stage of psychosexual development, and begins to suck on the uncut nuggets like gold-veined nipples.

The Big Weird Woman can't go that far. A glint of human awareness flashes across her face.

She drops her invisible child and covers her cracked chest with both hands. With a shudder and a moan, she hulks off into the blackness.

A helicopter can be heard.

EXT. DESERT CLIFF--LATER THAT NIGHT

Milton, the Indian in the Bermuda shorts and Hawaiian shirt, still squats and smokes cigarettes at the edge of his high sandstone cliff. He blows smoke at the stars and looks quite happy with his lot in life.

He hears and sees the Samaria helicopter rising up from the

desert floor.

He flicks his cigarette off the edge, watching it sail down into nothingness like a firefly on the way to Hell.

Then he stands up, brushes some sand from himself, and comes to attention, more or less, to the extent possible for a man with his clothes and attitude. Milton seems to expect someone important to be on that chopper.

It comes up to his level, lands, and Elijah jumps out.

Milton waits a few seconds.

MILTON
Where's your daddy at? Does he know about this?

ELIJAH
Geronimo!

Elijah karate-kicks Milton's midriff, causing him to follow his cigarette off the cliff.

SIMON
(sticking his head out of the chopper)
I didn't see that.

Simon and the Big Weird Woman jump out, leaving the chopper idling and ready for a quick take-off.

Elijah approaches the cavern over which the late Milton has been standing sentry. He jimmies the padlock, opens the grate, and throws a switch that lights the stony interior.

INT. CAVERN--MINUTES LATER

Elijah takes his time wandering through the tunnels, selecting "toys" from his father's impressive arsenal.

He wistfully strokes certain items which would be too large to fit into the chopper, such as a Bradley Urban Assault Vehicle and a tank.

INT. SAMARIA BOYS' ACADEMY 12TH-GRADE ROOM (FLASHBACK)

We are reminded of where this Teen Cadet obtained his expertise.

His Classy Teacher looks on with approval as he examines charts on the classroom wall that expose the inner workings of most of the stuff he's requisitioning tonight.

INTERCUT BETWEEN CHOPPER AND CAVERN

Simon supervises while the Big Weird Woman does all the heavy lifting.

She loads the chopper with lethal devices selected by Elijah, including M-16s, sniper rifles with big scopes, bazookas, fragmentation grenades, shoulder-deployed heat-seeking ground-to-air missile launchers, plus some canisters marked SARIN and PHOSGENE, all bearing the letter-A logo.

Being in a state of hypnosis, the Big Weird Woman's already strapping body is unnaturally strong, and she slings crates full of lead and steel almost as if they were stuffed with marshmallows.

She doesn't seem to notice the cuts, bruises and blisters that her hands, arms and tattooed chest are sustaining throughout this exercise.

ELIJAH
Your moose feels nothing.

SIMON
It's an old stage hypnotist's trick. Goes back to the time of the great Baron Dupotet. He used to stitch his subjects' lips together with carpet thread, and he never heard a complaint.

ELIJAH
At least not a clearly enunciated one.

EXT. HELICOPTER--HALF AN HOUR LATER

Just as they're ready to slam the hatch and take off, Elijah runs back to steal one last item.

It's a cardboard box, marked RED HERRINGS, full of assorted Arab headdresses and cheap paperback editions of the KORAN.

SIMON
Your old man was always such an expert on religion.

EXT. DIRT ROAD--A BIT LATER

Ahab walks alone, with only the moon and stars and coyotes to keep him company. He sinks into a dark night of the soul, falls to his knees in the sand, and looks imploringly to the heavens.

To his ecstatic joy, he sees his own initial floating up there, like a sign from God.

He begins to leap with sublime joy, then grasps his head and falls down dead of a sudden massive brain hemorrhage.

The sign from God turns out to be the logo on the Samaria Corporation chopper, which is flying off, due west.

As Ahab lies there, bleeding out the ears, eye sockets and nostrils, it sounds as though some natives nearby might be singing him a dirge. But it's not a very sad sounding dirge.

EXT. "BIG HEAP O' WAMPUM" PARKING LOT--NIGHT

The little Brown-Haired Girl is the last passenger to be loaded onto the last bus. One purple cellophane feather remains in her hair. She is deep in thought. Just before she mounts the steps, a slight smile creeps across her lips.

INT. LAST BUS--A MOMENT LATER

When the little Brown-Haired Girl gets to her seat, she looks disappointed not to find the Big Weird Woman waiting for her.

The Drudge climbs aboard to get the vehicle moving.

Her unweaned Two-Year-Old clambers up the steps after her. Sleepily, he tries to crawl into his mommy's lap, which is almost non-existent due to her pregnant belly, and is occupied in any case with the large steering wheel.

EXT. DIRT ROAD--A BIT LATER

The silver Mercedes leading the Samarian convoy, with Jez inside, rolls over the patriarch's corpse and presses it into the loose sand.

It's possible that none of the Drudges driving the other vehicles notice their hubby's ever-flattening shape as they run over him, again and again.

INT. LAST BUS--A BIT LATER

The Two-Year-Old is expected to sleep on his feet all the way home, leaning his military-capped head on the speedometer, receiving a concussion with each of the frequent bumps in the dirt road.

One particularly gooshy-sounding bump wakes him up, but just a little.

He whimpers, looks longingly at his mother's torso, places his thumb in his tiny mouth, and dozes off again.

Already this polygamist child is learning to hold his body stiff, and his appetites more or less at bay.

INT. PAPAL AUDIENCE CHAMBER, VATICAN--DAY

The little Jewish Boy allows himself to be lifted into LaFontaine's arms. But the stiffness of his posture indicates that it's only because he needs to be rescued, not because he submits to being loved--not yet, anyway.

Very bravely, LaFontaine turns his back on Pope Pius IX--a grave offense in itself. He could be chopped to bits any moment.

Without genuflecting, groveling, or even asking leave, LaFontaine vacates the Papal Audience Chamber, taking the Jewish Boy with him.

The Colossal Guard makes a lunge, as if to cut the great mesmerist down in his tracks. But the Pope stops him.

POPE PIUS IX
I wouldn't advise you to raise hands against that man.

The Colossal Guard is stunned by his god-like boss' warning.

COLOSSAL GUARD
Is he Satan's henchman, Your Eminence?

POPE PIUS IX
We should be so fucking lucky.

INT. TYKE'S BEDROOM--NIGHT

Glowing in an electrical outlet on the wall is a Cow and Chicken night-light.

Phil gets to tuck the little fellow in.
The Tyke rolls over with a soft, contented grunt, and places his thumb in his mouth.

Phil ponders him fondly.

PHIL
(to the Tyke's Mom)
I should go see my dad. And my agent.

EXT. "OFF-OFF-STRIP" NIGHTCLUB--NEXT NIGHT

The marquee reads--

PROFESSOR PERCIVAL and SHIT-HEEL the DUMMY!

Situated at the edge of an interstate off-ramp in the middle of the Nevada wasteland, the "Off-Off Strip" is the end of the line for failed Las Vegas acts.

An endless stream of eighteen-wheelers screams by, abusing their klaxon horns, toying deliberately with Doppler effect to annoy the few patrons of this night club.

Phil's car has no problem finding a parking spot.

INT. "OFF-OFF-STRIP" DRESSING ROOM--A MINUTE LATER

In the mirror, surrounded by light bulbs, about half of

which need changing, a decrepit face looks at itself with self-loathing and terminal hopelessness.

PROFESSOR PERCIVAL, Phil's dad, is the unlucky owner of this face. He's dressed in a baggy old academic gown, black. On the makeup table at his elbow, next to a bottle of cheap whiskey, is a black mortarboard-type graduation cap with a frayed brown tassel.

A ventriloquist's dummy, namely SHIT-HEEL, lies in a box on the floor. He's a college freshman, complete with a letter sweater and a dunce-cap, which has been stapled to his head at a pugnacious angle.

Via the mirror, Professor Percival sees a string of turquoise nuggets hovering in mid-air. Then the person around whose neck they're strung comes into focus.

PROFESSOR PERCIVAL

My son, the hypnotist. I don't suppose you can hypnotize the cock-sucking manager to turn off the boob tube over the bar.

PHIL

Are you kidding? On the night of the big game?

PROFESSOR PERCIVAL

What big game?

PHIL

How the fuck should I know?

The Deacons are one of those families who act gruff instead of hugging after periods of separation.

PROFESSOR PERCIVAL

It's bad enough for me, but for you TV's a thorough ass-fuck. They're already a mile under before you come on.

PHIL

If only the power would go off. A statewide blackout. We could work wonders by candlelight.

PROFESSOR PERCIVAL
Wonder-working's your gig. I just piss people off. Or try to. If they ignore me again tonight, I'm fixing to do my patented Christ Climax.

PHIL
Well, like they say, red makes green. No, wait, that's the World Wrestling Federation.

Professor Percival sucks on his cheap whiskey.

PHIL
Come on, now, Dad. Don't you remember what that stuff tastes like?

Phil makes the same hand gesture that he uses to put hicks, troubled teens and nice Indians under.

PROFESSOR PERCIVAL
Sure. Mmmm. Delicious.

Even as the professor gulps, Shit-Heel's voice emanates from the box on the floor.

SHIT-HEEL
You should never have told him it was unleaded.

Phil looks unhappy as his old man takes yet another swig.

PROFESSOR PERCIVAL
Don't worry, sonny-boy. You're a good healer.

SHIT-HEEL
(from the box)
Certain filthy old lushes are just incurable.

INT. "OFF-OFF-STRIP" NIGHTCLUB--A BIT LATER

Professor Percival and Shit-Heel the Dummy are doing their routine. The latter is on the lap of the former, whose ass is on a spot-lit folding chair up front.

Phil watches from the bar, wincing already.

The bleached old BAR MAID brings him a beer.

BAR MAID
Your daddy's just the cutest little old thing. Shit-Heel, maybe not so much.

A moderate earth-temblor rattles the bottles behind the bar and clinks the ice everyone's cocktails. Not that anybody notices--the television above the bar is on.

Nevertheless, as if the temblor is his cue, Shit-Heel goes into a panic.

SHIT-HEEL
We'll all be killed!

He buries his head, dunce-cap and all, in Professor Percival's gown.

SHIT-HEEL
(voice muffled)
You can really feel those H-bomb tests way out here in the middle of Butt-Fuck Egypt.

PROFESSOR PERCIVAL
(a kindly, if pedantic, old gentleman)
This is technically still the Las Vegas Strip, you know. I-15 is a continuation of--

SHIT-HEEL
(sticking his head out)
Shut the fuck up, geezer.
(sticking his head back in)

PROFESSOR PERCIVAL
(apparently hard of hearing)
In downtown, Las Vegas, the nuclear bomb tests often tend to be far less noticeable, what with all the asphalt holding things together.

A big fart puffs out the professor's gown. Shit-Heel

scrambles out, reeling.

SHIT-HEEL
You could use something to hold the fault in your ass together.

So far, nobody in the audience has acknowledged the dummy's existence, much less the professor's.

Even the Bar Maid looks as though she's reconsidering her opinion of Phil's daddy's cuteness.

Another nuke goes off, and the dummy dives for cover again. This time he comes up with a giant boner pushing up the front of his pants like a tent-pole.

SHIT-HEEL
Sorry, everybody. Power excites me.

PROFESSOR PERCIVAL
It's the ultimate aphrodisiac, as Dr. Henry Kissinger once remarked to Chairman Mao Ze--

SHIT-HEEL
(screaming, with sincere hate)
Didn't I tell you to shut the fuck up? Why don't you just die, old man?

Professor Percival ponders Shit-Heel's suggestion. Then he pauses a bit longer to survey the unresponsive audience.

PROFESSOR PERCIVAL
Okay.

He has opted for the Christ Climax.

Professor Percival gets up and turns the dummy loose on the biggest, drunkest BRUISER in the room, hoping the guy will kill them both.

SHIT-HEEL
Come on, fudge-packer. Pay attention. Grampy wants you to get miffed and rise up and beat him to death. You know, suicide by mongoloid.

The Bruiser hardly notices. Neither does his aging GIRLFRIEND, who is seated next to him.

SHIT-HEEL
All right, lard-ass. Just sit there.
(to Girlfriend)
Madam--and I use the term lightly--would you happen to have a loaded Glock concealed between those rolls of gut, or breasts, or whatever you want to call them? Let me check.

Shit-Heel commences groping her.

She just flicks his little wooden hand off, not even looking away from the television, which is showing an ad for an enormous SUV.

It's cool silvery-blue vehicle, and seems to float in slow motion through the Earth's most beautiful scenery. The vehicle itself has been photographed so skillfully as to make you hardly notice its gorgeous surroundings.

The music is intoxicating, and the girl behind the wheel has hair like liquid sunshine and a really nice rack.

Even videophobic Phil's looking.

EXT. DIRT ROAD--DAY (FLASHBACK)

His car struggles through sand and rocks, just barely crawling along.

He's sweating at the wheel, and choking on a throat full of grit.

INT. "OFF-OFF-STRIP" NIGHTCLUB

Shit-Heel won't stop groping the Girlfriend. He gets another boner, a really big one this time--modestly clothed, like the previous one, in his trousers.

SHIT-HEEL
Sorry. Decrepit trailer trash excites me, too. I'm sick that way.

He waves it in their faces.

BRUISER
(absently)
Yeah. Nice. Real good. Thanks.

Without thinking or removing his eyes from the screen, he brushes Shit-Heel's boner aside.

The Girlfriend doesn't even do that. She just cranes her neck around it.

BRUISER
Those are some sweet wheels.

GIRLFRIEND
Really.

The life leaves the professor's eyes, once and for all. Relaxing his dummy arm, he walks silently off, dragging Shit-Heel like the chunk of dead wood he is.

INT. PHIL'S CAR--WEE HOURS

Phil is driving his dad home.

Professor Percival sits in the death seat, withering into himself with despair till he looks no bigger than Shit-Heel, who remains parasitically fastened onto his lap, hissing Chopin's Funeral March into his ear with great cruelty.

EXT. RUN-DOWN LAS VEGAS NEIGHBORHOOD--DAWN

It's a zone of vacant lots and abandoned cars. The whole block on the verge of being reclaimed by the desert.

Phil's car passes the STAR DUST TALENT AGENCY, located in a shabby office on top of a garage.

SHIT-HEEL (VO)
Are you going to drop in on our so-called agent while you're in town?

PHIL (VO)
Why? Just in case he's found some rich and powerful movers and shakers who want to be hypnotized? I doubt Mo's got a time machine in there.

The car pulls into a raunchy trailer park.

INT. PROFESSOR PERCIVAL'S TRAILER--A FEW MOMENTS LATER

Phil is trying to tuck the professor in bed, academic gown and all, but the dummy is reluctant to leave his lap. Shit Heel seems to sense that it might be the last time he gets to straddle and torment the old man.

As Phil tries to pull him off, Shit Heel looks askance at the Medicine Man's turquoise necklace.

SHIT-HEEL
(with a camp lisp)
Looks like a certain somebody has come out since we saw her last. I hope you haven't brought AIDS into our home, you slut.

When Phil finally manages to wrench him loose, Shit-Heel yelps like a patient at the climax of a proctology examination.

SHIT-HEEL
Yow! Just 'cause Dad always liked me best!

Phil holds the obnoxious chunk of wood at arm's length, and tries to ignore its chatter.

PHIL
I've always wondered if it's the college-boy son you never had.

PROFESSOR PERCIVAL
(gasping from his pillow)
Fuck college...

EXT. SAINT PETER'S SQUARE, VATICAN--DAY

LaFontaine exits the Papal apartments, carrying the little Jewish Boy.

PROFESSOR PERCIVAL (VO)
...It just would've been nice to have a son who followed in my footsteps.

Gently, LaFontaine deposits the boy in a carriage, says a few words to the driver, and gets in.

They rattle off down the sanctified cobble stones.

INT. PROFESSOR PERCIVAL'S TRAILER--A MOMENT LATER

There's an uncomfortable silence, during which Phil and his dad both gaze at Shit-Heel, the professor wistfully, Phil with a hint of sibling rivalry.

Shit-Heel, finding himself surrounded, shakes his head, as if to say, "What a couple of matched assholes."

Professor Percival chooses this moment to breathe his last. While cruel snickers emanate from the dummy in Phil's hands, the old man commences his death rattle, hideously loud.

SHIT HEEL
(to Phil, over the death rattle)
Way to go. You broke his poor old heart. How hard would it have been to invest in a dummy and learn to throw your voice? Just a couple feet? You as good as killed him. And another thing--

Shit-Heel goes on and on.

But Phil's not listening because, through the frayed rayon curtains, he has caught a glimpse of a TV in the trailer next door. There's a skinny, huge-mouthed, husky-voiced woman on it, and she talks earnestly about something or other.

Taking a seat on the edge of his father's death-bed, holding a yammering Shit-Heel on his knee, Phil Deacon, the World's Greatest Stage Hypnotist, digs in for a few hours of voyeuristic television.

INT. PROFESSOR PERCIVAL'S TRAILER--NEXT MORNING

Phil's heading out the door, looking a little confused.

Shit-Heel's been chattering nonstop the whole time.

SHIT HEEL (OS)
(from under the bed, where Phil has stuffed him)
--and thanks, by the way, for finishing Dad off. I was getting sick of him. Now let's go dig up several casual sex partners. There's a lumberyard just up the road, if you take my meaning, and--

INT. STAR DUST TALENT AGENCY--LATER THAT DAY

Phil's agent is MO KATZ, an antiquated hustler in a loud plaid jacket.

On the wall of his office, Mo keeps a gallery of his clients' publicity shots: mostly dead hoofers, jugglers, magicians, hypnotists, one-man bands, etc. There's even a photo of pre-TV Professor Percival, a freshly manufactured Shit-Heel on his knee.

Phil stands and looks at this last picture.

MO KATZ
Your old man was even less funny then, if you can imagine that.

A helicopter is heard landing in the vacant lot next door.

MO KATZ
Must be Wayne Newton dropping by to pick up his new cut-outs. Fat morfadyke.

PHIL
(listening absently to the chopper)
I've been running into Simon a lot lately.

MO KATZ
(eagerly)
Paul?

PHIL
Magus.

MO KATZ
(disappointed)
Does that creep still poke through people's trash looking for gigs to hijack? If your dad really wanted to get people to beat him to death, he'd carry around an oil painting of Magus' mug. That'd be rich. Unroll it in their faces when they're least suspecting it.

PHIL
Speaking of Dad, he died.

MO KATZ
He does that every time he goes on.

PHIL
No, I mean for-real died. At least I think he did.

MO KATZ
(heartbroken to hear it, eager to change the subject)
I got you a gig in the H-place.

Phil perks up.

PHIL
The "H-place"? What "H-place"?

MO KATZ
(being evasive)
Well, the H-place I've booked you in ain't Hell, exactly. Some show-biz folks think it's pretty near Heaven, though.

He hands Phil a contract and some promotional materials.

MO KATZ
It's right next door to Hollywood, at any rate.

PHIL
(looking at the documents)
Are you insane?

MO KATZ

What insane? Working with underprivileged youths at a bona-fide Community Center? This is the kind of thing that might get the Christers out of your face.

Phil holds the contract at arm's length, with just his fingertips, like a turd.

MO KATZ

Come on, it's a fantastic opportunity. You put it in your promo material and wave it in their face next time the Jesus freaks try to bar your way into some stinking high school. I heard they almost closed you down in Wyoming.

PHIL

Colorado.

MO KATZ

One of those big square butt-holes. We'll say all proceeds went to a worthy charity of your fabrication. It'll be a good career move.

PHIL

(signing on the dotted line)

Assuming I'm ever heard from again.

Moments after Phil walks out, Simon Magus' face appears in the doorway.

He enters, and, with a single flick of a finger, seems to put Mo Katz under hypnosis.

Mo is petrified.

SIMON

Where's Saint Philip the Deacon going this time?

Mo hands over the promotional material, and goes promptly back to being petrified.

SIMON
(laughing)
"This I gotta see," as you'd put it.
(thinks about it)
You got him into this, Mo. Do you think he can handle it? But why am I asking you? You're under hypnosis. You don't have any opinions.

He takes Mo by either cheek and aims his face straight on.

SIMON
Say, "Gosh, Mr. Magus, sir. I don't know if Mr. Deacon can handle it. Maybe you'd better go check it out for yourself."

Mo says it.

SIMON
Say, "Here's my MasterCard, Mr. Magus, sir. Use it in good health to refuel that handsome aircraft which idles out there in the neighboring vacant lot."

Mo says it and hands over his plastic.

SIMON
Say, "Mr. Magus, sir, after you return from Los Angeles, relaxed and refreshed, would you permit me to book your act for a month in the Imperial Deluxe Dictator Room at fabulous Caesar's Palace, situated on the dazzling Las Vegas Strip?"

MO KATZ
(snapping out of it)
In your wet dreams, weirdo.

In response, the muzzle of a big black handgun is jammed into the nape of Mo's neck.

We see that he hasn't been petrified by hypnosis at all, but by Elijah, who's been standing behind him, fully prepared to blow his head off.

Elijah cocks the gun.

SIMON
Whoah, whoah. It's okay. Mo's right. We need to prove ourselves. We'll bring L.A. to its knees first. We'll slay 'em, Mo, you wait and see. And then you can decide whether, in your considered professional opinion, we're ready for the Imperial Deluxe Nazi Rim-Ram Room at blah-blah-blah...

On the way out, Simon nods at Elijah, who karate-kicks Mo in the gut, sending the old agent flying across the office.

He smashes into the wall. The show-biz photos fall and bury him.

EXT. LOS ANGELES COMMUNITY CENTER--NEXT DAY

The place is on the border between an African-American neighborhood and an Hispanic.

The ground-floor windows have been barred to foil intruders.

Something that sounds like an aural gang war roars from those barred windows. A couple dozen boom boxes can be heard belching a black "gangsta-rap" radio station full blast, while a roughly equal number of ghetto blasters shriek an Hispanic salsa station, also cranked all the way up.

Phil's glittery cut-out is propped against the front stoop of this Community Center. In his right hand, where a mike once was, this cardboard Phil holds an undersized, flounder-pale dick, expertly spray-painted, graffiti-style.

The World's Greatest Stage Hypnotist quivers as the earth-quaking vibrations of the rap and salsa loosen the concrete blocks of which this front stoop is constructed. At least one large block has wobbled loose. Its cast-iron reinforcing rods poke out into open air.

A hot rod full of TROUBLED ETHNIC YOUTH drives by and stitches Phil's cut-out across the plum satin cummerbund with Uzi fire.

INT. LOS ANGELES COMMUNITY CENTER ENTRY POINT--SAME DAY

A big AFRICAN AMERICAN ADULT lounges together with a white SOCIAL WORKER in a secure booth. Through a circle of perforations in the bulletproof glass, they deal with a very nervous flesh-and-blood Phil Deacon.

AFRICAN-AMERICAN ADULT
(shouting over the racket, trying not to chuckle at Phil's electric-blue tux)
Sorry, Mr., er--
(looking at today's program notes)
--Dorkon. Your venue has been taken over temporarily by an impromptu meeting of a political nature. Please feel free to enter and make yourself comfortable--

The Social Worker starts laughing.

AFRICAN-AMERICAN ADULT
--and maybe the stage will open up for you in a few moments.

Just to get in off the perilous street, Phil does as suggested. He enters the foyer.

Posters on the walls announce barbecues, Viva la Raza dances, Southern Baptist gospel ministries, performances by El Teatro de los Campesinos as well as their native African counterparts, and so on. This Community Center is the rope in a subcultural tug-o'-war, and it's ready to snap any minute.

Trying to be as inconspicuous as possible in his pale skin, Phil tiptoes past a pair of clinics, labeled AIDS and METHADONE respectively. Two open barrels stand nearby, one freely offering condoms, the other disposable hypodermic syringes.

Phil chooses to cower on a bench by the Legal Aid Nook. A white LEGAL INTERN hides behind a desk against the wall.

Phil's just trying to hang onto his bench and not be shaken off by the double boom-box din that blasts through a nearby door, marked DANCE HALL.

PHIL
(to the Intern)
Tough room, eh? I go on in a few minutes.

He tries to forget his jitters by absorbing himself in the reading material, a pamphlet entitled, "Six Quick Questions to Ask Your Court-Appointed Lawyer."

INT. DANCE HALL--DAY

The situation could be described as a seething mass of humanity, except it happens to be two seething masses of humanity, with a definite dividing line down the middle.

One side is composed of amazingly scary BLACK STREET GANG MEMBERS, male and female, and the other of no less scary HISPANIC BIKERS, both sexes.

It's all black leather, chains and frightful tattoos, with the bright insignia of either gang defining the left and right sides of the hall.

Everybody's huge. Their already broad, muscular shoulders are augmented by jumbo battery-operated radios.

This is an unstable situation, to put it mildly: two equally matched organizations, death-rivals, competing for turf.

For the moment, the aggression is strictly musical, but physical violence impends.

The two SUPREME LEADERS of the gangs climb onto a raised dais in front and start jockeying for position, in a similar but far more macho manner than Phil and Simon did in the casino dressing room.

BLACK SUPREME LEADER
(a head-splitting shout)
Shut the fuck up!

The Blacks get quiet, and the Hispanics do, too, more or

less. Both sides turn their shoulder-deployed eardrum-pulverizers down, but not off.

HISPANIC SUPREME LEADER
We called this truce because a couple of bee-yatches wanna show us what they got.

Two POLITICAL ACTIVISTS, one Black, the other Hispanic, both disguised as gang-bangers, climb onto the dais from opposite sides. They head straight for each other, looking angry, as if about to engage in a knife fight.

Everybody gets interested.

VOICE FROM THE HISPANIC SIDE
Now we're talking.

VOICE FROM THE BLACK SIDE
Some single combat action.

INT. LEGAL AID NOOK--AT THAT MOMENT

Phil notices the sudden relative silence. The jitters leave him, and are replaced with professional curiosity.

PHIL
(to himself)
Who reined in that herd?

He goes and peeks through the chicken-wired window in the dance hall door, but can only see broad backs emblazoned with gang colors.

Phil's such a pro that he forgets his fear with the possibility that he could learn something from whatever virtuoso is working the room.

Without thinking, he steps in.

INT. DANCE HALL

He can't see much, as everyone's so huge. So he climbs onto a folding chair against the wall.

Phil's head rises above the mob just in time to see the two Activists stop short in the middle of the dais, facing each other. They extend their right hands, and clasp each other's forearms in a greeting of solidarity.

The two Activists link arms, and turn to face the rival gangs, their free hands held high in a closed-fist salute of proud bi-racial unity.

Some of the gang-bangers on both sides shut up, but others jeer.

VOICE FROM THE BLACK SIDE
We ain't buying your bullshit guerilla theater tactics.

VOICE FROM THE HISPANIC SIDE
Yeah, that's so sixties. Try it on my grandpa.

VOICE FROM THE BLACK SIDE
I try it on yo mama.

A race riot starts to flare up. Physical feints are made along the dividing line, displays of valor.

BLACK ACTIVIST
(trying to restore order)
No, wait! That's just what the Oppressor wants us to do! Fight among ourselves!

Nobody listens. Guns are drawn and cocked.

HISPANIC ACTIVIST
(one last desperate shouting plea before diving for cover)
Our own flowing blood distracts us from the weakness of the Oppressor! He teeters on the brink of collapse at this very moment!

As if on cue, Phil's chair chooses right now to fold under him. He falls with a crash.

Everybody turns to stare.

He sits there flat on his ass on the floor in stage drag: electric-blue tuxedo, face made up, hair done big, a string of turquoise Indian nuggets tangled up in his bow tie.

PUZZLED GANG-BANGER
(gawking)
Who the fuck is she?

Phil clambers to his feet, simpering apologetically.

PHIL
I was just looking for the, ah, dentist's office.

The tiny buckles on Phil's cummerbund give way. He seems to explode in a burst of plum satin, like a sissy suicide bomber. This nearly gets him pulverized by several itchy trigger fingers.

He turns to flee for his life, nearly tripping over the glamorous garment. But then he hears something that stops him in his tracks.

It's music to any professional entertainer's ears: laughter.

This is more laughs than Phil's dad ever got in the whole lifetime that maybe just ended...

INT. "OFF-OFF-STRIP" NIGHTCLUB--NIGHT (FLASHBACK)

Shit-Heel stands on Professor Percival's shoulder, kicking him in the ear.

Four out of the five "Off-Off-Strip" PATRONS are watching the TV over the bar. The fifth stares at Professor Percival in bored puzzlement.

We hear peals of laughter, which are not coming from these stiffs, but rather--

INT. DANCE HALL--DAY

--from the Gang Members, who are unified, for the moment, in hilarious scorn for this honky.

Phil can't prevent himself from taking a bow; it's in his genes. He gets up on the dais to do just that.

The Political Activists, who are the only people not laughing, bar his way.

BLACK ACTIVIST
Where do you think you're going, Clown?

HISPANIC ACTIVIST
Weren't we just discussing you?

PHIL
(excitedly, already bowing)
Me? I'm not in the oppressing business. I'm in the entertaining business. I come from a long line of show-biz types. My dad is--was--a Vegas ventriloquist. You may have heard of him: Professor Percival...
(starting to get emotional)
I'm a pro, just like my dad, if I do say so myself. And pros like us never miss a gig as long as we can move our bodies. So you better break both my legs right here and now, if--

Phil realizes what an idiotic thing he's saying, and changes the subject. He tries to get his act off the ground.

PHIL
Good afternoon, ladies and, er, gentlemen. It's so nice to be here in the "City of Angels," as they say, heh-heh...

He finally notices that his cummerbund is dangling around his knees. Without thinking, he untangles the thing and tosses it to a young CHICANA, like Elvis bestowing a sweaty hankie on an old lady in the front row at Caesar's Palace.

It hits her in the face. Too late, just as it slides to the floor, he comes to the conclusion that tossing a cummerbund in these circumstances might not have been such a good idea.

PHIL
Um, never mind. Okay?

With the heel of her engineer boot, the Chicana crushes a cigarette out on it.

Her man, a GIANT CHICANO, is just about ready to do the same to Phil's head.

A few people are still laughing at him. Some stare in puzzlement, others in amazement at his guts, still others in aesthetic revulsion at the white skin on his face and hands.

A few are getting angry--they begin to see the Activists' point. But several remain politically unconvinced--

VOICE FROM THE HISPANIC SIDE
This pendejito oppress me? Not on his best day.

The Giant Chicano comes up to throw Phil out the window.

GIANT CHICANO
That's enough chuckles for today. Now you go through those bars like a hard-boiled egg through a slicer.

PHIL
Jesus Christ.

GIANT CHICANO
That's right, Spencer, say your prayers, 'cause some major damnation is coming your way.

PHIL
No, I mean you. You're Jesus Christ, and they just nailed you.

He plants an index finger on the Giant Chicano's chest--and is even more surprised than everybody else when the guy freezes in his tracks.

PHIL
(to himself)
Damn. It worked.

The Giant Chicano has stiffened into the crucified position, feet crossed, arms out, head dangling to one side, eyes rolled back, tongue lolling.

Phil spins him around to face the crowd.

BLACK GANG-BANGER
Is that some creepy shit?

HISPANIC GANG-BANGER
It's just like the big splatter-flick
with all the words at the bottom, man.

PHIL
Now, if these chairs don't collapse...

The Giant Chicano seems just stiff enough for Phil to try stretching him out, like LaFontaine did with the lovely young Noblewoman at the Paris opera.

The chairs groan and sag a bit, but hold up.

Phil's got everybody's attention now. He's getting a handle on this difficult audience, and the professional pride begins to show in his face and bearing.

He invites a petite, but very tough-looking BLACK CHICK, wearing a mean Afro-puff, to stand on the Giant Chicano's tummy.

Phil offers her a hand.

BLACK CHICK
(climbing up handily enough)
Back off, Cracker.

Everybody cheers.

VOICE FROM THE HISPANIC SIDE
You tell him, girl!

The Blacks turn their ghetto blasters back up, and the Chick dances all over the Chicano.

The Blacks jeer at their counterparts.

VOICE FROM THE BLACK SIDE
One of our women has found a use for a
beaner!

When the Hispanics start looking angry, Phil calls for a Black man and a Hispanic woman to repeat the process in reverse.

The scariest "gangsta" of all, a BUFFED BLACK YOUTH, shirtless, with an Olympic build, offers to stiffen himself without the aid of hypnosis.

BUFFED BLACK YOUTH
I don't need no magicking, peckerwood.

PHIL
Oh, but sir. It's not magic. It's hyp--

He's already a human plank.

PHIL
Never mind.

A lovely LATINA kicks off her footwear and mounts him. Her homeys crank up the salsa, and she dances.

At first she has some difficulty finding footholds among the Buffed Black Youth's pronounced abs. But she's a talented young woman, and soon masters the difficult terrain.

The sonic race-war has recommenced, loud as before. But both sides seem to be getting in a good mood, especially when the go-go girls eye each other's bodies appreciatively and begin to trade moves.

EXT. COMMUNITY CENTER ENTRY POINT--A FEW SECONDS LATER

Simon Magus shows up, alone.

He smuggles himself past the Black Adult and the Social Worker, in the same way he infiltrated the Colorado High School--without anyone noticing.

Simon follows the sound of the pounding rap and salsa to the dance hall door. He peeks in the window and sees Phil grinning between a couple of stiffs with girls on them.

SIMON
(to himself)
The old trick. Gets them every time.

Been getting them every time for about a hundred and thirty years, since the great Baron Dupotet pioneered the technique.
(shouting, unheard, over the din)
Oh, Phil, Phil, time to update your act with some fresh material!

Then he steps in--

INT. DANCE HALL--DAY

--and sees exactly what kind of audience the old trick has gotten this time.

We see Simon's first reaction to this show: disbelief.

PHIL
Do we have any more volunteers?

Some VOLUNTEERS from both sides come up and he begins bopping them on the forehead and murmuring into their ears.

Phil starts off easy. He causes one HISPANIC VOLUNTEER to fall back trustingly into the arms of a BLACK VOLUNTEER.

When both young men come to, they're embarrassed, and pretend to be angry. But they look at each others' faces with curiosity.

Phil causes another mixed-race pair of Volunteers to mistake each others' gang insignia for their own, and to greet each other warmly.

As the Activists watch with interest, he leaves these two under hypnosis, chatting together in an Afro-Latino dialect of their own spontaneous invention.

Next, Phil causes a MEXICAN YOUTH to sashay across the dais with exaggerated black mannerisms, and a BLACK YOUTH to do the opposite.

At first there's some anger in the hall at what appears to be mockery and racial stereotyping, but it gives way to laughter and--to Phil's delight--applause.

This applause brings the second reaction from Simon Magus

as he watches from the back: professional despair. He knows he could never work this crowd half as well.

INT. DANCE HALL--ALMOST AN HOUR LATER

The girls still dance, and the rap and salsa still roar.

Simon watches Phil's show, the despair digging deeper into his face with each uncanny triumph on the dais.

Two of Phil's subjects currently believe themselves to be caught in a blizzard in some town way up north--

EXT. SNOWY STREET CORNER--DAY

The young black FEMALE SUBJECT is cold and shivering on the sidewalk.

The HISPANIC SUBJECT, passing by, removes his biker jacket with its bright Spanish gang colors. Showing great gallantry, respect and solicitude, he drapes it over her shoulders.

HISPANIC SUBJECT
(just audible over the boom boxes)
Stay warm, my sister.

Other Subjects live out edifying mini-dramas elsewhere--

EXT. GENERIC SLUM ALLEY--NIGHT

The Mexican Youth writhes with heroin withdrawal and/or bullet wounds on the concrete.

Two BLACK YOUTHS come to help. They lay hands on him, and he is miraculously healed. Together, arms linked, the three of them ascend straight into the sky.

The two Activists stroll onto the scene, and watch them disappear into the clouds.

BLACK ACTIVIST
Do you think Phil Deacon is a member of the party?

HISPANIC ACTIVIST
If not, our cell needs to sign him up

quick, while he's still hungry.

EXT. AFRO-LATINO GANG-BANGER HEAVEN--DAY

It's a bright, warm, but otherwise vague place, except for a few pink hammers and sickles and red stars floating around on thin wires.

Gang-bangers of both races beam at each other, embrace and smile. They look into each other's eyes--

INT. DANCE HALL

--and see themselves.

As this glorious climax fills the dance hall with warmth and multicultural camaraderie, an ominous change comes over Simon.

All of his previous reactions to Phil's superior talent now crystallize into borderline-psychotic envy. Every human emotion is subsumed under a single desire: to destroy where he can't create.

EXT. COMMUNITY CENTER FRONT STOOP--A MOMENT LATER

Simon Magus goes back out onto the street, with desperation in his stride.

He pauses to sneer at Phil's glittery cardboard cut-out, Uzi bullet holes still smoldering about the midsection.

He examines the loosened concrete block upon which the cut-out is propped. Then he ponders the bars over the dance hall window.

Something like a smile plays across his envious mouth.

Simon snaps his fingers once and, in a splash of rats, the Big Weird Woman materializes from the shadows behind an overflowing dumpster.

SIMON
(pointing to the concrete block)
Do you like that heavy thing?

If she responds, it's only visible to a pro, like Simon.

EXT. L.A. SLUM STREET--A FEW MINUTES LATER

The two of them move along one of the saddest fringes of the Walk of Fame, embedded with the worn stars of forgotten Hollywooders.

They enter a zone populated by the grotesqueries who coagulate around the bleeding edges of the movie industry.

Almost like a window shopper, Simon looks delightedly around at all the PIMPS, JUNKIES, TRANSSEXUALS, TATTOO MONSTERS, BODY-PIERCING MASOCHISTS, LEATHER FREAKS, and drug-addled SLUMMERS from Bel-Air.

He also casts and appreciative eye on the BEGGARS, FLASHERS, trolling PEDOPHILES, sundry SURGICAL ADDICTS, including three or four VOLUNTARY MULTIPLE AMPUTEES who skitter along on makeshift wheeled conveyances, plus assorted MADMEN, and even crazier LAPD ASSHOLES, both uniform and plainclothes.

SIMON

This is going to be too easy. It's like being back home in the Rotten Apple. I'll hardly need to bop any foreheads around here.

EXT. PEA-GREEN BUILDING--A MOMENT LATER

Simon and the Big Weird Woman start climbing up a clanking fire escape which is coming unbolted from the side of an abandoned and boarded-up building.

Fifteen stooping stories high, its rotted bricks having been painted pea-green in the remote past, this the loftiest and most conspicuous structure in the whole depressed neighborhood.

It's not far from the Community Center, just on the next block, in fact. As we follow Simon and the Big Weird Woman up the precarious fire escape, Phil's venue heaves into view. The boom boxes can be heard all the way up here.

From the roof of this pea-green building, growing stronger as we ascend, come the sound and artificial wind of the Samaria helicopter's idling engine.

Elijah's excited face peeks over the parapet.

ELIJAH
Can I offer you nice folks a lift somewhere?

EXT. HELICOPTER--HALF AN HOUR LATER

The sun has just barely begun to go down. Orange light, tinged brownish with a touch of smog, bathes Ahab's scarlet chopper as it hovers over a hill at the edge of the city.

A big chunk of Los Angeles is visible, just starting to switch some of its lights on.

INT. HELICOPTER--AT THAT MOMENT

Elijah, the recent military academy dropout, looks right at home behind the controls.

The cabin is crowded with Samarian materiel, everything bearing the letter-A logo. We can see the Big Weird Woman hanging out the hatch, ready to drop something.

Simon is loosely strapped in a passenger seat behind Elijah, leaning over the former Cadet's shoulder and chatting to him as they survey, through the cockpit window, the city that sprawls at their feet.

SIMON
See the funny little Los Angelinos, Elijah my boy? They're all sunk in a permanent state of hypnosis...

INTERCUT AMONG PRIVATE HOMES, MOVIE THEATERS, PHIL'S SHOW

NUCLEAR FAMILIES sit stuporous before boob-tubes.

MOVIEGOERS do likewise before silver screens.

One RAP-LOVER at the Community Center is oblivious to Phil's show, as he sways to the sounds coming from his radio. He falls even deeper into a trance when a commercial comes on.

SIMON (VO)
I'd love to see what I could do without

the electronic competition.

INT. HELICOPTER

SIMON
How about if I snap my fingers and find out?

He does just that, and the Big Weird Woman drops the object she had in her hand, which turns out to be a fragmentation device.

EXT. HILLTOP BENEATH THE CHOPPER--THREE SECONDS LATER

A Los Angeles Power and Light sub-station, over which Simon and his associates have been hovering, blows up.

INT. HELICOPTER--A SECOND LATER

Simon and Elijah (but not the Big Weird Woman, who's too weird to notice such things) watch in delight as the power goes out, starting at the base of this hill, and fanning out, grid by grid, in a chain reaction, across much of the city.

Just before they fly off, almost as an afterthought, Simon reaches into the RED HERRING box and sprinkles a bunch of Arab headdresses and paperback Korans over the disabled power station.

A SERIES OF INTERCUTS ACROSS BLACKING-OUT LOS ANGELES

In a Beverly Hills beauty salon, the hair dryers stop, and the fat, pampered CUSTOMERS start screaming at the poor Vietnamese BOAT LADY who just sweeps up the place.

A whining drill stops in mid-torment and lodges in a wretched PATIENT'S molar. The DENTIST puts his foot on the edge of the chair to brace himself while he tries to muscle the bit free.

A SWEET OLD WHITE COUPLE in a lower-middle class, but cozy studio apartment, are puzzled when their modest supper fails to come out of the toaster.

INT. GOVERNOR SCHWARZENEGGER'S OFFICE--SAME MOMENT

The man himself is in his shirtsleeves, tie loosened, trying to stay in shape on an electric treadmill.

The apparatus is quite snazzy, and has a dashboard with speedometer, odometer, EKG readout, and a VHS, on which a Chuck Norris action movie is being pointedly ignored.

GOVERNOR SCHWARZENEGGER
(to his secretary)
Phone Jeb and see if he want to play a little online poker later on. Tell him I kick his redneck azz.

The power goes out, and the treadmill stops. But the sheer momentum of the Governor's physique carries him forward, straight through the front of the thing.

He winds up on the other side of the room, holding the dashboard, wires dangling, Chuck Norris tape unspooling all over the floor at his feet.

GOVERNOR SCHWARZENEGGER
Gott in Himmel. What has happened?

INTERCUT BETWEEN RAP AND SALSA RADIO STATIONS

Broadcasting stops.

INT. DANCE HALL--SAME MOMENT

A sea of white noise washes over both gangs. Boom-boxes are shaken in attempts to restart the music. Batteries are checked.

Phil thinks fast and seizes this opportune moment. He holds out his hands, palms down, and lowers them slowly, seeming to fine-tune something in the air.

When all is ready--

PHIL
(stroking the turquoise necklace)
I relinquish control.

He surrenders the stage to the two Activists.

HISPANIC ACTIVIST
(only half-joking)
Did you turn out the lights?

EXT. TOP OF PEA-GREEN BUILDING--HALF AN HOUR LATER

It's dark night now.

The chopper returns to its roost. Through the cockpit window, Elijah can be seen manning the controls.

ELIJAH
(shouting)
And Simon, the Magus, arrived in his flying chariot!

Once the engine has been shut down, the powerless city is as close to being silent as it ever gets, except for the sound of looting.

The blades still whirling on their own momentum, Elijah and the Big Weird Woman begin to unload, but Simon stops them.

SIMON
Wait. Those aren't for us.
(pointing to his own eyes)
I've got these.
(holding out his hands)
And these. That's all we need.

Whimpering in a kind of animalistic protest, the Big Weird Woman puts back a double armload of bazookas.

She holds up a pair of bleeding forearms, and hands full of blisters and smashed fingers. She displays the seismic crack tattooed between her deflated breasts, which has been lacerated by the edges of ammo crates.

SIMON
(tenderly)
Yes, yes. I know. You like simple, brainless, hard labor, don't you? Burns off some of that sick energy without scorching holes in your soul.

He reaches up to stroke her forehead with his left hand.

SIMON

Don't worry, love. Down below I have a bit of heavy lifting for you to do. Heavy throwing as well. And soon after that you'll be able to unload these goodies to your heart's content, into some grateful, dark arms.

The Big Weird Woman acquiesces in her mute way.

Leaving Elijah hunkered in the hatch of the chopper, an M-16 close at hand, they descend the precarious fire escape, the Big Weird Woman slopping gory handprints all over the pea-green bricks.

The sounds of breaking glass and cheers of inhuman glee rise up from the blackness to greet them. It's the LOOTERS.

SIMON

They've started the party without us.

Simon's stage-performer's body responds involuntarily to the cheers. He lets go of the railing to wave down at his unseen fans, and only avoids falling to his death when the Weird Woman reaches out one hand and catches him by the collar.

He dangles awhile in mid air, looking up into her face with a mixture of gratitude, horror and bent love.

Then he grabs hold of the clanking rails, and Simon, the Magus, descends into Hell.

INT. DANCE HALL--ABOUT THE SAME TIME

Having already forgotten Phil's presence, most members of both gangs listen to the Political Activists deliver their spiel.

They hardly notice the darkness of the dance hall, which is relieved only by the glow of Looters' bonfires, seeping between the window bars.

BLACK ACTIVIST

Look at yourselves--which is the same as saying, Look at us. We are such strong young men and women...

EXT. NEARBY STREET--SAME TIME

The moon secretes jaundiced light upon porn movie palaces and peep-show holes.

Their lurid images having vanished with the electricity, these institutions disgorge onto the sidewalks their TWISTED CLIENTELE, pale as slugs and even physically deformed, like Fellini extras.

BLACK ACTIVIST (VO)
Look at us, I say. We're the pride of our respective communities...

A mass of withered and bloodless STREET-MAGGOTS huddle in front of a shop window that features rows of used televisions, switched on all night--but not tonight.

L.A. Power and Light Company having failed them, these Street Maggots turn around and show us their mad, colorless faces, all misshapen from being pressed forever against plate glass.

HISPANIC ACTIVIST (VO)
Within our proud bodies and minds, we contain all the potential in the world...

Dangerously unoccupied now, the Street Maggots commence looking for trouble, and Simon Magus is right there to steer them in its direction.

He begins bopping pasty, blue-veined foreheads left and right, imitating Phil's technique.

HISPANIC ACTIVIST (VO)
Forget L.A. Power and Light. All the political power we need, and all the spiritual light in the cosmos, is already contained within our beautiful bodies and bright minds...

Simon Magus mucks about in the dripping alleys, conjuring up all the usually unseen SLEAZE. They crawl out of the cracks in the pavement, ready for a street orgy.

Simon recruits and encourages all manner of UNDESIRABLES to

behave badly.

For example, he creates four IMPROVED VERSIONS OF THE SAMARIAN BANGING BOY, and causes them to use their heads as battering rams, to rattle and dent the aluminum shutters of a Mom-and-Pop Korean barbecue shop.

HISPANIC ACTIVIST (VO)
But we must reclaim our dignity, and stop sinking to the Oppressor's lowest expectations...

Simon moves through the darkness with a growing entourage of NOCTURNAL CREATURES, every bit as pallid as their counterparts in the "Smoldering Gehenna" nightclub back in New York. Though this is sunny California, there's not a hint of a wholesome tan, nor so much as a freckle, among them.

For her part, the Big Weird Woman attracts any number of NECROPHILES. A ZOMBIE BATALLION constitutes the honor guard of her fan club.

Simon selects a half-dozen specimens of these Zombies and transmogrifies them into BIG CITY-STYLE GRIMACING BOYS. He dispatches them in the direction of a NICE YOUNG COUPLE who are only trying to get indoors and have protected sex.

NICE YOUNG MAN
Take my money. Just don't hurt Debbie.

They're not interested in the money, or in Debbie. They just want to hulk alongside and make ugly faces.

BLACK ACTIVIST (VO)
My sisters and brothers, with your exaggerated manners and your primitive music, you do the Oppressor's job for him. He laughs at you, even while fearing you...

Simon makes good use of the Big Weird Woman. Terrifying as she is, with her entire big body flexed like a jaw muscle, she serves as sheep dog.

Through her, Simon sees to it that much nastiness moves in the direction of the Community Center, with frequent pauses to offend LAW-ABIDING MOTORISTS stuck at non-functioning traffic lights.

Simon decrees mass-lickings of many cars. Windshields and door handles glisten appallingly in the moonlight.

INT. DANCE HALL--SAME NIGHT

Gradually, as the Activists speak, their audience grows more and more attentive.

Phil is quite pleased with how this potential catastrophe is turning out. Getting that dreamy look he wears when reading his LaFontaine book, he stands on the dais and gazes grandly across the sea of black and brown faces.

EXT. LONDON ZOOLOGICAL GARDENS, 1884--DAY

We see a sea of white faces, including those belonging to QUEEN VICTORIA, her Prime Minister BENJAMIN DISRAELI, her pet poet ALFRED LORD TENNYSON, and assorted other royalist BIG-WIGS of the period.

They are all seated comfortably in armchairs under a grand silken pavilion which shades them from the pale English sun.

Her Majesty seems to be enchanted, perhaps even mesmerized, by something that is taking place before her eyes.

HISPANIC ACTIVIST (VO)
This is our neighborhood. Why should those bars on the window be necessary?

Ribbons of red and blue silk are spiraled around the bars of the lion cage, which have been gilded for the occasion.

Inside this cage stands LaFontaine.

At his feet, an enormous lion lies flat on its back, its four mighty legs sticking straight up in the air.

BLACK ACTIVIST (VO)
Soon, my virile brothers and fecund sisters, this will be our city. And then, by virtue of sheer numbers alone, it will be our state. And by the time

our sons have grown fine and handsome
and strong...

The little Jewish Boy is in the cage, too, grown a couple well-nourished and -loved years' worth. He looks considerably more comfortable in the company of a large carnivore than he was in the Pope's.

He is splendidly dressed in a red velvet Little Lord Fauntleroy outfit, and has been well-educated and trained.

The Jewish Boy is obviously having the time of his life. He possesses all the stage presence of a professional two or three times his age.

INT. DANCE HALL

HISPANIC ACTIVIST
...it will be our country!

The sounds of chaos approach outside: the chilling vocalizations of the Street Maggots and Undesirables, the Perverts and Zombies, the Sleaze and the Nocturnal Creatures, who constitute Simon Magus' entourage.

Phil's the only person in the dance hall oblivious to this ominous noise. He looks down at his harmonious handiwork with pride and delight.

PHIL
(in a voice like LaFontaine's)
Savagery is being subdued.

VOICE FROM THE BLACK SIDE
What did that motherfucker just say?

EXT. LONDON ZOOLOGICAL GARDENS

LAFONTAINE
(in his grandest voice)
The vital fluid fills all space and all
beings.

JEWISH BOY
(to the lion)
Gauche!

On that command, the lion's paws move left, and Queen Victoria murmurs in admiration, as do the members of her entourage.

INT. DANCE HALL

Phil waves his hand, and some of the less attentive Hispanics begin to listen to the Black Activist.

EXT. LONDON ZOOLOGICAL GARDENS

LAFONTAINE
To control the vital fluid is to control all things, and all beings.

JEWISH BOY
(to the lion)
Droit!

The lion's paws move to the right, and Alfred Lord Tennyson begins to applaud, even before his Queen sets the precedent.

INT. DANCE HALL

Phil snaps his fingers, and certain restless African-Americans start paying attention to the Hispanic Activist.

HISPANIC ACTIVIST
For our daughters and sons of the future, and for ourselves, right now, we can create a good, fresh world!

From the bad, rotten world outside the barred windows, the sounds of Simon Magus' wild devotees rattle the windowpanes, louder and louder.

Meanwhile, Phil remains unaware of anything but this gig of his, and how swimmingly it's going.

INT. STAR DUST TALENT AGENCY--DAY

He's shaking hands with Mo Katz. They both grin and give the "thumbs up."

A picture of Phil, dressed in a safari suit, has been added to Mo's photo gallery, right next to Professor Percival.

BLACK ACTIVIST (VO)
We need be trammeled no longer by the White Oppressor!

INT. DANCE HALL

Everyone is staring at Phil, the closest thing they have to a White Oppressor at the moment.

But he's oblivious. Indeed, his eyes are shut.

He stands there, his necklace of gold-veined turquoise Indian nuggets gleaming in light borrowed from Looters' bonfires. He moves his arms in grand LaFontainian gestures, back and forth, as if conducting a symphony played by lion's paws.

EXT. LONDON ZOOLOGICAL GARDENS

LAFONTAINE
(in unison with the Black Activist)
Will is limitless!

JEWISH BOY
(to the lion)
Epees mortelles!

The lion's huge claws pop out, and Her Majesty gasps.

QUEEN VICTORIA
Jesus Christ!

INT. DANCE HALL

The concrete block from the front stoop comes crashing through the barred window, blasting the frame away and leaving a huge hole in the side of the Community Center.

QUEEN VICTORIA (VO)
Look at those big sharp cock-suckers!

Standing on the other side of the hole, backlit by the lurid glow of bonfires, still recoiling from the throw, is the hulking figure of the Big Weird Woman. The black crack in her chest is gilded with bloody abrasions from the concrete block's naked reinforcing rods.

She's backed up by a semi-circle of leering faces that seem to have crawled straight from Hell's lightless crannies.

Something that resembles a Phil Deacon doppelganger follows the concrete block into the hall. Flying like a frisbee in a cloud of loose glitter, it's his cardboard cut-out, Uzi-holes and all.

SIMON (OS)
(screaming from the shadows)
Come out and play, Philip the Deacon!

EXT. LONDON ZOOLOGICAL GARDENS

The Big Wigs begin to applaud, thinking the claw display must be LaFontaine's climax. They are unable to imagine anything more spectacular.

But then the great mesmerist nods at his little assistant.

LAFONTAINE
You may do the honors, my esteemed colleague.

The Jewish Boy flicks an index finger in the air.

The lion leaps to its feet and claws the red and blue silk ribbons off the gilded bars.

Queen Victoria squawks, soils her regal drawers, and faints.

EXT. COMMUNITY CENTER--A SPLIT-SECOND LATER

Leaving their ghetto blasters to sputter white noise on the dance hall floor, the Gangsters and Bikers come pouring out of the hole in the wall and onto the street, like a single pride of lions.

The Street Maggots, Undesirables, Perverts, Zombies, and all the others take to their heels, shrieking and squealing in ecstasy.

INT. GOVERNOR SCHWARZENEGGER'S OFFICE--A FEW MINUTES LATER

We see the Governor's face, its rugged handsomeness nicely accentuated by emergency candle-light. But he's looking uncharacteristically haggard tonight.

He is seated at his gubernatorial desk. Like the Big Weird Woman, he's backed up by a semicircle of demonic faces, which wobble grotesquely in flame-shadows.

They are ADVISORS, PROFESSIONAL POLITICOS, YOUNG REPUBLICAN INTERNS, and so forth. Though pencil-necks all, they have been browbeating him, causing him to look frazzled and wimpy. His shirt seems too big on him.

GOVERNOR SCHWARZENEGGER
No, no. I am telling you. I cannot declare ze martial law. Peoples vill say I am ze Nazi azzhole.

EXT. COMMUNITY CENTER FRONT STOOP--A FEW MOMENTS LATER

Just about everyone's gone, and the scene's comparatively peaceful. The screams and sounds of breaking glass have spread to other streets.

The night canopy is pretty visible, as tonight there is no light pollution to refract off the L.A. smog, which is light at the moment.

Phil peeks out from the dance hall. He climbs through the window-hole, brushes some glass and broken metal away from what used to be the windowsill, and sits, feet dangling.

PHIL
(speaking into the night)
That's quite a subject you've got there.

He's not surprised to hear his would-be rival's voice.

SIMON (OS)
She is rather good, isn't she?

Phil takes a moment to examine the concrete block and the breach it blasted through the wall.

PHIL
I don't even want to think about the post-hypnotic suggestions you must be using to maintain these levels of

adrenalin.

SIMON
(revealing himself)
It's not a matter of suggestion, or adrenalin. Not exactly.
(to the Big Weird Woman)
You can come out now.

PHIL
(in a Tarzan voice)
Phil good. Phil friend.

She looms up from behind a bush and dumbly displays herself.

PHIL
(shrinking back a bit)
Is she a maniac?

SIMON
(pausing, thinking)
I'm going to say...no.

PHIL
Not methamphetamine. Simon, even you wouldn't--

SIMON
She's a Latah.

At the mention of that strange word, as if in response, a car bursts into flames in the next block. A crowd of females start to do the timeless tongue-fluttering third-world cheer.

PHIL
A Latah? Give me a break. I've never seen one in my whole career.

SIMON
You see one now.
(squatting adoringly at her feet)
A prime specimen. Natural-born Latah. One for the journals. Total kinesthetic recall and flawless mimicry, involuntarily reproduced, on cue, like

a videotape--no, a hologram--in response to pre-selected stimuli. Allow me to demonstrate.

Simon begins to sing "Great Balls of Fire," doing a very mediocre Jerry Lee Lewis impression, but adequate for its purpose.

The Big Weird Woman becomes Biff, the husky farm boy from Kansas, complete with an invisible overturned water-trough for a piano. To the sound of the classic fifties recording that only she, and we, can hear, she does Biff better than Biff did Jerry Lee Lewis.

Simon lets her go on awhile until Phil seems suitably impressed. Then he glances wickedly at her and snaps his fingers, shutting off the music.

The Big Weird Woman suddenly becomes Phil in the rodeo corral. She holds an imaginary microphone to her big face and talks into it with Phil's voice.

BIG WEIRD WOMAN
(uncanny impression)
Wasn't that fantastic, ladies and gentlemen?

Phil gasps and shudders, and Simon laughs.

BIG WEIRD WOMAN
Biff's a splendid lad, but you know as well as I that he couldn't have given us such a stellar performance without a little help. And where did that help come from?...

SIMON
(over the Big Weird Woman)
Yes, Phil Deacon, you do, indeed, sound like that much of a dork...
(watching her with tender awe)
In a healthy society she'd be welded into in a padded cell and fed through a narrow slot in the door.

Phil is appalled to see himself as he is, but he can't take his eyes off the Big Weird Woman.

INT. PHIL'S CAR--DAY (FLASHBACK)

He's speeding through some remote no-place, his LaFontaine book in hand, emotionally scavenging off the great mesmerizer in the same parasitic way that the Big Weird Woman feeds off him right now.

EXT. COMMUNITY CENTER FRONT STOOP

Simon sees Phil's despair, and profits off it.

SIMON
Don't feel bad, Phil. When it comes right down to cases, none of us show-biz types is much more than a glorified Latah, right?

Phil has no reply to that.

BIG WEIRD WOMAN (CONT)
...I'll tell you where. Inside his own head. In the same place where every human being has limitless stores of talent and energy, which most of us are never aware of, and...

Phil has broken into a sweat. He wipes his forehead with the palm of his right hand, and then strokes the Medicine Man's necklace, as though it were an amulet to ward off evil.

He notices something strange. The Big Weird Woman makes exactly the same two motions: wiping her forehead and stroking an invisible necklace, with her right hand--her microphone hand.

The imaginary mike, as far as she is concerned, no longer exists, even though she's still delivering Phil's Kansas spiel verbatim.

He realizes that her body, if not her mouth, is under his influence, not Simon's.

SIMON
(oblivious)
I like this bit. Listen to the self-pity.

BIG WEIRD WOMAN
...and you're abandoning me faster than most sod-busters do. Must be time to change the filters in your backyard meth labs.

As if casually, Phil sticks a pinky-finger up his right nostril and moves it around. The Big Weird Woman does the same, without missing a syllable.

Simon fails to notice this ominous development, because he's too busy laughing.

SIMON
Backyard meth labs? Great line, Phil.

EXT. PEA-GREEN BUILDING--SAME NIGHT

A combined force of Street Maggots, Undesirables, Perverts, Zombies, etc., have linked up with some generic LOOTERS, and are wreaking senseless destruction around the base of the pea-green building.

They've ripped the boards from the windows and doors and used them to fuel bonfires, rousting even more addled and deformed SQUATTERS than L.A. rats.

Meanwhile, unseen in the lurid shadows behind them, many furtive figures, dressed in black, deploy militaristically up the fire escape, which hangs from the crumbling pea-green bricks by a few cast-iron threads.

These furtive figures ignore the chaos on the street. They have eyes only for what's happening up higher.

We follow them up, rising gradually above the smoke of the Looters' fires, and can soon make out letters on the backs of their black Kevlar vests: FBI, ATF and, oddly, MHS.

We follow these COMMANDOES still further up the fifteen stories, till we see two black helicopters overhead, deep in whisper mode, hovering silently at opposite corners of the roof.

EXT. STREET IN FRONT OF PEA-GREEN BUILDING--SAME TIME

A group of relatively healthy Street Maggots are

overturning vehicles parked in the vicinity, just for the hell of it.

They come to a black van and try to flip it, but are amazed at how heavy it is.

The Street Maggots step back, and seem puzzled by the van's black windows and the complicated array of antennae that bristle from its roof.

INT. BLACK VAN--AT THAT MOMENT

This is the command center of the triple deployment that's taking place outside.

At a console of microphones, computer display terminals and radar screens that flash like the dashboard of a Trident submarine, three COORDINATORS, one each from the FBI, the ATF, and the Ministry of Homeland Security (MHS), jockey for position. They're bickering and slapping each others' hands away from the fancy hardware.

FBI COORDINATOR
We go first.

ATF COORDINATOR
Us first.

FBI COORDINATOR
Would you stop being such a dink?

ATF COORDINATOR
How about I call the Governator and get him to come down here and break one of your arms off?

MHS COORDINATOR
No, for god's sake! Arnie will send Guardsmen. We can't afford to have amateurs underfoot.

Flustered, the MHS Coordinator drops a mike, causing feedback to shriek across the secure lines of communication.

EXT. PEA-GREEN BUILDING FIRE ESCAPE--AT THAT MOMENT

Several Commandoes, from all three federal agencies, grab their wired heads in aural agony. One or two almost fall to their deaths among the ravenous Looters.

INT. BLACK VAN

FBI COORDINATOR
Way to go.

ATF COORDINATOR
I've never seen such stupidness.

MHS COORDINATOR
Enough. This is the Ministry of Homeland Security's show.

He holds up one of the Arab headdresses which Simon earlier sprinkled over the blown-up L.A. Power and Light sub-station. In his other hand he brandishes the blackened stub of a paperback Koran.

MHS COORDINATOR
We go first.

FBI COORDINATOR
(peeking out one-way glass)
Whoops. Too late. The guys started without us.

EXT. PEA-GREEN BUILDING FIRE ESCAPE--AT THAT MOMENT

The rusty ladder is rapidly working itself loose under the weight of our nation's protectors.

EXT. STREET IN FRONT OF PEA-GREEN BUILDING--SAME TIME

All around the periphery of the Looters' orgy, Black Gang-Bangers and Hispanic Bikers can be seen. They, too, are moving in to do their job, but with a lot more panache than the feds.

Steadily, with all the sleek, concerted stealth of stalking lions, they encircle the Looters and close in, awaiting just the right moment to pounce.

EXT. COMMUNITY CENTER FRONT STOOP--A FEW MINUTES LATER

Phil is trying out his new toy, namely the Big Weird Woman.

He bends slightly at the waist, and she does the same, looming over Simon, who still squats at her feet, looking a bit worried now.

Phil puts out his right hand and lowers it, and she imitates him, laying her strong, bloody mitt on the back of Simon's neck. He shudders.

Phil makes a fist, and the Big Weird Woman grabs a handful of Simon's collar.

PHIL
She's just like one of those glove-boxes they use to change tiny diapers on the preemie ward.

Phil causes her to lift Simon off his feet.

SIMON
(trying to hide his fear)
Cute. Now put me down.
(to the Big Weird Woman, tenderly)
Please put me down.

Phil makes her swing him around a little bit.

SIMON
Come on now, Phil! Don't play games! I'm no Shit-Heel!

PHIL
That's a matter of opinion.

SIMON
She's not very predictable at times like this!

PHIL
And I bet you put the poor creature through times like this quite regularly.

Phil moves his left hand, and she swats Simon on the side

of the head.

EXT. PEA-GREEN BUILDING--A MOMENT LATER

The fire escape on the lower floors peels free from the rotting bricks.

A good half of the feds fall into the hands of the Looters. Zombies and Perverts descend on them like piranhas on a wading tapir, and commence stripping them of everything but their attached teeth.

A LITTLE HONEY-BLOND GIRL in a stained yellow pinafore squats over an MHS COMMANDO who's either unconscious or dead. At any rate, his helmet has been cracked like a black egg by a cast-iron landing which used to be attached to the fourth floor.

LITTLE HONEY-BLOND GIRL
Does this bite, or what? There's a ceramic plate missing from this asshole's flak jacket.

INT. BLACK VAN--AT THAT MOMENT

The FBI and ATF Coordinators peek out the one-way window and snicker.

FBI COORDINATOR
There's one to write home to Mom about. Stripped to your skivvies by a white-trash slum child.

MHS COORDINATOR
(defensively)
So what? Big deal. He's just a private contractor.

EXT. PEA-GREEN BUILDING--AT THAT MOMENT

The Little Honey-Blond Girl's YOUNGER BROTHER has joined her. He's a pudgy kid, wearing thick glasses and a Cow and Chicken tee shirt.

YOUNGER BROTHER
No wonder our President is finding it so difficult to build a proper nation

on the sandy banks of the Euphrates, with dog-shit fucking gear like--

Suddenly the sound of automatic weapon fire is heard overhead.

All the Looters look up, and the flash of tracer bullets lights up their horrible squinchy faces.

The Little Honey-Blond Girl and her Younger Brother skitter away with the other Looters. But they don't make it back to their subterranean nests, because strong black and brown arms are waiting to intercept them.

MEXICAN YOUTH
(to the Little Honey-Blond Girl)
Now you just turn right around, Missy, and give the shoddy equipment back.

EXT. TOP OF PEA-GREEN BUILDING--AT THAT MOMENT

A rousing fire-fight has commenced.

INTERCUT BETWEEN FIRE-FIGHT AND FLASHBACKS AT BOYS' ACADEMY

Young Elijah throws a bit of everything at the Commandoes: frag grenades, bazooka shells, and plenty of good old all-American M-16 fire, clips and clips and clips of it.

He takes a few government bullets right off, but performs like the excellently trained trooper he is.

Starting as a lad, back at the Samaria Boys' Academy, Elijah excels at firearms and theory.

But he's a little wimpy in martial arts class. The Honor Guardsmen kick his brunette butt, and make fun of him for being a weenie and a fag. This only serves to stoke his ardor.

What he lacks in bulk he compensates for with malignancy. Many developing sets of gonads fall victim to Elijah's ready heel.

His Classy Woman teacher/mother/sister, looking hot in a judo suit, disapprovingly observes his poor performance from the back of the room.

INT. VICTORIAN LONDON WORKING-CLASS DIVE--NIGHT

LaFontaine, incognito, caped and hooded, a perfumed handkerchief shielding his nose, disapprovingly observes a poor performance of Baron DuPotet.

The Baron's audience is composed of STREETWALKERS, PICKPOCKETS, HOUSE-BREAKERS, and other sundry wretched members of Victorian London's lumpen-proletariat. Unwashed, very pale, everybody's swilling gin, bellowing sea chanteys and mostly ignoring Dupotet.

He stands on a stage contrived of broken boat planks laid across empty gin barrels. He's looking the worse for wear, clothes rusty and rumpled, face unshaven. The self-styled "animal-magnetizer" seems to have fallen on tough times since pissing off Pope Pius IX.

Dupotet has selected, or coerced, an OLD WHORE to be his subject--rather victim.

INTERCUT BETWEEN DUPOTET AND ELIJAH

To the dull amusement of the sodden clientele, Dupotet grabs a pepper shaker from a fat COCKNEY who's gobbling meat pies, and shoves a handful up the Old Whore's nose. She doesn't react at all. Due to post-hypnotic suggestion, her body remains insensate.

Elijah throws sarin canisters, and phosgene, while the feds respond with pitiful squirts of pepper spray, designed to keep order in queues outside G-rated movies.

Baron Dupotet bows, giving a flourish of the pepper shaker, and gets nothing but a few burps in response. He determines to escalate his assaults on the Old Whore, because he is starved for applause.

With a shoulder-deployed surface-to-air heat-seeking missile, Elijah removes one or of the black whisper-mode choppers from the sky.

Dupotet approaches the Old Whore with a loaded and cocked pistol in his hand.

With another missile, Elijah removes a whole corner of the roof.

The cardboard RED HERRING box takes a direct hit. Arab headdresses and paperback Korans are scattered all over the neighborhood.

Finally, with several bullet holes in him, Elijah takes refuge in his father's chopper. It looks as though he intends to get it into the air.

EXT. TOP OF PEA-GREEN BUILDING--A BIT LATER

The eastern sky is beginning to grow sickly pale with the dawn, but still the fire-fight continues.

A MERCENARY in the employ of the Ministry of Homeland Security is seated behind a parapet, pretty much out of the line of fire. He chats with an ATF MAN, showing him a big, shiny new knife.

MERCENARY
Isn't she a peach? See the extra-deep blood gutter, for those really moist kills?

ATF MAN
That's quality craftsmanship.

MERCENARY
All us contractors are getting 'em these days. Real useful for faking A-rab and Eye-racky decapitations.

ATF MAN
The extra-deep blood gutter's a bit redundant on those occasions, I should think.

A bit of friendly fire whizzes past.

MERCENARY
(rattled)
I'm not getting paid enough for this. It's just a job.

ATF MAN
Really? I thought it was like a calling for you guys.

MERCENARY

You mean, "Cry havoc and unleash the dogs of war"? Oh, you bet. Here's the depth of my vocation--

Without bothering to poke his head up, he lifts his automatic weapon over the edge of the parapet and fires blindly in Elijah's general direction.

One of his rounds happens to hit the chopper's fuel tanks, igniting them and discharging the explosive cargo.

Just as the sun peeks over the horizon, the whole top half of the building and everything on it, including Elijah and every member of the combined federal forces, is atomized in the most orgasmic explosion you could ever hope to imagine.

INT. VICTORIAN LONDON WORKING-CLASS DIVE--NIGHT

Dupotet discharges his pistol right up next to the ear of the Old Whore.

EXT. COMMUNITY CENTER FRONT STOOP--AT THAT MOMENT

The Big Weird Woman is just as insensible as Dupotet's subject. She doesn't even blink when the pea-green building in the next block goes straight up into the sky.

But Phil, on the other hand, has not been hypnotized, and he is certainly no Latah. By reflex, he slaps his right hand to the side of his head, to protect his ear from the blast.

PHIL

What the hell was that, Simon? Um...Simon?

He sees that the Big Weird Woman has slapped her right hand to the side of her head, too.

The only problem is that Simon happens to be clutched in that hand. She appears to have knocked him cold against her own skull, if not broken his neck and finished him off altogether.

In either case, he dangles from her hand like a damp hankie.

INT. GOVERNOR SCHWARZENEGGER'S OFFICE--AT THAT MOMENT

Having noticed the sun peeking over the horizon, his baggy-eyed STAFFERS are sluggishly snuffing out the emergency candles--when the flash of the explosion across town startles them.

They look out the window just as the concussion arrives and rattles the glass.

After a stunned pause (his reactions are a bit slow, as he's been up all night), the Governor swings into action.

GOVERNOR SCHWARZENEGGER
So I declare the martial law. Send out many, many storm troopers.

His Staffers begin to scurry all over the place.

INT. VICTORIAN LONDON WORKING-CLASS DIVE

Dupotet is stitching the Old Whore's lips together with carpet thread. She utters no complaint.

INT. GOVERNOR SCHWARZENEGGER'S OFFICE

The pea-green building in the distance collapses like a miniature World Trade Center while the Governor watches, shocked, from his window.

GOVERNOR SCHWARZENEGGER
I wait here...
(looking around his desk)
...in case the phone rings.

INT. VICTORIAN LONDON WORKING-CLASS DIVE

BOBBIES, tin whistles shrieking, come in and close down Baron Dupotet's show, taking him into custody, respectfully. He is a baron, after all.

They permit him a final bow, to which nobody responds.

On the way out, manacled, he tries to engage LaFontaine one last time.

BARON DUPOTET
Come for the gin and pies, Monsieur?

LaFontaine, keeping his perfumed handkerchief to his nose, doesn't even look at Dupotet.

LAFONTAINE
(to the Bobbies)
I am ashamed to say that the Baron is, loosely speaking, my colleague. I'm obliged to linger here and repair his damage.

LaFontaine waits for them to escort Dupotet away.

Then he approaches the makeshift stage. With infinite gentleness, he reaches out a hand toward the Old Whore's ruined face.

EXT. L.A. POWER AND LIGHT HILLTOP SUBSTATION--DAWN

A TECHNICIAN, wearing a bright L.A. Power and Light jumpsuit on his body and the world's most reassuring smile on his face--a ringer for Jack LaLaine in his prime--emerges from the stricken power station.

He flips a thumbs-up, and the lights go back on in Los Angeles.

INTERCUTS ACROSS L.A., POWER GOING ON

Televisions, toasters, dildos, everything springs back into action.

In the Governor's office, his busted treadmill starts up, spitting sparks and wobbling across the floor.

Shrieking like girls with a mouse in the room, everybody climbs up on his desk, where there's not much cowering space.

In the crush, the Governor's hand gets stapled to his blotter. He sucks up the pain, because it makes him stronger.

At the salsa and rap radio stations, DEEJAYS cheer at the resumption of service, and scramble to get some especially obnoxious CDs lined up.

EXT. COMMUNITY CENTER FRONT STOOP--AT THAT MOMENT

The dawn sky is still dark enough to glow from the burning ruins of the pea-green building in the next block, yet light enough to display its cloud of black, syrupy smoke.

Phil is quite jumpy, as he's not sure whether the Big Weird Woman has killed Simon by smashing his head against hers.

She still holds him up with her right hand, so Phil causes her to slap his face a few times, more or less gently, to see if he can be revived.

PHIL
Simon, are you dead?

He causes her to grab Simon's dangling wrist.

PHIL
Damn, I'm not getting a pulse.

Suddenly, the rap and salsa radio stations blast back on the air. The boom boxes on the dance hall floor explode with ear-destroying racket.

Phil slams his left hand down on the windowsill upon which he is seated, to anchor himself for what seems to be a nuke or an earthquake.

The Big Weird Woman, still checking Simon's pulse, does the same thing, jerking her left hand violently down. This makes a great cracking noise in his shoulder-socket. It looks as though she might have removed Simon's arm altogether.

Phil sees this, and recoils. She does the same, dropping Simon in a heap at her feet.

Phil freezes, fearing more catastrophes if he moves again.

PHIL
Um, okay... Now I guess we wait for the forces of social order to arrive.

EXT. MAJOR LOS ANGELES INTERSECTION--LATER THAT MORNING

A National Guard troop truck, on its way to spread the balm of civility upon a suffering community, gets stuck. The traffic signals are still out, and cars going the other way refuse to stop.

The back is full of scared WHITE COLLEGE BOYS and their very pudgy SERGEANT.

COLLEGE BOY
(desperate for reassurance)
This is gonna be safer than Eye-rack, right Sarge?

SERGEANT
(the voice of experience)
Don't bet on it, son. Just stick close by me, and do like I do, and I believe you'll be okay, probably.

COLLEGE BOY
(beaming)
Gee, thanks, Sarge!

EXT. COMMMUNITY CENTER--ABOUT LUNCHTIME

Governor Schwarzenegger's finest finally arrive, only to find they're not needed. The Sergeant and his College Boys stand up in the troop truck and survey the scene in astonishment.

Order has been restored, and is being firmly maintained, by disciplined, but not goose-stepping, patrols of young Black and Hispanic men and women.

At this point it would be unjust to call them Gang-Bangers and Bikers. Even though their black leather, tattoos, chains and insignia remain, these young people's demeanor has been transformed overnight. It would be better to call them Members of Two Affiliated and Coordinated Community Youth Groups.

Zombies are sweeping up glass from broken shop windows and returning stolen merchandise, under the strict but fair supervision of the Giant Chicano.

Nocturnal Creatures, squinting in the sun, have been sat firmly down on a bus bench. The Buffed Black Youth with the Olympic build is adjusting their attitude.

BUFFED BLACK YOUTH
You people need a time out. Some vitamin-D won't hurt you, either.

Several Street Maggots have been issued large plastic bags.

HISPANIC BIKER
Police the area and gather up any religious paraphernalia that might have fallen from the sky recently.

One SARCASTIC PERVERT, still a bit frisky from last night's excitement, hasn't learned her civics lesson yet. She tries on a smoldering Arab headdress, one of those nice biq ones with the sort of Levantine hound's-tooth check pattern. She pretends to pray like a Muslim.

SARCASTIC PERVERT
(groveling, thin butt in the air)
Allah-Wallah, siss-boom-Ballah.

BLACK GANG-BANGER
That's not funny. When you learn to respect yourself, you'll respect other people's beliefs and customs. Mecca's that way.

The mood of this quadrant of Los Angeles resembles that of a young, healthy person just waking up to a life brim-full of interesting possibilities. One neighborhood of America, at least, is in good order.

It doesn't matter to Phil, as he stands on the Community Center's front stoop, that nobody is paying any attention to him. He considers himself the author of this harmony, and is blissful.

LAFONTAINE (VO)
Your will is not your own, but has merged with the vital fluid that emanates from my mind...

INT. VICTORIAN LONDON WORKING-CLASS DIVE--NIGHT

The Old Whore has powder burns on the side of her head from the pistol DuPotet discharged next to it; she has blood coming from her nostrils, due to the caustic pepper he forced into them; her lips are a mass of carnage, held together with coarse sutures of carpet thread.

LaFontaine passes his right hand over her three times. On the third pass, his hand stops, covering her poor face.

LAFONTAINE
Universal forces hold your astral body
in suspension, like a pearl dissolved
in ocean water...

EXT. COMMMUNITY CENTER FRONT STOOP

Phil gazes with compassion at the Big Weird Woman's ruined hands and arms. He offers the Medicine Man's necklace to her, and she takes it, apparently of her own free will.

PHIL
Why don't you take a nap now?

Her big body, which has been maniacally flexed all this while, softens. She curls up into a fetal position on the sidewalk at Phil's feet, next to Simon Magus, who's already at least as stiff as LaFontaine's lovely Noblewoman.

Like the Indian Tyke, the Big Weird Woman begins to suck on the turquoise nuggets.

INT. VICTORIAN LONDON WORKING-CLASS DIVE--NIGHT

LAFONTAINE
I transmit the vital fluid from my mind
to your body.

When LaFontaine withdraws his hand, we see that the Old Whore's nose has stopped hemorrhaging. Not only the blood and powder burns, but the dirt, scars and pock marks of her previous depraved existence are all smoothed away.

She still has plenty of wrinkles, but they're the laugh-lines of someone's sweet old granny having an afternoon nap.

LAFONTAINE
(a gentler, more intimate tone)
And, of course, my good woman, you instinctively know the other name for the vital fluid.

Dreamily, she shifts her dear old head to one shoulder. When she smiles, the carpet thread puffs away like so many filaments of angel hair. Just barely audible, her reply is more of a sigh than a syllable--

OLD WHORE
Love.

EXT. COMMMUNITY CENTER FRONT STOOP

There on the ground in her fetal position, the Big Weird Woman has already graduated from pacifier to teething ring. We can hear the nuggets crunching and popping between her grinding molars. The muscles in her broad back begin to flex again. She's like a lioness fixing to pounce.

But Phil is oblivious. He takes a bow, for he has miraculously healed a whole neighborhood.

INT. PARIS OPERA--EVENING

The angelic Noblewoman in the white satin gown is suspended between the two rosewood chairs.

The great mesmerist is absorbing all the admiration and love of a standing ovation, delivered by the most beautiful human beings on the earth.

He takes a final bow.

PHIL (VO)
Thank you very much, ladies and gentlemen.

LEMUR

Lemuria was the home of the first physical Human Stock, the Third-Race Men...the Sweat-Born, the Egg-bearing, the Androgyne. Almost sexless, in their early beginnings, they became bisexual or androgynous... very gradually, of course.

--Madame Blavatsky, The Secret Doctrine

FADE IN

EXT. LEMUEL'S FAMILY RESTAURANT--DAY

It's in a smallish town in the USA's Industrial Corridor.

The name is written cursively across the roof in orange and turquoise neon.

Placards propped against the front stoop advertise patty melts, bottomless cups of coffee, lemon meringue pie, etc.

When the front doors open to admit or expel CUSTOMERS, we hear bits of the piped-in muzak: the kind of "audio architecture" designed to get bodies in and out of the booths sooner rather than later.

Out comes a NUCLEAR FAMILY: DAD and MOM in Hawaiian shirts and Bermuda shorts, and a few KIDS in tee shirts emblazoned with the restaurant's cartoon logo, LEMMY THE LEMUR.

This creature is pictured wearing nothing but an orange vest and turquoise neckerchief. His eyes are perfectly circular and vacant. His hands are a bit odd: they seem to belong on a tree frog rather than a lemur.

The Nuclear Family hops in their SUV.

INT. SUV--DAY

DAD
(at the wheel)
The National Safety Council urges everyone to buckle up for safety!

Everybody laughs together, and sings--

NUCLEAR FAMILY
Put your mind at ease,
tell your riders please--

Nobody can remember the rest of the words.

EXT. BEHIND THE RESTAURANT--A FEW SECONDS LATER

On its way out of the parking lot, the SUV side-swipes a large dumpster which stands against the back wall, slightly jostling a clique of picturesque BUMS.

Most of them are just browsing. But one SIMPLE-MINDED BUM speedily ransacks to the rhythm of the muzak, heard through an open window nearby.

The largest Bum of all, the BOSS, takes this fellow gently by the shoulders, and looks deep into his eyes.

BOSS BUM
Slow down. You must experience this with all the senses.

The Simple-Minded Bum just stares blankly.

EXT. BEHIND THE RESTAURANT--NIGHT

The neon sign on the roof is switched on, bathing everything in orange and turquoise light.

A YOUTHFUL BUM makes a significant find: an intact kiddy place-mat featuring a large portrait of Lemmy the Lemur.

He hustles this treasure up to the Boss Bum, who holds the place-mat up high, so everyone can see and adore it. He strokes the image of Lemmy the Lemur as though it were the icon of a saint.

BOSS BUM
Say, "Thank you, Lemmy."

SIMPLE-MINDED BUM
Ank-hoo, Reema-a-argh.

BOSS BUM
(chanting, like a priest)
All hail to Lemmy.
He comes up with the gooooooooods.

The Boss Bum has to ponder awhile before he can compose the next verse of his hymn. He examines the divine lemur's wardrobe.

BOSS BUM
Depicted semi-nu-u-u-u-u-u-ude.

Several Bums join in, catching the gist of the words as

they go--

BUM CHORUS
... ooood... ooooooooood...

The Boss Bum waits for more poetic inspiration.

Through the window, we hear slamming lockers.

INT. RESTAURANT EMPLOYEE LOCKER ROOM--NIGHT

Various WAITRESSES, BUS BOYS and BUS GIRLS, all suited up in turquoise Lemmy vests and orange Lemmy neckerchiefs, are just heading out into the dining area.

One of the lockers hangs open.

A 1977 newspaper photo of the legendary serial killer, the Son of Sam, is scotch-taped to the inside of the door. With his round-eyed, mindless grin, the Son of Sam resembles a lemur, just like Lemmy.

BOSS BUM (OS)
(heard from the window)
He lends us yummy fooooooooods.

The whole interior the locker is papered with the usual pictures of famous psycho murderers, real and imagined: Ted Bundy, John Wayne Gacy, Jeffrey Dahmer, Hannibal the Cannibal, Vlad the Impaler, et al.

BUM CHORUS (OS)
oooooooooods...

This locker has been assigned to a bus boy named SPENCER SPROUL, according to the name tag safety-pinned to his vest. Running a bit late, he's stowing his backpack and suiting up for work.

Spencer is the most nondescript person in the world. It's impossible to assign him an age--somewhere between twenty and forty.

He lingers to stare at his gallery.

BOSS BUM (OS)
Better than Qualu--u-u-u-u-u-ude.

SIMPLE-MINDED BUM (OS)
Glooooooooog...

INT. RESTAURANT DINING ROOM--HALF AN HOUR LATER

It's the peak of the dinner rush.

The place is full of DINERS, plump but not morbidly obese.

The muzak hisses overhead, giving everyone, including the Employees, an unconscious itch to escape.

The decor is orange and turquoise, and glares just enough to augment the effects of the muzak.

A sweet bus girl named TRISHY labors elbow-to-elbow with Spencer. She constantly makes eyes at him, and finds every excuse to rub up against him in the rush. He's unaware of her existence.

In a booth near the toilets sits DETECTIVE FURTWANGLER, middle-aged, heavy-set. His bottle-green polyester-blend blazer is too small, and inadequately conceals a snub-nosed revolver in a shoulder holster.

With him are three uniformed officers, his henchmen: one FAT COP, one SKINNY COP, and one tiny FEMALE COP. The latter's ambition is to be the toughest creature on earth.

Spencer, doing his rounds, comes to a halt right at their booth and freezes. He stands there for the longest time, doing his best to give Detective Furtwangler a chance to memorize his face.

The Female Cop squashes a fly on the table, using unnecessary force. She flicks it away, and it caroms off Spencer's Lemmy vest.

The MEAN WAITRESS, a teen with a long, lizard-like physique and a face devoid of humanity, elbows Spencer aside.

MEAN WAITRESS
Stop trying to creep out the nice police officers, Spazzer. Go carry some plates back and forth or something... Good evening, Detective Furtwangler. Boys.

On that last word she eyes the Female Cop, who stares straight ahead and does not react.

The Mean Waitress lays out huge glazed doughnuts and black coffee for all of them, except the Fat Cop. He has ordered a BLT.

FAT COP
Did you tell the chef to hold the bacon?

MEAN WAITRESS
Just like always.

FAT COP
How about the mayo?

MEAN WAITRESS
Fuck.
(gathering the plate back up)
I mean--
(reciting by rote)
--please accept our apologies, honored patron, sir. Your replacement order will be out shortly, along with a complimentary side order of Lemmy fries.

SKINNY COP
I don't think you should accept those free Lemmy fries.

FAT COP
I know. You guys can have them. They're not on my diet.

SKINNY COP
That's not what I mean. You're being duped by the power structure. It's with such meaningless largesse that the free enterprise system creates the illusion of well-being among the proletariat.

FAT COP
Yeah, and they're way greasy, too.
(to the Female Cop)
You want my free Lemmy fries?

FEMALE COP
Would you guys keep it down? You're embarrassing me. You sound like a couple sister-boys.

Detective Furtwangler just looks at all three of them as though he can't believe he's sitting at the same table.

MEAN WAITRESS
(sighing)
Will there be anything else?

INT. RESTAURANT DINING ROOM--A FEW HOURS LATER

Loaded down with a giant tray of dishes, covered in coffee and condiments, looking degraded and exhausted, Spencer hobbles toward the flapping double doors that lead into the kitchen.

The Mean Waitress rushes to get there ahead of him.

INT. KITCHEN--A SECOND LATER

She cues the bully FRY COOK, who drops a mass of lard in his path.

Spencer comes in, slips, and falls spectacularly, smashing most of the stuff he's lugging.

MEAN WAITRESS
(to Fry Cook)
Look what you did.

A teen DISH WASHER chimes in.

DISH WASHER
Now I know why his mom named him Spazzer Sprawl.

FRY COOK
I bet that's gonna come out of your paycheck.
(stomping on the few items that aren't already broken)
And that. And there's another.

Spencer gets up and gives them what he obviously considers

a terrifying serial killer-type look.

They stare back. For a moment it's not clear what they're feeling, perhaps horror.

But, no, they start smirking.

MEAN WAITRESS
Prozac for the twitch, maybe?

Spencer growls menacingly--or tries to.

FRY COOK
Nice burp. You been pilfering onion rings off people's plates, Spazzer? The boss-man says that's a no-no.

Spencer glances at a door near the deep-fry vats, which is marked MANAGERIAL OFFICE.

INT. MANAGERIAL OFFICE--NIGHT

It's a tiny room, with a single minuscule window.

MELVIN, the Manager--a large, soft MBA-type--stands in front of a wall-mirror about the size of a piece of typing paper.

Many identical managerial clip-on ties are draped across a knob screwed into the doorjamb. They feature images of Lemmy the Lemur.

Melvin carefully selects one and clips it on.

He pauses to admire a painting hung next to the mirror.

It's a reproduction of a misty landscape by Thomas Kinkade, featuring several dollops of pigment "applied by the master himself," according to the Certificate of Authenticity scotch-taped to the frame.

On his desk Melvin maintains a collection of elegantly packaged Henry Mancini CDs. A screw-top jug of wine is perched on a doily nearby.

After a swig or two, Melvin decides it's time to deal with the commotion in the kitchen.

INT. KITCHEN--NIGHT

He comes looming up in front of Spencer, who stands alone among the wreckage.

By now the whole KITCHEN STAFF is snickering.

A few Waitresses and Bus Girls peek through the flapping doors. Most of them giggle, but Trishy looks sad.

MELVIN
(playing to the audience)
Are you going to stand there all shift breathing through your teeth, Bus Bitch?

Melvin gets some scattered applause on that last pithy phrase, so he tries it again, encore-wise.

MELVIN
Bus Bitch?

More applause.

INT. RESTAURANT EMPLOYEE LOCKER ROOM--AN HOUR LATER

His shift finally over, Spencer goes to his locker to stow his Lemmy vest and neckerchief.

He listens to the Bums snoring and sleep-talking outside. Some of them are having bad dreams.

SIMPLE-MINDED BUM (OS)
(moaning)
Ah gah ho-o-ome. Ah gah ho-o-o-o-ome.

After pondering his psycho killer pictures for a while, Spencer grabs his backpack and quietly closes the locker.

INT. KITCHEN--A COUPLE SECONDS LATER

Making sure nobody's looking, he sidles up to the wall where the Cooks hang their paraphernalia on hooks, like tools in a handyman's shop.

Spencer quickly steals a wicked butcher knife and a very massive potato masher. He stuffs the latter in his backpack, but risks taking an extra moment to hold up the butcher knife and admire its workmanship. He slashes it around, just a bit.

As he tests the edge against his thumb, Spencer tries hard to leer in an evil way. It's like watching someone who just got a cast off his leg try to bend his knee.

On his way out, he skulks past the waitress station and pockets several small blister-packets of ketchup, bearing Lemmy the Lemur's likeness.

Trishy observes this act of pilfering.

TRISHY
(to nobody in particular)
The sad guy. He must be very poor and hungry.

Spencer slips out the back door.

EXT. SPROUL-NUSSBAUM DUPLEX--NIGHT

It's puce stucco over a wooden frame, located in a lower-middle class residential neighborhood.

Lemuel's Family Restaurant is within sight.

MR. and MRS. NUSSBAUM, a nice old Jewish couple, Holocaust survivors, share the place with Spencer. They are sitting on their front stoop.

Spencer drives up in his busted jalopy and parks on the street.

When he gets out, the potato masher slips from his backpack and lands on his toe. He gathers it back up before the Nussbaums can see.

Limping a bit, he heads for his front door.

SPENCER
Hello, Mr. and Mrs. Nussbaum.

MR. NUSSBAUM
Good evening.

MRS. NUSSBAUM
Have you injured yourself, Mr. Sproul?

SPENCER
Oh, quite well, Ma'am. Yet thank you for the proffer.

He goes in.

The Nussbaums exchange puzzled looks.

MR. NUSSBAUM
A kind of oral dyslexia, maybe?

INT. SPENCER'S LIVING ROOM--MUCH LATER THAT NIGHT

The place is poorly lit and cheaply furnished.

His living room is crammed with serial killer memorabilia. Lining the walls, filling every corner, are candle-lit shrines to all the psychos whose pictures we saw in his locker at work.

Spencer has every book, magazine and newspaper article about his idols, plus videos, DVDs, tee shirts, action figures, lunch buckets--at least one example of every novelty item ever marketed off the reputations of these sickos.

In the middle of the room is an uncomfortable-looking red vinyl couch. A coffee table is positioned in front of it.

Upon this coffee table sits a scrapbook, labeled ROSTER OF TALENT. It's full of pictures and information about famous homicidal maniacs.

MAHALIA, a large, provocatively-dressed African-American woman, sits on the couch, while Spencer stands behind it, dressed in his food-stained bus boy shirt.

At his direction, she leafs through the scrapbook and examines its horrific contents. She is supposed to turn the pages only when he says so.

Bored to the point of death, Mahalia suppresses yawns even as she tries to look and act scared.

Behind his back Spencer holds the potato masher. He intends to brain her with it, when the right moment arrives.

SPENCER
Turn the page, please... This man, Fish, Albert Fish, he poked needles deeply inside his own, um, you know--

MAHALIA
Not his wee-willy-winkums?

SPENCER
(blushing)
No, no. His, er, crouch area. And he kept them there for years and months. To keep him--

Spencer briefly forgets what he's saying, because he has decided to adjust his stance. He places his feet just so.

SPENCER
--focused. The needles kept him--

MAHALIA
You don't say. Really? I find that so shocking and scary. Like to give me the chills all the way up and down my spinal cord.

SPENCER
Next page, please.

Spencer squints at the scrapbook and attempts to read aloud the text of a pasted-in newspaper article.

This isn't easy, because he is quite uncomfortable with the printed word. He contorts his face with mental effort, and laboriously sounds out each syllable.

SPENCER
"For three years, this sc--scoun-n-n-ndrel terror--terrorized Cincinnati with a string of"--turn the page--"bru--talities that defy descrip--"

MAHALIA
Not Cincinnati! My Auntie Louanda lives

sort of by there. Well, actually, she's
a bit further out, on Route--

Spencer clears his throat, and she clams up.

He raises the potato masher over his head and starts closing in, pushing his pelvis against the back of the couch.

SPENCER
Yes, all these master geniuses, they
always leave a clue. Each has his own,
the same, sort of, um, you know...
clue.
(glancing down at his feet)
They leave it over and over again. Like
a whatchamacallit--

MAHALIA
Try "calling card."

SPENCER
Like that. One of those. Some
psychiatrical doctors say it's because,
deep down inside, they want to get
caught.

MAHALIA
Get caught? By the po-lice?
(under her breath)
And get their heads busted? Sure, you
bet, white boy. Tell me another.

SPENCER
Other psychiatrical doctors say it's
like a mind game thing with the--

He loses his train of thought again. There's something amiss with the way he's holding the potato masher. He adjusts it to a more threatening angle.

MAHALIA
I'm listening. I hear you back there.
It's like a mind game thing with the
who? Try to tighten up, lover.
(under her breath)
So we can get this boresome shit over

with.

SPENCER
--with the cops. A mind game with the cops. Like, what do you call, matching witticisms.

MAHALIA
"Witticisms," huh? Mm, mm, mm. If that don't beat all.

SPENCER
Still other psychiatrical doctors say it's more like an artist signing his work.

Spencer obviously expects a strong reaction to this startling revelation. He nudges the back of the couch with his knee. Mahalia does her best.

MAHALIA
Nawwww. You don't mean it. Like art work? Get the fuck out. Like an oil painting or poem or concerto? Who would imagine such an immoral thing?
(yawning outright)
Serial killers thinking of themselves as artists. Is that just the limit of surprising evilness, or what?
(doing an impression of a nasal Caucasian honk)
I mean, totally.

Spencer tries to up the ante; he just wants an unfaked reaction.

SPENCER
Jack the Ripper--

MAHALIA
Damn.
(looking about the room)
Where?

SPENCER
He sent pieces of kidneys--no, it was livers, I think--something like that. He mailed them to the Pope over in

Portugal.

MAHALIA
Now what kind of twisted intellect would mail terrible things to that little old sweetheart? The world is so very sincerely full of badness...
(looking about the place, pretending to shudder)
And such a house of horrors you run here, Sugar! Like a spook alley. But not in the racist sense of the term, of course.
(flipping a few pages)
In fact, I ain't seen one colored face all evening.

She comes to the Ted Bundy chapter.

SPENCER
The policemen only caught this master genius by matching his dentist recordings with bite marks on a dead person's, um...

Spencer can't bring himself to say "buttocks" in mixed company.

Mahalia turns to a photo of the bitten ass in question.

MAHALIA
(finally put off)
Crazy honky motherfucker... oops. Excuse me. Goodness gracious.

SPENCER
(climaxing, or trying to)
Page! Turn it! This master genius' only tool was a double-edged razor blade, less than an inch square--
(reading over Mahalia's shoulder)
"...with which he inf--inf--flicted more dam-m-m-mage than any twelve axe murderers--
(creeping up slowly)
--because he took his time."

Spencer's got the potato masher in both hands, and is wound up tight as Tiger Woods before a big drive.

MAHALIA
That is the most disturbing thing I have ever heard. I am sure it's gonna give me goosenights and bumpmares--I mean nightbumps and maregooses--

She starts to laugh, spoiling the mood for Spencer. His potato mashing arm goes limp.

MAHALIA
(glancing at her watch)
Look, honey. Let's get to the point. For another twenty bucks I watch you jack off, and we call it a night.

He does not respond.

MAHALIA
(turning to look him in the eye)
Not a secretor?

Embarrassed, he glances at a great mass of ketchup blister-packets piled high on the floor nearby. He has evidently been pilfering the condiment from Lemuel's Family Restaurant for years.

Lemmy the Lemur seems to leer at him from the labels.

He gives Mahalia what he thinks is his scary look.

MAHALIA
Oh, my. And how am I to interpret that facial expression? You know, we working girls are experts at interpreting facial expressions. Part of on-the-job safety. OSHA regulations.

He growls.

MAHALIA
Getting a bit pugnacious, are we? Well, how about this?
(standing up, looming over him)

In return for fifty bucks, I refrain from knocking you on your cracker ass and emptying your wallet altogether.

He tries to get his potato masher back up.

MAHALIA
(belly-laughs)
That's a very im-PO-tent looking blunt object. Yes, and you a very im-PO-tent man, I can tell. You act im-PO-tent. You dress im-PO-tent.

She reaches out, caresses his weapon and strokes his stained shirt.

MAHALIA
Ketchup is the closest you ever gonna come to being drenched in red, darlin' I suggest you cling to them individual servings and squeeze with all your tiny might.

She turns her back on him.

MAHALIA
I won't even bother robbing your weak-ass money. Take it to the grocery store, the bag boys will just laugh at me.

She leaves.

INT. LEMUEL'S FAMILY RESTAURANT--NEXT DAY

KRYSTELLE, the cashier, stands at her post.

Unlike the other Employees, she has no Lemmy vest or neckerchief. But Manager Melvin compels her to wear an unflattering orange and turquoise uniform dress, very tight on her prematurely matronly figure.

Customers stand before her. They would like to pay and leave, but Krystelle keeps miscounting the their change.

She's distracted by the sight of Spencer.

He's working like a demon, busing dishes at two or three times his normal rate of speed. If his face wasn't incapable of expression, it might be full of humiliation and rage.

Trishy, the sweet Bus Girl, just strives to keep up, so she can continue trying to make him notice her.

Manager Melvin hovers behind the cash register, watching Spencer's performance appreciatively. His large, soft body interferes with Krystelle's duties.

MELVIN
Looks like that pep talk I gave Spencer last night had a positive effect on his company loyalty.

KRYSELLE
I'm sure he'd take a bullet for LEMCO, now that everybody's calling him Bus Bitch.

MELVIN
Yup, no doubt. Pep-talking is a skill I learned at the College of Business. You could have learned it, too, Krystelle, but you weren't paying attention. Too busy flirting with that Accounting major who somehow neglected to marry you.

KRYSTELLE
Did you ever see that episode of Rockford Files where he breaks a guy's face with a roll of nickels?

Melvin walks off quickly.

He doesn't forget to drop a couple nickels in the fake crystal brandy snifter which Krystelle maintains next to the complimentary Lemmy toothpicks, just in case anybody wants to leave her a tip.

She looks resentful, and determined to get her own someday.

EXT. THE STANDISH MANSION--SAME DAY

It's an old, opulent, three-story house, the most splendid structure in the town's rich neighborhood.

INT. MRS. BELVA STANDISH'S VAST BEDROOM--DAY

She's an ancient society matron, who also happens to be sole owner, publisher, and Editrix-in-Chief of the local newspaper.

Mrs. Standish is surrounded by furniture, carpets, tapestries and pricey bric-a-brac, all bearing an imposing "S" monogram with curlicues and fancy flourishes.

She's decked out in an expensive robe of beige satin. A sapphire-studded editor's visor is perched like a tiara among the face-lift nips and tucks on her venerable forehead.

Sitting at a dressing table that's been converted to a desk, Mrs. Standish lays out tomorrow's edition on a big desktop computer.

RALEIGH STANDISH IV, her forty-year-old live-at-home son, sits on her spacious canopy bed nearby, looking bored.

He's dressed in an elegant suit with a gigantic old lady-style diamond brooch weighing down the left lapel.

RALEIGH
Why can't I be the restaurant critic?

MRS. STANDISH
(without looking from the screen)
You tell me why, Raleigh.

Continuing to manipulate the mouse with her right hand, she reaches out her left, opens a gilded drawer, and produces a copy of the local telephone directory, which she hands over to her son. The yellow pages are pitifully paltry.

MRS. STANDISH
When your dearly departed father purchased the paper, he was certain that something would come of this burg.

Raleigh throws the phonebook on the floor without even looking at it.

RALIEGH

So, anyway, I sit at table and eat and drink and mock the bus boys, and call in my poignant criticisms via my little cell phone. And you be here, at the other end, typing everything out, sprinkling commas like tiny shrimps on canapes. There's no other method possible, Momsy, because I'm borderline illiterate, just as dead Daddy always told me.

(going for the guilt angle)

You never protected me from that emotionally distant, physically abusive, excessively butch tyrant.

MRS. STANDISH

(impervious to guilt of any kind)

Cell phone? Dear love, Raleigh, the whole point of restaurant criticism is that it's done by stealth. They're not supposed to know you're there.

RALEIGH

You never want me to have any fun!

MRS. STANDISH

But, heart of mine, I am awfully busy with cotillions and debutante balls. Not to mention journalism.

Raleigh throws himself face down on his mother's bed and commences kicking his arms and legs in a tantrum.

RALEIGH

(shrieking)

Poopoo Momsy! Poopoo Momsy-y-y-y-y!

Gradually he starts moving his limbs less and his hips more, thrusting deep into his mother's lace counterpane. His shrieks segue into muffled moans.

MRS. STANDISH

Raleigh! Calm yourself.

(looking out the window)
Our guests are arriving.

Between the lace curtains, several limousines can be seen expelling RICH OLD LADIES.

Mrs. Standish moves to the bed and sits next to her offspring. She holds his head to her withered bosom and rocks him awhile, tunelessly quavering an unidentifiable lullaby.

MRS. STANDISH
My sweet, why restaurant criticism? Your father would have wanted you to do sports writing. A young man of genius, such as yourself, has so much more leeway for linguistic invention in sports writing. All those lovely adjectives! For example, a softball game is scheduled this afternoon between the Girl Scouts and--

RALEIGH
Bristly dykes.

MRS. STANDISH
Now, now...

She looks nostalgically at a large framed photographic portrait of KATHARINE GRAHAM, the late, legendary publisher of the Washington Post. A dried-up rose is attached to the frame. The picture is inscribed with the words--

IS BELVA MY "FRONT-SPOILER," OR WHAT?!?!

MRS. STANDISH
(sighing)
Ah, well. We're young only once.

RALEIGH
You'll do it?
(in ecstasy)
You be my amanu-, um, amanu--you write my words in sentences on your motherly lap. Top.

Chuckling fondly at his own little joke, Raleigh flips

through the "R" section of the yellow pages.

RALEIGH
Hmm. I see your point, Momsy. Mighty slim pickings. The competition in this town must be cut-throat, if not downright stiff. I'll have to be especially cruel.

EXT. LEMUEL'S FAMILY RESTAURANT--45 MINUTES LATER

Krystelle has abandoned her post, and is ducking out the front door.

She sneaks across the street, leaping the traffic island in the middle with surprising agility for someone with such a prematurely matronly figure.

She dodges SUV's intent on playing chicken with such an irresistible target.

Krystelle's destination is--

EXT. DAGBERT'S FAMILY EATERY, FUTURE LOCATION--DAY

--a construction site directly across from Lemuel's.

We see and hear cement mixers, hammers, saws, WORKERS, etc.

The billboard out front offers an artist's prospective view of a place that looks about the same as Lemuel's, but with a violet and yellow color scheme, and a different cartoon character logo: DAG THE DINNERSAUR--

He's depicted on the billboard as a violet stegosaurus who can walk on his hind legs and use his front paws like hands. Instead of reptilian scales on his spine and tail, Dag has a double row of yellow dinner plates, and instead of horns on his head he has salad forks, also yellow.

Krystelle heads for a temporary office in an aluminum shack at the periphery of the construction site, upon which a large HELP WANTED sign has been hung.

INT. LEMUEL'S FAMILY RESTAURANT--DAY

Melvin and most of his Employees are gathered at the front

door. They peek out and scowl resentfully at the rival establishment taking shape across the street.

They observe Krystelle's progress as though she were a rat switching sewers.

MELVIN

Some company loyalty, eh, people?

Suddenly, their view is obscured by a large canary-yellow Mercedes Benz. It bounces over the curb and stops about three feet away from the front door.

EXT. LEMUEL'S FAMILY RESTAURANT--DAY

Raleigh Standish IV has arrived in his mother's car to commence his new career.

His liveried CHAUFFEUR runs around to assist the master.

Raleigh emerges from the Mercedes and notices the many pairs of eyes inside the restaurant that seem to have gathered to admire him.

His vanity flattered, he takes a moment to primp and preen his high-fashion garb and accessories, in particular the diamond brooch that nearly tears his lapel out by the roots.

RALEIGH

(into his gold-plated cell phone)

Restaurant criticism is done by stealth, eh, Momsy? You sent the gardener ahead by city bus to trumpet my approach, didn't you? You're such a little dickens. If that's the term.

His Chauffeur opens the restaurant door. Raleigh steps inside--

INT. LEMUEL'S FAMILY RESTAURANT--DAY

--and is faced with a sour-puss pink-collar mob.

MEAN WAITRESS

(loudly)

I didn't know Elizabeth Taylor was in

town. I hope we have plenty of chicken.

RALEIGH
(to his Chauffeur)
When I yank on the air hose, you pull me up fast. The bends be damned.

Melvin shows the new arrival to a booth, looking back often and clenching his buttocks tightly shut as he walks.

Once seated, Raleigh produces a white silk handkerchief, embroidered with the imposing "S" monogram. With a flourish, he wipes the flatware, then discards it in the ashtray.

In the next booth sits the Nuclear Family: Dad and Mom in Hawaiian shirts and Bermuda shorts, and the Kids in their Lemmy tee shirts.

Raleigh looks at them for quite some time.

Meanwhile, Customers are stacking up at the cash register. It's been disabled for the moment by Melvin. He's trying to teach the Mean Waitress how to work the keys.

MELVIN
I have the sneaking suspicion that Krystelle's no longer with us. So, until I can dig up someone with a more matronly appearance, you get a promotion. You get to play with rolls of nickels. See here? You whack it against the coin tray and it spills its guts just like a raw egg.

She cracks ten dollars worth of nickels onto the floor.

MELVIN
Is it too much to ask you to pay attention?

He sees why the Mean Waitress isn't paying attention: she's busy staring at Raleigh.

MEAN WAITRESS
Isn't he cruising the wrong end of town?

MELVIN
Now, why would you ask me such a question?

When Spencer buses by, Raleigh doesn't acknowledge any aspect of his existence, except to gasp at his Lemmy vest and neckerchief.

Spencer hears the gasp, looks down, and sees himself as if for the first time. He holds his neckerchief up like a hangman's noose and inspects it through the corner of one eye.

RALEIGH
(into his cell phone)
How simply, um--
(searching for an adjective)
--unremarkable the bus boys are, Momsy. I must say.

INT. STANDISH PARLOR--AT THAT MOMENT

Mrs. Standish sits at a lace-covered card table, playing canasta with the other Rich Old Ladies.

Her proud, elegant body and face perform amazing contortions as she tries to wedge a princess extension against her ear with one shoulder, balance a laptop on her knees, play canasta, eat tiny cucumber sandwiches, sip tea, chit-chat, and take dictation from her son, all at the same time.

Among the Rich Old Ladies is MRS. COVENTRY, a UV radiation-ravished crone with curly red hair. She's comparatively athletic, but not nearly enough to justify her short white tennis skirt and panties.

Mrs. Coventry harps on her only topic, oblivious to everyone's unhappy sighs. They've heard this a million times before--

MRS. COVENTRY
If the Vietnam war was still going, my husband Harvey would still be in the SDS, instead of owning his own exclusive tennis club, and--

MRS. STANDISH
(loudly, into the phone)
Raleigh Standish the Fourth! Did you say something about boys?

Her guests try not to hear this.

MRS. STANDISH
Remember what the terrible police detective said!

INT. LEMUEL'S FAMILY RESTAURANT--AT THAT MOMENT

Raleigh's cell phone battery dies.

INT. STANDISH PARLOR--DAY

MRS. STANDISH
Hello? Raleigh?... Hello?

Anxiously, Mrs. Standish looks around the parlor until her eyes alight upon a woman in a white uniform, who's lugging a large silver tray laden with fresh and delicious-looking hors d'oeuvres.

This is RUTH, the caterer.

INT. LEMUEL'S FAMILY RESTAURANT--DAY

In a snit, Raleigh bangs his pricey cell phone on the table till the guts start coming out.

MELVIN
(to the Mean Waitress)
I suspect that customer is well-to-do.

MEAN WAITRESS
No. Really?

MELVIN
Darn it. I knew I should be pooling the tips and giving the house a cut.

MEAN WAITRESS
Learn that in the MBA program, did you?

Raleigh drops his shattered cell phone into a complimentary glass of ice water.

RALEIGH
Oh, isn't it just dandy? I'll have to return to this potty-chair at a later date.
(on his way out, to Spencer)
Boy, you can keep the hankie. It's genuine moire silk, if you even know what that means.

Spencer obediently latches on to the handkerchief and stuffs it in his pocket.

INT. LOCKER ROOM--SEVERAL HOURS LATER

It's the end of Spencer's shift, and he's hanging the Standish hankie, trophy-wise, in his locker. He takes care to display the "S" monogram prominently.

While he does this, we see that he has added some more killer pix to his locker's mini-gallery: a few newcomers, and more of the old "master geniuses" as well.

INT. STANDISH KITCHEN--THAT NIGHT

Ruth is packing up a lot of catering gear. Mrs. Standish hovers near.

MRS. STANDISH
Ruth, you simply outdid yourself today, as usual. I will have you cater all my functions henceforth. Oh, by the way--

She produces a paper bag full of hundred dollar bills.

MRS. STANDISH
(handing it over)
Tell your brother that Raleigh is still trying to overcome his little habit. You're a blessing, dear. You aren't planning to charge full price for the Gruyere canapes, are you? They were a bit skimpy today.

INT. RUTH AND HER HUBBY'S BEDROOM--LATE THAT NIGHT

The face of one of Spencer's scary "master geniuses" is splashed across the front and back covers of a book, along with the bold-print words--

2ND EDITION!
NEW DNA EVIDENCE
INNOCENCE POSTHUMOUSLY PROVED!

Ruth--food slave to the wealthy by day, by night just an average unloved wife--has her nose buried in this sensational publication. A white sticker on the spine reveals it to be a library book.

She's in the sack with her HUBBY, who's just as average as she, but mean.

HUBBY
How about not reading gruesome shit in bed? I can't sleep when you leave your lamp on all night to protect you from the boogie-man.

Ruth feigns girlish fear in a forlorn attempt to get a pity lay.

RUTH
I'm so scared. Can't I have the light? Please?
(trying to make him jealous)
I got chills from this terrible dude.

She strokes the mug shot on the front cover.

HUBBY
Asshole.

He rolls over, making sure to rake a couple red stripes out of her calf with his unclipped toenails. Then without further adieu, he commences snoring.

Ruth is also snoring soon, in spite of the sounds of a very clumsy intruder grappling with the window in the next room.

The book lies open, face down, across her chest.

INT. RUTH'S KITCHEN--AT THAT MOMENT

As a housebreaker, Spencer's a serious spaz. He falls all over himself climbing in the window, getting tangled in the curtain, and raising all manner of ruckus.

INT. RUTH'S BEDROOM--A MINUTE LATER

He looms over the sleeping couple, wielding the stolen butcher knife.

Just as he is about to strike, Spencer sees something that brings horror to his face--or at least the closest approximation he can manage.

SPENCER
Second edition? Innocence?

He's so upset that he snatches the book off Ruth's chest without even being sneaky about it.

Her breasts jiggle under her nightie, but she doesn't wake up. Indeed, she smiles and purrs in her sleep, dreaming that her Hubby is groping her.

Spencer stands over the bed, butcher knife raised in one hand, library book in the other.

He reads frantically over the next few hours, moving his lips, frowning, and struggling over each syllable.

He begins to have a one-way discussion with his intended victims, over their snores.

SPENCER
It's like they're saying this master genius never should of been born, that he's a fraudulency, that he couldn't--
(choking up)
--pop a chubby!

Spencer raises his voice on that last phrase, disturbing Ruth a bit. She stirs in bed.

He holds the knife higher, remembering his murderous plans --just until she's settled back in.

Then he promptly gets reabsorbed into the book. He dog-ears pages. He clenches the butcher knife in his teeth or holds it between his knees, in order to free up both hands for ripping out illustrations and sticking them in his pockets.

By the first hint of dawn, Spencer has had enough. Despair falls on him as he closes the book. He has lost one of his gods.

He tosses the book back down on Ruth's breasts.

As she purrs again with pleasure, he raises the knife, very high.

INT. RUTH'S KITCHEN--DAWN

The kitchen table is covered with dishes, ashtrays and beer cans. Ruth's hubby's worn-out wallet is flopped in the middle, a few bucks and one or two credit cards hanging out.

On his way past, Spencer briefly considers this wallet.

SPENCER
No. It's not about stealing. I'm not a stealer.

He takes time to pop a pilfered blister-packet of Lemmy ketchup, spread some on the floor, and step in it, precisely and with care.

While he is thus occupied, the butcher knife slides from his back pack, unnoticed, and lands on the table.

Spencer exits through the window, leaving it open behind him.

INT. RUTH'S KITCHEN--EARLY THAT AFTERNOON

Detective Furtwangler sits at the table.

He's in shirtsleeves, his bottle-green blazer hung over the back of the chair. His holster, bearing the snub-nosed revolver, remains strapped to his back.

The butcher knife is laid out before him.

He frowns, rubs his eyebrows, and grunts with internal effort. He appears to be contemplating the weapon, using all his deductive powers to unlock its deadly secrets.

Then he farts. The tension leaves his face and he starts looking at the ceiling, twiddling his thumbs.

Ruth comes in, all in one piece.

She bears a big beautiful baked fish on a platter, smothered in lemon slices, steamed broccoli bits, toasted almonds, and other fresh and healthful trimmings. She slides it down in front of his face, shunting the knife to one side.

DETECTIVE FURTWANGLER
Ah, God. Thanks, Sis. Food for a change. Nothing like that dioxin at Lemuel's.
(burping painfully)
I don't know why I keep going back there.

He sees the book lying on the floor nearby, and picks it up.

DETECTIVE FURTWANGLER
What did I tell you? Good read, huh?
(notices the dog ears)
Wow, you're almost finished. I didn't know you had such good reading skills.
(sees the mutilated pages)
You chopped through this like a lumberjack. Serial killer fan, eh, Sis?

RUTH
(puzzled)
I guess so... I was pretty sleepy.

DETECTIVE FURTWANGLER
Did it give you bad dreams?

RUTH
Looks like it sure did. I must have been thrashing around pretty serious... But I still can't say I know what DNA is.

Neither does he--but he speaks authoritatively:

DETECTIVE FURTWANGLER
It's hair and spit and stuff.

RUTH
(a tad grossed out)
You do this all day? For a living?

She scoops up some dishes and flatware off the table, including the butcher knife, which she pays no particular attention to, and tosses everything into the sink.

She loads her arms up with ashtrays and beer cans.

RUTH
Great hubby I got, eh? It's not the rudeness and neglect so much as the sloppiness. Leaving windows hanging open for all the bugs in the neighborhood--
(she shuts Spencer's point of entry and exit)
--not wiping his feet--

Ruth squats down and wipes away Spencer's careful ketchuppy clue with a dishrag.

DETECTIVE FURTWANGLER
(chewing with his mouth open)
Yeah, that son-bitch is a slob, all right.

EXT. RUTH'S HOUSE--HALF AN HOUR LATER

It's in a slightly less squalid residential neighborhood than Spencer's duplex.

Detective Furtwangler is leaving. Ruth sees him off.

DETECTIVE FURTWANGLER
I'm a new man.
(loosening his belt)
If the chow you fix for the rich folks is anything like that fish I just destroyed, no wonder they're superior to us in every way... Sis, I want you

to tell that no-good hubby of yours to shape up and get more tidy. And also he better give you a tumble in the sack every couple weeks. Or else his Bro-in-Fucking-Law's gonna bring the full weight of the law down on his case.

The NEXT-DOOR NEIGHBORS hear that, and peek out.

RUTH
Just take off his shirt and make him go outside. That'll be punishment enough.

DETECTIVE FURTWANGLER
I'll do better than that. I'll sic my trio of uniformed henchmen on him.

Those individuals wait in and around a squad car double-parked out front.

The Fat Cop sprawls on the hood, uniform unbuttoned, sunning his ample breasts and unwrapping a stick of sugarless gum.

The tiny Female Cop stands on Ruth's front lawn, practicing groin-jabs with a billy club and shrieking rhythmically.

The Skinny Cop is curled up on the back seat with Trotsky's LITERATURE AND REVOLUTION.

SKINNY COP
Listen to this--
(reading aloud)
"If the Revolution has the right to destroy bridges and art monuments, it won't hesitate to lay its hands on any tendency in literature which threatens to arouse the proletariat, the peasantry and the intelligentsia against one another."

FEMALE COP
You really are a prissy pants, aren't you?

Nobody seems to notice Spencer standing on the sidewalk nearby.

Detective Furtwangler brushes past him on the way to get behind the wheel.

Ruth runs out before they can drive off. She's waving around the paper bag full of money that Mrs. Standish laid on her.

RUTH
Bro! One more thing. A new bag from the old bag. She wants you to cut her baby boy some more slack.

DETECTIVE FURTWANGLER
(putting on an upper-crust accent)
Oh, really?

RUTH
Raleigh.

The bribe is passed through the car window, blatantly, as if Spencer's not standing right there to witness it.

INT. SQUAD CAR--AT THAT MOMENT

Detective Furtwangler looks at him, and something seems to click. But, after peering a bit closer at Spencer's face, he shakes his head and decides to ignore such an obvious nobody.

INT. LEMUEL'S FAMILY RESTAURANT, LOCKER ROOM--NEXT DAY

It's break time.

Waitresses, Dish Washers, Bus Boys and Bus Girls smoke cigarettes, try to convince one another to have sexual intercourse, and traffic in baggies of methamphetamine.

Spencer alone is constructively occupied. He sits on a bench, slowly writing on the back of a Lemmy the Lemur place-mat.

He grimaces and struggles, as if each word is being dragged from his forehead with a hook and chain. Writing is no easier for Spencer than reading or talking.

We hear the words shaped by his pencil--

SPENCER (VO)
Dear Mr. Manson. Hello from the hole of the Lemur. I, Spencer Sproul, wish to pour out my ardent admiration feelings upon your mutual heart. I fall into your tried-and-true arms, Mr. Manson, because--

INT. RUTH'S BEDROOM--NIGHT (FLASHBACK)

Spencer stands over the bed, knife poised. The library book jiggles on Ruth's breasts.

SPENCER (VO)
--no enormous number of DNA-gallons will ever prove YOU posthumously impotent. You were never proved pre-humously potent in the first place.

INT. LOCKER ROOM--DAY

The Dish Washer, the Fry Cook and the Mean Waitress quietly gather behind Spencer. They read over his shoulder, glance back and forth at each other, whirl index fingers around their ears, and make coo-coo eyes.

Oblivious, he continues to write.

SPENCER (VO)
I find you, Mr. Manson, to be the greatest creative one in the whole Roster of Talent. Especially your innovating advancement known as "creepy-crawling"--

INT. RUTH'S BEDROOM--DAWN (FLASHBACK)

A beam of sunlight seeps through the drapes and hits Ruth square in the face, waking her up.

Spencer backs off.

SPENCER (VO)
--the inspired technique of leaving the bedridden victimological sleepers untouched--

INT. RUTH'S KITCHEN--DAWN (FLASHBACK)

SPENCER (VO)
--but only rearranging their furniture pieces a bit--

On his way to the window, Spencer steps in the kitty litter, accidentally "rearranging" this "furniture piece."

SPENCER (VO)
--in order to "freak them out," as you so very sixtily say, when they wake up from their exposed slumberings--

Ruth stumbles in, half-asleep, in her jammies. She stubs her toe on the kitty litter.

SPENCER (VO)
--allowing them to thank their luckiness that you, invisible you, spared them this time a special sticky death. It is a master genius stroke, Mr. Manson, for being no stroke at all.

Ruth pays no heed beyond kicking the cat.

INT. SPENCER'S LIVING ROOM--NIGHT

Spencer sits on his red vinyl couch. On the coffee table, the ROSTER OF TALENT is turned to the Charles Manson chapter.

The OFFICIAL CHARLES MANSON FAN-CLUB WEBSITE is called up on Spencer's rickety old laptop. A sound-file of the man himself repeats over and over again on the tiny speakers--

CHARLES MANSON (VO)
I don't play music for chicks. And it's not about money. I play music for God, man... I don't play music for chicks. And it's not about money. I play music for God, man...

Spencer listens to this wisdom while continuing to write on the back of the Lemmy place-mat.

Over the Manson sound file, we hear his words as they

slowly form--

SPENCER (VO)
Now in my solitary evening duplex I bleed my uttermost desires. I would tell you my life's program--

When his text calls for a period or comma, Spencer dips his pencil-tip into the guts of a Lemmy ketchup blister-packet which lies, burst, on the coffee table. It almost appears as though the letter is punctuated in blood.

SPENCER
I want, with all my life, Mr. Manson, to do this: spread the worst sensations, to all people everywhere--

INT. SPENCER'S LIVING ROOM--DAWN

He's been writing all night, and has finished the thing. The place-mat being large, the paper thick, Spencer must fold it with force, smash it down hard on the coffee table, and muscle it into an envelope.

SPENCER (VO)
--and yet, at also the same time, to fascinate all people everywhere. Like you, Mr. Manson.

Spencer has a hard time getting stamps to stick. But he manages with the help of Lemmy ketchup.

SPENCER (VO
Like the manager of a family restaurant. His photo is framed behind the cash register for all to thank his grand blessings of heartburn, blessings of heart attack, deep loss of red heart tissue, stripy like bacon with glisten-globs of grease. I want to be much like that manager, Mr. Manson. I want to be much like you.

INT. POST OFFICE--DAY

He mails it.

The POSTAL CLERK, a lovely young woman with a face full of compassion and understanding, looks deep into Spencer's eyes with kindly concern.

EXT. SPROUL-NUSSBAUM DUPLEX--SEVERAL MORNINGS LATER

Spencer comes out, checks the mail, only to find that his epistle to Charles Manson has bounced back, marked INSUFFICIENT POSTAGE.

INT. POST OFFICE--LATER THAT MORNING

Spencer has returned to repeat the process.

This time he insists on his literary production being weighed several times, and metered.

He makes the lovely Postal Clerk check the postage over and over again.

SPENCER (VO)
That is what I want, with my life, to be, for all people everywhere. I want to draw all people in my image, and to my image--

Spencer pauses to examine the FBI'S TEN MOST WANTED on the Post Office wall.

SPENCER (VO)
--and gain a myth-like type of notorietablilty for my very self.

Spencer sits on a bench near the counter, and spends the next few hours staring at the Postal Clerk. She's the only person our would-be killer has managed to terrify, so far.

EXT. SPROUL-NUSSBAUM DUPLEX--DAY

He stands by his mailbox, waiting for the postman to come.

SPENCER (VO)
So, what is your thought on me and my life program, Mr. Manson?

Mr. and Mrs. Nussbaum sit on their front stoop, watching him wait. They look concerned.

EXT. SPROUL-NUSSBAUM DUPLEX--NEXT DAY

Spencer checks his mail. Only a gas bill.

SPENCER (VO)
I would love to dearly hear.

EXT. SPROUL-NUSSBAUM DUPLEX--NEXT DAY

Still no word from the great man.

SPENCER (VO)
I do remain your true Spencer Sproul.

Mrs. Nussbaum hobbles up and stands next to him. She reaches out her dear old hand and almost touches his shoulder. At the last moment, something tells her that's not such a good idea.

MRS. NUSSBAUM
Is a young lady being lax in her correspondence, Mr. Sproul?

SPENCER
Oh, yes, Ma'am. Quite max. Thank you for your respite.
(to himself--but speaking straight into her face)
I guess I tried to break in the bigness league too soon. Better grow back to the basics.

He looks at a convenience store down the block.

SPENCER
Do you folks need anything out from the store?

Not waiting for a reply, he wanders off.

MR. NUSSBAUM
The poor fellow's oral dyslexia, or whatever it would be called, seems to worsen with stress.

MRS. NUSSBAUM
Or heartbreak.

EXT. CONVENIENCE STORE--DAY

Rather obviously holding a pistol at the ready under his orange Lemmy vest, Spencer approaches.

He almost trips over a PUNK GIRL squatting among puddles of crankcase grease in an empty parking space out front. When he bumbles into her, she arches her back and hisses like an alley cat.

She's a tattooed teen, short and squat due to childhood malnutrition, with about nine pounds of crumbly metal embedded in her eyebrows, nose, ears, lips, chin, nipples and navel. She gobbles methamphetamine.

This Punk Girl has a pistol concealed under her threadbare Cow and Chicken tee shirt, almost as obviously as Spencer's. She's plainly plotting to rob the place, just as soon as the speed kicks in.

To get inside the convenience store, Spencer has first to negotiate his way through a mob of MORBIDLY OBESE FOLKS, both sexes, all ages. The place is very popular with their physical type.

Just as he manages to squeeze within arm's length of the automatic door, Spencer's feet are whisked off the ground, and he's washed inside on a tidal wave of cellulite.

INT. CONVENIENCE STORE--DAY

Inside are more Morbidly Obese Folks. They make the plump Customers at Lemuel's look like starved fashion models.

The counter help is a lanky COLLEGE BOY with the pure face of a Buddhist monk. He's having the time of his life.

COLLEGE BOY
(crying out to everybody at once)
Here! Let me help you with that!

He slides between car-sized love handles to assist in the great feed. He slops chili on three-quarter-pounder pork sandwiches, and ladles sour cream all over bushel-baskets full of nachos.

When the Morbidly Obese Folks ingest what pleases them,

they seem to enter a higher realm of being. They look like colossal sphinxes.

At these moments, religious bliss fills the College Boy's eyes. It's as though he's witnessing the Olympian gods feed on nectar and ambrosia.

Once in a while, THIN, or AVERAGE-BUILD, or even PLEASINGLY PLUMP PEOPLE manage to fight their way in, and attempt to buy, say, a pack of sugarless chewing gum. The College Boy ignores them as one would ants.

AVERAGE-BUILD PERSON
How 'bout come change, Slick?

COLLEGE BOY
Whatever.

Not removing his eyes from a MAMMOTH CREATURE with a foot-long fried chicken burrito, the College Boy throws a handful of twenty dollar bills in the Average-Build Person's direction.

Spencer will not allow himself to be distracted by these strange circumstances. Fingering the trigger of his pistol, he strains to be seen and heard around the moving mountains.

SPENCER
(shouting)
Do you want go in the back room with me?

COLLEGE BOY
(irritated at the interruption)
What?

SPENCER
Um... can I use the bathroom?

COLLEGE BOY
You can fire-bomb the bathroom and grind the ashes underfoot, for all I care.

Spencer takes that as permission.

INT. BACK ROOM--DAY

Even though there are industrial-sized containers of the stuff back here, Spencer removes a blister-packet of Lemmy ketchup from his own pocket.

SPENCER
I'm not a stealer. It's not about stealing.

He pops it and carefully lays down his customary tomato slick. Spencer plants his shoes, ever so precisely, in the redness.

Here among the crates of lunch-meat pizzas and microwave-friendly fish burgers, Spencer assumes the cliched shooter-stance: pistol held solidly in both hands, poised at arm's length.

When, and if, the College Boy comes back here, Spencer wants to be ready. So as not to be caught off-guard, he keeps an eye on his intended victim via the security monitor that hangs from the ceiling.

INT. BACK ROOM--ABOUT AN HOUR LATER

Spencer's waiting yet, body and gun patiently poised.

On the security monitor, the College Boy can be seen, in blurred black and white, still slopping the gods.

There's no sound on the monitor, so Spencer quickly disengages one hand from the pistol, just long enough to reach out and open a refrigerator case. Resuming his stance, he eavesdrops between popsicle shelves that open onto the sales area.

Not only are the Morbidly Obese Folks fatter than the Lemuel's crowd, but they're much more prone to walrus-like flopping violence. The stuff they consume makes them mean.

Disputes constantly flare up.

On the monitor, a slight shadow dives between vast gray blobs--

INT. CONVENIENCE STORE SALES AREA--DAY

The College Boy's in heaven as bellies and breasts squash him flat. He weeps and quakes in spiritual ecstasy.

COLLEGE BOY
Believe me, more than any sex activity I could ever imagine--
(choking up with deep emotion)
--I would love to see you folks fight. But the boss would fire me if I punched out leaving major structural damage to the building. Then I could no longer be priest in this temple which was built and consecrated to serve you!

INT. BACK ROOM--TWO HOURS LATER

The gun's getting heavy.

Eventually, the College Boy comes in, and walks his nose right up into the barrel of Spencer's gun.

COLLEGE BOY
Oh, hi. How was the bathroom? I'm sorry, but I don't have time to fall on my knees and plead for my life just now, because--
(beaming with bone-deep pleasure)
--I need to fetch more pabulum for my lovely God-Babies.

He grabs a couple bales of beef-byproduct nuggets and jumbo Bavarian gristle-muffins.

The gun still trained on his head, the College Boy casts an affable grin at Spencer.

COLLEGE BOY
What you just witnessed was only the afternoon snack rush. Unless you are emotionally strong, I suggest you clear out before--

He shudders, and can't speak for a moment. He drops the bales and peers deep into Spencer's eyes, holding out both hands in helpless, bewildered supplication.

COLLEGE BOY
(whispering hoarsely)
--b-b-before--

He grabs the tiny orange lapels of Spencer's Lemmy vest and hangs on like a drowning man.

COLLEGE BOY
(barely able to mouth the word)
--suppertime.

Beaming, he wipes his eyes, half in embarrassment, half in astonished pride.

COLLEGE BOY
I see you like to watch on the small screen. That's wonderful, too. It has is own charm, making the God-Babies seem--

No more words are possible, as the College Boy spasms from his toes to his head.

After recovering from that, he pulls up a cream soda crate, sits, and scoots over to make space for Spencer.

Spencer stares at him for the longest while, immobilized. Someone has just invited him to sit down. This has never happened before.

SPENCER
You want me on the soda pop box? Right nearby you?

COLLEGE BOY
(eyes on the screen)
Yes, yes. This is a good place to watch from. Come see...

Spencer hesitates a bit longer, then sits, keeping the pistol embedded in his intended victim's rib cage.

COLLEGE BOY
I'm sorry your gun doesn't scare me more. It's just that, when you receive a calling to minister to the God-Babies, you gain a realistic

perspective on small caliber fire.

He settles in to enjoy the show with Spencer. But soon, strangely, the College Boy's sublime joy dissolves into soft sobs and tears.

SPENCER
What are you being sad for?

COLLEGE BOY
I'm sad for my God-Babies. See how they constantly belch, and then wince in agony? That's because the loveliness has blossomed so deep on their waists, it's pushing their tummies inside-out. They're scorching away their throats with their own digestive acids, and guaranteeing themselves terminal cancer in the meantime. And the only way they can make the burning go away, if only for just a short while, is to come to me. I gently soothe it and coat it with more grease, like a sunburn with cocoa butter, or diaper rash with baby oil. It's sad, and beautiful... and an exciting privilege.

Spencer starts checking out the lists of ingredients on the surrounding cartons and packages, moving his lips and knitting his brow, as he always does when confronted with the alphabet.

SPENCER
M... S... G...

He sees those three particular letters on absolutely everything. MSG even impregnates the few token pre-fab salads in their styrofoam caskets.

COLLEGE BOY
I keep those around as visual puns.

The Punk Girl chooses this moment to come in and rob the place--or try to. She is just barely visible on the monitor as a tiny smudge.

PUNK GIRL (OS)
Everybody face down, flat on the floor. Now! What are you waiting for?

COLLEGE BOY
Ah! Finally! It's about time! Watch this! Homer's clashing rocks! You can only pity the poor stunted creature.

The Morbidly Obese Folks close in. They're not even slowed down by the single round the Punk Girl manages to squeeze off before they crush her.

This is Spencer's big chance to see death happening. But his eyes are not on the security monitor. He's looking at the College Boy's face.

COLLEGE BOY
Ah, God! Oh, Baby!

That clinches it. Spencer is a convert. He has caught the College Boy's enthusiasm.

He hurries out the back door, leaving his firearm on the floor.

INT. LEMUEL'S FAMILY RESTAURANT--DAY

It's the lunch rush.

INT. KITCHEN--DAY

Cooks hustle in every direction, trying to work around Spencer, who is seriously underfoot.

A College Boy-type gleam just noticeable in his eyes, he explores the kitchen as if it were a wonderful alien planet.

Mouth writhing, he sounds out the list of ingredients on a big carton of LEMCO'S DEEP FRY BATTER MIX.

He struggles through the catalogue of additives on a slab of processed lard, bound for the vats that seethe on all sides.

He passes over the few bags of frozen carrot slivers and

flaccid lettuce leaves--

SPENCER
Visual buns. Treat like orange and turquoise confetti. Except more sparing

Spencer examines the dead meat with both attraction and revulsion. He gingerly approaches a defrosting hamburger patty, and is just reaching out a large meat fork to prod it, when--

FRY COOK
Hope I'm not in your way, Spazzer.
(elbowing him aside)
You got it bass-ackwards. I make the shit, you shovel it. This is the shit-making zone.

DISH WASHER
Yeah. The Board of Health would close us down if they saw something like you crawling back here.

SPENCER
(brandishing the fork)
What are you nothings, that you know of this business? Soon you'll follow the humbling orders off me.

DISH WASHER
"The humbling orders"? You sure got a way with the Anglo-lingo, Bus Bitch.

FRY COOK
Put the sharp pokey-pokey thing down and get the fuck out.

Just as Spencer's knuckles whiten on the handle of the fork, Manager Melvin appears.

He's passing through on his way to a certain door by the sinks.

FRY COOK
Wait for it--

Everyone hears the sound of a toilet stall slamming and being latched.

DISH WASHER
Goof-off time.

MEAN WAITRESS
(peeking in from the dining area)
Melvin was trotting along pretty knock-kneed. I'd say half an hour, at least.

All the Employees come pouring in to goof off, brushing Spencer aside.

INT. MANAGERIAL OFFICE--A MINUTE LATER

The little room is deserted.

Spencer pokes his head in and looks around. He admires the elegant Mancini CDs, the screw-top wine jug perched on its lace doily, and the misty Thomas Kinkade oil painting with its Certificate of Authenticity.

After glancing back into the kitchen to make sure nobody's watching, Spencer sneaks into the office.

A bit nervous, he fumbles with the CD player till "Moon River" slithers out.

He stands before the painting and peels off some glops of paint.

SPENCER
There. Much better. Smoother.

He unscrews the lid and takes a furtive swig of wine. Then another.

Spencer tries to do Anthony Hopkins, straining to arch his eyebrows and droop his eyelids at the same time. It's pretty embarrassing--

SPENCER
Two generations of nutrients have given you some long bones, Clarence. Except I shall dine off your several kidneys with a nice, um--

(squinting at the label on the jug)
--Car-lo Ros-si Mus-ca-tel.

He borrows one of the surplus managerial ties and clips it underneath his Lemmy neckerchief.

Admiring himself in Melvin's typing paper-sized mirror, Spencer prances awhile, stiffly and grotesquely.

After a further swig--

SPENCER
Looking suave. So suave.
(rhyming it with "wave")
Looking Europeanesque.

Then he gets an idea. He goes out--

INT. KITCHEN--DAY

--passing the toilet on his way to the locker room.

Some Bus Girls with nothing better to do loiter by the door, giggling and eavesdropping on the boss.

In a grand, beautiful, sonorous tenor, Melvin belts out the 1938 romantic ballad, "You Go to My Head"--

MELVIN (OS)
You go to my head, like a sip of sparkling Burgundy brew--

Trishy is among the gigglers. She gives Spencer the eye as he brushes by. Or at least she tries. He doesn't see her, or anybody else, it seems.

INT. LOCKER ROOM--DAY

From his locker, Spencer fetches Raleigh's silken white handkerchief.

INT. KITCHEN--DAY

On his way back to the Managerial Office, he passes again through the kitchen.

MELVIN (OS)
(crooning)
I find you spinning round my brain, like a bubble in a big-ass glass of pink champagne--

INT. MANAGERIAL OFFICE--DAY

Spencer tries to flit the Standish hankie in front of the mirror like a rich dandy.

SPENCER
(addressing his own reflection)
A wealthy associate provisioned me with this neckerchief. Like a gratuitous tip. See? They wrote "S" on it, for Spencer Sproul.

He ties it around his throat, but finds the look less than satisfactory.

He presses the hankie down on Melvin's blotter and flops it around, messing up the boss's pencils, envelopes and invoices, and upsetting a framed photo of Melvin's prepubescent daughter, JAZMYNNE.

Spencer finally comes up with a pretty fair approximation of how the privileged classes might fold a handkerchief. He tucks it in his Lemmy vest pocket, with a precise triangle of while silk poking out.

He tries to make an effete, ever-so-sophisticated and bored face, like Raleigh's.

From out behind the restaurant come voices--

BOSS BUM (OS)
(singing)
Oh, they feed on chicken pie,
if you eat it you will die.
And the meat, you cannot cut it with a swo-o-o-o-o-o-ord--

SIMPLE-MINDED BUM (OS)
--schwo-o-o-o-orrzzch.

SPENCER
Ah, the simpleton medleys of the poor pleasant class.

He pilfers another hit off the jug.

Now that he is suave and Europeanesque, Spencer feels the need to read something more intellectually challenging than lists of food additives and wine labels.

His eye alights on a copy of today's newspaper, flopped on Melvin's managerial desk. It's opened to the SOCIETY PAGE. The lead article's headline reads:

YOUTH SYMPHONETTE TO PERFORM IN STANDISH MANSION THIS AFTERNOON

It's accompanied by a full-color photo of the local MUSIC CONSERVATORY, which is housed in a defunct and yuppified train station.

In the foreground of the picture stands an athletic, rich, late-middle-aged man.

He has one arm stiffly wrapped around the shoulder of a little boy with the same sort of curly red hair that we saw on Mrs. Standish's canasta partner, Mrs. Coventry.

The caption reads:

HARVEY COVENTRY, SR., ANTICIPATES THE PERFORMANCE OF HIS GRANDSON, HARVEY COVENTRY III.

Perhaps by coincidence, this page also prominently displays an advertisement for COVENTRY'S EXCLUSIVE TENNIS CLUB.

Suddenly, we hear the sound of a toilet flushing.

Before leaving, Spencer rips off Melvin's Society Page.

He returns, on second thought, and latches onto the wine, too.

EXT. LEMUEL'S PARKING LOT--DAY

Spencer stalks toward his busted jalopy, his backpack bulging with the jug.

Eyeing him uneasily from the dumpster, the Boss Bum continues to lead his comrades in a group-sing. They hoot and bawl obliviously along.

BOSS BUM
Undertaker, hang around,
'cause there's work here to be found--

BUM CHORUS
(in unison, more or less)
At that all-go-hungry hash house
where we bo-o-o-o-o-oard.

INT. SPENCER'S CAR--DAY

Spencer sits at the wheel. Placing the Society Page on the death seat, he considers the photo of the Music Conservatory.

Then he unscrews the lid, removes another inch from the jug, and focuses, more or less, on little Harvey Coventry III.

Spencer tunes his radio to an all-Mancini station, meanwhile narrowing his eyes in a high-tone way.

SPENCER
(to his own reflection
in the rearview mirror)
The flute player doesn't do music very good. So I shall sup on his gimlets and wash them down with a sparkly burgomeister muskratelle... For I am a scoundrel.

He opens the glove compartment, revealing a mini-arsenal: brass knuckles, a can of mace, a straight-edged razor, etc.

From among these items he selects a piano-wire and wooden-peg garrote, which he coils around the death-seat sun visor, tucking the pegs up inside, to be at the ready.

EXT. LEMUEL'S PARKING LOT--DAY

Spencer pulls out and drives unsteadily off.

Across the street we see Dagbert's Family Eatery, all built

and ready to go. The place is just gearing up for its grand opening later today.

Krystelle perches in a welcoming position on the front stoop. She wears a uniform every bit as tight as the one she cast off when deserting Lemuel's. It's violet and yellow, adhering to Dagbert's color scheme, and even more unflattering to her full figure.

EXT. MUSIC CONSERVATORY--DAY

Spencer's car idles among swank vehicles containing CHAUFFEURS and NANNIES who are waiting for the bell to ring and their little prodigies to come out.

INT. SPENCER'S CAR--DAY

While he waits, he uses the time productively, tapping away at his rickety old laptop.

Spencer might be a spaz with words, but, loosened up with alcohol, he's not too bad with nonverbal things that glow and flash and slide when you tickle the track pad.

He calls up the LEMCO National Headquarters Homepage and lifts the official image of Lemmy the Lemur.

He does the same with a John Wayne Gacy fan-site, getting a good shot of that all-time champion boy-killer in his clown greasepaint.

Spencer hits the jug another time. It gets his fingers really hopping.

He's morphing the lemur and the psycho with a dead alligator and Dr. Condoleezza Rice, when--

EXT. MUSIC CONSERVATORY--DAY

--the bell rings, and RICH KIDS start tumbling out of the former train station's grand portals.

They're in uniform blazers, school ties and cute plaid shorts.

INT. SPENCER'S CAR--DAY

Spencer stashes his laptop on the dash. Outmaneuvering a legit parental car, he pulls up, rolls down the window and accosts a HELPFUL YOUNG LAD.

This trusting little soul leans his head, shoulders and most of his torso into the death-seat window. He winces at Spencer's boozy breath.

It's his first kidnapping, so Spencer's a bit nervous.

SPENCER
Hello, youngster. Can you answer my question?
(trying to sound out the names on the Society Page)
Har-vey Co- Coven-, you know, er, Senior, he told me I should drive here and get his junior youngster on my seat with me. Right here...

Spencer pats the death seat.

One of the wooden pegs of the garrote slips from under the sun visor with a "boing" from the piano wire. Spencer tucks it back up, fumbling drunkenly.

SPENCER
I am supposed to take the talented--
(squinting at the article)
--hair? The talented hair? Um--to the exhaustive Coventry Tennis Club for--
(pause, thinking hard)
--for his exhaustive Coventry tennissing lesson.

HELPFUL YOUNG LAD
Oh, you want Harvey, sir? Everybody wants Harvey, believe me. And it's easy! He's right over there! The one toting the slide trombone!

EXT. MUSIC CONSERVATORY--DAY

Little HARVEY COVENTRY III walks among his CLASSMATES.

The latter are about what you'd expect: mini-pencil-necks with translucent skin from staying indoors their whole lives practicing.

But the Coventry boy, on the other hand, is ruddy, a splendid specimen, with delicious heft to his bones and an appetizing sheen to his curly red hair and dimpled flesh.

The Classmates carry measly violins and sissy piccolos; but this boy has a hale and hearty trombone, golden as he is.

INT. SPENCER'S CAR--DAY

Because the prey is a musician, Spencer turns up the Mancini on his car radio, as an enticement.

He pulls up alongside Harvey and attempts to engage him.

SPENCER
I'm hungry--er, rather peckish. Quite, like, so--

Harvey takes plenty of time to consider Spencer's Lemmy vest, Lemmy neckerchief, and busted jalopy.

Then he sees something that sparks a certain amount of interest--

HARVEY
(eyeing Spencer's laptop)
You've got quite a funny old dinosaur there.

SPENCER
It's supposed to be a scary lemur. Don't you think it's just scary a little, boy?

A violet and yellow helicopter passes overhead.

HARVEY
What's with the chopper? Turn that sickening noise off, eat a whole bunch of these, and follow that chopper.

Harvey tosses Spencer a roll of breath mints, stuffs his trombone in the back seat, and hops in.

Spencer obeys all three directives without question or hesitation, making Harvey smile.

EXT. SPENCER'S CAR--DAY

They follow the chopper, ducking in and out of side roads through various parts of town, trying to keep up.

Their progress is not aided by Spencer's drunkenness. In fact, several times he nearly fulfils his homicidal ambitions.

EXT. DAGBERT'S FAMILY EATERY, PARKING LOT--DAY

DAG THE DINNERSAUR--or, at any rate, a seven foot tall, three-D, living, breathing polyester-plush version of him--arrives in the violet and yellow helicopter, much to the manic glee of an unruly mob of BRATS.

Just as Spencer and Harvey pull up, Dag starts to thrash his dinner plate-studded stegosaurus tail around.

He works the Brats into a frenzy, like a blood festival. One of them gnaws on Dag's toes, while others hump his legs like over-excited spaniels.

INT. SPENCER'S CAR--DAY

Spencer grabs his laptop off the dash, calls up DAGBERT.COM, and morphs a bit of the Dinnersaur into his revamped Lemmy.

Both Spencer and Harvey gasp at the result.

SPENCER

A nibble more scary now, eh, little trumpetist?

(trying to be debonair and seductive)

The youngsters out there look very excitable. Shall we walk among them and feel their scaredness, I and you?

HARVEY

I'm too old for Dink the Dorkysaur. Let's go inside and see what they have for the grown-ups.

(climbing out)
Grab my instrument. Wouldn't want to leave it unattended in this neighborhood.

Like a Bus Boy in a good restaurant fetching a silver finger bowl on demand, Spencer does as he is told.

Harvey's finding it amusing to have his own prole to boss around.

EXT. LEMUEL'S FAMILY RESTAURANT FRONT STOOP--DAY

The Fry Cook, the Dish Washer and the Mean Waitress are discreetly passing a hash-pipe back and forth. Trishy stands nearby trying not to notice.

They watch Spencer follow the child into Dagbert's.

MEAN WAITRESS
Look, Spazzer's got a boyfriend. And I do mean "boy."

DISH WASHER
And it's a rich boy. That's really offensive.

FRY COOK
I knew he was a fag. Didn't I tell you he was a fag? But I had no idea he was a pendergast.

Trishy gasps at that last word and begins to weep softly, as if she's been slapped in the face.

DISH WASHER
We should call Detective Furtwangler right now.

Trishy volunteers to go inside to do the phoning, with her own quarter.

INT. DAGBERT'S FAMILY EATERY--A FEW MINUTES LATER

Except for the colors and the mascot, this place is barely distinguishable from its rival across the street.

The biggest difference is Krystelle's beaming photo, framed and hung behind the cash register, with a brass-colored plastic plaque at the bottom that says MANAGERESS.

It's opening day, and already this formidable career woman has clawed her way to the top.

Spencer, Harvey, and the trombone are jammed in a booth.

A grotesquely swollen bacon and cheeseburger has been set in front of the boy. Even the bun jiggles with clots of grease.

SPENCER
(more Anthony Hopkins)
You know, the French people over in Europeanesque lands, they enjoy pressing lots of exquisite filly-minions and things down a goose's neck. It makes his kidney extra fat for, um, like liverwursty-matter. You wipe it on your soda cracker. And it's majorly expensive.
(trying to look snooty)
It's a required taste.

He looks at the screw-top wine selection, sees the word "Chianti," moves his lips to sound it out, gasps at the price, and changes his mind.

SPENCER
So, with that in your mind, please do eat up, my, er, stout laddy.

HARVEY
(wincing up at the ceiling speakers)
Eat? Here? I couldn't hold down milk-toast. The Muzique company's diabolical.

Harvey takes up his trombone. A string is attached to the slide because his arm is not yet long enough to reach the lowest notes.

HARVEY
You'd never believe it in this dive,

but there's actually no such thing as a bad tune. Listen to this bit--

He stands on the seat and hoots along with the piped-in music.

HARVEY
The bass line doesn't need to be quite so idiotic.
(plays a few measures)
See? You can imply all kinds of more or less interesting modulations. Up on top, you can extend the chords and do ambiguous passing dissonances--

Harvey somehow makes the giant horn produce some high, piercing shrieks.

HARVEY
But that sort of thing only makes people want to sit around and listen awhile, instead of getting in and out fast, and making room for more saps!

Harvey follows that last word with a loud honk, jostling several Customers, and causing the trombone to expel a quantity of condensed lung mucus onto the table.

Obeying the natural-born instincts of his socioeconomic class, Spencer reaches for something to wipe it up with. Harvey watches, amused.

The Standish hankie happens to be the closest thing to a rag available, so Spencer removes it from his Lemmy vest pocket and sops up the mess.

Then he folds the silken thing and tucks it neatly between the Dag the Dinnersaur ashtray and the saltine-stuffed sugar shaker, taking care prominently to display the fancy "S" monogram.

HARVEY
Why do you think the finer restaurants have either no music at all, or actual good stuff? It's because wealthy diners expect to sit at their tables as long as they wish, and not be tortured in

the meantime.

Right behind Harvey, seated in the adjacent booth with his back to the child, is none other than our favorite restaurant critic.

Raleigh discreetly pokes a new ruby-encrusted cell phone over his shoulder.

RALEIGH
(whispering)
Are you getting this, Momsy?

HARVEY
The lower and middle classes are constantly being dragged and shoved around by the ears, and they don't even know it.

RALEIGH
My god, a child prodigy. He's writing this week's review for me!

INT. STANDISH MANSION, RECEPTION HALL--AT THAT MOMENT

A charity bash is going on, featuring the local Youth Symphonette. The second trombone seat is empty.

Mrs. Standish occupies the seat of honor, front and center. The symphonette is playing a soft bit, and her shriek echoes all over the place--

MRS. STANDISH
(into a princess extension)
Raleigh Standish the Fourth! Who is that little boy you're with?

This draws stares, gasps and harrumphs from the audience, and snickers from the players.

INT. DAGBERT'S FAMILY EATERY--DAY

Harvey flubs a low note.

MRS. STANDISH (OS)
(filtered)
That sounds like--

INT. STANDISH MANSION, RECEPTION HALL--DAY

MRS. STANDISH (CONT)
--Mrs. Coventry's little grandson!

She furtively eyes that very woman, who's seated next to her.

Mrs. Coventry ignores the concert and bends ANOTHER OLD LADY's ear with her only topic--

MRS. COVENTRY
My husband didn't compromise his political principles. Not at all. He just saw no further reason to be in the SDS when the Vietnam war ended...

INT. DAGBERT'S FAMILY EATERY--DAY

The boy has climbed onto the table, the better to drown out the ceiling speakers with his bellowing trombone.

HARVEY
These poor dupes all around us are just as irritated as we are. But they're not well-to-do, and they can't bring themselves to leave till they've done justice to the paltry tab. They're in agony in the meantime. And here's the most diabolical bit of all... Are you ready?

SPENCER
(just barely keeping up)
Ready?

HARVEY
The agony is the biggest draw of all! They wouldn't come near this place without it!

This is all a great revelation to Spencer. In his mind, he sees--

INT. LEMUEL'S FAMILY RESTAURANT (A SERIES OF FLASHBACKS)

--himself at various times throughout his busboy career,

getting twitchy and angry, even on break time, teeth gritting, knuckles whitening on the edges of trays in unconscious rhythm, and not knowing why.

INT. DAGBERT'S--DAY

But now that he knows it's all the fault of the Muzique Company, instead of being resentful, Spencer is fascinated.

Leaving the intended victim stomping around on the table and tooting full blast--

INT. DAGBERT'S BACK ROOM--DAY

--Spencer infiltrates his nondescript self into the back of the restaurant.

As violet and yellow-clad EMPLOYEES scurry all around him, he inspects a wall console full of knobs and dials.

He starts to sound out a label which reads--

CENTRAL NERVOUS SYSTEM IRRITANT TUNES
FOR RAPID HIGH-VOLUME CUSTOMER TURNOVER

INT. DAGBERT'S DINING AREA--DAY

Raleigh turns around and ogles Harvey over the back of the seat.

MRS. STANDISH (OS)
(filtered)
You bring little Harvey the Third
straight here this instant!

INTERCUT BETWEEN DAGBERT'S AND STANDISH MANSION

MRS. STANDISH (CONT)
(squinting at the symphonette)
He's supposed to be filling out the T-
bone section!
(glancing at Mrs. Coventry,
switching to a whisper)
Raleigh, I beseech you. His grandfather
is one of our biggest advertisers!

RALEIGH
Fuck off, Momsy, you mercenary old slag. I'm taking the plunge.

MRS. STANDISH
(simpering, to Mrs. Coventry)
Isn't this adagio pure heaven?

MRS. COVENTRY
Tennis is plenty revolutionary, as my husband always says. After all, what is the net but a barricade?

Raleigh drops his cell phone, rubies and all, into a glass of iced tea.

His mother winces at the resulting burst of static. She hangs up and looks at Mrs. Coventry for a moment.

MRS. STANDISH
My god, you're an ignorant bitch.

INT. DAGBERT'S FAMILY RESTAURANT--DAY

RALEIGH
(to Harvey)
Have you had dessert, little one? There's a positively scrumptious item on the kiddy menu--

Raleigh opens the document in question--which he has never laid eyes on until this moment--and jumps back with a whoop when a cardboard pop-up Dag the Dinnersaur reaches out its fangs and tries to bite off his nose.

Spencer comes back into the dining area looking very preoccupied. Forgetting about Harvey, he heads straight for the door.

INT. DAGBERT'S ENTRANCE--DAY

Just as he reaches the vestibule, Krystelle stops him.

KRYSTELLE
Sick of marshmallow Melvin's abuse, too, just like me, Spencer? Well, all our openings for bus boys are filled

just now. But if you want to work your way up the ladder here at Dagbert's, you can collect litter in the parking lot, on spec. I might be able to toss you a nickel a pound. Nothing contractual, of course. And just till I can dig up some wet-backs who aren't organized.

Spencer is so absorbed in thinking about the music lesson he just got from Harvey that he can come up with no reply to Krystelle's offer. He just stares at her.

KRYSTELLE

Well, think about it. So to speak. And let me know. Better not dilly-dally, though. Someone might just fill your shoes before you've had a chance to step into them.

SPUD, one of Krystelle's slower bus boys, slops by, shedding ketchup. Spencer very carefully steps in it, leaving a perfect footprint, as in blood.

Spencer and Spud exchange a long, lingering look.

INT. DINING AREA--DAY

Raleigh's trying to read between cardboard stegosaurus fangs.

RALEIGH

Yes, here it is. Dag the Dinnersaur's Double Dutch Delight... per Deux!

(tittering at his own bilingual alliteration)

Trust me, darling. I'm a professional restaurant critic. I know about these things, and I assure you, it's to die for. If you wish, my lad, I shall abuse my status as arbiter of taste in this burg, and prevail upon the waitress to supply us with an extra cherry on top. And then the pair of us will just dig in and wallow around like a couple of nauseating--

Suddenly, the front door swings open--

INT. ENTRANCE--DAY

--and Detective Furtwangler's three uniformed henchmen barge in, one by one.

First comes the Fat Cop. He takes up a vigilant stance immediately to the left of the entrance.

The Skinny Cop follows. He stands at full-parade attention on the right.

The Female Cop is next. She jockeys for position beside the Fat Cop, who elbows her away.

She scampers across, jostles around with the Skinny Cop for awhile, and winds up wedging herself between him and a Rotary Club gum-ball machine that features a picture of a mentally challenged boy.

After a pause, during which the three officers scan the restaurant to make sure the area is secure, Detective Furtwangler makes his big entrance.

Squinting importantly, he brushes past Spencer--

INT. DINING AREA--DAY

--and sleuths among the booths.

Raleigh nearly cries out in horror. He turns quickly around and buries his face deep in the kiddy menu. It looks like Dag's swallowing his head.

With an expert investigator's eye, Detective Furtwangler doesn't have too much trouble locating Harvey--the only kid sitting without a mommy and daddy.

DETECTIVE FURTWANGLER
Oh, you poor little tiger. Did the bad man give you marijuana?

Harvey shrugs. He eyes the snub-nose revolver peeking out from under the detective's jacket.

DETECTIVE FURTWANGLER
Did you get a good look at the mean man?

HARVEY
Well, duh.

DETECTIVE FURTWANGLER
Can you describe him?

HARVEY
(thinking about it)
Actually, no.

DETECTIVE FURTWANGLER
(reaching out a comforting hand)
Oh, you sad little fella. You caught Regressed Memories Syndrome.

Harvey looks him up and down, appraising in his clothes and shoes.

HARVEY
Oh, yes. That's right, Officer. I must have caught "Regressed Memories Syndrome."

DETECTIVE FURTWANGLER
(finally noticing the trombone)
You like music?

As if on cue, the Muzique starts oozing an arrangement of the classic "Let it Be," for ocarina and electronic rhythm-box, adjusted to a sultry bossa-nova beat.

Sitting down uninvited, Detective Furtwangler sings along. He couldn't be further off key--

DETECTIVE FURTWANGLER
When I get myself in real big trouble,
Hairy Larry comes to me...

Raleigh's frozen in his seat, listening to all this going on behind his back, shocked out of his wits, only three inches of plywood and vinyl separating him from the Gestapo.

INT. ENTRANCE--DAY

The three uniformed henchmen stand sentry, sort of.

The Female Cop is kicking the Rotary Club's gum-ball machine.

FEMALE COP
This hunk of crap stole my quarter!

She unsheathes her night stick and winds up like a baseball player.

The Skinny Cop has buttonholed Spud, the slow bus boy, who's off work now.

SKINNY COP
(attempting to raise Spud's class consciousness)
It's not the same man who first works and reposes; but it's because the one works that the other rests. Do you understand that you're the light infantry of capitalism?

Spud responds by pulling something out of his nose and carrying it out the door on his index finger.

The Fat Cop winces as a TEEN squeezes past on Spud's heels lugging a huge take-out pizza in a cardboard box. It belches thunderheads of steam that leave globules of grease wherever they condense.

FAT COP
You might want to drink a glass of grapefruit juice with that.

The Teen ignores him and leaves.

The Fat Cop sticks his face out--

FAT COP
Unsweetened!

He sees someone in the parking lot who makes him smile.

EXT. DAGBERT'S PARKING LOT--DAY

It's Mahalia.

She's accosting Spud, barring his way to the bus stop. She

tries to work her charms on him while he picks his nose some more.

INT. DAGBERT'S--DAY

FAT COP
Hey, guys. Guess who's tricking out there.

The Female Cop stops in mid-swing and looks out the window.

FEMALE COP
Mahalia!

The three of them scamper out.

EXT. PARKING LOT--DAY

The Female Cop slams Mahalia, who's twice her size, against a parked car, and commences shaking her down.

FEMALE COP
Long time no see, girlfriend!

INT. DAGBERT'S--AT THAT MOMENT

DETECTIVE FURTWANGLER
(still crooning)
Let 'im bleed, let 'im bleed, let 'im bleed, let 'im--

Noticing the Standish hankie by the sugar shaker, he reaches out to touch the wet thing.

DETECTIVE FURTWANGLER
--bleed?
(recoiling in disgust)
God almighty. Talk about DN-fucking-A.

He snatches a Dag the Dinnersaur fork from a NAUGHTY CHILD who's trying to chip formica off a neighboring table, and skewers the handkerchief.

Immediately, his skilled law-enforcer's eye recognizes the embroidered "S" monogram.

DETECTIVE FURTWANGLER
(under his breath)
Standish, you sick old fuck.

Raleigh nearly faints. He thinks that was addressed directly to him.

HARVEY
(the pure lamb)
What's a "sick old fuck," Officer?

Unable to withstand the child's inquiring gaze, Detective Furtwangler must avert his eyes. He looks out the window--

--and sees what his three uniformed henchmen are up to.

DETECTIVE FURTWANGLER
I may need to interrogate you at a later date, son. Write your phone number--
(looking hurriedly about the table)
--on this place-mat. Leave it with the cashier when you pay.

He rushes out, casting back a single reluctant glance.

Raleigh's face is still buried in the kiddy menu, petrified and very puzzled.

RALEIGH
(whispering, over his shoulder)
Is the bad man gone?

EXT. PARKING LOT--DAY

Detective Furtwangler trots onto the scene, brandishing the fork like a dowsing wand, Raleigh's hankie tangled in the tines.

Mahalia's bent ninety-degrees forward over the hood of the car, and is having her inner thighs ransacked with great thoroughness by the Female Cop.

DETECTIVE FURTWANGLER
(as if he didn't know)
What do we got?

The Female Cop, over-excited, reports with Nazi-click of the heels.

FEMALE COP
Suspicion of solicitation! Sir!

MAHALIA
Lemme go, and I'll tip you off about the lair of a evil serial killer, right here in the neighborhood.

DETECTIVE FURTWANGLER
That makes eight evil serial killer lairs this month, on this block alone. What is it, a running joke between you and your girlfriends?

MAHALIA
Naw, honest, Detective Fart-Wrinkler. It's the real thing this time. You gonna find all kinds of off-putting clues in there. This guy was talking dirty about the Pope.

DETECTIVE FURTWANGLER
Do you realize what a pain in the butt it is to get a warrant, Mahalia? Now, if he was political...

MAHALIA
What?

The Skinny Cop opens his mouth to chime in, but--

DETECTIVE FURTWANGLER
(to Skinny Cop)
Not a word, Ho Chi Minh.

MAHALIA
Political?
(catching on)
Ohhhh. Like a terrorist? Um... yeah! Yes, sir, Detective Fat-Wanker. Oh, baby, was he ever po-o-o-litical. He was reading the Kareem.

DETECTIVE FURTWANGLER
The which?

SKINNY COP
She's referring to the Koran.

MAHALIA
That's what I'm talking about.

DETECTIVE FURTWANGLER
The what?

SKINNY COP
It's the sacred book of Islam. While providing justification for many of the feudal tendencies of contemporary Muslim culture--

Raleigh and Harvey, and Harvey's trombone, sneak out of Dagbert's without anybody seeing them.

SKINNY COP
--there are adumbrations, in the late chapters, of a primitive communism which, if untangled from its theocratic outgrowths--

They hop into Mrs. Standish's canary-yellow Mercedes Benz.

SKINNY COP
--could provide the basis for true revolution in the Middle East.

There is a pause, during which everyone, including Mahalia, stares at the Skinny Cop.

DETECTIVE FURTWANGLER
Are you done?

SKINNY COP
Trotsky said all revolutions are verbose.

MAHALIA
(to the Skinny Cop)
Man, if you so down on democracy, why the fuck did you sign up to bust

niggers' heads in its name?

The Skinny Cop takes a deep breath, in preparation for what promises to be an interminable and incomprehensible reply.

But, before he can get a word out--

MAHALIA
(to Detective Furtwangler)
Yeah, I saw tons of Mid-East stuff around that dump, honey. You just go on over there and shake that terrorist down within an inch of his three-and-a-half- inch life. But take li'l Ms. Tomb Raider to watch your back--

The Female Cop lunges at Mahalia, and has to be restrained by the Fat Cop.

MAHALIA
--'cause he's one unabombing, box-cutting, American Civil Liberties-trashing, kamikaze peckerwood maniac butt-hole. And that is the god's-honest truth.

DETECTIVE FURTWANGLER
(whispering to his henchmen)
In the name of homeland security, fuck the warrant.
(to Mahalia)
Aim us in the general direction, my dear, and we can be on our separate ways.

MAHALIA
It's that ass-ugly puce stucco abortion right over there.

She points at the Sproul-Nussbaum duplex.

Standing on the sidewalk, right in everyone's line of vision, is Spencer. Just as he did outside Ruth's house, he's displaying himself to the police--or trying to, at any rate.

Nobody bothers to focus on him.

As the forces of law and order march off to do their patriotic chore, the Skinny Cop lingers behind, to raise Mahalia's political awareness a bit further.

SKINNY COP
Under true socialism, when eroticism ceases to commodified, you and your fellow sex-workers will be reeducated like any other members of the lumpen-proletariat.

MAHALIA
(yelling after Detective Furtwangler)
On second thought, forget about the serial killer. Shoot this asshole forty-seven times instead.

EXT. DAGBERT'S FAMILY EATERY--DAY

The Standish Mercedes speeds out of Dagbert's parking lot, nearly running over Melvin, who's trying to cross over from his own restaurant as furtively as possible.

He's so pale and soft, it looks as though this might be his first time outdoors.

Melvin approaches Spencer.

MELVIN
Doing a little industrial spying, eh, Sproul?

Spencer says nothing.

MELVIN
I'm impressed. That really shows me some gumption. I couldn't come over here and hang around myself. Not sporting. The Better Business Bureau would never give me that Merchant of the Month Award. But you, Bus Bi--I mean, Spencer--you can loiter around anyplace, just as you please. You're permanently incognito with that empty mug of yours. I don't mean anything by that, of course, heh-heh... You'll have

to drop by the house sometime, and meet
the wife and--

Spencer walks away, heading toward home.

EXT. SPROUL-NUSSBAUM DUPLEX--DAY

Mr. and Mrs. Nussbaum's door is ajar. But the Female Cop uses that horizontal sledge hammer known as a "skeleton key," anyway, just for the pleasure of splintering private property.

INT. NUSSBAUM HOME--A MOMENT LATER

Detective Furtwangler is preceded by the three Cops, just as before in Dagbert's--only this time the area they survey to make sure it's secure is occupied by nobody but a terrified old couple.

The Female Cop immediately goes into overdrive, while her colleagues stand back at a safe distance and watch the one-woman show.

DETECTIVE FURTWANGLER
(to the Fat and Skinny Cops)
See, they're so busy playing with dollies and chit-chatting during recess, they're never forced to choose between learning the rules of playground honor and getting their asses kicked, as we did in school. This is why, after they grow up, they're so scary when you turn them loose. We could use about eight or nine more of them on the force. The nutty murderers would leave town because they couldn't compete.

The Female Cop slams the old man up against the wall.

MR. NUSSBAUM
I demand to see some badges and a warrant, and to be informed of the charges against us.

FEMALE COP
Tell it to the commandant at

Guantanamo. Maybe he'll even read you
your rights. No, wait a minute. I guess
he won't, come to think of it, 'cause
you don't have any!

When she hears that, Mrs. Nussbaum crouches on the floor and goes into hysterics.

The Skinny Cop approaches her, bringing what he considers words of comfort:

SKINNY COP
One day everyone will recognize that
religions are nothing more than
different snake skins cast off by
history, and that Man is the snake who
sloughed them.

MR. NUSSBAUM
(with deep bitterness)
Fool. You should be quoting MEIN KAMPF,
not DAS KAPITAL.
(to the Female Cop)
As for you, young woman, you're a mere
amateur compared to the Gestapo. By
this point in the so-called
"investigation," they had my father
doubled up on the floor already, a jack
boot in his stomach.

FEMALE COP
I'll be glad to oblige, Ali-Baba.

Getting pumped up for some serious law enforcement action, she rolls up her sleeves, draws back her foot and takes aim at the old man's midriff.

DETECTIVE FURTWANGLER
Whoa.
(taking the Female Cop aside)
Did he say "Gestapo"?

FEMALE COP
Goose--something like that.
(eager to get back and
kick the old man)
Whatever.

DETECTIVE FURTWANGLER
Er, boys, let's wrap it up. Our work is done here.

He hustles his people out the door. It's necessary to drag the Female Cop away.

EXT. SPROUL-NUSSBAUM DUPLEX--A MOMENT LATER

DETECTIVE FURTWANGLER
Good thing we didn't let him see our badge numbers. He's probably a lawyer.

Spencer sits on his own front stoop, immediately next door, less than ten feet away.

He tries to put on one of those supercilious "Catch me if you can" looks that psychos in the movies are always giving to the authorities.

Detective Furtwangler looks at him. Something seems to click, yet again. Then he decides to continue ignoring this trivial creature.

INT. SPENCER'S LIVING ROOM--DAY

Spencer kneels over a cardboard box where he keeps his arsenal, comprising the expected firearms, knives, black jacks, brass knuckles, etc., also an aluminum rat-tail comb, a Martha Stewart-brand hot glue gun, a very nasty-looking soldering iron, and some tweezers.

From among these and other items, he selects a bottle of chloroform and a rag, plus a large cattle prod.

He stuffs these in his backpack, slings it casually over one shoulder, and goes--

EXT SPROUL-NUSSBAUM DUPLEX--DAY

--next door.

The Nussbaum's splintered door hangs by one hinge.

Spencer peeks in and sees the old lady hunkered on the floor, her arms clenched tight across her belly, moaning in anguish, deep in a Holocaust flashback.

Her husband kneels next to her, rubbing her back and shoulders.

SPENCER
Are you okay, Mr. and Mrs. Nussbaum?

MR. NUSSBAUM
Physical injuries are minimal, thanks be to God.

Spencer's starts to remove the chloroform from his backpack.

SPENCER
(hopefully)
Did they make sundry questions about me?

Mr. Nussbaum didn't hear that.

MR. NUSSBAUM
You are a nice person, Spencer. I know you will listen to me, and try very hard to get my words, somehow, into your poor brain... A terrible time is coming in this country. I know, because I saw the same thing happen, long ago, in another place.

SPENCER
(eagerly)
You mean the Germany people? Back in history times?

Excited, Spencer pulls out the cattle prod and holds it in front of him, in both hands. He flips the switch, and it begins to hum and vibrate.

SPENCER
The germy people that electrified all those hundreds of homoerotic Egyptian children and ladies?

Mercifully, the old folks are a bit hard-of-hearing and near-sighted. In any case, Mrs. Nussbaum is too upset to notice much of anything, and her husband is intent on imparting his wisdom.

Spencer sits down on the floor and settles in, like a child at story time, cattle prod at the ready.

MR. NUSSBAUM
Spencer, there will come a time, soon, when your only defense--

EXT. PUBLIC LIBRARY--NEXT DAY

MR. NUSSBAUM (VO)
--will be knowledge.

Spencer is walking up the steps to the main entrance.

MR. NUSSBAUM (VO)
It is the only dependable weapon when a country goes in this terrible direction.

The library's next-door to the BETTER BUSINESS BUREAU, whose marquee reads--

MERCHANT OF THE MONTH AWARD BANQUET TODAY

INT. PUBLIC LIBRARY--DAY

MR. NUSSBAUM (VO)
The content of your mind is the one thing they cannot take away from you, without killing you outright.

Spencer wanders past various deserted sections of the library, marked LITERATURE, PHILOSOPHY, RELIGION, and HISTORY.

Eventually he comes to the BUSINESS shelves, the only part of the library that has any visitors.

Spencer looks at the illustrations in a book on SUBLIMINAL ADVERTISING. He stares at--

--reproductions of magazine ads where images of people copulating and killing each other are subtly blended into the shiny bits of soda pop cans, SUVs, handguns, etc.

MR. NUSSBAUM (VO)
Knowledge will sharpen your sense of

honesty and fair play, Spencer--

He bumbles, completely at random, into the LAW stacks.

MR. NUSSBAUM (VO)
In particular, my friend, you must master the profound and beautiful law of your own civilization. How it works, how it is applied, how it can be used and abused, and twisted into a travesty of itself.

Spencer glances through a book on CIVIL RIGHTS LEGISLATION, but grows bored after ogling a few illustrations of lynched southern Blacks.

He tries to read a word here and there, but it's such a chore. It makes him sweat as much as he does when busing tons of filthy plates. He grinds his teeth in mental discomfort.

Spencer's mind soon wanders. He looks out the window, just in time to see--

EXT. BETTER BUSINESS BUREAU--DAY

--HARVEY COVENTRY, SR., little Harvey's grandpa, arriving in a taxi. He wears white tennis shorts and carries a graphite tennis racket in one hand, a boxed tuxedo in the other.

He is welcomed at the door by the Better Business Bureau's pretty young female RECEPTIONIST.

HARVEY COVENTRY, SR.
Is there anyplace I can change?

RECEPTIONIST
(trying to be funny)
From SDS to the BBB? I'd say you've already changed quite enough for one lifetime, Mr. Coventry!

Harvey Coventry, Sr., looks as though he's about to brain the girl with his tennis racket.

Krystelle walks by on her way to the library.

INT. PUBLIC LIBRARY--DAY

She heads straight for the Business shelves, apparently using her lunch hour to bone up on some management skills.

She's surprised to see Spencer in such a place.

KRYSTELLE
Well, Mr. Sproul. Fixing to supplant the marshmallow?

SPENCER
Huh?

KRYSTELLE
He's so sexist.

SPENCER
I don't know because I'm not a gay person.

Krystelle takes Spencer by the hand like a lost child, and leads him to--

INT. TAX LAW STACKS--DAY

She sits with him at a study table, a Tax Law book open before them. She points to a page with words, and he stares dumbly. She slides her finger to a column full of numbers, and he kicks right into action, absorbing the data like a loofa.

Krystelle sits back and watches awhile in mild astonishment.

KRYSTELLE
Hey, Rain Guy. Looks like you and me better hit the Black Jack tables in Vegas sometime.

Experimentally, she flops one of her breasts over part of the page, keeping an eye on him for any reaction. He cranes his neck around it and continues sucking in the numbers.

KRYSTELLE
(unsurprised, undisappointed)
Never mind.

EXT. PUBLIC LIBRARY--A COUPLE HOURS LATER

They part company on the front steps.

Krystelle has loaded Spencer down with materials on accounting tricks, tax loopholes, everything one needs to cheat the government like a proper merchant.

He strains under the weight.

KRYSTELLE
Good luck bringing Melvin to his dimpled knees. You'll have to pop across the street and pay us a visit sometime. Let me know what he's up to.
(glancing furtively around)
You know, sort of like an industrial spy?
(pausing, getting no reaction)
Well, I'm sure I can suborn one of the other lemurs.

She notices Spencer staring at the Better Business Bureau next door.

We can hear the Merchant of the Month's amplified acceptance speech.

HARVEY COVENTRY, SR. (OS)
When I bombed the Draft Board, not two blocks away, little did I suspect that, thirty-five years later, I'd be standing here accepting this trophy from you bourgeois pigs--

Through the walls and windows of the Better Business Bureau, it's difficult to tell if he gets any laughs.

KRYSTELLE
Do you think I'm not worthy to be in there eating tuna casserole with those guys?

SPENCER
Thank you for saying if you also wish, Ma'am.

He walks off.

KRYSTELLE
(shouting after him)
How else do you think a woman can snag that award?

INT. SPENCER'S LIVING ROOM--NIGHT

Seated among devotional candles at his shrine to famous killer Ted Bundy, Spencer inches, letter by letter, through the library books.

Taped on the wall are newspaper clippings about Ted Bundy's "career." One features a picture of this psycho in his law school days. The headline reads--

"GIFTED" BUNDY DREW UP "EXQUISITE" LEGAL BRIEFS

MR. NUSSBAUM (VO)
Most importantly of all, Spencer, knowledge of the law will enhance your love of humanity.

Thumb-tacked nearby is a police photo of one of Bundy's victims. Her head has been bashed out of shape with a tree branch.

Spencer, his own head visibly reeling from all the hard studying, stares at this gruesome splatter shot.

Suddenly, in his mind--

--he sees it morph into Lemmy the Lemur.

He jumps up, dashes over to the red vinyl couch, and starts whacking away at his laptop.

He's working on the revamped Lemmy that he began while waiting for little Harvey to come out of the Music Conservatory.

We witness developments ON THE LAPTOP SCREEN:

--Lemmy's perfectly circular eyes remain lidless, but Spencer gives them a slight inward angle along the top, a hint of a hateful scowl.

--A tiny, almost unnoticeable rim of scarlet makes Lemmy's eyes glow with subliminal mania.

--His formerly cute rabbity buck teeth are sharpened, just a tad, to suggest vampire fangs.

--His whiskers and fur begin to spike and bristle, and Lemmy develops the faintest slouch, almost the beginnings of a hump-back.

--Lemmy's already creepy tree-froggy fingers grow nails at the tips, nearly thick and sharp enough to be called claws.

--His ears are raised, the tufts of fur on top twisted to a point, to suggest vampire bat sonar or maybe devil horns.

Most people, unless they were told to look twice, wouldn't consciously notice much change in Lemmy the Lemur--though they would walk away filled with uneasiness, combined with a sick titillation.

EXT. MELVIN'S HOME--A COUPLE WEEKS LATER

Manager Melvin parks his nice car in the driveway of a two-car garage, attached to a solid upper-middle-class suburban house.

He and Spencer get out of the car and enter--

INT. MELVIN'S HOME--DAY

It's large, fancy, crass, and bookless. There's more Mancini, a couple slightly bigger Kinkade paintings, and some fatter jugs of screw-top vintage.

Melvin introduces the WIFE, whose face is even blanker than Spencer's.

INT. MELVIN'S BASEMENT DEN--DAY

At a wood-veneer desk, Spencer uses his newfound knowledge to cook the books.

He spends several hours with an adding machine and a big orange and turquoise leatherette-bound LEMCO ledger, embossed with Lemmy.

Melvin lounges on a day bed nearby and shakes his head in admiration.

Each time Spencer pulls the crank that totals up the figures, Melvin sees, in his mind--

EXT. MELVIN'S HOUSE--DAY

--a new elephant-sized SUV in the driveway.

--a boat attached to it.

--a crew of swimming pool builders just pulling up.

--Melvin himself arriving in a new convertible sports car.

--his Wife and pudgy prepubescent daughter, JAZMYNNE, coming out to meet him.

MR. NUSSBAUM (VO)
Through your study of the law, Spencer, you will develop a love of truth and honesty that will see you through the most chaotic of times.

INT. BASEMENT DEN--A FEW HOURS LATER

Cigars have been broken out, along with some kid of brown distilled liquor.

MELVIN
I was thinking of promoting you to the food-prep section, Spencer. But I can see you're talented at cooking things other than patty melts and onion rings.

The smile leaves Melvin's face while he burps painfully at those last five words.

MELVIN
The sky's the limit in this company. I started out bussing just like you, and worked my way up. Look at me now.

Spencer obediently looks at him.

MELVIN
(thoughtfully)
You know, I could use a right-hand guy around the place.

Spencer betrays no more enthusiasm than he did when this same man dubbed him "Bus Bitch."

JazMynne comes in with a tray of Lemmy snacks. She's wearing a Lemmy tee shirt, from which her belly protrudes.

MELVIN
JazMynne, meet Mr. Sproul. Spencer, my little girl here is an artist. She's entering the "Give Lemmy a Total Makeover Contest." JazMynne, show Mr. Sproul your Crayola creation.

The kid forks it over.

Spencer immerses himself in the Official Entry Form and Contest Rules, which are stapled to JazMynne's drawing. He pores over these documents, sounding out the words, for a rudely long time.

MELVIN
(clearing his throat)
So, Spencer, what do you think of JazMynne's new Lemmy? My daughter is showing you her art work. Don't hurt her feelings, Bus Bi--I mean, Spencer.

Spencer finally gives the picture a glance.

JazMynne's drawing is crude. She's covered the lemur in flowers and butterflies, and given him long eyelashes and a cute simper.

In Spencer's mind, he sees--

--his own ratcheted-up version barging onto the page and devouring JazMynne's.

Spencer gazes back and forth from the child's protruding navel to a sharp letter-opener on her dad's desk blotter.

MR. NUSSBAUM (VO)
God bless you, my friend, and preserve you in the troubled times ahead.

INT. POST OFFICE--NEXT DAY

Spencer stands at the counter, stuffing a manila envelope with a color printout of his own revamped Lemmy the Lemur.

The lovely young Postal Clerk looks anxious. She's expecting a repeat of his earlier bizarre behavior.

Spencer has written a cover letter to be mailed with the printout, which he proof-reads, word by agonizing word.

As the Postal Clerk keeps a nervous eye on him, we hear the words formed by his moving lips--

SPENCER (VO)
Dear Sirs of LEMCO National Headquarters. Please insert my entry inside your wide national Give Lemmy a Total Make Out contest, even though employees of LEMCO and their relatives are not ineligible because I have no relatives like an uncertain manager with nameless remains. Sincerely, I remain your company-loyal Spencer Sproul.

He approaches the Postal Clerk, who has broken out into a sweat.

SPENCER
What's the stamps for special mail to Des Moines? Check many, many times. Many times.

As before, Spencer sits on a bench and stares at the poor woman, just to make extra-double sure his new Lemmy makes it all the way to Des Moines.

After the second or third hour of being stared at, she looks pretty terrified.

INT. LEMUEL'S FAMILY RESTAURANT, KITCHEN--SAME DAY

The Fry Cook pretends to work, but is actually listening to a conversation taking place behind the door of the Managerial Office.

MELVIN (VO)
So, you personally watched Mr. Sproul having rectal intercourse with the red-haired tyke?

INT. MANAGERIAL OFFICE--AT THAT MOMENT

Melvin's sitting behind his desk, feet up, a coffee cup half-full of wine in his hand, Mancini's "Love Theme from Romeo and Juliet" on the CD player. He's relaxed to the point of drooping around the edges of his chair like an amoeba.

Trishy the bus girl stands before him. She has tears in her eyes, and is on the verge of sobs.

TRISHY
Well, no. But--

MELVIN
But? But what? But you called the cops on him, anyway?

TRISHY
Mr. Sproul's such a nice man. What he has is a sort of health problem. People with his sort of health problem need prompt emergency medical care. Or else they won't stop, um, having his health problem. Sort of.

MELVIN
So why didn't you call the doctor instead of the cops?

Having no reply to that razor-sharp logic, Trishy breaks down into sobs.

MELVIN
That man is a regular artistic savant with the numbers. And he's got the most

company loyalty to me and LEMCO of
anyone on the roster. For example, I
expect you, treasonous Trishy, to go
the way of our ex-cashier any day now.

Melvin nods toward his little window, and Dagbert's Family Eatery beyond.

He's sitting too low to see between the orange and turquoise curtains, but Trishy, and we, can see an act of industrial espionage going on at this very moment.

The Mean Waitress is moving her long, lizard-like physique across the street to the rival dining establishment, where Krystelle waits for her on the front stoop.

EXT. DAGBERT'S--DAY

The two women have a quick conversation. When Krystelle hands over a few bucks, it becomes clear that the Mean Waitress is serving as her eyes and ears at Lemuel's.

INT. MANAGERIAL OFFICE--DAY

MELVIN (CONT)
Mind your own business, trashy Trishy.
To help you do that, I'm removing you
from mine. Clean out your mind and your
locker.

Trishy gasps, runs out the door--

INT. KITCHEN--DAY

--and brushes past the eavesdropping Fry Cook.

He drops his basket of onion rings and dogs her steps, more out of curiosity than compassion.

MELVIN (OS)
(shouting)
Say hi to Krystelle! And tell her she
better not send spies over here, now
that Spencer's ratcheting up the place!

INT. DINING AREA--A FEW MOMENTS LATER

Trishy walks out of Lemuel's Family Restaurant for the last time.

Instead of using the back door, she has chosen to leave by the front, to give herself an excuse to pass through the dining area and see Spencer once more.

She casts a loving eye on him, trying to let him know that she sympathizes with his "health problem."

This time his lack of response is unsurprising, because she's looking not at Spencer himself, but at his icon.

His photographic portrait, complete with spiffy clip-on Lemmy tie and blank facial expression, hangs next to Melvin's behind the cash register.

The brass-colored plastic plaque on the bottom of Spencer's frame says ASS. MNG.

The Dish Washer is contemplating the new Spencer.

DISH WASHER
"Ass Mange" is right. He's putting on the airs.

TRISHY
(through a sob)
I feel he looks distinguished.

The Mean Waitress comes barging in, all sweaty, from her traitorous sprint across the street. She joins them.

MEAN WAITRESS
Now that he gets to have a tie, he turned into a peacock.

FRY COOK
Little fag. I bet he's a fag. What do you want to bet he's a fag? I bet he is.

DISH WASHER
Where is Spazzer, anyway?

MEAN WAITRESS

Now that he's Chief Executive Vice President in charge of looking like a retard, I'm sure he's got better places to be than here, with us.

INT. POST OFFICE--AT THAT MOMENT

To help him pass the time productively while he monitors the Postal Clerk, Spencer has brought his laptop along.

He googles "SUBLIMINAL USE OF COLOR," and calls up a website that has a VIDEO CLIP of an experiment with rats--

--They head straight for the most garishly painted part of the maze, and immediately start in with the cannibalism, infanticide, coprophagy, etc.

Spencer plays one bit back, over and over again--

--One rat opens another's jugular with a single slash of the teeth, and the whole maze is soaked in bright red.

INT. LEMUEL'S FAMILY RESTAURANT--DAY

Spencer, all dressed up in his Assistant Managerial tie, greets a PAINTER and an UPHOLSTERER.

He examines their sample books and selects some paint chips and swatches. These adhere to the official LEMCO color scheme, but the hues and saturations grate even more viciously on the retina.

PAINTER

(wincing)

It's not Ornery Matisse, but it'll do the trick.

Spencer reports to the boss.

INT. MANAGERIAL OFFICE--DAY

Melvin's at his desk, feet up, amoeba-relaxed.

Spencer stands before him, holding the paint chips and swatches in a beam of sunlight from the window.

Melvin winces and laughs in cheerful pain at the glare.

He exerts himself just enough to slide the leatherette-bound LEMCORP checkbook across his blotter and into Spencer's hands.

Then Melvin settles into a near-vegetative state surpassing any we've yet seen. He's on the verge of not breathing, and it makes him blissful.

The next few scenes are INTERCUT with shots of Spencer writing check after check.

INT. DINING AREA--DAY

TECHNICIANS countersink sinister-looking electronics into the ceilings and walls.

INT. KITCHEN--DAY

Just inside the double doors that open out into the dining area, a LIGHTING EXPERT installs a large, elaborate control panel.

He's getting in the way of a man in a jumpsuit brightly marked MUZIQUE, who's doing the same thing.

Both control panels bristle with knobs and levers and dials. The Muzique console is even higher-tech than the one at Dagbert's.

The MUZIQUE MAN rummages around in his tool chest and comes up with a couple of death-black CDs, which he holds at arm's length like suicide pills.

MUZIQUE MAN

This is what we pipe into second-run movie theaters during intermission to drive them out to the snack bar. I'll be glad to install it, but only if you promise to give me a chance to clear out before you switch it on.

EXT. THE DUMPSTER--DAY

The Bums hear the new tunes.

The Simple-Minded Bum starts to weep and moan. He buries his head in a pile of refuse.

INT. EMPLOYEE LOCKER ROOM--MIDNIGHT

All the Cooks have been called from their beds to attend a secret meeting. They sit on the benches, rubbing their eyes sleepily.

In front of them is a television set hooked up to a VHS.

Spencer makes his entrance, and pops a tape into the machine. It's a security video from the convenience store, showing the Morbidly Obese Folks disporting themselves awesomely among the snacks.

SPENCER

See our target market? Look what they're putting inside them. And look how fast. And look how unstoppable.

He has gotten the Cooks' attention.

INT. KITCHEN--WEE HOURS

Under Spencer's supervision, WORKMEN install big bins of pure crystal MSG over the deep fry vats.

Spencer encourages the Fry Cook to dump in borderline-homicidal amounts by the heaping handful.

The Fry Cook looks resentful and doubtful at first. But, eventually, swayed by Spencer's enthusiasm if not his eloquence, he starts nodding his head and shoveling the shit.

INT. MANAGERIAL OFFICE--A FEW WEEKS LATER

Melvin's relaxing at his desk, as usual these days.

INT. DINING AREA--DAY

Already there's a bigger than usual line of Customers waiting for a booth.

Not only are there more of them, but they're behaving more impatiently than before. They unconsciously wince at the colors and sounds that gnaw on their eyes and ears.

When they're finally seated, the Customers attack their gristly deep-fried meat entrees with a violence that is starting to approach Convenience Store levels.

Spencer, pretty much running the show now, hovers among the booths and surveys the dining action.

He ponders the token salad bar, and observes how everybody walks right past, laughing at the few flaccid bits of leaves and carrot slivers.

Inspiration lights up his face, sort of--

INT. DINING AREA--MIDNIGHT

It's a secret Waitress' meeting. They are no happier about this than the Cooks were.

While they stand around and watch, OTHER WORKMEN install hidden aerosol spray nozzles under the salad bar's sneeze guard.

These nozzles are attached to a plastic pipe that leads behind the salad bar to a big vat, labeled LIQUID NICOTINE.

Spencer instructs the Waitresses first to encourage the Customers to load the "salads" down with giant sponge-like croutons, then to press a hidden lever and drench everything with a fine subliminal spray of the addictive substance.

INT. LEMUEL'S DINING AREA--NEXT DAY

The nicotine isn't particularly increasing traffic at the salad bar.

So, when nobody's looking, Spencer gives the sneeze guard a good kick, which redirects the drugged aerosol into the general atmosphere, particularly the NO SMOKING area.

INT. KITCHEN--DAY

A newly hired ASSISTANT COOK is starting to trim the gristle off some meat. But Assistant Manager Spencer shakes his index finger in a gently but firmly scolding way.

He removes the knife from the Assistant Cook's hand, and suddenly becomes fascinated with it, forgetting where he is and who's watching.

Spencer starts slashing it about.

EXT. LEMUEL'S FAMILY RESTAURANT--DAY

Cars are lined up around the block, and Customers spill out the front door as they queue for a table.

A fist fight or two breaks out--nothing too serious, just yet.

EXT. BEHIND LEMUEL'S--NIGHT

MR. CLEAVE, one of the top local fashion designers, is let in by the back door, followed by a few of his TOADIES.

Their big hair and skin-tight leather outfits draw murmurs of admiration from the dumpster Bums.

MR. CLEAVE
(upset)
I told that creature Sproul I didn't want anyone seeing me here!

He rushes in.

A small crew of fawning ASSISTANTS drag in bolts of cloth, rolls of vinyl, a sewing machine, and boxes full of buttons, buckles, zippers, etc.

INT. LOCKER ROOM--NIGHT

The Mean Waitress has been drafted, against her will, to serve as dressmaker's dummy. She stands on a bench, stark naked and very resentful, trying to give everyone erections with her lizard-like physique. She's not having much success.

Mr. Cleave takes up his position in a chair near the wall, surrounded by his Toadies.

Propped against a locker nearby is an official LEMCO promotional cardboard cut-out of a fresh-faced model in a waitress uniform, complete with Lemmy vest and Lemmy neckerchief.

A printout of Spencer's revamped, computer-enhanced Lemmy is pinned to an easel nearby, for easy reference.

Using a lot of colored pencils and pastel chalks, Mr. Cleave draws up any number of ratcheted-up waitress outfits, with amazing rapidity.

His Assistants bring these visions into three-dimensional reality on the Mean Waitress' body.

Mr. Cleave's Toadies look over his shoulder, clapping their hands and cooing in aesthetic ecstasy.

FIRST TOADY
I'd eat there if she brought the stuff to me.

SECOND TOADY
Really?

FIRST TOADY
(whispering)
Well, no. But you know what I mean.

Mr. Cleave expresses his esthetic philosophy as he creates, and everyone except the Mean Waitress listens--

MR. CLEAVE
Clothes, makeup, hair and accessories can, should, and simply must, express all manner of sickness and health--

By means of aquamarine eyeshadow, the Mean Waitress is made to appear to have perfectly circular lemur eyes. They're rimmed with scarlet mascara, lending a hint of mania.

MR. CLEAVE
--all manner of passiveness and aggression--

Referring to Mr. Cleave's drawings, the Assistants do her hair to look like lemur ears.

They pull tufts up to resemble bat ears, or horns. The whole is held in place and given a cold, hard luster with sealant from a huge spray can.

MR. CLEAVE
--conscious hate and unconscious love, and, best of all, that helpless state which quivers and twitches between the two.

The Mean Waitress is provided with gloves that look tree-froggy, with a hint of claws at the tips.

MR. CLEAVE
Fashion can, should, and simply must, repel and allure simultaneously, like a powerful, lovely, lethal drug.

As it takes shape on the Mean Waitress' body over the next few hours, the new waitress uniform looks a bit like what the Munchkins of the Lollipop League wear: the sleeves and skirts flounce up, stiff and pointed as scimitar blades, looking like they'll slice off a limb if you get too close.

The Mean Waitress is fitted out with boots, thigh-high, pointed toes and extreme stiletto heels. If they were black, they would look too scary on the toughest dominatrix.

But the patent leather is dyed peach and aquamarine, and embossed with Lemmy faces, so the sado-masochism is cloaked under something that appears, at first glance, to be cutesy.

The total effect, juxtaposed with the Mean Waitress' own inhuman face and reptilian body, causes the Toadies to cover their faces in unaffected awe.

EXT. BEHIND LEMUEL'S--NIGHT

Their work done, Mr. Cleave and friends sneak out the back door.

The Mean Waitress slips out behind them. Her new getup and the nighttime excite her. She looks around for trouble.

EXT. DUMPSTER--A MOMENT LATER

Everything is bathed in orange and turquoise neon from the

sign on the roof.

The Simple-Minded Bum is just waking up from a sad dream. He weeps, very softly, so as not to disturb his sleeping comrades.

Suddenly, a pair of lemur hands clasp the horizon of his world. A horrific lemur face looms up before him, as the Mean Waitress chins herself on the dumpster's rim.

MEAN WAITRESS

Goof!

Leaving the Simple-Minded Bum in convulsions of terror, she creepy-crawls like Squeaky Fromme around the side of the restaurant.

INT. MRS. STANDISH'S MERCEDES--AT THAT MOMENT

The liveried Chauffeur is at the wheel, under orders to cruise aimlessly through the night streets.

There's a trombone on the back seat next to Raleigh.

Both men look unbelievably bored.

EXT. LEMUEL'S FAMILY RESTAURANT--NIGHT

The Mean Waitress jaywalks toward Dagbert's, scaring mild-mannered motorists with her strange makeup, hair and outfit.

She screams obscenities at a taxi driver, and plays chicken with an eighteen-wheeler which is happy to oblige.

EXT. MERCEDES--NIGHT

The canary-yellow vehicle moves sluggishly down the road, drawing resentful stares from less privileged PEDESTRIANS and MOTORISTS.

It approaches Lemuel's and Dagbert's.

EXT. TRAFFIC ISLAND--NIGHT

The sight of the Standish Mercedes fills the Mean Waitress with class resentment.

She leaps off the traffic island and positions herself, spread-legged, tongue protruding, right in the path of the car.

It screeches to a halt.

INT. MERCEDES--AT THAT MOMENT

Raleigh and the Chauffeur watch through the windshield as this bizarre creature peels aside her form-fitting vinyl vest and flashes a pair of lizard breasts.

There is a moment of silence.

INT. MRS. STANDISH'S VAST BEDROOM--NIGHT

Mrs. Standish is asleep in her broad canopy bed.

Moonlight slips through the lace curtains and plays across her face, which is buried two inches deep in a mud pack.

Thick cucumber slices are wedged like monocles into her eye sockets, for cosmetic purposes.

Without removing the vegetable matter, she reaches out to answer her princess extension, which is ringing on the bedside table.

RALEIGH (VO)
(filtered)
Wake up, Momsy. Dictation time.

MRS. STANDISH
(sleepily)
Where are you?

She lifts one cucumber slice, just enough to provide a peripheral view of the empty pillow next to her.

MRS. STANDISH
I assume you have the chauffeur.

RALEIGH (VO)
(filtered)
No, I'm on a skateboard.

EXT. MERCEDES--NIGHT

Raleigh, cell phone to his ear, watches the Mean Waitress scamper across to Dagbert's.

RALEIGH
I feel a feature coming on.

EXT. DAGBERT'S FAMILY EATERY--AT THAT MOMENT

Krystelle opens the door to admit the Mean Waitress.

Before it can close on the two women, we hear explosions of the most antisocial rock 'n roll, and glimpse blinding blasts of violet and yellow light.

RALEIGH (VO)
Not just a review this time, Momsy, but a proper essay. Pulitzer Prize, that sort of thing.

INT. MRS. STANDISH'S BEDROOM--NIGHT

She sits up in bed with her laptop, cucumbers still wedged in her eyesockets.

MRS. STANDISH
You're lucky I can touch type, dear.

RALEIGH (VO)
(filtered)
I want to address the whole idea, so to speak, behind the genre, if you will, of family restaurants. The mise en scene and so forth.

MRS. STANDISH
(yawning)
Literary ambition descends on my little boy.

INT. MERCEDES--NIGHT

Raleigh sits a bit straighter than usual in the back seat, clears his throat, and tries to look authorial.

RALEIGH
Well...

INT. DAGBERT'S FAMILY EATERY--AT THAT MOMENT

The Mean Waitress walks in to find that Manageress Krystelle has been doing some ratcheting of her own.

RALEIGH (VO)
The decor in these places is, of course, perfectly dreadful...

Krystelle has fitted out the walls with a system of yellow and violet neon tubes that flash an animated cartoon. It rages around the room, repeating itself in a loop.

Dag the Dinnersaur goes after meal-robbing cave men, chomping on their heads, splitting them wide open and retrieving the meat entrees that engorge their bellies.

Over and over again, Dag emits a single electronically synthesized noise that's supposed to resemble a dinosaur shriek-roar. It's painfully audible over the ear-destroying heavy metal music that Krystelle has piped in.

She stands near the idle cash register, trying to hear the Mean Waitress' latest bit of industrial espionage.

KRYSTELLE
(screaming)
What? Say that again?

RALEIGH (VO)
And you can't hear yourself chew... Not that you'd want to, necessarily. But, to each his own...

The only customers Krystelle has managed to attract are the Nuclear Family: Dad and Mom in their Hawaiian shirts and Bermuda shorts, and the Kids in their Lemmy tee shirts.

RALEIGH (VO)
Perhaps the greatest challenge posed by this whole dining milieu is the creatures by whom one finds oneself surrounded...

They keep coming up and screaming complaints into Krystelle’s face.

FIRST KID
Can you turn the music down? It makes the inside of my head feel full of lumpy blood.

SECOND KID
Could you take this patty-melt back, because it tastes like burning styrofoam?

DAD
Can you do something about the lights? They make my eyes feel like a couple lid-baggies full of sand.

MOM
Could you turn off that cartoon on the walls? It’s giving the kids bad burps.

They bail out before dessert.

RALEIGH (VO)
And yet--

INTERCUT BETWEEN MRS. STANDISH’S BEDROOM AND MERCEDES

MRS. STANDISH
And yet what, love? I’m tired.

RALEIGH
And yet, and yet--
(searching for adequate expressions)
--and yet, the ensemble in toto possesses a certain subliminally masochistic irresistibility.

MRS. STANDISH
Can you spell that, love?

RALEIGH
No.

MRS. STANDISH
As Editrix-in-Chief, I have to ask whether "masochistic" might be too strong a term in this context.

RALEIGH
Oh, yes? Well, just ask yourself this, Momsy. Why do we keep coming back to these places?

MRS. STANDISH
Sweetheart, I've never set foot in a family restaurant.

INT. DAGBERT'S--NIGHT

RALEIGH (VO)
Be that as it may. As I was saying--

Krystelle stares dejectedly into an empty cash register.

KRYSTELLE
(screaming over the noise)
I don't get it. I stole all Spencer's ideas and implemented them according to every qualitative marketing book in the stinking library. And now I've got to get a second job. How does the retard do it?

MEAN WAITRESS
(also screaming)
He's a fag. They have that subtle feminine touch. I guess. What the fuck do I know? I'm just a waitress.

RALEIGH (VO)
Why do we return to family restaurants again and again--

INT. MERCEDES--DAY

RALEIGH
--in the same way we cannot stop picking at an icky scab on the tip of our--

MRS. STANDISH (VO)
(filtered)
Let's make that "nose," sweetie.

RALEIGH
(enraged)
Well, if my talent has to contend with arbitrary censorship, all I have to say is--

INT. MRS. STANDISH'S BEDROOM--NIGHT

A very loud honking noise blasts over the phone, making her wince. The cucumber slices pop out of her eye sockets and stick to her laptop screen.

INT. MERCEDES--NIGHT

His literary ambition already tapped out, Raleigh has laid his cell phone aside and taken up the trombone.

He is trying to master the instrument. The sounds are horrible, like an old elephant being cruelly sodomized against its conscious will.

INT. LEMUEL'S FAMILY RESTAURANT, KITCHEN--DAY

Spencer stands before the Muzique and light control panels. He turns the levels way down.

INT. DINING AREA--DAY

The place is closed.

All the Employees are seated in booths, the Waitresses squirming about uncomfortably in their new uniforms.

Balloons and party hats fill the dining area, and Melvin's right in the middle of it all. It's his retirement party.

He's giving his valedictory speech--

MELVIN
A family restaurant is like a movie, only with smells and tastes added. And feelings. In a way. What I mean is--

He's interrupted by a sudden late arrival.

Krystelle crashes the party in her tight violet and yellow Dagbert's Manageress dress.

Apparently she has mistaken this for a date-type shindig, for she leads Spud, her slow bus boy, by the hand. She has gotten him into a kind of suit, his hair slicked down, and the condiments pretty much rinsed and scraped from his body.

Krystelle hands Melvin a Dag the Dinnersaur ashtray. A piece of paper is stuck to it, upon which is written, in comical, colorful letters, CAN I HAVE MY HORRIBLE FUCKING JOB BACK?

He accepts the ashtray graciously enough, but lays it immediately aside, allowing the paper to slip to the floor.

Melvin has the perfect excuse to brush her off like this, because he's right in the middle of giving the climactic speech of his career in the food services industry.

MELVIN
--touch feelings is what I mean, not the emotional kind--

Krystelle takes a seat in an unoccupied booth near the toilets. Nobody will sit next to her. But maybe that's because Spud is a compulsive nose-picker, and he insists on clinging to her side, due to a dim sense of shyness.

Spencer has taken a shine to the slow-witted bus boy. He slides in next to Spud.

SPENCER
(whispering)
Want to come work for me--I mean, Melvin?

Spencer looks at the farewell complimentary chicken-fried steak with a large side order of Lemmy fries that waits to be eaten by Melvin, just as soon as he finishes his speech.

Then Spencer looks at his own photographic portrait behind the cash register. The ASS has been removed from the brass-colored plastic plaque on the frame. Now it just says MNG.

Spencer's picture has supplanted Melvin's, which has been removed--

INT. PASSAGEWAY TO THE TOILETS--DAY

--and hung among the GALLERY OF FORMER MANAGERS that lines the walls between the men's and ladies' rooms.

Melvin's PREDECESSORS all look like Fellini extras.

INT. DINING AREA--DAY

Spencer corrects himself again, in a loud, proud voice--

SPENCER
(to Spud)
No. I mean, work for me.

It's the first time Spencer truly realizes the position he has attained in the world. He comes as close to smiling as he ever does in our eyeshot.

In reply to the job offer, Spud picks his nose and leaves early on Krystelle's elbow, before Melvin even has a chance to finish his speech.

Through the window, Spencer watches Spud go.

MELVIN
--although I guess you can have emotional feelings, too. If you want. Anyway, if you could smell and taste a movie--

Crossing the street, Spud repeatedly looks back at Spencer, nearly causing himself and Krystelle to be run down a couple of times.

MELVIN
--and, like, touch it, it would be a restaurant. So, right there, we're already two up on Hollywood, right?

No response from the Employees.

Melvin clears his throat, in order to get the incoming Manager's full attention and support.

MELVIN
Right, Spencer? Or maybe three.
(pausing to tally
on his fingers)
Anyway, Robert Redford wishes he could
be us--I mean, you.
(tears)
So, even though I'm gone--
(more tears)
--please keep on pulling together, and
don't disappoint him.

After a very brief moment of puzzled silence, everybody leaves except Spencer, the Fry Cook and the Mean Waitress.

INT. KITCHEN--WEE HOURS

The Mean Waitress loiters around very bored, smoking joints. Her new uniform, though a Mr. Cleave original, appears to be itchy everywhere, especially between the upper thighs.

Spencer supervises the Fry Cook as he prepares a mess of all-out, full-tilt Convenience Store cuisine. The only thing missing is the styrofoam packaging.

Spencer unscrews the MSG bin from the wall and dumps all of the stuff into the deep-fat fry vat.

After he helps Spencer load a huge tray with the result, drag it out to the dining area--

INT. DINING AREA--WEE HOURS

--and plop it on a table near the toilets, the Fry Cook heads straight for the door.

FRY COOK (OS)
(calling over his shoulder)
I wasn't here tonight.

Spencer looks puzzled, but lets it pass, as he has more important things to do than unravel that paradox.

EXT. THE DUMPSTER--WEE HOURS

Spencer stands at the back door.

He waves a menu around, pointing at the screw-top wine section and doggy-whistling at the Simple-Minded Bum, who peeks over the rim, sucking his finger shyly.

After glancing back to make sure the Boss Bum is asleep, the Simple-Minded Bum succumbs to the temptation.

Just as Spencer is closing the back door on himself and his little guest, the Youthful Bum wakes up the Boss.

BOSS BUM
Where you taking my worthy constituent?

Spencer slams the door--

INT. LOCKER ROOM--A SECOND LATER

--and latches it.

He goes to the window and opens it a crack.

SPENCER
(calling out)
He'll be back. With presents for everybody.
(closing the window)
Probably. Maybe.

INT. DINING AREA--WEE HOURS

The place is nearly dark and almost silent.

Spencer leads the Simple-Minded Bum to the booth and sits him down before the giant tray full of evil food.

The Simple-Minded Bum picks up a menu and points to the wine pictures. He makes supplicating sounds at the base of his throat, and yearning cocker spaniel eyes.

SPENCER
No. That is badness for you.

Spencer hurries toward the kitchen.

On the way he passes the salad bar and switches on the aerosol nozzles, spraying the room with another kind of poison, for good measure.

INT. KITCHEN--A MOMENT LATER

Stationing himself just inside the flapping doors, he holds both hands up, at the ready, before the Muzique and light consoles.

Wedging the doors open, just a tad, with his foot, Spencer peeks out. He waits till the Simple-Minded Bum feels brave enough to dip a finger in the grease, and lick it.

Just as the little guy winces in agony--

--Spencer removes his foot, allowing the doors to flap safely shut. Then he cranks up the light and sound all the way, till the needles bang against the maximum limit of the red danger zones on the dials.

The Mean Waitress waits nearby.

SPENCER
(covering his ears)
Go, go.

That's her cue, but--

MEAN WAITRESS
These boots pinch me, and my butt itches.

SPENCER
It's howcome LEMCO discovered the overtime. Now, go.

MEAN WAITRESS
He's a wino. He's gonna make sour barf on this outfit.

INT. DINING AREA--A MOMENT LATER

The Simple-Minded Bum sits there, on the verge of a seizure.

His body is reeling from the horrible food, his eyes nearly blinded by the vicious orange and turquoise glare, his ears almost deafened by the second-run movie theater Muzique that shrieks from speakers overhead.

Suddenly, a grotesque lemur comes looming up, buggy eye-makeup, tree-froggy gloves, scimitar-edged uniform, dominatrix boots, and all.

MEAN WAITRESS
Will there be anything else?

INT. KITCHEN--AT THAT MOMENT

Even over the Muzique, Spencer can hear the scream.

He uncranks the sound and light systems, and peeks out.

INT. DINING AREA--NIGHT

The poor Simple-Minded Bum lies under the table in a puddle of piss and puke, silent and motionless, to all appearances, dead.

MEAN WAITRESS
(standing over him)
Can I go now?

Finally, Spencer has managed to get a psycho killer look on his face, worthy of framing and hanging among the shrines in his living room.

He approaches the victim with a big meat fork. He gets on hands and knees, crawls forward and reaches out, intending to nudge, or maybe even poke, this, his first and only kill, so far.

Spencer can't quite do it.

He ponders the apparent corpse with perfectly normal distaste. Spencer's trying hard to force himself to be titillated by Death, three-dimensional, as opposed to pictures in a scrapbook.

It's no easier for him than it would be for any average, or sub-average, Joe.

The victim suddenly snaps out of it, making Spencer jump a few feet in the air.

SIMPLE-MINDED BUM
(moaning pitifully)
Ank-hoo, Reema-a-argh, ank-hoo, Reema-a-argh...

SPENCER
(after he catches his breath)
Not quite sublunary enough. The levels need to be adjusted.

MEAN WAITRESS
You think?

EXT. BEHIND LEMUEL'S--NIGHT

The Simple-Minded Bum stumbles out the back door, loaded down with Lemmy artifacts, paraphernalia and fetishes, Lemmy kiddy menus and kiddy favors, Lemmy toy packets, coloring books, disposable board games, and other cheap Lemmy crap.

The guy can barely walk. Terrified, babbling for comfort and reassurance, he needs to be lifted back into the dumpster.

SIMPLE-MINDED BUM
Ank-hoo, Reema-a-argh, ank-hoo, Reema-a-argh...

BOSS BUM
(tenderly)
That's right. Thank you, Lemmy, thank you, Lemmy.
(sees Spencer peeking out the back door)
What did you do to him?

Spencer slams the door. We hear it being bolted on the inside.

INT. MRS. STANDISH'S VAST BEDROOM--DAY

Seated at her big desktop computer, sapphire-studded editor's visor propped, tiara-wise, among the face-lift tucks on her brow, Mrs. Standish is trying to compose the SOCIETY PAGE for tomorrow's paper.

After inserting the obligatory ad for SALIBURY'S EXCLUSIVE TENNIS CLUB, she realizes that she has nothing to report.

Just in time, this commercial comes on her fabulously huge mahogany cabinet television--

EXT. LEMUEL'S FAMILY RESTAURANT--DAY (TV COMMERCIAL)

Standing in front of a placard advertising--

LOW, LOW PRICES FOR SUPPER SPECIALS

--a LOCAL ACTRESS with a fashionable speech impediment tries to feed Spencer his line.

LOCAL ACTRESS
Mishter Shproul, how ish it poshible to offer shuch shurprishingly low, low prishesh for you shupper shpecialsh?

SPENCER
Huh?

She points to the words on the sign, but he reads no better than she speaks.

SPENCER
Huh?

INT. MRS. STANDISH'S VAST BEDROOM--DAY

After pondering the man's face on TV for awhile, Mrs. Standish types the headline for the lead story--

SPENCER SPROUL SPREADS SPLENDID SPUDS

EXT. LEMUEL'S FAMILY RESTAURANT--DAY (TV COMMERCIAL)

The Local Actress pantomimes eating, then reaching into her pocket.

SPENCER
Oh.
(straightening up to deliver his line)
It's not about stealing. I am not a stealer.

INT. MRS. STANDISH'S VAST BEDROOM--DAY

Mrs. Standish types this caption under his photo:

I AM NOT A STEALER

EXT. LEMUEL'S FAMILY RESTAURANT--DAY (TV COMMERCIAL)

In the background, many Morbidly Obese Folks can be seen, lined up to get in. They look dangerously impatient.

INT. CONVENIENCE STORE BACK ROOM--DAY

The College Boy is watching the commercial, too.

Heartbroken over being abandoned by his God-Babies, he shakes his fist at the image of Spencer on the screen.

COLLEGE BOY

Not a stealer? You're a liar AND a stealer!

INT. STANDISH MERCEDES--DAY

Raleigh's not making a great deal of progress learning the trombone.

The slide accidentally barges over the seat and bops the Chauffeur's uniform cap awry, causing the Mercedes to swerve drunkenly.

RALEIGH

(wincing at his own obscene racket)

I can't imagine how the little brat does it.

He throws the trombone out the window.

EXT. MERCEDES--DAY

It bounces off the windshield of a patrol car that follows close behind, seriously pissing off the driver and passengers, who happen to be--

INT. PATROL CAR--AT THAT MOMENT

--Detective Furtwangler and his three uniformed henchmen.

INT. MERCEDES--DAY

The Chauffeur looks into the rearview mirror and nervously clears his throat.

Raleigh glances languidly over his shoulder, and does a double take. He sits up straight, trying to look like a solid citizen.

EXT. PATROL CAR--AT THAT MOMENT

Detective Furtwangler rolls down his window and waves the Standish hankie.

INT. MERCEDES--DAY

RALEIGH
Give him the slip... No time for tranny jokes.

A very low-speed car chase commences, during which Raleigh phones home.

RALEIGH
Momsy, you cheap old carpet-muncher, did you skim a few pounds off Furtwangler's cash-bag this month?

EXT. PATROL CAR--DAY

The Female Cop hangs out the door screaming into a megaphone--

FEMALE COP
How many quarts of spooge are we gonna find when we pump your stomach today, Nancy?

MRS. STANDISH (OS)
(filtered)
Oh! My word!

INT. STANDISH TOILET--DAY

The old lady's moving her bowels.

MRS. STANDISH
(into a princess extension)
Who was that vulgar little shrike?

She farts one time, demurely.

EXT. THE STREET--DAY

The Mercedes manages to get out of sight of the cop car, just long enough for Raleigh to bale sluggishly out.

He hangs onto his cell phone like a boozer falling downstairs with a cocktail.

Raleigh lands in some bushes and struggles through them, looking a bit like Jane Goodall cruising for monkeys.

He pulls some branches aside and peeks his face out, looking for a place to hide.

Raleigh finds himself in front of--

EXT. BETTER BUSINESS BUREAU--DAY

The marquee reads--

MERCHANT OF THE MONTH AWARD BANQUET TODAY

RALEIGH
(looking at the Public
Library next door)
I guess I could flip a coin...

INT. BETTER BUSINESS BUREAU, MEN'S TOILET--DAY

Spencer and Spud piss, side by side. Impressively, the latter is able to pick his nose at the same time.

SPENCER
This day, Spud, you will glimpse what a future can hold in storage if you strive of a muchness and keep its true faith on your standard issuances.

Together they zip, exit the men's room, and enter--

INT. BETTER BUSINESS BUREAU BANQUET HALL--DAY

A banner is stretched across the wall up front:

CONGRATULATIONS SPENCER SPROUL!
MERCHANT OF THE MONTH!

The place is filled with PILLARS OF THE LOCAL BUSINESS COMMUNITY, seated at tables with their WIVES.

They wear party hats emblazoned with the motto--

I AM NOT A STEALER

Everyone applauds as Spencer takes his seat at the table of honor, front and center.

Spud's place is at his right hand.

An IMPORTANT BUSINESSMAN mounts the podium and speaks into a mike--

IMPORTANT BUSINESSMAN
Today we honor the man who ratcheted up the local family restaurant scene, making it more relevant to today's lifestyle. He lured butts back into the booths when it looked like the convenience stores--

A CONVENIENCE STORE MANAGER looks unhappy.

IMPORTANT BUSINESSMAN
--and snack stands--

A SNACK STAND OWNER looks offended.

Both of them get up and head for a wet bar tucked in a nook at the far end of the banquet hall.

IMPORTANT BUSINESSMAN
--had seduced butts away forever from the sit-down dining experience, with napkins, forks, spoons--
(pause for effect)

EXT. PUBLIC LIBRARY--DAY

The patrol car screeches to a halt.

The Skinny Cop jumps out to return an overdue copy of Lenin's NATIONAL LIBERATION, SOCIALISM AND IMPERIALISM.

IMPORTANT BUSINESSMAN (VO)
--and a few paper-thin carrot slices.
(pause for laughter, applause)
So, having said that--

INT. BETTER BUSINESS BUREAU PODIUM--DAY

IMPORTANT BUSINESSMAN
--without further adieu--

He pauses for really big applause.

EXT. BETTER BUSINESS BUREAU--AT THAT MOMENT

From the bushes, Raleigh watches the Skinny Cop scamper up the library steps.

No longer feeling the need to flip a coin, Raleigh dives into a side door of the Better Business Bureau--

INT. WET BAR--A SECOND LATER

--and, to his utter horror, finds himself in the tiny space behind the bar, squeezed right up against the prematurely matronly torso of the barmaid, who happens to be Krystelle.

She's moonlighting as a temp.

As always, she has been dressed, by her current employer, in a dress that is unflatteringly tight.

Raleigh gasps like a suffocating man. His eyes roll back into his skull.

INT. BANQUET HALL--DAY

IMPORTANT BUSINESSMAN
--the triple-B Merchant of the Month--

The former holder of that title, Harvey Coventry, Sr., gets

up and follows the Convenience Store Manager and the Snack Bar Owner.

INT. BANQUET HALL FRONT ENTRANCE--DAY

Suddenly, the door to the banquet hall swings open, right in the middle of the most important speech of Spencer's career--or, at any rate, the introduction to it.

Detective Furtwangler has arrived.

As usual, he is preceded by his uniformed henchmen--just two this time.

The Fat Cop comes in first and stations himself on one side of the entrance.

He is followed by the Female Cop, who skitters in and jockeys for position.

FAT COP
There's plenty of room on the other side.

INT. PUBLIC LIBRARY CIRCULATION DESK--AT THAT MOMENT

The Skinny Cop hands the Lenin book and a couple bucks to the LIBRARIAN.

On his way out to resume his civil duties, he gets distracted by a copy of Engels' ROLE OF FORCE IN HISTORY.

INT. FRONT ENTRANCE--DAY

Detective Furtwangler makes his big entrance.

IMPORTANT BUSINESSMAN (OS)
--Spencer Sproul! Spencer Sproul, ladies and gentlemen! Spencer! Sproul!

The detective hears that name, and his ears perk up. With suspicious eyes, he looks toward the front of the hall.

INT. PODIUM--DAY

The lights go down a bit.

Spencer comes up, nudges the mike and gets some feedback.

SPENCER
Is this thing off?

INT. FRONT ENTRANCE--AT THAT MOMENT

Detective Furtwangler eyeballs Spencer, seeming to recognize him.

INT. PODIUM--DAY

Spencer eyeballs him right back.

As the Businessmen and their Wives settle in to enjoy Spencer's acceptance speech, we see, in his head--

--the famous police helicopter videotape footage of the legendary serial killer, Night Stalker, sprinting full-out for two miles, scaling ten-foot retaining walls, crossing eight lanes of traffic, in his final naked animal-scramble for freedom.

The Banquet Hall gets quiet, except for the sound of Harvey Coventry, Sr.'s voice.

HARVEY COVENTRY, SR. (OS)
You guys have heard why I quit the SDS, right?

Spencer steps out from behind the podium, ready to fly from Detective Furtwangler.

INT. WET BAR--AT THAT MOMENT

Raleigh has retreated to the safe side of the bar, and has wedged a stool between his buttocks. He glances uneasily at Krystelle's physique.

He's trying to be butch and blend in with the Convenience Store Manager, the Snack Bar Owner, and Harvey Coventry, Sr.

RALEIGH
(slapping everyone on the back, bellowing like a truck driver)
Aw, hell no! I ain't heard one single

damn butt-flippin' word 'bout that!
Why don'tcha tell me all about it,
buddy-pal o' mine?

Raleigh is surprised to hear his voice echo throughout the Banquet Hall.

INT. FRONT ENTRANCE

Detective Furtwangler hears his voice, too, and follows it, forgetting about Spencer.

INT. WET BAR--DAY

Unlike Raleigh, the Convenience Store Manager and the Snack Bar Owner have heard Harvey Coventry, Sr's reasons for quitting the SDS, a couple thousand times.

CONVENIENCE STORE MANAGER
(to Snack Stand Owner)
Let's go back and hear what the retard
has to say.

HARVEY COVENTRY, SR.
(undeterred, to Raleigh)
I didn't compromise my political
principles. Not at all. As a matter of
fact--

He's interrupted by the amplified voice of today's guest of honor--

SPENCER (OS)
I am bringing to mind by what my creme
de mentor said one time only. A family
restaurant is like a movie--

INT. PODIUM--DAY

Spencer has resumed his position behind the podium, and is reading, with great difficulty, a written speech,

SPENCER
--except with smells. Like that one
with Miss Divine and Tab Hunter, also
Edith Massey amongst mothers, plus a
Camembert roll by Stiv Bators.

Spud has already reached the extreme limit of his attention span. He gets up from the table of honor and wanders away.

Spencer doesn't notice because he's struggling with his text.

SPENCER
Except you just don't only scratch and sniff the little card that comes inside the video box. Except it doesn't. But you also lick it, because food tastes, you know? And maybe chew it some.

INT. WET BAR--DAY

Harvey Coventry, Sr., hunches over Raleigh, talking directly into the side of his head.

In sympathy for his suffering, Krystelle brings Raleigh a complimentary brandy Alexander.

HARVEY COVENTRY, SR.
--and if the Vietnam war was still going, the furthest thing from my mind would be owning my own exclusive tennis club.

RALEIGH
Looks like the barmaid could use a few tennis lessons.

She almost upsets the delicate glass with her bosom.

RALEIGH
Or maybe a couple basketball lessons.

HARVEY COVENTRY, SR.
(interrupting his own spiel)
We could have gotten someone less matronly, if you know what I mean. But the temp agency charges more for that sort of thing. Now, back to more pressing matters--

SPENCER (OS)
And soda pop and coffee, also. They taste, too, like food. All the senses,

four or five or whatever.

INT. PODIUM--DAY

SPENCER (CONT)
Like a sort of movie. That's what a family restaurant is like, you know? A movie? Except you put it in your mouth? Spud?
(departing from the written text)
Spud? ...

INT. WET BAR--DAY

Detective Furtwangler approaches, waving the Standish hankie around--

DETECTIVE FURTWANGLER
Raleigh! Yoo-hoo! Raleigh Standish the Sick-Fucking Fourth! You old deviant! Where can you be-e-e-e-e?

Raleigh reacts with mortal horror. He crawls under his bar stool, and phones home.

RALEIGH
(whispering, whimpering)
Momsy! Come save me! I'm at the Better Business Bureau! Bring lots and lots of cash! Hello? Pick up, Momsy! Please pick up!

INT. STANDISH MANSION, BASEMENT--AT THAT MOMENT

Baseball stadium organ music rattles the stone walls.

The Chauffeur has been caused to shed his livery and don a hot-dog vendor's get-up.

CHAUFFEUR
(trying to sound the part)
Get your red hots! Red hots, right here!

Mrs. Standish wears a genuine 1930's professional baseball player's uniform.

She approaches a rack of bats, and takes her own sweet time selecting just the right one.

This time it's a Louisville Slugger, with exquisite hairline cracks in the varnish.

On a table nearby, the princess extension rings and flashes, unnoticed, unheard, among a selection of fine ointments.

SPENCER (VO)

Spud?

INT. BANQUET HALL--DAY

SPENCER (CONT)

Spud?

(a few tears)

Spud? ... Spud?

All the BUSINESSMEN are surprised and, quite frankly, moved to hear that name.

FIRST BUSINESSMAN

Sproul's quite a guy. This is his big moment, and he's sharing the spotlight with his prodigy, or whatever that's called.

SECOND BUSINESMAN

Yeah, he's decided to take Spud under his wing and introduce him to the subtleties of the contemporary food services industry.

THIRD BUSINESSMAN

I wonder how much he's charging Spud's folks.

INT. WET BAR--DAY

Detective Furtwangler looms over Raleigh's barstool, around whose legs he's coiled like a fetus.

DETECTIVE FURTWANGLER

(dangling the hankie in his face)

You're killing your dear old Momsy with

this. You know that, don't you,
Raleigh?

RALEIGH
Why? Is she stroking out from lifting
your giant bags of payola?

Detective Furtwangler reaches down and makes the standard bad-cop testicle grab--to no discernible effect other than a complacent sigh from Raleigh.

Meanwhile, Spud shows up and wipes something under the bar.

Harvey Coventry, Sr., turns to him.

INT. FRONT ENTRANCE--AT THAT MOMENT

The Skinny Cop is just arriving from the library.

He has checked out the Engels book, plus Bakunin's STATISM AND ANARCHY and one or two others.

He hears a voice coming from the wet bar--

HARVEY COVENTRY, SR.
I'm in the business of making people
feel better about themselves, through
tennis. And that's political. You can't
tell me that isn't political--

The Skinny Cop goes to check it out.

INT. WET BAR--DAY

Krystelle shoves a plate of beer nuts in front of Spud's face, in a forlorn attempt to distract her former employee from the contents of his nostrils.

HARVEY COVENTRY, SR.
(to Spud)
What's your name again? Spud? Can you
sit there on your barstool, Spud, and
tell me that the business of making
people feel better about themselves,
through tennis, is not political?

Spud sure can't.

The Skinny Detective approaches, and offers this--

SKINNY DETECTIVE
I understand your position perfectly. Marx himself said, "The bourgeoisie has, historically, played a most revolutionary role." Your business provides you with a taste of the personal fame which the declining bourgeoisie crave as a substitute for the self-respect which capitalism fails to provide.

HARVEY COVENTRY, SR.
Who are you calling bourgeois? I'll off you, pig!

He grabs his graphite tennis racket and brains the Skinny Cop.

Up till this moment, we have only gotten the tiniest taste of what the Female Cop is capable of.

She's got Harvey, Sr.'s head beaten out of shape before the rest of him has a chance to bounce off the wall a second time.

In the confusion, Spud picks his nose, and Raleigh slips away.

INT SUV--DAY (A WEEK OR SO LATER)

The Nuclear Family cruises aimlessly, almost comatose with boredom. Dad is dropping off at the wheel.

All the other cars pass them, honking angrily at their sluggish progress.

FIRST KID
(from the back seat)
Let's go to Dag's!

All the Kids begin to scream gleefully.

DAD
We're not radical punks. That's not the sort of people we are.

MOM
Lemuel's has a more family-like atmosphere.

SECOND KID
Let's go to Lemmy's.

Everyone bares their teeth.

NUCLEAR FAMILY
(in unison)
Yeah!

EXT. STREET--DAY

The SUV speeds off toward the orange and turquoise Lemuel's Family Restaurant sign.

EXT. LEMUEL'S FAMILY RESTAURANT--DAY

There's a huge, long queue of Morbidly Obese Folks waiting to get in. They're in a surly mood.

In fact, a riot is on the verge of breaking out. If not for the frenzied shrieks and billy-club jabs of the Female Cop, this whole end of town could collapse into chaos.

The Nuclear Family tries to get in line, but they're elbowed aside like insects.

Next to the front door, a seven-foot-tall fiberglass effigy of Lemmy the Lemur has been installed. It's Spencer's own ratcheted-up version, brought to three-dimensional reality.

Riveted to its base, a brass plaque dedicates this monument to Spencer. There's an engraved citation from LEMCO National Headquarters in Des Moines, formally thanking him for creating Lemmy's "new, more appetizing look."

The Fat Cop stands sentry, along with the Skinny Cop, whose head is bandaged. Neither of them can stop staring at the big Lemmy.

SKINNY COP
Marx said that a commodity appears, at first sight, to be a very trivial thing. But analysis shows that it is, in reality, a very queer thing, abounding in metaphysical subtleties and theological niceties.

FAT COP
(appalled)
You can say that again.

Spencer and Spud stand together, side by side on the front stoop, watching Dagbert's Family Eatery being torn down for lack of interest.

SPENCER
It was merely a flesh in the frying pot. For staying power, you need subtleness and, um--
(drawing an unconscious hand across his own groin)
--potency. Also
(doing Anthony Hopkins again, a little better this time)
--also ex-quee-zeet concentration. Plus stealth.

SPUD
Like that Hannibal the Cannonball?

Spencer chuckles fondly, and gives Spud a patronizing pat on the buttocks.

SPENCER
Close enough. For now.

Together, they go inside.

Before the door closes behind them, Spencer and Spud are bathed in an intense orange and turquoise light.

We hear human sounds underneath the Muzique, something between gratified grunts and anguished howls.

FADE OUT

BOMB BABY

...in the day of atonement shall ye make the trumpet sound. And ye shall hallow the fiftieth year, and proclaim liberty throughout all the land, unto all the inhabitants thereof. It shall be a Jubilee unto you, and ye shall return every man unto his possession, and ye shall return every man unto his family.
--Leviticus 25:9-10

FADE IN

EXT. PRE-WORLD WAR II HIROSHIMA -- NIGHT

An UNWED MOTHER moves along the street, keeping in the shadows. She carries bundled-up pair of beautiful NEWBORN TWINS.

She creeps along the back wall of an ancient Buddhist temple and approaches the baby abandonment drawer. Sunken into the wall just above ground level, it's designed to accommodate up to a half-dozen unwanted babies at a time.

The Unwed Mother deposits her sleeping infants in the drawer and gives it a gentle shove, sending them through to the other side of the wall, into the safety of the temple enclosure.

EXT. BUDDHIST TEMPLE -- DAWN

A shaven-headed MONK meditates at the edge of an ornamental lotus pond.

Roused from his prayers by the babbling of the babies, he goes to collect them.

EXT. HIROSHIMA CITY -- YEARS LATER

The atom bomb goes off.

The temple is flattened, except for the back wall.

EXT. HIROSHIMA CATHEDRAL CONSTRUCTION SITE -- MONTHS LATER

Catholic missionaries are overseeing the construction of a cathedral on the former site of the temple. They are incorporating the old wall as a memorial of the blast.

Work proceeds very slowly, as everybody suffers from radiation sickness, except FATHER GAUDI. He's a young Spanish priest.

EXT. ALLEY BEHIND CATHEDRAL -- NIGHT

A JAPANESE WOMAN, burned and sickened by gamma rays, tucks something in the baby abandonment drawer.

Weeping, she limps off into the scorched rubble.

EXT. OHTAGAWA RIVER -- NIGHT

She makes her way to the bank of the shallow river that flows sluggishly through the ruined city.

She crawls onto a makeshift raft, shoves weakly off, and drifts into the smoky darkness, moaning.

EXT. CATHEDRAL -- NEXT MORNING

Father Gaudi is trying to start a vegetable garden in the radioactive soil. Nothing grows but strange weeds with little blue flowers.

He hears odd sounds coming from a tangle of weeds along the back wall. It sounds like a baby, sort of.

He goes to check it out.

EXT. CATHEDRAL -- FIFTY YEARS LATER

It's Sunday morning, August sixth, 1995: exactly half a century after the bomb.

A lavish Japanese WEDDING PARTY is gathering in the cathedral compound. A professional VIDEO CREW, formally dressed, tapes the whole affair.

ISHIDA-SAN is the local crime boss, also father-of-the-bride. Slightly bored, he flips an expensive, half-smoked cigar into the parking lot.

It lands behind a black stretch limo, sizzling in a red puddle of transmission fluid.

Beyond the limo, a poinsettia bush is growing against the back wall. It more or less conceals the baby abandonment drawer.

The drawer squeaks open a crack, and KARA-KUN peeks in from the street. He's a tiny, simple-minded bum, fifty years old. He has folded his very limber body into the drawer.

Silently and rapidly, Kara-kun smuggles himself into the churchyard, and heads for the cigar.

A few crows swoop down from the gray sky.

After a struggle, Kara-kun emerges from behind the limo. He's brushing black feathers off his rags and chewing on the cigar.

Mumbling contentedly, he approaches the Wedding Party with the intention of mingling. Nobody notices him, just yet.

EXT. CATHEDRAL PARKING LOT -- DAY

Parked at the side of the cathedral are five or six flashy vans belonging to the Yakuza (Japanese Mafia).

FILIPINAS and Filipino TRANSVESTITES hang out of the windows, chatting. They are prostitutes enslaved by the Yakuza. The Transvestites are in full drag, their Sunday best.

Yakuza THUGS fidget behind the steering wheels of the vans. They wear dark glasses. Colorful dragon tattoos peek from under the cuffs of their rental tuxedos.

A couple dozen expatriated FOREIGNERS from every part of the world are descending the side steps that lead to the crypt chapel. Among them are two Americans.

POLLY EDWINE is dark and strong-looking -- a daunting figure to any man not assured of his own worth.

HANK is dressed in a spiffy stone-washed, brushed-denim suit. A chic ponytail sprouts from the back of his head. His position in the R&D department of a major American automotive company requires this appearance of creativity kept under tight wraps.

HANK

It's nice to see the girls get a little air. But why are the thugs dressed up so fancy?

POLLY

In case they're needed to quell disturbances at the wedding. Their boss is marrying off his oldest daughter.

HANK

No, really? Is that him?

POLLY

That's the great Ishida-san.

HANK

He does look more angular than most fathers-of-the-bride, now that you mention it.

POLLY

It comes from sampling his own shipments of methedrine.

HANK

Does he sample his own shipments of Filipinas? They'll rent this dump to anybody!

INT. CRYPT CHAPEL -- DAY

The NIGERIAN ACOLYTE props a fake silk screen in front of the altar.

The customary Sunday morning social hour gets underway. It's a regular Tower of Babel. A single language, English, echoes among the pews, but it's an English rich with an astounding array of accents.

Hank rousts a pregnant Chinese BOAT PERSON from a folding chair in the back.

He confiscates the few thin cushions which the poor girl was sitting on, and hustles them up to the American Automotive Executives' WIVES in the front pew. These turquoise-rinsed ladies have staked out the most pious place in the crypt for themselves.

Hank joins Polly in a pew further back.

HANK

The faithful are banished to the basement so Ishida-san can desecrate the place with his daughter.

POLLY
You're not one of the faithful. Your bosses' wives drag you here.

HANK
They need a man to protect them from the underworld figures.

POLLY
What about their husbands?

HANK
On the golf course with Japanese counterparts. Automotive joint venture is a most delicate affair.

POLLY
I can imagine.

HANK
Luckily for me, I'm in the creative end of things. Nobody expects me to know my chipper from my putter. I'm allowed to spend my only free day worshiping.

He picks up a hymn book and pretends to ponder some inspirational verses. He offers to share with Polly.

POLLY
In other words, Hank, your masters' wives drag you here. By the ponytail.

HANK
Well, you drag your hubby here, too. At least as far as the parking lot. Isn't that where you left the professor? Sleeping off Saturday night in the family death trap?

POLLY
Who says he's sleeping? Sammy could be praying out there among the thugs.

HANK
Or magically levitating that poor Mazda three feet in the air. With him inside, the shocks could use a rest.

Giggling is heard, and a clatter of spike heels, as three Filipinas come scurrying down the stairs to join the party. They are welcomed by everyone, except the Wives, who consider themselves too good to pray with mere prostitutes.

NIGERIAN ACOLYTE
Finally, the mobsters let some lovelies escape from the vans.

FIRST FILIPINA
Everybody come! It's wonderful! You must come see!

Everyone, except the Wives, scampers out.

EXT. HIROSHIMA CATHEDRAL GROUNDS -- DAY

Thugs, in formal dress, armed with lead pipes and jack handles, are chasing Kara-kun around, at the instigation of Ishida-san. They are terrified of coming into contact with such an unlucky creature, but they fear the wrath of their boss just as much.

With much agility and speed, Kara-kun scales the wall of the compound.

He perches on top, hooting and jeering. Ishida-san's cigar stub is still clenched between his lips, and it oozes transmission fluid down his chin. He bumps and grinds like a Filipina stripper in a Yakuza nightclub.

The Foreigners watch from the safety of the crypt steps. They cheer Kara-kun on as he prances along the top of the wall.

HANK
Sanctuary! Sanctuary!

Kara-kun leaps over the Thugs' cowering heads, and grabs onto a large elevated brass bust of Pope John Paul II that adorns the churchyard.

Several Thugs approach the Rectory. They bang and kick the door.

It opens, and Father Gaudi appears. He's old now, but still vigorous. He wears a full-length black cassock and carries the Gospels in one hand, a silver cup filled with consecrated bread in the other. He views the Thugs with gentleness. Perhaps he's even a little bored.

ISHIDA-SAN
Look what that animal did!

The BRIDE sobs in the arms of her BRIDESMAIDS. Her train is smeared with muddy footprints.

ISHIDA-SAN
The kid's going to bitch in my ear about this for the rest of my life!

FATHER GAUDI
I'm truly sorry. But, at the moment, I'm more concerned with your other kids. Or should I call them your slaves?

ISHIDA-SAN
What are you talking about? Those entertainers have legit work-visas.

Father Gaudi says nothing. Gently but firmly, he elbows Ishida-san aside and begins working his way through the parking lot. He is performing a kind of drive-in ministry, slipping communion to the Filipinas and Transvestites through rolled-down van windows.

Ishida-san follows along.

ISHIDA-SAN
How can you charge one-point-five million yen to rent this hall, when it's infested?

FATHER GAUDI
It's not a hall. It's the house of God. And you'll have to discuss parish finances with the Bishop. My job is to minister to the foreign community.
(to a PRETTY FILIPINA)
The body of Christ.

PRETTY FILIPINA
Amen.

FATHER GAUDI
If Kara-kun behaves a little unpleasantly sometimes, it's only because he happened to be in his mother's womb when the Americans pulled their hideous prank on this town. His brain was irradiated.

Kara-kun is sitting cross-legged on top of the brass pope's head. He hoots and blows kisses at a BIG THUG.

FATHER GAUDI
The gamma rays seem to have affected his sense of decorum.

ISHIDA-SAN
That's not all that's going to be affected!

Ishida-san grabs a club from one of his men and stomps a few menacing yards in Kara-kun's direction.

Several Filipinas and Transvestites poke their heads out the van windows.

The SMALL TRANSVESTITE is a delicate, pretty boy: Audrey Hepburn with a golden-brown complexion. He is too high-strung even in the best circumstances. Today he's on the verge of tears.

SMALL TRANSVESTITE
(worried about something else)
Father! Please don't let them do bad things to Kay-kay!

FATHER GAUDI
No danger of that. No matter how loudly Ishida-san screams into their ears, they'll never get close enough to touch our mascot.

PRETTY FILIPINA
(giggling)
He does run fast, doesn't he?

FATHER GAUDI

He could be a double amputee confined to a broken wheelchair, and still be safe from the likes of them.

The LARGE TRANSVESTITE boldly steps out of the van and reveals himself. He's a strapping youth, well-muscled, with a fine baritone speaking voice, and he looks right at home in his slinky dress, nylons and high heels.

LARGE TRANSVESTITE

The Yakuza think Kara-kun's an evil spirit in disguise. Our country may be poor, but even the pygmies on Mount Pinatoba aren't so superstitious.

Kara-kun flips the cigar into the Thugs' midst, and they all dive for cover.

Several of the Foreigners laugh scornfully from the crypt steps.

SMALL TRANSVESTITE

God bless Kara-kun's happy soul...And also the soul of my baby brother!

FATHER GAUDI

Mother of God. What's happened now?

SMALL TRANSVESTITE

They forced him to make the flame dance!

LARGE TRANSVESTITE

There was no time for practicing because the natives were getting restless. He did his best, Father, but his arms weren't strong enough for the benzine goblets.

SMALL TRANSVESTITE

My baby brother has burns so horrible, and nobody nurses him!

As discreetly as possible, so the Thug DRIVER won't notice, the Large Transvestite slips Father Gaudi a piece of paper.

LARGE TRANSVESTITE
Boys and girls are dying at this address, four or five on a tatami mat.

PRETTY FILIPINA
You must do something, Father!

FATHER GAUDI
I'll be there as soon as I can, I promise you. The body of Christ.

SMALL TRANSVESTITE
(sobbing)
Amen.

Ishida-san returns from blustering around the base of the pope's bust.

Father Gaudi distracts him from the distraught transvestite by taking his elbow and proceeding to the next vehicle.

Someone passes a charming, racially-mixed BABY through a side window. Delighted, Father Gaudi takes it into his arms and carries it to a bench situated just off the parking lot.

Ishida-san follows, looking askance at the Baby's round eyes and darkish skin. He's affected by the Baby's beauty, in spite of his own racism. He sits down next to the priest and looks out across the cathedral compound.

The Foreigners, including Hank and Polly, climb all the way out of the crypt with a couple of guitars for the Filipinas in the vans.

Ishida-san listens to their lovely song.

ISHIDA-SAN
How would your Bishop feel if werenters took our daughters someplace else?

FATHER GAUDI
Not likely. Your weddings are theater. And this building, hideous as it is, happens to be the most photogenic backdrop in town...With the exception of the Mercedes Benz dealership.

ISHIDA-SAN
(impressed by Gaudi's nerve)
You don't talk like somebody that just got handed one-point-five million yen in cash... Okay. You got me where you want me, Priest... But I have another daughter ripe for marrying. She's my youngest, my favorite.

The Bride has stopped weeping, and is now having a temper tantrum. She screeches and kicks viciously at the shins of the Video Crew.

ISHIDA-SAN
My favorite, by far.

FATHER GAUDI
A second daughter. Congratulations. Please urge her to attend my Saturday Bible class for non-believers. It's conducted entirely in Hiroshima dialect.

ISHIDA-SAN
I've also got friends on the city council. All I need to do is suggest they start regulating river traffic. That's where your precious animal lives, right? On the river? Well, the Ministry of Health would just love to burn his raft. No more mud-minnows for supper. He'll be chased up into the hills like a three-legged dog that farts too much.

FATHER GAUDI
Kara-kun doesn't fear mountain heights. That's not why he's chosen the river as his habitat.

ISHIDA-SAN
Then what does scare him?

After a moment's thought, Ishida-san pulls out a solid-gold cigar lighter. It's a beautiful thing, an antique, engraved with dragons and phoenixes and chrysanthemums.

He fiddles with it fondly a few seconds, then adjusts it to full flame and waves it in front of Father Gaudi's face like a blow torch.

Father Gaudi casts a protective glance in Kara-kun's direction.

ISHIDA-SAN
I should have guessed. He's scared of flames, just like all animals.

FATHER GAUDI
I wouldn't blame him if he was, with his pre-natal history.

ISHIDA-SAN
No wonder he lives on the water. If he tried pitching camp on the streets with the other bums, he'd be doused with gas and fricasseed on the first night.

FATHER GAUDI
Courtesy of the teenaged bikers. Your fond recruits.

ISHIDA-SAN
Sit tight. This won't take a second.

Ishida-san crosses the parking lot, summoning his Thugs.

On the way, he happens to pass by a rusty, bashed-up Mazda, ineptly parked among the vans. It's difficult to see through the smudged windows, but someone inside is snoring so loudly that the car vibrates on its overloaded, worn-out shocks.

Ishida-san forgets what he's doing and stares at this odd sight.

But he is distracted by his Thugs, who gather about him, awaiting his orders. They draw him aside to form a huddle.

Ishida-san sends a LITTLE THUG to confiscate bouquets from the bewildered Bridesmaids.

Polly and Hank, plus a few other Foreigners, approach Father Gaudi.

POLLY
I don't believe this. They're not going to --

FATHER GAUDI
Of course not. Too many witnesses. And if Kara-kun comes down, that's no cause for concern, either. Our mascot has a top-secret escape route.

In the Yakuza huddle, the expensive bouquets have been dismantled, the blooms stripped away, and the stems twisted together to make a couple of torches, which Ishida-san has lit. He arms himself with one, and hands the other to a TALL THUG.

Ishida-san marches to the pope's bust with his Thugs. He waves the fire around Kara-kun's legs and feet. Smoke from the second torch billows up from behind.

Far from being afraid, Kara-kun coos like a dove in fascination. He reaches down and passes his hand through the fire. Without warning, he grabs the torch.

Ishida-san flicks his precious cigar lighter ablaze and tries to set Kara-kun's rags on fire.

Kara-kun is enchanted. He tosses the torch like a bridal bouquet into the arms of a HOWLING THUG, and snatches the beautiful golden thing.

Shrieking in triumph, he conceals the prize in his rags, leaps down among the Thugs, scrambles between their cringing legs, and vanishes behind the poinsettia bush.

The baby abandonment drawer's characteristic squeak is heard.

EXT. STREET OUTSIDE CATHEDRAL -- DAY

Kara-kun zips down the traffic-jammed street, heading for the river.

A few Thugs follow, without enthusiasm, hopelessly outpaced.

EXT. CATHEDRAL COMPOUND -- DAY

HANK
Back to the raft, Huck.

POLLY
He didn't even get a chance to come downstairs and pray with us.

FATHER GAUDI
We'd better have a conference.

With broad arm gestures, he summons the Foreigners into the crypt. They all crowd happily down the stairs.

Several more Filipinas and Transvestites take advantage of the confusion to escape from the vans.

Hank rushes to get down the steps ahead of them.

Ishida-san is left to stomp about the compound, cursing and screaming in Hiroshima gutter-dialect.

INT. CRYPT CHAPEL -- DAY

At the front pew, Hank fusses over his bosses' Wives as the despised Filipinas come into their presence.

HANK
It's just for a few minutes, I promise. Father has called a kind of powwow. Immediately afterwards these, um, ladies will be on their way back to the parking lot. Okay?

He goes to join Polly in their customary position further back.

POLLY
Do you know the distinguishing characteristic of harem attendants?

HANK
I'm sure you'd volunteer to perform the alterations on me.

Father Gaudi mounts the pulpit. He clears his throat. Everyone shuts up, more or less.

FATHER GAUDI
My friends, we have a problem. A legalistic one yet. After four centuries of wholesome anarchy, I'm afraid that Kara-kun's beloved Ohtagawa River is about to come to the attention of the city council. Today he finally spoiled the wrong wedding.

VARIOUS FOREIGNERS
The cops want to corner Kay-kay on the streets some night... They'll institutionalize him... Around here, "institutionalize" means the same as "disappear" in Argentina...

POLLY
I think I know which institution would take him.

HANK
Your hubby's very own university. Right, Mrs. Edwine? Their med school's mental health clinic has plenty room for one more. I hear they're bountiful with the thorazine.

FIRST FOREIGNER
Would Kara-kun be willing to dock in one specified place night after night?

SECOND FOREIGNER
Do you think he'd be welcomed by his new neighbors at the marina?

THIRD FOREIGNER
Getting his raft up to code would take a miracle.

HANK
Yeah. After he performs that miracle, we'll get John Paul II to beatify him.

The Wives titter at this remark, while some of the more pious Foreigners murmur in dismay.

POLLY
(trying to keep things serious)
If the boat regulations are enforced anything like the car regulations, being up to code will matter less than paying the inspection fee.

HANK
The professor's wife speaks from experience.

FATHER GAUDI
Perhaps, if we open our hearts and our pocketbooks...

A collection is taken. The pledges and donations pour in from everyone in the crypt, except for the Wives. They hesitate to contribute.

But then the Large Transvestite swishes up among them.

POLLY
(to Hank)
Snap to. An underworld figure is invading the harem.

HANK
Drag queens don't count. The ladies simply adore drag queens. Especially this moose. Watch how he handles them.

The Large Transvestite has perched himself among the Wives.

LARGE TRANSVESTITE
Listen, Lovie-Dovies, if we let the police "disappear" Kara-kun, who knows what will happen? With no unlucky spirit to scare them away, my handlers might just start coming down here and sharing this bench with you luscious honey-dearies.

STUPID WIFE
But your, um, handlers are Japanese. Japanese don't have any religion. Why would they want to invade our chapel?

LARGE TRANSVESTITE
Who can say? Who can say, my little buggy-yummers? You never know. But I can tell you, Sweet-licks, once the Yakuza take over a place, they can be such brutes, such cruel savages. Ooo-ooh!

He flutters his hand on the Wives' knees.

LARGE TRANSVESTITE
And it helps to look at things from Kara-kun's point of view, doesn't it? The poor little bomb baby...

EXT. BOMBED HIROSHIMA -- DAY (FLASHBACK)

We see the horrible scenes he describes.

LARGE TRANSVESTITE (VO)
Imagine what it must've been like to bounce around inside somebody's tummy on that morning... His mommy tried to jump in the water to bathe her burns, except the atomic blast had parted the river from its bed... Nothing was left behind but glowing mud, not even much good for a poultice... Just a whole bunch of people were overwhelmed and washed away when the boiling Ohtagawa flushed back...

EXT. CONTEMPORARY UPSTREAM SUBURBS -- DAY

The river is shallow and lazy, almost lumpy, in the late summer heat.

LARGE TRANSVESTITE (VO)
The old fishermen's wives say this explains Kara-kun's life-long love affair with the river...

On the flood plain, NATIVE FAMILIES are having picnics and ball games, attempting to enjoy the week's few moments of freedom. YOUNG SONS recreate politely with FATHERS who are strangers to them.

Everybody avoids coming into contact with the polluted water, except for TWO SMALL CHILDREN, who know no better than to try to go wading.

Their OLDER SIBLINGS drag them away and dry their feet with handkerchiefs, which are promptly discarded into the river.

A barely buoyant raft, improvised from bamboo slats tied together with rags, slides from a bank of diesel exhaust. The pilot is none other than Kara-kun.

Mothers try to ignore him, and quietly scold their children for staring at his strange face.

LARGE TRANSVESTITE (VO)
They say something in him yearns to be washed away with his own beloved townsfolk...

He drifts awhile among turquoise industrial suds. Then he scoops a half-dead fish off the surface and aims it at the sky.

A pair of crows appears overhead, croaking loudly. They take turns swooping down to feed on the fish. Occasionally a talon or beak opens a gash in one of Kara-kun's fingers, but this only makes him laugh.

The longer he laughs, the more people abandon the flood plain in superstitious fear.

INT. CRYPT CHAPEL -- DAY

LARGE TRANSVESTITE
Now, ladies, I know that our little Kay-kay makes weird noises from time to time, and is not the most spiffy dresser in all of East Asia. But he's no butch, nipple-tweaking organized crime figure, is he? It's a question of the lesser of two evils, don't you agree, Kissy-poops?

The Wives agree, and come up with a little money.

HANK
(to Polly)
What did I tell you? Such consummate finesse, such, such --

POLLY
Interpersonal dynamics.

HANK
Yeah! If only we could straighten him up. Square him away, just a tad. Get him into a reasonable shade of mascara and some un-laddered nylons. I'm positive there'd be a position waiting for him in our personnel department.

The Nigerian Acolyte brings the collection plate to Hank and Polly's pew. Hank looks in and pretends to marvel at the Wives' generosity. He casts an adoring grin in their direction.

The plate is passed into the hands of the only native who worships here. The JAPANESE AMATEUR ARCHEOLOGIST wears a beard and rumpled clothes, very self-consciously in the western academic style. He loads the collection plate with wads of paper money.

FIRST FOREIGNER
Whoah. Easy. We're not buying the little monster his own yacht.

ARCHEOLOGIST
(very confidentially)
Soon I'll be able to afford to drop ten times that much. Just ask Ishida-san in about seventy-two hours.

FIRST FOREIGNER
Don't tell me. You're gonna visit his new gambling den and break the bank.

ARCHEOLOGIST
You could say that. The site he's chosen to build it on has great

archeological importance -- assuming my research and calculations are correct.

The collection plate is passed to a group of Filipinas. These impoverished girls have no bills, just copper coins.

FIRST FILIPINA
I will share my money, to help Kara-kun stay free and keep making Ishida-san crazy.

SMALL TRANSVESTITE
(still weeping about his burnt brother)
I hope Ishida-san has twenty fat daughters, so Kay-kay can be nasty to each of them.

FATHER GAUDI
Come, come. Let's be charitable. These Yakuza are not free, either.

LARGE TRANSVESTITE
Oh? Who holds Ishida-san in bondage? I don't see any of his fingers missing.

SMALL TRANSVESTITE
I don't see patches of his skin scorched away.

FATHER GAUDI
Ignorance holds Ishida-san in bondage. And pride compounds that ignorance sevenfold. But he is not completely chained yet. Occasionally I see something else shine through his eyes.

Just as the Transvestites' scoffing threatens to get out of hand, the hackneyed wedding march from "Lohengrin" starts to rumble down on everybody's heads.

INT. UPSTAIRS CHURCH -- DAY

Ishida-san's guests are important CIVIC LEADERS, RULING PARTY DIET MEN, and PILLARS OF THE BUSINESS COMMUNITY, along with their lovely WIVES and MISTRESSES. Everyone is arrayed in the correct occidental fashion.

The Bridesmaids have tried to dab Kara-kun's footprints away from the Bride's train, but evidence remains, discoloring the lace. Her face is puffed with weeping and a hateful expression.

Ishida-san is giving his eldest away, finally, and can't wait to indulge in a cigar. He digs around in his coat for the means to light up, and comes up empty-handed. No gold lighter.

His LIEUTENANT, a reptilian fellow in a rental tux, quickly reaches over and obliges the boss with a lit match.

In the flare of the flame, we see that Ishida-san's face is exploding with a borderline-psychotic rage.

INT. CRYPT CHAPEL -- DAY

The collection plate is passed up to Father Gaudi.

FATHER GAUDI
So, let me see... Ah! My friends, I am pleased to announce that the inspection fee on Kara-kun's raft will be covered.

Cheers are heard from the congregation.

POLLY
I don't want to spoil the party--

HANK
Here it comes.

POLLY
--but I have to point something out. Kara-kun likes to grab minnows by hand. That isn't a method the Fishermen's Union will be likely to approve. Somebody should at least show him how to pretend that he can use a line and sinker.

FATHER GAUDI
Mrs. Edwine's observation is, as usual, perfectly astute. Who will volunteer to teach Kara-kun to pretend to fish?

All eyes are averted. Nobody wants to do it.

HANK
I just happen to know someone who's perfect for the job. This person's a Ph.D., so he's an expert at pretending to do things.

POLLY
Oh, hell. Sorry I mentioned it.

HANK
Since he has a plush university job with unlimited free time, and since he isn't here to defend his interests, I nominate this certain person.

FATHER GAUDI
A show of hands?

The certain person is elected -- with one abstention. Polly tries to decline on his behalf, but she is ignored.

HANK
So, we've got ourselves an Official Emissary. I volunteer to be the Chairman of the Angler's Education Committee. That means, Polly dear, that I'll be on him like a cocklebur from now on.

STUPID WIFE
Who are they talking about?

LARGE TRANSVESTITE
Your guess is as good as mine, Snugglebumps.

EXT. HIROSHIMA CATHEDRAL PARKING LOT -- DAY

Some of the Thugs are gathered around the bashed-up Mazda.

To entertain the remaining Filipinas, they unwrap sticks of gum and try to toss the foil wrappers through the car's open window, into the gaping mouth of SAM EDWINE, who's producing the same huge snores that almost deafened Ishida-san.

Wedged in the death seat, he's an enormously tall, heavy-set man, with a flame-orange beard and shaggy hair thinning on top. He is dressed in worn-out professorial tweeds, several sizes too small, the leather elbow patches scuffed and hanging by individual threads.

So far, three gum wrappers have made it into Sam's mouth. They adhere to his tongue.

He suddenly awakens. He rolls his eyes with bashful seductiveness, but doesn't bother to spit the foil wrappers out. Indeed, he chews on them awhile, then swallows, neither breaking eye contact with the Thugs, nor relaxing his sweet smile.

EXT. CROWDED DOWNTOWN HIROSHIMA STREET -- DAY

The Mazda moves slowly through the congestion. A bamboo fishing pole sticks out from the side window, interfering with traffic.

CYCLISTS and PEDESTRIANS must duck to avoid decapitation.

SAM (VO)
Why me, for Christ's sake?

INT. MAZDA -- DAY

Polly is driving. Sam is wadded double in the death seat, a can of lively earthworms squeezed between his knees.

SAM
I've got animals in my lap! Who do they think I am? Saint Fisting Francis? I don't do church work. I'm not even baptized.

POLLY
I tried to decline this honor on your behalf, Dear, but the parishioners wouldn't hear of it. You should have seen the Detroit dames. They were thrilled to take on the Hiroshima Mafia.

SAM

Ouch! God damn it! I can't even look a fishhook without injuring myself!

POLLY

I don't understand what you're so worried about. How hard can it be to dangle a piece of string in the dinkum wawa?

SAM

Dinkum wawa? I can't believe you said that. This is a major artery we're talking about, emptying into fathomless deeps.

In the hazy distance between two skyscrapers, we see a slice of the crowded sea.

SAM

All kinds of awfulness could happen out there on your dinkum wawa.

POLLY

You'll be okay. Just use one worm at a time. Sea serpents have much bigger appetites than that.

She turns at a major intersection, opening up a view of a huge traffic jam ahead.

Bicycles, cars, taxis, buses and people clog the entrance to Peace Park, site of world-famous Ground Zero.

POLLY

Oh... Guess what day it is.

SAM

Already?

POLLY

The Golden Anniversary. The Jubilee.

SAM

Call me Mr. Over-Achiever, but I feel like I should spend Sunday filling out applications for jobs in a real country. You know, contributing to our survival.

POLLY
You're about to do God's work. That's much more important.

SAM
Hanging out with river riff-raff counts as God's work? Does the Bible tell me so? If I do this, will your God get us off these carcinogenic islands? Will he reach down and magically make me employable in the real world?

Polly reaches across, puts her hand on his knee and looks very gently into his eyes.

POLLY
Don't worry, Sammy. I don't mind living here. It's not that nasty a country. You're a perfectly good provider.

SAM
The big P. What a ridiculous word.

POLLY
The whole point, Dear, is this: today you will have a chance to know the inner contentment that comes from doing good works. As the Bible says: "Whatsoever you do to the least of my brothers you do unto me."

She pulls up to the curb.

POLLY
(whispering)
We'll get home someday.

They exchange a long look...

POLLY
Don't let him keep you out all night. There's squid tentacle sushi for supper.

The car lurches three feet into space with Sam's exit.

EXT. PEACE PARK ENTRANCE -- DAY

Just as the car is pulling out, Sam remembers to reach in and grab the bamboo pole and can of worms.

SAM
(shouting to Polly)
Okay! I guess I'll be a nice guy, just this one time, and show Kara-kun how to fool the Fishermen's Union!

He towers over the crowd of INTERNATIONAL PEACE LOVERS, who have come to commemorate A-Bomb Day.

SAM
Hmm. The joy of doing good works. Never thought of that. Sounds pretty wild. I'll try anything once.

He drops the fishing stuff, shoots his cuffs, sucks up his gut and tucks in his shirt, which comes untucked again when he exhales. He lunges off into the mob.

He comes back, on second thought, gathers up the pole and worms, then lunges back into the mob --

But he's forced to skid to a halt because some uniformed HIGH SCHOOL STUDENTS cross his path.

Even on this hot August Sunday they're buttoned into stifling woolen uniforms and loaded down with book-stuffed satchels.

SAM
Ah! Suffer the little children to come unto me. Study hard, babies, and maybe someday you'll be my disciples at the big important university!

They don't even glance at him. Distracted by neither the giant American nor the holiday celebration, the High School Students move in joyless lockstep, like haggard robots, down the block.

Sam watches them in amazement as they vanish into a weekend cram school. Over the door is a garish sign that reads --

"LET US LEARNING THE ENGLISH!"

EXT. PEACE PARK -- DAY

The MAYOR OF HIROSHIMA stands on a raised dias.

He's a diminutive codger with a Hirohito-Hitler mustache. All dressed up for the big Jubilee, he wears white gloves, a silk ribbon sash, and a blood-colored carnation which obscures almost the entire front of his boy-sized morning coat.

He somberly releases clouds of diseased doves from chrome-plated cages.

Directly upon release, the poor animals, which have plastic olive branches stapled symbolically to their upper beaks, skid straight into the grass like overloaded sailplanes.

They're trampled to grease spots by stampeding International Peace Lovers.

EXT. MIDDLE OF PEACE PARK -- DAY

By far the most conspicuous member of the motley multitude is Sam Edwine.

On his face is an expression of religious ecstasy, because he's doing God's good work, bringing comfort and joy to the heathen.

He dances little jigs, nudging everybody aside with his gyrating pelvis. He leaps into the air with all the bashful-eyed grace of the hippo ballerinas in Disney's Fantasia.

He swings the bamboo fishing pole around like the fairy godmother's wand, and sprinkles worms from the can like banana peels in everyone's path.

SMALL SCHOOLCHILDREN on a field trip break ranks and scatter in terror at Sam's approach.

TEACHER
(in Japanese)
Get back in line, or the big devil will eat you up!

Somewhat farther along the path, standing at full attention among barbecued cuttlefish booths, is a platoon of MALE COLLEGE CHEERLEADERS, Sam's students.

These junior fascists are dressed in WWII-style military uniforms of dark-blue wool. They're rallied under giant radiating-sun flags and banners emblazoned with reversed and righted swastikas.

Their boom-box blares martial music and racist propaganda.

A couple of these Cheerleaders hold up a big placard which reads, in both Japanese and English --

WE ARE A DIVINE NATION WITH THE EMPEROR AT OUR CENTER!

BULLDOG-LIKE CHEERLEADER
(screaming into a megaphone)
Japan is a tiny rice paddy! America is a treeless peak! Flood control is paramount!

Everyone is terrified of these fanatical boys -- everyone except Sam, of course. He barges through their ranks.

Among the Cheerleaders is a thin boy with glasses, who looks frazzled. He is Sam's NERVOUS STUDENT.

SAM
(shouting)
Why aren't you at home studying your English? It's a required course, you know!

The Nervous Student almost faints from embarrassment. He gobbles some pharmaceutical amphetamines from a little prescription bottle. It looks like he's got quite a habit.

Feeling really holy now, Sam prances deeper into the A-Bomb Golden Anniversary Celebration, heading toward Ground Zero.

EXT. DEEP IN PEACE PARK -- DAY

Tucked behind a row of ornamental azalea bushes is a shanty town where some of Hiroshima's BUMS live in washing machine cartons.

A few of them are Kara-kun's age, and are deformed or brain-damaged because they were exposed to the A-bomb's radiation inside their mothers' wombs.

A proud platoon of Hiroshima city COPS comes marching up in full Jubilee regalia: white gloves and gaiters, silken shoulder braids, golden epaulettes, and so on. They've come to roust the Bums.

Sam dances onto the scene, his whole head aglow with divine inspiration.

A few Bums break away and hobble over to greet him, their old pal. They stand on tiptoe, stroke his beard, and babble like pleased babies.

Sam interposes his vast body between them and the clutching claws of the police. He's getting joy from good works.

SAM

Whatever you pricks do to my little bros, you do to me! Why not let them join the party? This is their home! These cats are Ground Zero's regular and rightful residents!

He slaps a white-gloved hand from a grimy Adam's apple.

SAM

Why are you doing this? To prettify this dump? For the benefit of today's visitors? Are you kidding? Have you even bothered to look at your foreign guests?

Sam calls the cops attention to the throng of International Peace Lovers, liberals to an individual.

SAM

It would tickle them pink to be spare-changed by genuine native hoboes! It's my fascist students you should be giving the bum's rush to! They're the ones jeopardizing municipal tourist revenue!

The Cops eventually recover from their shock and start looking angry. So Sam gets scared and decides to move off.

He looks pretty sheepish at first, but gradually recovers his divine inspiration. Sam's prancing again by the time the crowd swallows him up.

The Cops are left to do their job. Wielding spotless ivory dress-truncheons, they bust several heads, smash up the shanty town, and hustle the poor guys off.

Only one little cardboard bungalow remains standing.

INT. BUM'S HOUSE -- DAY

A DEFORMED BUM squats on his haunches, staring in puzzlement at a needle jammed deep in his arm.

His blood is being harvested by MAMOON, a small, twitchy Bangladeshi.

Dressed in a white lab coat several sizes too big, Mamoon is an assistant radiation effects researcher. He comes equipped with a little black bag such as doctors once used for house calls. The bag clinks with glass vials and hypodermic syringes.

He peeks out a hole in the cardboard wall to see if the cops are gone yet.

EXT. GROUND ZERO -- DAY

Wearing a look of saintly ecstasy, Sam is doing the Boogaloo at the epicenter.

Mamoon catches up and tugs on his coattails. Under Mamoon's arm is a well-stuffed Manila envelope.

SAM

Why, bless my wholesome soul. If it's not the Pakistani radioactivity guy.

MAMOON
Oh, please, Dr. Edwine. Must we go through this every time? It's the Bangladeshi radioactivity guy.

SAM
Who said you could come down from the Mountain of Slow Death?

Mount Hijiyama hulks in the polluted distance.

The Radiation Research Foundation can be seen in the middle of an acid rain-ravaged bamboo grove at the summit. It's a squalid and sinister place, housed in several large dilapidated WWII-vintage Quonset huts.

SAM
Did you bring your locally famous boss, the illustrious Bruiser?

MAMOON
My supervisor's name happens to be Valentina. Nobody but you calls her the Bruiser. And she rarely leaves her lab.

SAM
That makes you the only sane resident of Hiroshima within five blocks of this shindig. Besides me, of course... And I, if you must know, happen to be on a divine mission.

MAMOON
I have a delivery to make on the far side of the park.

SAM
A delivery, eh? And a pick-up, too, I'll just bet. Sucking on radioactive arteries like a bumblebee on flowers.

Sam throws down his fishing tackle and snatches the Manila envelope. Ignoring Mamoon's whimpers of protest, he rips it open and examines the contents.

It's a sheaf of illustrations xeroxed from medical textbooks: gory postmortem photos of botched thoracic and brain surgery.

SAM
Damn! Some kind of ugsome!

MAMOON
Such pictures make Kara-kun's face light up.

SAM
You gene-jammers cherish him, don't you? He's the most exquisitely futuristic mutant this glamorous town has to offer. But you'll never be able to probe his secrets.

MAMOON
Oh, I wouldn't be so sure about that. He's willing to hold still for three minutes or so, in exchange for a stack of postmortems, like those you're holding in your hand.

SAM
Three minutes?
(rolling up the pictures and sticking them in his pocket.)
That's barely long enough to get a syringe unwrapped and his stringy biceps tied off. How frustrating for you... Could you hold this for a second?

He gathers the fishing stuff back up and shoves it into Mamoon's hands, causing him to drop his black bag. The glass vials inside break and dozens of samples slosh out, soaking Ground Zero with mutant blood.

Then Sam moves in on Mamoon, chasing him in circles. Sam reaches down, digs his fingers into the folds of Mamoon's lab coat, and tickles the unfortunate Bangladeshi without a hint of mercy.

Mamoon cringes in an agony of embarrassment. He's so flustered, it doesn't occur to him to drop the pole and worms and defend himself. He can only hold his elbows tight against his sides.

Several dozen assorted LOVERS OF INTERNATIONAL HARMONY gather to stare, unsure as to how they should react to this sight.

MAMOON
Please, Dr. Edwine! In my culture, men don't touch so readily!

SAM
Oh, gee. I didn't know that. I thought this was normal behavior on the subcontinent. I guess I'd better stop doing this, huh? Huh?

Sam stops when he feels like it.

MAMOON
(shakily composing himself)
It's time I kept my appointment with our little friend. The pictures, please.

SAM
Oh. I almost forgot.
(peeking again at the postmortems)
I've got to hand it to you gamma ghouls. Till now he only came ashore to spoil bourgeois weddings.

MAMOON
What's your secret reason for befriending such a specimen, Dr. Edwine? Somehow I can't believe you're running a divine errand for the Christians, or even for your wife.

SAM
My wife? Did you mention my wife, Moony? Don't talk to me about being hen-pecked. You, who dance attendance on the Bruiser for a living.

MAMOON
Her name happens to be --

SAM
I never understood why your country needs radiation researchers in the first place.

MAMOON
We don't want to be caught unprepared for the only disaster that hasn't befallen us yet.

SAM
How prudent of you.

Mamoon is trying to calculate an efficient way to hold the fishing pole and can of worms, from which several specimens are escaping. They crawl up the white sleeve of his lab coat, leaving gray trails. He fails to notice them.

MAMOON
Besides, Valentina gives me free run of the pharmacology lab on Sundays, to do my --
(pausing and leering)
-- private research, so to speak.

SAM
Don't tell me about whatever designer poisons you're cooking up. As a professor at Boom Town U., I'm expected to behave myself. And I only associate with guys who do likewise.

MAMOON
Then take my advice and shun your wife's pew-mate.

SAM
She has several pew-mates. Are we talking about a first-, second- or third-worlder?

MAMOON
We're talking about Hank.

SAM
Oh, sure. Hank's a real wild man, with his perfect ponytail. A creative artist, a savage. Watch out!

A worm has made it all the way up to Mamoon's lapel. Sam eyes it and tries not to laugh. He has to look away.

He squints through the smog at the Radiation Research Foundation.

SAM
Do you really expect that dump to stay standing for 200 years?

MAMOON
That's how many generations of natives we need to study. They don't call it "long-term genetic damage" for nothing. In the meantime, Dr. Edwine, if you'd be so kind as to allow Valentina and me to do our work...

He looks down at his little black bag, which lies in a pool of gore on the ground. He pokes it sadly with the fishing pole, causing the shattered paraphernalia inside to clink.

MAMOON
...maybe we can unearth a few really spectacular mutations here and now. We could get some serious funding for a change. Spacious labs, air conditioning, a proper commissary with a vegetarian menu.

SAM
Altruist.

MAMOON
Please give me the pictures back.

SAM
Nope. Sorry. This is one bloodletting I can prevent. Today you're just going to have to report back to the Bruiser empty-handed. Oh, you're in for such a spanking, Moony. Cruisin' for a bruisin'... Are you done playing with Kay-kay's toys yet?

Sam snatches the fishing gear and hulks off into the crowd, Mamoon's postmortems poking from his pocket.

MAMOON
(shouting)
Don't forget to tell Kara-kun where the pictures came from! Please? Dr. Edwine? Sir?
(lowering his voice)
Thieving infidel dog, Sir. Filthy American imperialist bully bastard swine. Sir.

Mamoon stomps off in the direction of Mount Hijiyama. His little black bag clinks as he goes. He sounds like a midget milkman.

INT. RADIATION RESEARCH FOUNDATION -- SAME DAY

It's a dreary, dank, under-funded institution, olive-drab. The furnishings and filing cabinets look like leftovers from the days of General MacArthur.

Even the various INTERNATIONAL RADIATION RESEARCHERS have a certain mid-1940's sense of style and grooming, as they slink up and down the gloomy corridors.

Ray Conniff's rendition of "Red Roses for a Blue Lady" hisses through cheap monaural speakers nailed to the cobwebby walls.

This is intended to soothe the nerves of the RADIATION VICTIMS who loiter listlessly outside the laboratories, waiting their turn to get poked and prodded. They have been dragged here weekly for the past half-century, for liver biopsies, blood tests and tissue samples.

INT. VALENTINA'S LAB -- DAY

VALENTINA is a fleshy and more-or-less voluptuous citizen of the former Soviet Union. Under her lab coat she has big protuberant middle-aged breasts and wide hips.

She busily flips the air bubbles out of a syringe.

An AGING RADIATION VICTIM hovers over his RETARDED SISTER, who is strapped down on a gurney. She squirms and hoots as he tries to calm her with a soft folk song, gently tapping time on her shoulder.

Oblivious to the Retarded Sister's cries, Valentina draws what seems like an excessive amount of blood. She labels the vial, and places it on the shelf among countless other vials, many of them labeled "K.K."

Mamoon shows up and quietly tries to stow his little black bag under a table, but its clinking catches Valentina's attention.

VALENTINA
No, no. You show me.

Trembling, Mamoon empties the bag on the table. He has no blood samples to show, only scabby glass splinters.

VALENTINA
So, you come up dry, little man? You dare penetrate my personal space empty-handed?

EXT. RIVERBANK BORDER OF PEACE PARK -- DAY (INTERCUT)

Kara-kun's frayed mooring line is lassoed around a utility pole. It straggles over the azalea bushes on the levee, and droops down through the mud to Kara-kun's raft, which looks like a load of trash and wood scraps bound for a bonfire upstream.

Sam crashes through the azaleas and proudly holds up his three gifts for Kara-kun: the can of worms, the bamboo fishing pole, and the sheaf of stolen postmortems.

Kara-kun dashes up the embankment and makes a beeline for the pictures. He peers at them, making compassionate sounds in the base of his throat. He strokes the pages, puts a tragic look on his face, and holds them up for Sam to share.

SAM
What's-his-name wasn't kidding. You really do like splatter-shots, don't you? Well, I'm delighted to be the one who was thoughtful enough to xerox them for you. They come from me. From Sam.

He writes those last two words on the envelope and tries to persuade Kara-kun to look at them and repeat them.

SAM
F-R-O-M S-A-M. Not the little man in the white coat who comes off the dark mountain. Stay away from him. He's so mean and dangerous...

INT. VALENTINA'S LAB -- (INTERCUT)

Mamoon is ashamed to look in his supervisor's eyes. He's like a little schoolboy confessing to Mommy that the bullies stole his lunch money. He flinches, expecting to be cuffed on the side of the head.

VALENTINA
Where are the pictures? You gave them to the moron and got nothing in return?

EXT. THE RAFT -- (INTERCUT)

Sam follows Kara-kun down into his floating home.

The raft's superstructure has been improvised from cardboard boxes and discarded tatami mats, rescued from mulch piles and slapped on the deck.

INT. THE RAFT -- DAY

It's a shadowy, smoky enclosure, with some chinks in the makeshift walls that let in a little light and air.

Having scooped a handful of mud off the bank before entering, Kara-kun is pasting up his new gory xeroxes.

MAMOON (VO)
(whining)
The big American took them away from me.

In the corner, Ishida-san's lovely golden cigar lighter is enshrined on a beer crate, surrounded by hundreds of burning jasmine joss sticks.

SAM
This place looks just like my bedroom back in high school. Same basic style of decor. Smells like it, too. Where'd you get all the hip incense?

As if in reply, Kara-kun squats before his shrine and makes the sign of the cross.

KARA-KUN
Bod-dy Chris'! Blood-dy Chri-i-is'!

SAM
Oh, you naughty boy! You snitched it from the sacristy, didn't you? Terrible little rapscallion, looting the sanctuary...

Sam picks up a joss stick, which burns his fingers. He drops it on the deck.

It bounces against several small plastic bags of yellowish crystalline powder stacked in a suspiciously neat pyramid against the wall.

INT. VALENTINA'S LAB -- (INTERCUT)

With a contemptuous grunt, Valentina turns her back on Mamoon.

He eventually gathers his nerve back up.

He sidles up to a stainless steel tray full of medical paraphernalia and blood-splotched cotton squares, like piles of tiny rising-sun flags. He snatches a couple ampules of something that looks like egg nog.

Valentina stands nearby, watching his every move through the corner of one eye, meanwhile testing the edge of a scalpel on her thumb.

Mamoon sneaks out of the room.

Valentina watches him go, and smiles fondly at his naughtiness. Then she closes in again on the Retarded Sister, this time for a hefty tissue sample.

INT. PHARMACOLOGY LAB -- DAY

Mamoom spasms among pyrex beakers and Bunsen burners. He mixes the contents of the stolen ampules with other noxious-looking materials.

He pulls a bowl of yellowish crystalline powder from a microwave oven, and begins spooning the illegal-looking stuff into small plastic bags, for retail distribution. It's the same stuff we see on the raft.

INT. THE RAFT -- (INTERCUT)

Puzzled, Sam takes out his own cigarette lighter to help him see the stack of little bags more clearly through the gloom.

By the light of the flame, we see that Kara-kun's walls are completely papered over with Mamoon's medical textbook illustrations.

Sam surveys this gallery of death in appalled amazement.

INT. PHARMACOLOGY LAB -- (INTERCUT)

Seated on a stool near Mamoon is Hank, the self-proclaimed Chairman of the Angler's Education Committee. He's flipping through a pile of photographs of Hiroshima's homeless people. He selects one in particular to wave gleefully in Mamoon's face.

MAMOON
(taken aback)
Please tell me you're not --

HANK
(laughing)
It's interesting. We're employing Pavlovian means, or whatever that's called.

The photo is of Kara-kun on his raft.

INT. THE RAFT -- DAY

Kara-kun is trying to steal Sam's cigarette lighter.

SAM
What are you, a man or a magpie? Don't be so greedy. It's just a disposable. See? Not even shiny.

Kara-kun collapses into a dejected heap and whimpers.

SAM
Okay, okay. Here.

Sam's attention has been distracted from the bags. He follows Kara-kun out onto the deck --

EXT. KARA-KUN'S RAFT -- DAY

-- and allows the bomb baby a few minutes to frolic in the smoggy sunshine with his new toy.

SAM
Now, before we begin our first fishing lesson, allow me to explain why it would be desirable to learn to hold this bamboo pole in such and such a way.

But Kara-kun is not listening. He squats and begins to scratch the mud away from certain flat stones on the riverbank, revealing the scorched silhouettes of carp skeletons in terminal agony.

SAM
I'll be damned! X-rays! So this must be the place where the river got blasted away. Is this where your poor neighbors fell for the old Red Sea ruse?

On the opposite bank, STREET URCHINS are gathering and cat-calling. They try to torment Kara-kun by pitching one-yen pieces into the water like tiny skipping stones, and daring him to dive for them.

Working-class GROWN-UPS join in on the fun. Copper fives and tens come sailing across.

SAM
(yelling)
Why are you worthless lowbrows trying to tease him?

FIRST GROWN-UP
Call it a protest against the consumption tax!

SECOND GROWN-UP

Yeah! If all our loose change is in the hands of idiots, there's no way the government can scrape another three percent of the flesh off our bones!

With a bribe of a handful of silver from Sam, Kara-kun is able to withstand the temptation.

So the Street Urchins and the Grownups shift tactics. They tear pages from a luridly sadomasochistic comic book, wad them up, and toss them into the river.

THIRD GROWN-UP

If money doesn't get a plunge out of the monkey, the manga never fail! He loves pictures of pain!

Finally seduced, Kara-kun wades out into the water.

SAM

Come back to the raft, Huck-san!

EXT. THE RAFT -- SEVERAL HOURS LATER

They haven't moved an inch. The fishing pole lies idle in the mud; the worms have escaped from the can; and Sam sits on the deck with his elbows on his knees, his head cradled dejectedly in his hands. Almost the entire afternoon has passed without a single line being cast.

EXT. A JETTY, NOT FAR UPRIVER -- LATE AFTERNOON

A banner can be seen unfurling. It reads:

ANNUAL LANTERN-FLOATING CEREMONY

DIGNITARIES of the liberal persuasion from all over the world are showing up with their personal VIDEO CREWS and retinues of TOADIES and PRESS AGENTS.

They hold silent prayer vigils and offer photo opportunities. Squatting on the bunting-festooned jetty, they launch lit candles in tiny, colorful floating lanterns, in order to secure a lasting world peace.

A NEWS CREW from a local TV station captures everything.

SOUND MAN

Wouldn't the lanterns be more effective if they were launched after dark?

CAMERAMAN

Sure. But then we couldn't get such excellent shots of these foreigners' solemn profiles. Aren't their noses wonderful?

The floating lanterns blunder a few feet downstream into the gathering gloom, and get mired in a miniature doldrum on the far bank. One lantern capsizes, setting the oily surface of this puddle faintly, bluishly ablaze.

Kara-kun appears from nowhere, delightedly vocalizes, and leaps in to bathe himself in fire.

The Dignitaries upstream shy back from the jetty when they hear Kara-kun babbling in the shadows.

SAM (OS)

Kara-kun tempura!

EXT. THE RAFT -- LATE AFTERNOON

Sam is lounging on the deck.

SAM

Does it bring back memories? Fifty years ago today, was your mommy's womb-water boiling like that? I think I'm beginning to understand what my wife's pew-mates see in you, my pal.

Kara-kun splashes awhile happily. But then his skewed eyes look out across the river.

Hundreds of flickering flames are descending upon him, more floating lanterns. This is too much fire even for a bomb baby.

He makes panicky sounds in the base of his throat and clambers up the embankment to hide in the bulrushes.

SAM
Oh, I forgot. This is your annual night to sleep ashore, isn't it?

Kara-kun responds only with whimpers.

SAM
Relax, will you? I never understood why you get so upset every year. All we have to do is position ourselves upstream. I'll show you. Let's row awhile, toward my place, and the fire will go away from us.

But Kara-kun hesitates to come out.

SAM
It must be like a recurring nightmare for you. This one night keeps rolling around every year, when your home seems to break out in flames... But you have to eat a little supper before bedtime. Otherwise your tummy might growl and give you bad dreams about unlucky ghosts and devils. Come back to the raft again. Let's catch us a school of juicy, nutritious rainbow trout before pitching camp. That's why God sent me here with this tackle and trim.

Kara-kun minces through the mud on cringing tiptoes and climbs aboard, rubbing his belly and making hand-to-mouth eating motions.

He pitches the fishing pole like a javelin deep into the shadows.

Together, they shove off from Peace Park. In the deepening evening light they navigate slowly up the lazy river, toward Hiroshima's suburbs.

EXT. OHTAGAWA RIVER -- DUSK

There's no regulation at all on this water, no right of way, not even an agreed-upon side to navigate on.

The wakes of the various craft are tangled together like strands of poorly braided hair.

EXT. THE RIVER, FURTHER UPSTREAM -- DUSK

With Sam's assistance, Kara-kun scavenges for his supper. He pokes among the bulrushes for shoreside carrion. He noses into a few marina dumpsters.

Superstitious NIGHT FISHERMEN occasionally float by and toss him a cold rice ball or two, to propitiate this unlucky spirit. They do double takes at the big foreigner on board.

Sometimes the Night Fishermen offer to tow the raft upstream a little way. Kara-kun casts them his mooring line and the raft is pulled slowly along.

At these times he croons like an angel in heaven. He lies on his belly and dangles his hand in the water.

Sam watches the bomb baby's face in fascination, maybe even in awe.

EXT. RIVERSIDE CONSTRUCTION SITE -- DUSK

Ishida-san's new gambling den is taking shape. A big billboard on the roof reads:

HOME OF THE BRAVE
GRAND OPENING SOON!

As furtively as possible, the Japanese Amateur Archeologist scales a CLANKING chain link fence at the periphery.

He creeps about in the shadows, pries back a couple slabs of reinforced concrete and snoops among the weeds.

He hears the raft being rowed up the river. It heaves into sight, just off the near bank.

Kara-kun, at the oar, notices the trespasser first. Babbling and tugging on Sam's coattails, he makes shoveling motions and happily points at the Archeologist.

Sam looks up and waves.

SAM
(shrieking)
Yoo-hoo! Digger man! Why on earth are you trespassing on the bloodthirsty mobster's property? Do you have a death wish?

KARA-KUN
(imitating Sam)
Igger-bah! Obberty! Bish?

The Archeologist panics. He holds a finger to his lips and makes frantic "shhhhh!" sounds. He dives into the weeds and crawls away before Ishida-San or one of the Thugs can see him.

EXT. HOME OF THE BRAVE -- DUSK

Ishida-san himself stands in the middle of things, personally overseeing the work, an unlit cigar clenched between his lips.

He is proudly showing the place to two AMERICAN AUTO EXECUTIVES, Hank's bosses, one skinny and one fat. Dressed in expensive business suits, they look like potential investors.

Hank hovers between them and Ishida-san, serving as interpreter.

Sam and Kara-kun row slowly by, like Huck Finn and Jim.

SAM
Hank! Ha-a-a-ankie! Hankums! Hoo-hoo! It's a lot easier if you get down on your knees!

Hank pretends the crazy goon on the river is screaming at someone else by that name.

Ishida-san does a slow burn. He stares at the raft and its two strange occupants, particularly Kara-kun, who's sucking on his solid-gold cigar lighter.

Sam stares right back at the crime boss and flips the bird.

He doesn't break eye-contact or lower his middle finger till they row out of sight.

EXT. THE RIVER, FURTHER UPSTREAM -- DUSK

The bomb baby is a bit hungry for dessert. He rubs his belly. So they run the raft aground in the shallows.

He hesitates. Then, with a gentle shove from Sam, he submerges himself and commences cupping up double handfuls of the sluggish minnows.

SAM
See? This night's no different from any other.

Sam lies on his belly on the deck, his chin comfortably cradled in the palms of his hands.

SAM
To hell with it. Right, buddy? To hell with the Fishermen's Union. To hell with Ishida-san and his goons and his pet councilmen. To hell with the churchy crowd and the gamma ghouls. To hell with everybody except us little ones. Eat hardy, Kay-kay, and God bless your half-hatched self.

INT. HIROSHIMA CATHEDRAL ORGAN LOFT -- LATER THAT EVENING

The two American Auto Executives have taken up uncomfortable positions in the Asiatic-sized choir stalls.

They've brought their underling Hank along. He stands.

Father Gaudi has seated himself on the organ bench.

FATHER GAUDI
So, we have a little boycott brewing, do we?

SKINNY AUTO EXECUTIVE
Our wives don't enjoy sharing their place of worship with hardened criminals.

FATHER GAUDI
Oh, I see. It's the hardened ones they don't like. Well, those particular criminals have voluntarily confined themselves to the parking lot.

SKINNY AUTO EXECUTIVE
So far. But what if the pimps decide to come in some Sunday? It's bad enough that our wives have to risk catching AIDS from sharing the communion cup with whores.

FATHER GAUDI
Excuse me, but I don't like the way your upper lip curled when you said "pimps" and "whores." In our efforts to survive, we all contribute to the defilement of this world, don't we?

Father Gaudi gestures across the loft railing at the interior of the cathedral. Automotive smog fills even this indoor space.

FAT AUTO EXECUTIVE
Great. A green priest. That's all we need.

FATHER GAUDI
Everybody, except your wives, heartily welcomes the Filipinas to church each week. And nobody -- again with the exception of your lovely wives -- has objected to learning The Lord's Prayer in Tagalog.

FAT AUTO EXECUTIVE
A birds-and-bees type. Never read the verse about being fruitful and subduing the god-damned earth.

FATHER GAUDI
Most of the parishioners don't get a chance to subdue anything. They're too busy being subdued themselves by men like you.

FAT AUTO EXECUTIVE

A god-damned lefty to boot! Where'd you say you're from?

FATHER GAUDI

(proudly)

I am Catalonian.

FAT AUTO EXECUTIVE

Where's that? Central America, right? What are you, one of those Liberation Theologians?

SKINNY AUTO EXECUTIVE

(in a stereotype Mexican accent)

Padre no been home to the hacienda for long, long time. Not since before us gringos nuked Boom Town.

FATHER GAUDI

(ignoring that and rising to his feet)

I can tell you that they are simmering inside, many members of our congregation. They're boiling with outrage against the feudal-minded culture in which they find themselves submerged every day of their exiled lives --

SKINNY AUTO EXECUTIVE

Every day except Sunday. Or at least those Sundays when no gangster weddings are scheduled overhead.

FAT AUTO EXECUTIVE

Oh, yeah. I heard about those high-tone bashes. No wonder the great Gaudi can afford to turn his nose up at our wives' offerings. He's got Nip Mafiosos for sugar daddies.

FATHER GAUDI

(gaining momentum)

As for the pimps, as you call them: is it possible to name anybody in greater need of grace than those men? Every day

of my life I pray that they may
overcome their superstitious fears and
descend the steps; that they may sit in
our little chapel and listen to us sing
and watch how we pray.

He looms over the Americans.

FATHER GAUDI

And, after I beseech God to provide
this small miracle, sometimes I even
remember to ask that you gentlemen, and
your associates, will follow on the
pimps' heels, your hats in your hands,
your eyes downcast in utter humility!

SKINNY AUTO EXECUTIVE

(overwhelmed)

Maybe we should make an appointment
with the Bishop.

The Americans retreat from the loft.

Hank hangs back long enough to flip a delighted thumbs-up, to which the priest does not respond.

EXT. CATHEDRAL SIDE GATE -- NIGHT

Two black stretch limousines are waiting. The first contains Ishida-san, who gets out, greets the two Auto Executives, and directs them to the second limo.

Hank rushes ahead and struggles with a THUG CHAUFFEUR for the privilege of opening the door for his bosses.

He succeeds, and reveals a GOLDEN-EYED GIRL and another bewildered PUBESCENT FILIPINA, huddled and quaking in the vast back seat. Before the Auto Executives close in on them, they crane their necks to get a glimpse of God's house.

FAT AUTO EXECUTIVE

(climbing in and panting)

You ladies smell pretty tonight. Clean
as a whistle. Just like a breath of
fresh air, after that church. Stank
like bent tacos in there.

When he lays hands on the Golden-Eyed Girl, she screams in revulsion, shoves him away, and bolts out the door.

She pushes past Ishida-san, who is waiting on the sidewalk, according to the cordial Japanese custom, ready to wave and bow until the honored patrons drive out of sight.

His face inscrutable, Ishida-san gives a nod of the head to a FLEET-FOOTED THUG riding shotgun in the Americans' limo.

The Fleet-Footed Thug chases the Golden-Eyed Girl about half a block, and stops her with a flying tackle. She screams again as her beautiful face scrubs into broken glass and gravel in the gutter.

SKINNY AUTO EXECUTIVE
Looks like that one's out of commission for the night. We're going to have to double up now. I hope this means we get a fifty-percent discount.

Ishida-san pretends not to hear that. He walks into the cathedral's side gate.

INT. HIROSHIMA CATHEDRAL -- NIGHT

The Lieutenant makes sure the place is secure before his boss enters.

Ishida-san comes in by the chancel door. He climbs the spiral staircase to the loft, and seats himself next to Gaudi on the organ bench. No greetings are exchanged. The mood is oddly intimate.

Ishida-san has brought a photo of his younger daughter.

ISHIDA-SAN
I'm sure you know, Priest, how hard it is to marry off Hiroshima girls. Genetic damage and so forth --

FATHER GAUDI
You are starting to cut into my free time, Ishida-san.

ISHIDA-SAN
-- but I managed to find her a real stand-up guy. Unlike her big sister, this girl is life to me. She's my beautiful princess. All her classmates had authentic weddings. Why should she be left out?

FATHER GAUDI
Let's get to the point, shall we? Kara-kun crawls over the embankment for one reason only. He has made a lifetime hobby of spoiling weddings in this cathedral. Yours was far from the first. Over the past generation he has infuriated every rich family in town at least once.

ISHIDA-SAN
Do you blame us for getting mad? That animal ruins the authentic mood of this hall --

We see the concrete walls, cheap abstract-expressionist stained glass, various inept depictions of Christ on the cross, etc.

ISHIDA-SAN
This stuff really impresses us Japanese. The kids today are nuts about authentic weddings. My beautiful princess has got to have one... You better cure your mascot of his bad habits before the time comes, or else.

FATHER GAUDI
Or else what?

ISHIDA-SAN
(pretending not to hear the question)
Have you noticed how kids these days got no religion, no respect the beliefs of their elders? Teenaged bikers aren't nearly as finicky as my men about mixing it up with an evil spirit.

FATHER GAUDI

Oh, come now, Mr. Ishida. A beating will have no effect on his behavior. This little one's mind can't associate causes with effects. You know that as well as I. His consciousness floats like an empty sushi box in a river. He's almost as bad as an American.

ISHIDA-SAN

I don't sympathize with that kind of mental laziness. I'm a businessman, the hardest worker in this workaholic town.

FATHER GAUDI

Yes, and thanks to your hard work, the city council will soon take Kara-kun's raft away. So he'll probably start attending receptions and rehearsals as well.

Ishida-san is filled with rage. He forces himself to stay calm.

ISHIDA-SAN

Do you know where this animal spends his nights?

EXT. RIVERSIDE DRIVING RANGE -- NIGHT

Hundreds of Japanese BUSINESSMEN are practicing golf shots from three tiers.

Their drives almost never make it to the far net, where Kara-kun has established his secret campsite.

He is bedding down for the night, wrapping himself in the lower billows and seams of the green net. He vanishes into greenness.

The raft is moored to the nearby bushes.

Sam lies flat on his back on the deck, fiddling with Kara-kun's crooked oar, waving it through the air like Toscanini's baton.

Directly across the Ohtagawa is a mammoth apartment building with purple plastic balconies.

Polly stands on a sixth-floor balcony. She holds out into space a large piece of sushi. It features a dollop of chartreuse horseradish peeking out from under a generous chunk of purple squid tentacle.

POLLY
(calling into the distance)
Suppertime, Sammy!

EXT. WEALTHY RESIDENTIAL NEIGHBORHOOD -- NEXT DAY

The hillside houses of the local rich are splendid, if scaled down by American standards.

We glimpse emerald-green back gardens between white stone walls. From the windows of adolescents' bedrooms, the most antisocial rock music can be heard -- but it's turned down to a furtive whisper.

A city bus pulls up and expels several Filipina DOMESTIC SERVANTS, arriving for work in the surrounding homes. They are not young or attractive enough to be forced into prostitution like their sisters. But their exhausted appearance makes it clear that they're being exploited in other ways.

Mamoon, the radiation effects researcher, follows these poor women off the bus. He totes his clinking black bag.

On his heels is IMELDA. She's a fat middle-aged Filipina who looks and acts a lot like Imelda Marcos. She wears a vulgarly sequined dress, the same shade of pale turquoise which swathes figurines of the Virgin Mary in Catholic churches. Her feet are pinched into the kind of spike heels favored by streetwalkers.

Imelda can barely lumber off the bus, so Mamoon is forced to hold her elbow, much to his distaste.

Slouching by are some of the High School Students who passed Peace Park on their way to the cram school. Buttoned up in their woolen uniforms, burdened with enormous book bags, they look far too haggard and cynical for their tender age.

They're coming up the hill, from the direction of the river.

IMELDA
(suppressing a smile)
Poor dears. They're allowed so little pleasure in their lives.

A few of the High School Students duck behind a bush for several seconds. They come out again, wiping their noses and looking much more chipper.

Mamoon watches them approvingly. Then he leads Imelda down the incline, in the direction the Teens came from.

EXT. OHTAGAWA RIVERBANK -- DAY

Mamoon and Imelda sneak into a bamboo grove, where Kara-kun's raft has been run aground in the mud. The bomb baby himself is squatting on the deck, and seems to be waiting for them.

Mamoon pulls out a fresh batch of gory pictures and waves them in Kara-kun's face, like a bone for a spaniel.

Kara-kun is pleased, and grabs the gift. In a grotesque caricature of gallantry, he offers his elbow to Imelda.

She looks like she'd rather handle worms, but accepts the offer, anyway, because she can hardly walk in the mud.

The three of them go inside the raft's superstructure, Imelda tiptoeing unsteadily. Mamoon watches his step, and tries to touch as little as possible. Unlike Sam, he is disgusted by Kara-kun's home.

After a few minutes Mamoon comes out on deck. He is placing wads of banknotes and vials brimfull of fresh ruby-red blood into his black bag.

Imelda soon follows, wiping her face and looking as though she needs to barf.

IMELDA
(snatching at the money)
Some of that belongs to me.

EXT. YAKUZA OFFICE -- A FEW SUNDAYS LATER

It's a two-story hub of organized crime, located blatantly in a lower-middle-class residential neighborhood.

A patrol car makes a U-turn rather than pass by this building, as dozens of Thugs brazenly punch in and out with bags full of drug money and crates of handguns. Ishida-san has the cops so firmly in his pocket that discretion is not necessary.

Some HOUSEWIVES are gathered around a laundry line next door.

FIRST HOUSEWIFE
(almost shouting)
This street is getting very busy lately, isn't it, ladies?

The others all concur, very loudly.

Meanwhile their HUSBANDS slink off to the driving range with golf bags, eyes fearfully averted from the Thugs.

Father Gaudi, dressed in his full-length black cassock, approaches the front door. He gently confronts the SENTRY, who's big and tough, but reluctant to face the old priest.

Father Gaudi touches his arm. After a silent moment, the Sentry's eyes fill with tears, and he stands aside.

INT. BACK ROOM -- DAY

Half a dozen Filipinas and Transvestites are crowded on the floor. All of them are suffering terribly from the injuries and diseases associated with the sick sex which native customers force them to perform.

Father Gaudi walks in and takes a look around. He does a double take at a shadowy figure propped in the corner. At first glance, it looks just like Kara-kun.

But it's actually the FLAME DANCER (the Small Transvestite's burnt baby brother). Tiny, blackened, ragged, babbling softly in delirium, he looks and sounds very much like the bomb baby.

Nobody is nursing any of these wretched young people.

Father Gaudi reaches into the high collar of his robe and pulls out a silver locket. He removes sacred bread and works his way around the room, slipping the sacrament into gasping mouths.

FATHER GAUDI
Body of--

INT. ANOTHER BACK ROOM -- DAY

IMELDA
Body of Christ, eh, Love?

Imelda is holding down the Golden-Eyed Girl with one hand, and trying to gag her with the other.

IMELDA
This is as close as you're getting to communion for a long time.

Unbathed and untreated, the Golden-Eyed Girl is barely recognizable through her cuts and contusions.

GOLDEN-EYED GIRL
I'm sorry, Den Mother, I'm sorry! I won't run again! It's just that the old American smelled so bad, like poisonous gas! I couldn't help it, I couldn't breathe!

The sound of some non-sidelined Filipinas practicing a hymn comes sweetly down the corridor.

IMELDA
Hear your older sisters' music? They sing for you. They've been through this, and I as well, and we survived. You will, also. It's part of the burden of being a grown-up lady. So don't spoil their song with unhappy sounds from your own throat. Bite this rag.

GOLDEN-EYED GIRL
But I want to pray to the Blessed Virgin for forgiveness. Please, Den Mother, may I?

IMELDA
Of course, Love. And I'll join you.

As they say the Lord's Prayer together in Tagalog, Ishida-san's Lieutenant approaches very slowly from the opposite corner, his stockinged feet whistling along the quaintly traditional tatami mats. Over his head he swings a stout bamboo rod.

The closer he gets, the wider the Girl's eyes grow. She's going to start screaming any moment.

IMELDA
There, there. It's not quite as much fun as running down the sidewalk in the night like a wild puppy-dog. But it's better than being back in our homeland, isn't it? Be strong now, and the old man might not have you deported.

Even while struggling to insert the rag, Imelda modestly averts her eyes. Her role model is the Virgin Mary, after all. She gazes soulfully out the window.

IMELDA
Come now, bite down on this rag. It's better than chewing your tongue off. And we wouldn't want to bother the neighbors.

She can see Father Gaudi taking his leave. He pauses to make the sign of the cross on the forehead of the Sentry, who still weeps.

IMELDA
(to the Lieutenant)
Okay, okay Godzilla, you made your point. Hurry up and get this Jezebel chastised. It's almost time for mass.

EXT. HIROSHIMA CATHEDRAL COMPOUND -- LATER THAT DAY

A wedding rehearsal is being conducted on this Sunday afternoon.

The Filipinas and the Transvestites are gathered around the Yakuza vans, singing their hymn.

Their TODDLERS bounce around in the drivers' seats, twist the steering wheels and beep the horns. The Thug drivers are nowhere to be seen.

A big spider has strung a web across the baby abandonment drawer. Dead black butterflies hang there. It has not been used for some time.

INT. CRYPT CHAPEL -- DAY

Father Gaudi gingerly inserts a consecrated wafer between the enameled lips of Imelda.

FATHER GAUDI
Body of Christ.

IMELDA
(chomping and burping)
Amen.

The usual Foreigners, including Hank, Polly and the Japanese Amateur Archeologist, are seated in their regular places.

Only the Auto Executives' Wives are absent. They have been driven away, and Thugs have taken over the front pew.

These are the same guys who wore rental tuxes at the previous wedding, and reluctantly chased Kara-kun.

Now they sport their customary crass mobster-style outfits and lounge around, comfortable as Christians. They seem pretty confident that the "unlucky spirit" will not be showing up today to scare them away.

A PLAYFUL THUG rises to his feet, sneaks up from behind, and pinches Imelda's big butt.

In response, she folds her hands over her matronly bust and raises her sopping eyes to the ceiling. She is doing an excellent impression of the saccharine painting of the Blessed Virgin scotch-taped to the concrete wall.

Imelda rises from the communion rail, genuflects, and turns to join the Thugs in the front pew.

FIRST FOREIGNER
Why does this greasy crone get to come in, and not the lovely young Filipinas?

SECOND FOREIGNER
It's the privilege of rank. She's the recruiter. She lures her little sisters out of the jungle with promises of legitimate work in the land of golden opportunity.

THIRD FOREIGNER
Chunky broad finally shows her face.

SECOND FOREIGNER
What's to stop her? She has all the bodyguards she needs, squatting right next to her.

A few Thugs kneel at the communion rail, and refuse to scoot over for the Foreigners. They open their mouths wide and arch their backs like trained seals at a marina, expecting to be offered a slug of nice wine.

But Father Gaudi just gives them the same tender forehead blessing he gives to sentries and babies.

THIRD FOREIGNER
While the cat's away...

FIRST FOREIGNER
Why don't they unlock their Sherman tanks and let the girls come in and be treated like human beings for forty-five minutes or so?

SECOND FOREIGNER
Think of the degrading acts the Filipinas must perform every night.

Feeling human cuts into the quality of
their work.

In the back of the crypt, some MUSCULAR YOUNG FOREIGNERS are removing their Sunday-best blazers and murmuring anti-Japanese sentiments in each others' ears.

The Nigerian acolyte nudges Father Gaudi, who looks up and sees a brawl brewing. He mounts the pulpit and clears his throat, bringing the place to order.

At the communion rail, the Thugs turn around and sit on the purple velvet knee-cushions, facing the congregation.

FATHER GAUDI
My friends, before our customary social hour gets underway, allow me to say one thing. I will speak over our guests' heads, as they're the only ones present who have no English... Please try to remember that these poor fellows fit no better into the mainstream than we do. So, even though they are indigenous to the region -- and even though we all love to Japan-bash from time to time -- let us try to tolerate their presence. Still better, let us welcome them as lovingly as we can.

FIRST FOREIGNER
Fine, but why isn't the Pimp-of-Pimps down here to bask in our snuggly love? Is he too good for our company?

SECOND FOREIGNER
Or just too busy destroying people's lives?

ARCHEOLOGIST
No. Ishida-San's too busy destroying the past.

HANK
What's that supposed to mean?

ARCHEOLOGIST
(singing)
O'er the land of the freeeeee, and the...

HANK
Been there.

ARCHEOLOGIST
The warlord who founded Hiroshima four hundred years ago kept his harem on that very spot. The soil bristles with priceless, sexy relics.

VARIOUS FOREIGNERS
Well, banzai to that! ... Bastard's a real patriot...

HANK
So, Gaudi, is that why the Godfather doesn't hang out with us? Because he's too busy burying Japan's proud cultural heritage under slabs of concrete?

FATHER GAUDI
Let's just say that, unlike his followers, Ishida-san instinctively knows that a non-believer shouldn't come too close to Christ's body and blood.

Father Gaudi gently slaps a Thug's hand away from the sacramental wine.

POLLY
(standing)
Speaking of blood, if anybody's still interested, I have my husband's first and, I guess, final report to the Angler's Education Committee. I've been assuming the committee was dissolved, by default, so to speak...

She looks pointedly at the Thugs and Imelda, and unfolds a scribbled-upon doughnut wrapper from her pocket.

POLLY
...but I might as well present Sammy's report to you now.
(reading aloud)
"Fish-hooks are too dangerous. The stupid little prick pokes himself."

FATHER GAUDI
So, the subject of Kara-kun has been officially broached...

Imelda, who has absorbed every word of the discussion so far, falls to her knees in feigned prayer so she can pretend not to listen to the rest.

FATHER GAUDI
You all seem to have figured it out by now. Our small, strange friend has finally fulfilled everybody's worst expectations, and vanished.

CANADIAN GIRL
What about contacting the proper authorities?

Everyone laughs at that suggestion.

SECOND FOREIGNER
Honey, you just try to get the Hiroshima fuzz interested in a transient on the slowest day of the year.

HANK
I move to reconvene the Anglers' Education Committee!

He meets little difficulty getting the motion seconded.

POLLY
Sammy has no time to conduct a man-hunt. He's a professor --

HANK
Exactly. He has more time than he knows what to do with. Besides, he knew Kara-kun better than anybody.

VARIOUS FOREIGNERS
Hear, hear!... Man-hunt, man-hunt!

Without comprehension, but cheerfully, the Thugs join in.

POLLY
(to Hank)
..."knew" Kara-kun?

HANK
(smirking)
Sorry.

The Nigerian acolyte props the fake silk screen in front of the altar. With a sigh, the social hour gets halfheartedly rolling.

The Thugs remain seated on the communion rail knee cushions, silently chain smoking. They watch Imelda trying to socialize like a normal Catholic society matron.

Nobody will talk to her, or even stand near her. Like a madwoman, she gossips and titters into empty space.

EXT. HIROSHIMA CATHEDRAL PARKING LOT -- DAY

Sam is snoring, as usual, in the death seat of the Mazda.

As Yakuza gum wrappers sail through the open window to collect on his lolling tongue, he has a nightmare...

INT. CRYPT CHAPEL -- NIGHT (DREAM)

Like a Satanist coven, the Foreigners squat in vulgar positions around the altar.

They yowl this cannibal hymn:

CONGREGATION
Pluck forth thy royal diadems.
Pluck forth thy locks entwined within.
Pluck forth from radiant brows the flesh
which pads the seams where head-bones mesh.

The Archeologist rummages among a treasure trove of sacred objects on the floor. He comes up shouldering a golden shovel.

CONGREGATION
Pry back thy scalp like fecund sod.
Expose thy rank farm's protein pods.
Chip free thy skull, let marrow drain,
Till one gray tegument remains.

Imelda climbs onto the altar with amorous intentions. She gropes the crucifix.

CONGREGATION
And when thy brain is amply shown,
and naught is left of skin and bone...

Father Gaudi has an insane look on his face. He wields a crude ceramic chalice.

CONGREGATION
...then serve thyself to Christus
Rex...

It sloshes with gobs of human gore.

CONGREGATION
...or suffer our collective hex.

EXT. CATHEDRAL PARKING LOT -- DAY

The Mazda convulses on its worn-out shocks as Sam lurches awake from this horrible vision. He sticks his face out the window, gasping for air, his whole body throbbing with panicked heartbeat.

Now we know why he sleeps in the car on Sunday instead of joining his wife in the crypt.

EXT. RIVERSIDE CONSTRUCTION SITE -- NIGHT

Work is being done around the clock, to realize Ishida-san's dream as quickly as possible.

Covering the fresh facade of his new gambling den is a bright array of neon lights, which reads --

HOME OF THE BRAVE

In the shadows at the periphery, the Archeologist turns over a few shovelfuls of mud, and does indeed discover a piece of ancient pottery.

No longer caring if he is seen trespassing, he pockets his find and treks out across the construction area, toward a large house trailer.

On its front awning is hung the sinister-looking emblem of Ishida-san's underworld organization, big and conspicuous in the artificial light.

EXT. HOUSE TRAILER -- NIGHT

The Lieutenant sits on the front stoop, chatting with a couple of teen biker PUNKS. They wear purple and green spike hairdos, brown lipstick, and buttock-exposing cutaway leather jeans. On the backs of their jackets is emblazoned the name of their motorcycle gang:

THE KELOID KROWD

When the Archeologist comes striding suddenly out of the night, the Lieutenant knocks him flat on his back and removes the contents of his pockets.

He passes the ancient artifact through the trailer window to Ishida-san, who has pulled back the curtain in mild curiosity.

ARCHEOLOGIST
(voice muffled under the Lieutenant's shoe)
Bribe me generously, or I go public with that pot shard and all work ceases around here!

Ishida-san nods his head gently at the Lieutenant, and retires from the window.

The razor-sharp blade of an exquisitely-crafted Samurai knife glints in the artificial light.

LIEUTENANT
(to the two Punks)

See now, you don't just jab straight on like this. His sternum gets in the way...

When the tip of the knife CLICKS against the Archeologist's breast bone, he looks more surprised than pained.

INT. HOUSE TRAILER -- NIGHT

It's a lavishly appointed place, complete with black-velvet paintings of golden-eyed tigers, a bar, and even a fake European-style fireplace with a deep mantelpiece.

As the lecture-demonstration continues outside, Ishida-san settles himself comfortably in a green leather armchair. He examines the pot shard.

LIEUTENANT (OS)
This is the angle, between these two ribs. Slice in, pretty hard, to get through those muscle fibers, and then up... You don't have to be so polite about it! I mean really up! Try again... Okay now, watch his eyes. Count to ten...

Ishida-san stands, crosses his office, and arranges his new curio attractively on his ersatz mantelpiece. He steps back, squints his eyes, and tilts his head, to check the effect in this particular angle of light.

LIEUTENANT (OS)
...See that? The life goes out at a relaxed pace, and he sort of snuggles into himself with a sigh, like a tired baby at bedtime. That's because you just sliced his left ventricle in two, in the efficient and effective manner of our proud Samurai ancestors.

FIRST PUNK (OS)
With his eyes bugged out like that, and that beard, he looks just like a foreigner.

LIEUTENANT (OS)
It's best not to look at their eyes too much after you've tucked them in. Their soul is looking for a place to hide from the devil, and it might just choose your body... And now, you ignorant punks, I want you to think hard. Under these circumstances, do I even need to ask how we dispose of our handiwork?

Ishida-san hears this last question, breaks into a small, fond smile, and gazes across the site of his future dream palace, at the roaring cement mixer.

EXT. OHTAGAWA RIVER, UPSTREAM SUBURBS -- DAY

Sam Edwine is standing in the stern of a noisy speedboat.

At the wheel is a teenaged Japanese BOATMAN. He sports an oily pompadour that droops over his face.

They speed up and down the rich neighborhoods upstream. Sam lurches from rail to rail, almost capsizing the boat. He is trying to make this man-hunt as conspicuous as possible.

Even on this chaotic river, Sam manages to create a nuisance. He nearly capsizes several small fishing boats with his wake.

SAM
Yoo-hoo, Kara-kun! Kay-kay-e-e-e-e!
Where on earth can the naughty boy be!

He waves and screams at the American Auto Executives' young BABY SITTERS.

These native girls are taking American TODDLERS for a stroll along the bank.

The Toddlers are average examples of their kind. But, to the local way of seeing, their blue eyes and blond hair epitomize everything perfect and lovely.

Every fisherman on the water and every pedestrian on the land stares at them in adoration.

SAM
(shrieking at the Baby Sitters)
Young ladies, do you see me? I am searching high and low for your mistress' muddy mouser! Now will you ask them to get out of my wife's face, please?

The Toddlers laugh at him, but Sam gets no reaction whatever from the Baby Sitters.

They barely raise their eyes. They are modest Japanese virgins of good social class, after all -- which makes it all the more surprising when they abandon the Toddlers and duck into a nearby bamboo grove.

EXT. BAMBOO GROVE -- DAY

A DOPE PEDDLING BUM has parked his rickety bicycle here.

He's one of the sweet old guys who stroked Sam's beard at the A-bomb Golden Jubilee celebration. But he's been corrupted in the meantime.

With hunger in their eyes, the Baby Sitters converge on him and purchase little bags of yellow crystalline powder -- Mamoon's concoction.

EXT. AMERICAN AUTO COMPANY'S R&D FACILITY PIER -- DAY

Sam orders the teenaged Boatman to make several especially obnoxious runs under the balcony of Hank's laboratory.

Hank is standing by the back door, whittling on a futuristic model car, a white lab coat protecting his spiffy brushed denims. His lab seems to be a buzzing hive of automotive creativity.

Through the windows, about a half-dozen Japanese LAB ASSISTANTS can be seen scurrying and scrambling among vats of hi-tech inorganic sculpting plasticine, extra-large computer display terminals, gyroscope-mounted drawing boards, etc.

SAM
Hank! Hankie-e-e! Have you seen Kara-kun, you prick?

(to the Boatman)
Is that all the louder you can rev this bathtub toy?

Sam kicks and dents the chrome exhaust manifold, hoping to jar the already ineffective muffler loose.

But, when Hank comes strolling out onto the pier --

SAM
(to the Boatman)
I changed my mind! Whoa! Steady, big fella! Holding pattern! Stop, for Christ's sake!

The Boatman puts it in idle.

HANK
Edwine? What are you doing up here in the suburbs? You're supposed to be cruising the docks. That's where a bunch of the other homeless types hang out. Kara-kun's probably on a bender with his colleagues.

SAM
(screaming over the outboards)
This teeny-bopper says we can't go to the docks! It's against Ministry of Tourism regulations! The city fathers will lose face if an important foreigner like me sees that the third world is alive and well, right here in Hiroshima!

HANK
Lies.

SAM
(screaming)
Beg-pardon?

Sam nudges his giant knee into the Boatman's spinal column. This persuades him to cut the engines altogether. He tosses a line to Hank, who makes no effort to catch it.

Hank seats himself on the pier.

HANK

I said, your sidekick is just lying through his teeth. You can take that boat wherever the water's deep enough to buoy the props out of the mud. That's the whole point, Edwine. The Angler's Education Committee appointed you to find Kara-kun before the city fathers start regulating river traffic.

SAM

Whatever. Why don't you invite me into your lab for a nice cup of tea or Jack Daniels or something? I'm a fellow American. Where's your hospi-goddamn-tality?

HANK

Top secret things in there. All the dope on next year's models. You could be an industrial spy.

SAM

So I'll give you beers. We've got an on-board ice chest. Join us in our man-hunt, and we'll scour the soggy slums together. Being all alone on a boat with someone like this is creepy.

HANK

I'm afraid I just can't up and desert. I work for industry. I'm involved in the research and development of useful things. Unlike you academic slobs, I have to punch in a certain number of hours each day. So I'll have to take a rain check on your invi --

Suddenly, the sound of loud martial music from the opposite bank cuts Hank off in mid-sentence.

It's the Male College Cheerleaders who we saw earlier at the A-Bomb Golden Anniversary Celebration. They are marching by, on maneuvers.

The thinner UNDERCLASS UNDERLINGS are being forced to trudge barefoot in the mud of the flood plain.

Sam’s Nervous Student straggles among them. He has neither the physical strength nor the emotional energy for this. The boy looks ready to collapse any minute. He pops a handful of his pharmaceutical uppers.

SAM
Smile and wave at the noodle-Nazis, Hankums!

HANK
(appalled)
Who are those horrible boys?

SAM
My campus is infested with them. As a matter of fact, I think I see one of my freshmen over there... Yoo-hoo, Freshboy-san! Have you done your homework?

HANK
Don’t do that! They’ll see us!

The Nervous Student pretends not to see Sam, and tries to disappear into the marching ranks.

The Cheerleaders approach a point directly across the Ohtagawa. To the accompaniment of a mammoth bass drum, they start to scream fascist songs from the thirties and forties.

Hank gets even more panicky. Something about these boys chills him to the marrow. He throws himself flat on his belly on the pier.

HANK
I can’t hear myself breathe!

SAM
Well, Hankie, if you’re sure you don’t want to join us, I guess we’ll be shoving off. Bye now. Take care of yourself.

HANK
You’re not leaving me here!

He leaps into the boat. A true professional, even in his panic, he is able to shout a few Japanese words of highly technical instruction to his native LAB ASSISTANTS, who have meanwhile gathered at the back door.

SAM
(to the Boatman)
Okay! Chart a course for the funkier distributaries!

EXT. OHTAGAWA RIVER -- DAY

They head downstream, weaving and veering in and out of the unregulated traffic, like a damp bumper-car ride.

After the horizon has swallowed up the Cheerleaders, Sam pops a couple beers from the on-board ice chest. Hank gradually regains composure.

The boat passes within sight of Hiroshima University, Sam's place of employment.

A mysterious shoe box-like structure occupies a brown knoll at the edge of the campus. It's the med school's mental health clinic.

HANK
Boom Town U. Loony Bin... You know, of course, Professor, that eventually you're going to have to look in there...

EXT. THE DOCKS -- DAY

We see campsites of Hiroshima's outcasts.

Tucked into every nook and cranny, they're jealously guarding vast, pointless accumulations of junk-wealth: washing-machine cartons bursting with bottle caps, bales of meticulously origamied ice cream wrappers, etc.

Here, too, as in Peace Park, we see some Bums of Kara-kun's age, who got A-bombed inside their mother's bellies and are deformed or mentally retarded.

HANK (VO)
I don't know about the women -- what few specimens there are -- but if the men are away from their families for more than seven months, they're declared legally dead. Juvenile delinquents are free to stomp them to mush and set them on fire, without fear of legal entanglement. And the old folks right here are in particular danger, living as they do on the border of --

The speedboat snuggles beneath a highway overpass.

HANK (VO)
-- Biker Land!

On the bank, the Keloid Krowd, in outlandish punk-derivative garb, are working on their motorcycles and hot rods.

These evil adolescent BIKERS have covered every surface with beautiful graffiti. Skulls and mushroom clouds are spray-painted everywhere with effortless clarity.

INT. KELOID KROWD CLUBHOUSE -- DAY

It's a lean-to built from scrap materials.

With a couple of rusty aluminum rat-tail combs, the two Punks are practicing the Lieutenant's ventricle-stabbing techniques on an aged WINO. So far, they've only succeeded in injuring him.

When they hear the sounds of the speedboat, they abandon their practice and run outside.

EXT. KELOID KROWD CLUBHOUSE -- DAY

The two Punks join their comrades in manning the throttles of their various vehicles. The Keloid Krowd revs in unison, trying to run the speedboat off with a blast of infernal racket from unmuffled engines.

HANK
(shouting over the racket)
I'm told the great Ishida-san recruits his assassins here.

SAM
What, these weenies on their whiny rice burners? Not in a zillion years. Let's go dig up some more honest, burping bums. Gun it!

Nothing happens.

The Boatman is paralyzed with biker-horror. It's necessary to pry his fingers from the steering wheel so Hank can get the boat moving again.

EXT. A BIT FURTHER DOWNSTREAM -- DAY

The Boatman has recovered the use of his body, and he's been ordered to cruise under grimy turnpike bridges.

Behind chain-link fences, on the graveled edges of destitute embankments, the homesteads of HOBOES can be seen.

Sam tells the Boatman to put it in neutral, and they drift awhile. The river has almost no current here.

HANK
Guess what's the leading cause of death among these homeless Japanese. I'll give you a hint. It's not exposure to the elements, and it's not --
(pausing significantly)
dangerous drugs --

SAM
Don't tell me about it. Not a word. I don't want to hear about the schemes you and Mamoon have got cooking.

The idling boat runs aground at the edge of a particularly strange campsite. This space has been staked out by the CAT RANCHER.

He wears thick aviator glasses and a nylon training jacket emblazoned with the legend BEEF-MASTER.

In his shaded spread he possesses two separate herds of one-eyed alley cats, and meters of random weeds strung up and curing over miniature styrofoam bonfires.

The boat sits motionless, while Sam and the Cat Rancher share what feels like a five minute stare-down.

SAM
(to Cat Rancher)
Do you think our Huckleberry friend hopped a freight barge for the balmy coral beaches of Okinawa?

The Cat Rancher makes no reply, but gathers an armload of cats to his breast. Only his tears betray him.

HANK
He's mourning for someone.

SAM
(to Cat Rancher)
You miss Kay-kay, don't you?
(raising his voice to address the neighboring Hoboes)
You all miss him, right?

While Sam sermonizes the huddled masses, Hank leans over the speedboat rail and peers deep into the nooks and crannies of the embankment. He clears his throat loudly, as if cuing someone to come out of hiding.

And, sure enough, Mamoon creeps from behind a pile of discarded futons, toting his little black bag full of blood-collecting paraphernalia.

SAM
(to Hank -- not noticing Mamoon)
These folks need Kara-kun as badly as Calcuttans need Mother Teresa. This is his home and his ministry. Somebody has to bring him back soon.
(noticing Mamoon)
Mamoon, my man! What a surprise! It's almost as though you had an appointment

to meet us here! How's the Bruiser
treating you? Any new welts under those
little britches?

MAMOON
As I've told you many times before, my
supervisor's name happens to be
Valentina. And she never touches me.

He squats down and ties off the Cat Rancher's biceps.

SAM
Don't be coy. I know the pair of you
are whipping up a race of tiny Paki-
Russky hybrids to continue your work
for the next 200 years.

HANK
Make that Bangladeshi-Russky hybrids.

MAMOON
(to the Cat Rancher)
Make a fist, if you would be so kind.
(glancing at Hank)
So, who -- rather, what brings you all
the way down here, Dr. Edwine?

SAM
God sent me to look for your main
source of plasma. I didn't know you had
so many backups, or I wouldn't have
bothered.

MAMOON
Yes, these tidewater transients are
fascinating subjects for liver biopsies
as well. Very promising. I can almost
taste the mutations.

He wrestles with the Cat Rancher, who's not fond of
needles.

MAMOON
And they're much easier to handle than
Kara-kun... Have you found him yet?

SAM

Do you think I'd be floating around with this ponytailed dip-wad if I knew where Hiroshima's real good-time boy was?

MAMOON

I suppose not...

He pokes around inside the Cat Rancher for an artery.

MAMOON

Did you know that the main cause of death among these unfortunate people is not the ingestion of --

HANK

Dangerous drugs. He knows, he knows.

Sam reaches into the on-board ice chest, grabs a sandwich, and tosses it to Mamoon, who catches it with bloody fingers, then drops it.

Two or three BUMS appear, snatch it up, and vanish back into the shadows, fighting over the gory thing.

Sam settles down comfortably on the deck with a couple beers for himself -- the last two. He leans over the boat rail, dangling a few languid fingers in the filthy water.

SAM

Speaking of the good-time boy... The strangest rumors have been circulating among the med students at my university's nut-house. They say Kara-kun was having an affair with an actual woman before his disappearance, a lady Russky who hangs out on top of a certain creepy-crawly mountain near here...

The smog parts briefly in the distance, revealing the Radiation Research Foundation on top of Mount Hijiyama.

SAM

Does that ring a bell or what, Mamoon, my man?

MAMOON

I'm sure the native interns would have no difficulty imagining Valentina alone with him. They are two of a kind, at least from the Japanese point of view: just a couple of irradiated aliens. Her own genetic material was scrambled during two helicopter rides over Chernobyl.

The Boatman is getting restless. He keeps looking back fearfully toward Biker Land. Besides being afraid of the Bikers, he has never been so humiliated in all his life: here he is wasting an afternoon among homeless people and weird foreigners.

He shudders and fidgets so much that the boat works itself frcc from the mud.

Just as Mamoon removes the needle from the Cat Rancher's forearm and stows the blood sample in his black bag, the boat begins to drift.

The conversation continues as the boat slides very slowly down the embankment.

Mamoon strolls alongside, occasionally tripping on a Bum or a pile of trash, stopping only when he comes upon a wretch too weak, drunk, or catatonic to resist being vampirized.

SAM

(to Hank)

Just look at your partner in crime, busily working his way from one wretch to the next. He looks just like Father Gaudi doing the drive-in ministry. Except Gaudi hands out God's flesh instead of stealing the blood of the damned.

HANK

(eager to get back to the point)

The word around the automotive community is that Valentina's interested less in Kara-kun's chromosomes than his white blood cells. She's supposedly been pumping him full

of HIV and sucking whole quarts of
serum from his veins in the name of
AIDS research.

SAM
Oooh! Gracious sakes, no! Bite your
tongue, Hankums!

HANK
Who are you to pooh-pooh these rumors
without checking the woman out first?

SAM
Wait a sec... You want me to check her
out?

The boat gets stuck in a mini-doldrum.

Mamoon takes advantage of the pause to squat down and drain a snickering old BAG LADY. He unwraps a syringe.

SAM
Is this an order? In the sense that my
wife won't be able to pray in peace
unless I obey?

HANK
It's a firm suggestion. Straight from
the mouth of the Chairman of the
Angler's Education Committee.

MAMOON
Valentina has a locked lab all to
herself at the Foundation. She calls it
her "personal space." If you're serious
about unearthing the poor pinhead, it
might be worth your while to insinuate
yourself in there.

SAM
Why don't you? You spend each working
day right under her nose.

Mamoon slaps the old Bag Lady's hand away from his crotch.

MAMOON

That's why it would be hopeless for me to try. She is, I fear, a racist. She treats me as though I'm infected with something even worse than AIDS.

SAM

Like, for example, halitosis?... Come on now! Deliberate HIV injections? The Foundation wouldn't allow their facilities to be used for such ghoulish procedures... Would they?

Mamoon does not reply, but averts his eyes and pokes the Bag Lady hard to make her squeal, as a diversion.

This does not reassure Sam at all. He stands up and paces the deck a bit nervously, rocking the boat out of its doldrum and making it drift again.

To keep up with the Americans, Mamoon has to abandon the Bag Lady, the needle still in her arm.

SAM

(trying to convince himself)

Besides, her results could be skewed by Kara-kun's relationships with those lovey-dovey Christers at the cathedral. The Bruiser could never be certain that he hadn't already been infected.

As he follows alongside the boat, tiptoeing among human refuse, Mamoon exchanges glances again with Hank. The two of them begin closing in on Sam like hyenas stalking a wounded giraffe.

HANK

I guess you're right, Edwine.

MAMOON

He might very well be infected at prayer.

The boat drifts a little faster, and Mamoon trots to keep up.

HANK
But not at play.

MAMOON
For example, dirty needles wouldn't be a consideration.

HANK
Kay-kay's not involved with dangerous drugs.

MAMOON
(beginning to get out of breath)
At least not from a consumeristic standpoint.

Mamoon reaches across the thread of river that separates him from the speedboat, and tosses several small plastic bags of his designer dope on the deck.

MAMOON
(to Hank)
By the way, here are samples of the new batch. And, if I do say so myself, it turned out quite nicely.

HANK
(grinning at Sam)
So, the ice is broken.

SAM
What, you think I'm surprised?

The Boatman helps himself to a bag and turns his back to self-administer the drug.

Sam looks away.

HANK
(to Sam)
Why do you think the kid was willing to float us down here to hell? Call it a tip.

SAM
Are you guys aware of the insane dope laws in this country? Half a joint on

your bathroom floor is the same as a yacht full of heroin. In prison they let you do nothing but sit on the edge of your cot all day. Not even any fun buggery.

Hank and Mamoon leer at each other.

SAM
You guys just keep hinting around. I'm no capitalist, and I have no interest in your enterprise. I'd much rather talk about the chief neck-biter on top of Mount Hijiyama...Do you really think she dorked Kay-kay?

Hank pulls up a deck chair and winds up for some serious coaching. He reaches into his pocket and takes out a snapshot of Valentina.

She's lugging a plastic bag of cheap plum wine out of a downtown Hiroshima Seven-Eleven store.

SAM
(disappointed)
Oh. Not my type...

HANK
You could invite yourself to the Foundation and pretend to interview her for a non-existent weekly back home. Russkies still consider themselves exotic in the free world.

SAM
I'd make a lousy spy. I've got no idea how to ask leading questions and be subtle.

HANK
(eagerly)
So fake it.

SAM
Such enthusiasm, Hankster. It's almost as though you've got your own secret

reasons for wanting me pawed by that
commie broad.

The boat bumps gently into an abandoned trash barge and stops drifting.

The Bag Lady is waddling after Mamoon with a sexy look on her face. She giggles and fingers the hypo that still dangles from her arm.

BAG LADY
(to Mamoon, in Japanese)
You're a little lover-man.

The Boatman, high now, switches on the on-board boom-box. He accidentally turns to a station that features the martial music and fascist songs which the Male College Cheerleaders play and scream.

Hank thinks the horrible boys he fears so much are in the neighborhood. He clings to the rail and nearly has a stroke.

Sam kicks the boom box into the water, where it bubbles and sputters awhile before sinking. Its racket is drowned out by real-life screams coming from further down the embankment.

To Hank's immeasurable relief, it's not the Cheerleaders coming, but another sort of teenager altogether.

A pack of Bikers, including the two Punks, are working their way up the riverbank. They are marauding into the Hoboes' campsites, stomping on everybody and threatening to set them on fire with blowtorches contrived from spray paint cans and cigarette lighters.

The Bikers are being egged on and cheered by the Working-Class Grown-ups who earlier threw money into the river for Kara-kun to fetch.

Mamoon is horrified. With the Bag Lady hanging amorously off him, he tries to scramble on board, dropping his little black bag.

The vials inside shatter. Blood splashes out and stains the embankment.

The Boatman is just as scared as Mamoon. He guns the engine before the Bangladeshi can get in.

Sam and Hank barely avoid being bounced overboard.

Mamoon leaps for it and winds up flat on his face in the mud, choking on a black cloud of outboard exhaust, the Bag Lady cackling and rolling on top of him.

The boat takes off. Mamoon is left behind, screaming to be rescued.

Hank is laughing.

EXT. RIVERSIDE CONSTRUCTION SITE -- SAME DAY

As usual, Ishida-san is personally overseeing the work on his new gambling parlor.

A van backs into the construction site and pulls up behind him.

THUG DRIVER
(sticking his head out the window)
Um, Boss? We got one on the way out.

Ishida-san continues watching the WORKMEN do whatever they were doing before this interruption. After a while he turns and nods to his Lieutenant, who deals with the problem.

LIEUTENANT
(peering into the back of the van)
Which one is it this time?

THUG DRIVER
What, you don't recognize him? A little too well-done on that side, I guess.

The Lieutenant is not prepared to exchange banter with a mere driver.

THUG DRIVER
It's the littlest cross-dresser's baby brother.

LIEUTENANT
The littlest cross-dresser?

THUG DRIVER
Yeah, you know. The one that's always pouting and whining and crying.

LIEUTENANT
They all do that. Even the big ones.

In the back of the van, the Flame Dancer is thrashing and babbling. He looks and sounds a lot like Kara-kun.

THUG DRIVER
This dumb spastic dumped a whole tray of flaming benzine goblets all over himself. He's a tough little guy, though. It happened about a week ago, and he's been hanging on all this time. Looks like it's finally catching up with him now. He keeps begging to be wiped with a special magic spirit oil or something. He says it can only be found at the foreigners' shrine.

LIEUTENANT
Oh, that. Wait a minute.

The Lieutenant reports back to Ishida-san.

ISHIDA-SAN
How was his work?

LIEUTENANT
Fine. While he lasted, he was a pleasure to work with, unlike his bitchy brother.

ISHIDA-SAN
All right. The old priest has enough sense not to make waves. Let the boy go see him. But get back here before dark...

The Archeologist's corpse can be seen, wrapped in plastic and stuffed behind the cement mixer.

ISHIDA-SAN
You've got a little disposal job to do.

The Lieutenant bows ninety degrees and returns to the van. He gets in the death seat and is about to close the door, when --

ISHIDA-SAN
(shouting)
Tell Father I said hello! And give him my best!

EXT. RADIATION RESEARCH FOUNDATION -- DUSK

A Hiroshima city bus pulls into the acid rain-ravaged bamboo grove at the summit of Mount Hijiyama.

Sam disembarks with dozens of aging RADIATION VICTIMS.

Among them are several of the Bums from Peace Park, Sam's pals. He's exchanging caresses with them and trying to buck up their courage to face the horrors of this place.

One by one, everybody but Sam heads for various flapping doors marked --

LIVER BIOPSIES
BLOOD SCREENINGS
FOETAL TISSUE SAMPLES
STOOLS
URINE

The Bums are enticed by ORDERLIES with trays of cold rice balls and cans of cheap chemical beer.

Sam wanders out back and approaches a Quonset hut marked with a sign that reads:

RADIATION EFFECTS CAFETERIA

To reach this goal, he picks his way through a medical wasteland: a forest of mops planted in buckets, sheaves of exposed X-ray film, discarded syringes, etc.

INT. RADIATION EFFECTS CAFETERIA -- DUSK

Sam shudders when Ray Conniff's rendition of "Red Roses for a Blue Lady" hisses down the back of his neck.

He scans the rows of pastel aluminum tables and easily picks out Valentina from among the dozens of INTERNATIONAL RADIATION RESEARCHERS. She's the one waving a bottle of cut-rate plum wine in his direction.

On her table are two ice-filled Mason jars and two bowls of macaroni and cheese. The chairs are the form-fitting fiberglass kind found usually in bowling alleys.

Valentina starts eating with one hand. With the other she pulls snapshots of grandchildren from a handbag and deals them like cards across the table.

VALENTINA

A budding anarchist, that one. But very clever... The words "amoebic dysentery" seem not to be in his physiological vocabulary.

SAM

Huh? Whose -- ?

VALENTINA

You know who I am talking about. Your pin-headed bomb baby virtually subsists on raw sewage. If you're looking for some evidence of mutation, tag a few of his leukocytes and trail them like rafts through his bloodstream.

SAM

There'll be no tagging anything on Kara-kun. He's vanished. I thought you'd heard. It's all over the, um, Christian community, and --

VALENTINA

Anyway, it does not matter. We two are all that matters. Correct? Look at us--

She grabs Sam's arm and pushes his tweed sleeve up to his elbow. She holds out her own equally pale forearm for comparison.

VALENTINA

See? Identical shades. We are the same. "Onaji-da," as the locals so primitively put it. Even our leaders are clones. Ignorant clones both of them. Handsome performers with red ball noses, like in the circus. Just clones.

SAM
Clowns or clones?

VALENTINA
Exactly!

Sam is at a loss for words. Since this woman is obviously drunk already, he swigs down his wine and pours more.

VALENTINA
Yes, now is indeed a time for clones. You and I, Samsha, we can be big blue-eyed clones, too. We must mount a performance. We have a responsibility to let the readers of your hometown weekly gazette know that the cold war is really over, so they can get back to their births, defecations and deaths in a peaceful frame of mind.

She reaches across the table and grabs him by the tweed lapels.

VALENTINA
And we must notify our Nipponese hosts that they are now redundant. A Pacific buffer between our two great Caucasoid civilizations is no longer necessary.

She waves her arm at the surrounding tables.

VALENTINA
These island dwarves are on their way down. Their pitiful spit-bubble has burst. Soon you and I will be riding rickshaws to work, Samsha, and paying the fare with half-smoked cigarette stubs. The natives will dive and scramble to suck the simple carbohydrates from our discarded chewing gum wrappers...

She hammers back her fourth jar with grace worthy of a Bolshoi ballerina.

VALENTINA
This is not Ukrainian "spiritus" in our glasses. Far from it. But, no matter. Friendship is the only intoxicant we need. Together let us now sing the Internationale.

SAM
Um... I never really learned that one.

VALENTINA
So we will sing something else in duple time. Tell me you're not too immature to have heard of Pyotr Seeger. And his smash hit...

They stand up, toast each other, link arms, and sing:

SAM and VALENTINA
May there always be sunshine!
May there always be blue skies!
May there always be Mommy!
May there always be me!

VALENTINA
(belching)
Drink to the first of two centuries on this squalid mountain!

They remain coupled, their bodies swaying with alcohol.

VALENTINA
Now, my Samsha, come, let us visit my personal space. I will show you secret things. One of my so-called patients is waiting just for you!

They lumber to their feet and she leads him drunkenly through the labyrinthine and creepy bowels of the foundation.

INT. VALENTINA'S LAB -- DUSK

The Aging Radiation Victim still hovers over his strapped-down Retarded Sister. The pair of them have been languishing here ever since the A-bomb Golden Jubilee.

VALENTINA
Let us dispose of these miserable creatures. And then -- ah! -- we have so many things to discuss! For example, the amusing pharmaceutical project on which our funny friend from Bangladesh has been working so hard, like a naughty elf... Samsha, as a professor with daily access to classrooms full of, shall we say, potential customers...

INT. SAM'S UNIVERSITY CLASSROOM -- DAY (FLASHBACK)

Sam has his feet up on the teacher's desk. He has a Coke and a doughnut balanced on his belly, and he's dozing off.

Most of his freshmen are asleep, too.

VALENTINA (VO)
...you might be interested in the commercial applications...

Everybody looks like they could use a central nervous system stimulant, except the Male College Cheerleaders.

These junior fascists sit ramrod straight, in full uniform. They seem very angry about their tuition money being used to pay this decadent American to sleep. Some of them look ready to rise up and awaken him in violent ways.

The only thing holding them back is Sam's ominous size, especially juxtaposed with the tiny East Asian teacher's desk. It would be safer to poke a hibernating grizzly bear with a stick.

VALENTINA (VO)
My little brown research assistant already has the high schools, how do you say, "covered." He is ready to graduate, Professor Samsha...

Sam's Nervous Student twitches among the Cheerleaders. He can't stand the tension. He reaches into his pocket and takes out his little bottle of pharmaceutical pills.

VALENTINA (VO)
Of course, as a citizen of the former Soviet Union, I am ignorant as a baby about concepts like supply and demand...

To the boy's horror, no pills are left.

VALENTINA (VO)
But Mamoon assures me there's plenty of the latter at your place of employment...

The Nervous Student scampers out of the classroom in panic, almost awakening Sam.

Out the window, he can be seen scrambling across the campus to the mental health clinic on its brown knoll.

The place is closed. He waves his empty prescription bottle around and kicks frantically at the doors.

Sam snores once and wakes himself up, just in time to spill the Coke all over his belly.

INT. VALENTINA'S LAB -- DUSK

VALENTINA
...I presume that's really why you have come to me, the vanished river tramp notwithstanding, and all coyness aside, eh?

The Aging Radiation Victim's Retarded Sister suddenly lets out a wail, causing Sam to jump.

Squares of red-splotched gauze are draped and patched across her face and neck. She is obviously the victim of out-of-control tissue sampling. Her eyes are full of animal fear.

VALENTINA
Back to work. Come, Samsha! You can assist...

She places her hand on his shoulder.

Sam scrambles for the exit.

INT. RADIATION RESEARCH FOUNDATION -- DUSK

He stumbles through the maze of lightless corridors, trying to retrace his steps.

He passes many labs and sees white-coated Researchers of every nationality and race performing ghoulish procedures on Radiation Victims.

Through drunken eyes, he thinks he sees the Bag Lady being vivisected in a broom closet.

EXT. RADIATION RESEARCH FOUNDATION -- NIGHT

He peers over the mountain's edge, looking for an escape route, then drunkenly lumbers down the slope.

EXT. HIROSHIMA CATHEDRAL -- SAME NIGHT

Sam enters the compound by the side gate, just in time for evening mass. He stands in the shadows for a while, observing Father Gaudi.

Yakuza vans slowly pull up and arrange themselves in somber rows. Father Gaudi weaves in and out among them, dressed in his full-length black cassock, performing his drive-in ministry.

The cannibal hymn seems to filter up from the crypt.

Sam starts to run away, but Gaudi is beckoning him.

He trails Gaudi through the automotive maze, watching him slip the holy communion through van windows to sleepy Filipinas, and bless their slumbering babies.

FATHER GAUDI
I never understood why they hated him so much.

(to Pretty Filipina)
The body of Christ.

PRETTY FILIPINA
Amen.

SAM
Why who hated him so much?

FATHER GAUDI
Did they fear his bringing ritual taint into their weddings?
(to Small Transvestite)
The body of Christ.

SMALL TRANSVESTITE
Amen... Father! You must look in that van over there!

FATHER GAUDI
(not hearing him)
Why do you never join us in the crypt, Dr. Edwine?

SAM
(startled by the abrupt change of subject)
Do you really want to know?

More echoes of the cannibal hymn.

SAM
Because the child inside me is sure I'll find gore in your holy cup.

Gaudi winces. He looks away from Sam and into the rear of a van. Then he winces again, twice as hard.

FATHER GAUDI
I think it is time for you to report back to the Angler's Education Committee, Dr. Edwine.

At first sight, it looks as though Kara-kun is lying back there. But it's actually the Flame Dancer, burnt, ragged and blackened. He nuzzles at the stem of a small pewter opium pipe.

FATHER GAUDI
The body of Christ.

FLAME DANCER
(very weak)
Amen...They are kind men... They give me the pipe to soothe my burns... Please don't be angry with them, Father... Please don't ban them from mass... or Den Mother...

He shudders at the mention of that vindictive demoness, then passes out.

FATHER GAUDI
(whispering to Sam)
I dare not call an ambulance. The police will get involved, and Immigration too. Ishida-san will tell them to deport all the young people from his village. His family will be blamed and the jungle will swallow them up. This child will never see his parents again.

Gaudi grabs Sam's elbow and pulls him out of the earshot of the Thug Driver, who sits in the driver's seat, fidgeting the rearview mirror up and down, checking out Sam's ominous dimensions in reverse.

FATHER GAUDI
We must get him to a private hospital. We need somebody discreet with a car. I'm sure that chauffeur is well armed. But, alone, the Yakuza are unbelievable cowards. On the other hand, his cronies may come out of the chapel at any minute. Where is your car?

Sam shrugs.

FATHER GAUDI
Whom do we know with a car?

EXT. DOWNTOWN HIROSHIMA STREET -- NIGHT

Hank's car unsteadily weaves in and out of traffic.

It's disguised as a standard off-white Japanese sub-compact, but under the hood is an experimental electric motor. The car is silent but for the SWISH of smog against its front bumper, and the light SUCTION SOUNDS of its tire treads kissing the asphalt.

INT. HANK'S CAR -- NIGHT

Sam is wedged into the death seat.

Hank's at the wheel, having been summoned from a party. Obviously high on some sort of stimulant, he's doing a Beaver Cleaver imitation.

HANK
Gee whillikers, Mom. How long before we're almost there yet?

In the back seat, the Flame Dancer is propped and, to all appearances, dying.

HANK
What, no pithy last words? Lawrence the fricasseed martyr said, "I'm done on this side. You can turn me over now."

SAM
Phoning you seemed like a good idea, at the time. To Gaudi and me both.

HANK
You guys were sure eager to dump your difficulties in someone else's lap.

SAM
Turn here.

Hank goes straight.

SAM
The burn-and-trauma clinic is that -- oh. You're going to --

HANK
Boom Town U. Loony Bin.
(laughing)

It's the only alternative. You're one of their sensei: old Doc Edwine, right? So the clinic can't turn this kid away. Do you think any other medics in town would even glance at a mere penniless Flip?

Sam looks in the back seat.

INT. BACK SEAT -- NIGHT

In a random flash from the streetlights, he hallucinates Kara-kun lying there instead of the Flame Dancer.

HANK (VO)
Besides, you're still the Official Emissary of the Angler's Education Committee, and I'm the Chairman...

Kara-kun leers and winks. He waves the Flame Dancer's opium pipe around, and makes dopey faces at Sam.

INT. FRONT SEAT -- NIGHT

HANK
We can snoop around in the varsity whacky-shack, and kill two crows with one stone, if you know what I mean.

As though it's not obvious what he means, he twists his face into a grimace resembling Kara-kun's.

SAM
But this person's not crazy.

HANK
This "person," as you call him, this craven little bugger-stuffer, is on his way out. He's way past the survivable percentage of flambeed body area.

SAM
That's your diagnosis?

HANK
You betcha -- as they say in one's hometown. So it doesn't matter where we

go. We're just doing this to keep Father Gaudi peaceful as possible inside. We Americans owe the old guy that much, after nuking him fifty years ago.

EXT. WEALTHY RESIDENTIAL NEIGHBORHOOD -- NIGHT

On the way to Hiroshima University, Hank's electric car silently prowls through the same elegant lanes that Mamoon visited with Imelda.

INT. HANK'S CAR -- NIGHT

HANK
Can you feel it?

SAM
I'm a solid bourgeois professor, and a husband.

HANK
So what? You can feel it, right?

SAM
It's the duty of a man like me to look blankly across the seat at a man like you, and say... Can I feel what?

HANK
Don't bullshit. We're Americans. Each of us knows exactly what's on the other's mind right now. No further word needs to be spoken. Just rolling blindly through this place, guys with our demographics can feel it.

The car is driving past many heartlessly affluent homes, cold and dead as gemstones.

SAM
All right. Fine. I'll say what you want to hear. Somebody with access to the adolescents of this neighborhood couldn't avoid making a fortune.

HANK
Did you hear how snooty your voice got when you said "adolescents"? You college professors really do consider yourselves a cut above us mere toilers in the teen trenches.

The car passes some High School Students slouching along the sidewalk.

Even though it's pretty late at night, they wear uniforms and carry satchels full of books. They're trudging home from compulsory after-hours cram school, looking exhausted, bored, hopeless and bitter.

Several of them crossed Sam's path at the A-Bomb Jubilee celebration. They are noticeably thinner and sicker now, due to substance abuse.

HANK
The kids are forced to lead such regimented lives. We couldn't find a single teeny-bopper with a free minute to work for us. And, with my white face and Mamoon's brown face, there's no way we could get involved on the retail end. Guys like us stand out like African-Americans at a ski resort.

Hank expects Sam to chuckle at this bit of racism, but he doesn't.

SAM
Why are you burdening me with this?

HANK
(ignoring the question)
So we thought we'd try resurrecting the old myth of the dirty degenerate pusher-man drooling in the suburban shadows...

The Dope-Peddling Bum who served the Baby Sitters' needs can be seen parking his rickety bicycle behind a bush.

HANK

For the sales force, we hire only rootless transients. The homeless don't officially exist in Japan, so nobody sees them. They're especially invisible in swanky neighborhoods like this. Rich Japanese eyes flinch from shabbiness like it was leprosy... And that's where the really big pain in the butt begins. We go through about one-point-eight distribution people per month.

SAM

What do you mean, "go through"?

The Flame Dancer starts to moan and babble deliriously in his native Tagalog.

Hank is unmoved by these sounds of pain and anguish coming from his back seat. He pulls up to the curb and parks, the better to take his time answering Sam's question.

HANK

I mean they disappear. Nobody seems to know what becomes of them. The law never catches them, that's for sure. If our people get arrested, they just fill out the standard apology forms for vagrancy and loitering, and that's as hot as it ever gets. It's not even necessary to pay anybody off. Only the flatfeet from the sub-station get involved, never prefectural police. And the flatfeet wouldn't know paraphernalia if it was jabbed in their jugular. They've been in Ishida-san's pocket for so long, they've forgotten what society's enemies look like. Especially freelancers like us.

(glancing back at the Flame Dancer)

It's really a privilege to live and do business in such a law-abiding society as this, don't you think?

SAM

To hell with you, and Mamoon, both at once.

He reaches his huge hand over the stick shift, grabs Hank by the spiffy brushed-denim collar, and offers to throttle him.

SAM

Enough. Take this child to a doctor.

EXT. HIROSHIMA UNIVERSITY PSYCHIATRIC CLINIC -- NIGHT

The old GATEKEEPER is puzzled at the silent car pulling up. He straightens his gold shoulder-braid and epaulets, and is about to come marching out to intercept the intruder. But he recognizes Professor Edwine through the windshield.

The Gatekeeper bows ninety degrees, and Hank noiselessly guns it over the curb.

Sam grabs the upper half of the Flame Dancer, Hank the lower, and they enter.

INT. HIROSHIMA UNIVERSITY PSYCHIATRIC CLINIC -- NIGHT

They kick off their shoes and step into plastic slippers.

HANK

I hate this ritual.

They pass into the waiting room. Its walls are lined with pheno-barbed STUDENTS, FACULTY and STAFF.

The walls are unadorned gray concrete, moldy here and there. A single-sex toilet is damply squeezed in a corner, its saloon doors affording a full view of the urinal.

HANK

If you ever need to be reminded that you're living in Asia, just visit the doctor.

Sam's Nervous Student is slouched in a chair against the wall. This boy is still dressed in the same WWII-style military uniform that he wore while marching with his fellow fascists on the riverbank. Toxic Ohtagawa mud is caked halfway up his scrawny calves.

A maturely attractive night-shift NURSE observes the Americans' entrance from her post.

She leads them down a gloomy, low-slung corridor to a tatami room, and has them lay the Flame Dancer out on a futon. Sam doesn't forget to gently tuck the boy's opium pipe nearby.

Hank leers at the Nurse, who looks straight into his eyes.

HANK
It's party time, I think.

He drags Sam --

EXT. HIROSHIMA UNIVERSITY PSYCHIATRIC CLINIC -- NIGHT

-- back out to the car, forgetting to put his shoes back on, and ruining his socks on the asphalt. He rummages around in the trunk.

HANK
Seduction kit, seduction kit... where the hell -- ah! Here it is.

He tucks bottles of mescal and absinthe under one arm, then ferrets out a Swiss Army Officer's pocketknife.

HANK
Universal lock pick. Just in case old Lotus Blossom in there doesn't have the key to the medicine cabinet... So, let's misbehave, Mr. Polly.

SAM
Somebody should watch over the boy. You go on without me.

HANK
Okay, go ahead and be that way. Like the syphilitic philosopher said: "What doesn't destroy me makes me horny." Maybe you should sort of poke around for our mascot, just so you can tell

Madame Edwine that you didn't waste the whole night mooning over a crispy corpse.

INT. FLAME DANCER'S TATAMI ROOM -- NIGHT

Sam crouches on the floor next to the Flame Dancer.

He tries not to listen to Hank's voice, which is echoing up the corridor.

HANK (OS)
Everybody knows they've been feasible for years. Why do you think you didn't hear me pull up? That baby parked outside isn't even a prototype. It's just my personal toy...

INT. ANOTHER TATAMI ROOM -- NIGHT

Hank is sitting on a futon, fully clothed. The Nurse is at his side, yawning and bored.

HANK
(very nervously)
...I've personally accepted bribes from a major oil company to help cap the technology. My bosses are all investing in Canada and Siberia. There's plenty of untapped oil up there ready to be sucked off like honey as soon as the tundra melts. So bring on the greenhouse effect! Speaking of atmospheric warming, how do you like these beverages, my dear?...

INT. FLAME DANCER'S TATAMI ROOM -- NIGHT

Sam tries to plump up the boy's rice-bran pillow, and serves him tiny sips from the pipe.

SAM
There, there... there, there...

Gradually, he stretches out on the mats and dozes off.

EXT. OHTAGAWA RIVERBANK -- SAME NIGHT

The Lieutenant and another Thug pull the dead Archeologist from the back of their van, ready to dump him in the water.

Through the darkness comes the sound of a raft being rowed up the river.

They drop the corpse on the muddy bank, cracking its cement overshoes on a culvert. In fright, they run to cower and cringe in the van.

INT. YAKUZA VAN -- NIGHT

Whimpering among blood puddles on the plush-carpeted floor, the Lieutenant rubs and puffs his Shinto fetishes, and tries to bribe his countless gods for deliverance.

INT. FLAME DANCER'S TATAMI ROOM -- NIGHT

Sam is unable to breathe, and unable to wake up.

INT. FLAME DANCER'S TATAMI ROOM -- DAWN

Hank comes to collect Sam.

The Nurse follows. Her hair is a bit disheveled, but only a few centimeters of the absinthe and mescal have been removed from the bottles.

Sam is calling Kay-kay's name in a nightmare. Hank has to stomp on his chest a few times before he sits up, rubs his eyes, and looks around.

Nothing remains of the Flame Dancer but a grease spot.

SAM
What happened to --

HANK
Come on. I've got something to show you.

EXT. WEALTHY RESIDENTIAL NEIGHBORHOOD -- DAY

Hank's car is passing back through, in the opposite direction.

INT. HANK'S CAR -- DAY

Hank is at the wheel, Sam in the death seat.

HANK
So, Edwine, guess who we decided to recruit for our sales force this year.

SAM
(mumbling to himself)
I shouldn't be surprised.

HANK
I asked you a question.

SAM
You son-of-a-bitch.

HANK
You got that right.

He parks just down the block from the Dope Peddling Bum, who's still stationed behind the bush, having camped there.

And, sure enough, Hank is right about Bums being invisible to affluent native eyes. A Teenager's FATHER cruises right past in a silver Mercedes and sees nothing.

Hank is also right about Hiroshima cops. A couple of them blunder by in a patrol car, just as blindly.

A uniformed HIGH SCHOOL GIRL, on the other hand, sees the Bum well enough. She drops her overstuffed book satchel in the gutter, and makes a beeline for him.

HANK
Now, let's pause a moment and have a look at that employee. We've come all the way here to check up on him, so...

Having given little bags of dope to two or three Teenagers, the Bum is trying to collect money from them. They ignore his pleas for payment.

HANK
I could point out countless flaws. But, guess what? There's a certain mutual

pal of ours whose sales technique shares none of those imperfections.

SAM
You're lying. I've seen the natives scatter at Kay-kay's approach. Even the tough Yakuza fear him. They think he's an evil spirit in disguise. Nobody in town could be less suited for your sales brigade than --

HANK
I'm afraid you're wrong about that. The younger generation have shed a good deal of their fathers' superstition. I chalk it up to the wholesome influence of American culture. Take the Keloid Krowd, for example. They didn't fear our mascot in the slightest. And neither did the coddled kids of this neighborhood. In fact...

EXT. OHTAGAWA RIVERBANK -- DAY (FLASHBACK)

HANK (VO)
...they thronged him.

Kara-kun is at his sales position in the bamboo grove which Mamoon and Imelda visited. His raft has been run aground, and the Teenagers are descending on him.

He's fetching Mamoon's designer drug from the superstructure and handing it out in exchange for ten thousand yen bills.

His behavior has a definite dog-like quality. There's almost no human intelligence involved. Someone has taken the trouble to train him very patiently.

SAM (VO)
I couldn't even get the little idiot to hold a fishing pole. How could you and Mamoon teach him to --

HANK (VO)
We employed Pavlovian means.

INT. HANK'S CAR -- DAY

SAM
What the hell is that supposed to mean?

HANK
I'll give you a hint. We needed a woman.

SAM
Oh, Christ.

HANK
No, just a woman. It had to be someone willing to, shall we say, positively reinforce Kara-kun, on cue, every time he fetched bags in response to money in dry runs...

INT. CRYPT CHAPEL -- DAY (FLASHBACK)

Father Gaudi is delivering a homily from the pulpit. Polly prays in the congregation.

HANK (VO)
Figuring we could never afford a native, I personally scoured the crypt one Sunday for a foreign woman.

SAM (VO)
Jesus. Sacrilege to boot...

Hank creeps on his haunches from pew to pew, whispering into the ears of certain FOREIGN FEMALES.

HANK (VO)
Absolute discretion was necessary, of course...

A LARGE THUG is dozing in the front pew. He almost awakens as Hank creeps over his toes.

HANK (VO)
...because neither Mamoon nor I is suicidal enough to tackle Ishida-san on his own turf.

INT. HANK'S CAR -- DAY

SAM
You're not going to tell me you got one of the Filipinas to help you do this!

They're Catholic girls, good and modest at heart, and --

HANK
I know, I know. To do what was required in Kara-kun's case, it took a special type of Filipina...

INT. CRYPT CHAPEL -- DAY (FLASHBACK)

Imelda kneels and weeps devoutly at the communion rail, crossing her matronly bust and fidgeting her rosary with great fervency.

EXT. RIVERBANK -- DAY

Hank's car descends at a leisurely pace, and pulls up at Kara-kun's former sales position. It's deserted.

INT. HANK'S CAR -- DAY

HANK
So, allow me to continue my tale of heartless exploitation of the innocent... A stimulus-conditioned Kara-kun was stationed on his raft behind that very mess of puckered bulrushes, there...

EXT. KARA-KUN'S SALES POSITION -- DAY (FLASHBACK)

The bomb baby is doing his job quite well.

HANK (VO)
...And, not only was he able to do it, but there was something about him, salesmanship or sheer novelty, that actually attracted new kids all the time.

A beautiful NEIGHBORHOOD GIRL is eyeing Kara-kun lasciviously.

HANK (VO)
Hire the handicapped, you know?

INT. HANK'S CAR -- DAY

HANK
Unfortunately, after a month or so, he disappeared with a canteen full of concentrated liquid product. Let's hope, for his sake, that he never takes a sip. His eyeballs would explode and splatter both banks... Needless to say, we'd really like to find him. And, in the meantime, our customer base needs broadening, too. We could use your services on so many levels, Professor Edwine.

He tries to press a roll of money into Sam's hand.

HANK
Mamoon allocated the funds himself. Five hundred thousand yen. Crispy, new banknotes.

Sam looks at the money as though it's a dead rat.

HANK
If you're too pure and good for our money, I'm sure you're not interested in this free month's supply I was about to offer you.

He stashes a packet of dope in the glove compartment.

HANK
But maybe you could see your way clear to accepting this --

Hank hands over a waist-up polaroid of Kara-kun undergoing behavior modification. The curly top of Imelda's head is visible at the bottom of the picture, undulating itself out of focus as she performs fellatio on him.

In Kara-kun's eyes are the first stirrings of self-consciousness, cynicism and greed.

SAM
You were the one pushing me the hardest to find this man...

EXT. KARA-KUN'S SALES POSITION -- DAY (FLASHBACK)

The dope is moving swiftly.

Kara-kun has a strange sneer on his face. His eyes are focused, and he seems to look with contempt at the young addicts.

Suddenly, something startles the Teenagers so badly that they drop their purchases and scramble away through the bulrushes like hunted animals.

SAM (VO)
He was lost before disappearing.

Kara-kun is left alone to face the music.

The male college Cheerleaders come marching along the flood plain in full militaristic uniform, chanting and waving their horrifying banners high.

Somebody forgot to train Kara-kun to be afraid of these young men. He fetches an armload of bags to offer them.

The Cheerleaders are not smiling. They thump their bass drum and scream their fascist songs as they descend on the bomb baby.

INT. HANK'S CAR -- DAY

As if on cue, the same Cheerleaders march up the riverbank and come to full parade rest in the mud about fifteen yards away from Hank's front bumper.

Sam's Nervous Student is among them.

Hank, terrified, slouches way down in the driver's seat.

SAM
Are these the potential customers everyone's been talking about?

The Cheerleaders commence practicing a wild, arm-flailing CHANT in praise of the dead Emperor Hirohito.

Trembling, Hank peeks out from under the steering wheel at the Bulldog-Like Cheerleader.

SAM
They seem to be patrolling the neighborhood.

HANK
You've got to find poor Kay-kay!

SAM
Woe to him who gives scandal to the little ones.

Sam climbs out of the car --

EXT. WESTERN SLOPE RIVERBANK -- DAY

-- and elbows through the Cheerleaders.

SAM
(to his Nervous Student)
Look in the glove compartment. Written report due first period, Monday.

He walks off.

Hank is left whimpering and trying to start his electric motor, as the Cheerleaders close in.

EXT. HIROSHIMA CATHEDRAL COMPOUND -- A YEAR LATER

It's Easter Sunday.

A spectacular WEDDING PARTY is congregating. The bride is Ishida-san's YOUNGER DAUGHTER. She's resplendent in a gown of Belgian lace.

The Filipinas and their Babies have decorated themselves with white lilies. They are still banished to the parking lot.

Sam fitfully dozes in the Mazda among the vans.

An eye pops open. He seems to have been awakened by the squeak of the baby abandonment drawer. He sits up, looks around, and thinks he sees Kara-kun wandering like a little ghost through the churchyard.

It's actually the Flame Dancer. Dressed in frayed clothes, his hands and face deformed by healed-over burns, he looks a lot like Kara-kun.

Ishida-san's Younger Daughter recoils from him and swoons into the arms of her BRIDESMAIDS.

ISHIDA-SAN

The animal's back!

He storms out the main gate, toward a fleet of limousines idling on the street.

The Flame Dancer approaches the Mazda and raps a finger on the window.

Sam, too, thinks it's Kara-kun. He reaches out a hand to verify the existence of this ghost.

FLAME DANCER

(shrinking back)

It looks like we both survived our night in hell, Dr. Edwine. I would congratulate you, but I can't shake your hand. My body is unlucky. The natives won't touch someone who looks as dead as I do.

Ishida-san is in the street, screaming into a limo window and gesturing in the Flame Dancer's direction.

Oblivious to the danger, the Flame Dancer inspects himself in Sam's side-view mirror. Then, bravely, he limps toward the steps that lead down to the crypt chapel.

The congregation below starts singing a hymn, and that stops him cold. He begins to weep.

FLAME DANCER
I want to pray!

Sam unfolds himself from the car and stands by his side, not two feet from the steps -- closer than he has ever gotten.

FLAME DANCER
I'm ashamed.

SAM
They're obligated to accept you. You won't be the first Magdalen they've embraced. See? Father Gaudi is down there all suited up...

Sam thinks he sees, at the bottom of the steps, Father Gaudi waving a crude ceramic chalice around, sloshing blood everywhere. The old priest seems to leer up at him, tongue extended.

SAM
...and he beckons you to be seated. Don't keep him waiting.

The limo door is opening.

SAM
You're only a few steps away from sanctuary.

FLAME DANCER
You never come to mass. If you come, too, everybody will be so surprised they won't notice me.

The cannibal hymn filters up the steps, Polly shrieking on top.

POLLY (OS)
Then serve thyself to Christus Rex...

Eight or nine Thugs are approaching in a tight formation, led by a SUMO-SIZED THUG who is armed with a crow bar.

Ishida-san runs alongside, hysterically urging them on.

POLLY (OS)
Or suffer our collective hex!

Sam grabs the Flame Dancer's arm and is beneath the ground before his knees can lock.

INT. CRYPT CHAPEL -- DAY

Bracing himself for the worst, Sam looks around. It's the first time he's ever been down here. He seems surprised to see no blood spattered on the walls, no gnawed human ribs underfoot.

Polly is approaching the lectern to read the Epistle.

The front pew is occupied by Thugs and Imelda.

The Flame Dancer quietly finds a bench against the back wall. He has barely arranged himself next to Sam, when he suffers a sudden fit of the shakes.

He reaches into his rags, produces his opium pipe, and starts taking discreet puffs.

SAM
What the hell are you doing?... Well, maybe it'll make you nod off. Then I can untangle our elbows and sneak off before Gaudi sprouts goat horns and breaks out the meat cleaver.

A gray haze is gathering. The Foreigners are coughing, glancing back, and doing double-takes as they think they recognize their resurrected mascot.

The Thugs are still oblivious.

SAM
That stinking pacifier of yours has got to go.

FLAME DANCER
But you have to stay with me. Please?

SAM

Listen, if you're hell-bent on making communion, you'll have to shuffle up that aisle under your own steam. Gaudi's goblet might be full of gore.

The Flame Dancer leans against Sam and nods off. Sam punches him, gently but firmly.

SAM

You have to be awake to take the Eucharist.

FLAME DANCER

You may not know it, big brother, but God is in your head. I'll eventually have to put him in my head, too, if I'm going up to Heaven without my body. But for now I need him inside me, here.

The Flame Dancer rubs his belly. He looks sadly toward the front of the church, then down at his rubbery legs.

Father Gaudi reaches out his hand and beckons this small soul toward home.

The Flame Dancer starts to nod off again.

Sam takes his elbow and proceeds slowly up the aisle, his other hand around the Flame Dancer's shoulder.

Behind them, shrieks are heard as the Thugs scramble for the exit in superstitious horror.

The familiar wedding march from "Lohengrin" rumbles down on everybody's heads from the church upstairs.

SAM

Here we go, little brother.

EXT. SAM'S RIVERSIDE APARTMENT BUILDING -- NIGHT

The purple plastic balconies glow strangely in the moonlight.

Sam is brooding on the sixth-floor balcony.

He hears the sounds of someone rowing a raft up the river.

He listens awhile, looking out across the Ohtagawa. A thick bank of diesel exhaust rolls in to obscure the view.

POLLY (OS)
Sammy, suppertime!

He goes in.

A cluster of sticks and weeds floats past. A few crows can be heard not far overhead.

other TOM BRADLEY books:

Elmer Crowley

We'll See Who Seduces Whom
(with David Aronson)

Hemorrhaging Slave of an Obese Eunuch

My Hands Were Clean

Calliope's Boy

Family Romance
(with Nick Patterson)

Vital Fluid

Epigonesia
(with Kane X. Faucher)

Even the Dog Won't Touch Me

A Pleasure Jaunt With One of the
Sex Workers Who Don't Exist in
the People's Republic of China

Bomb Baby

Put It Down in a Book

Felicia's Nose
(with Carol Novack)

Lemur

Fission Among the Fanatics

Hustling the East

The Curved Jewels

Kara-kun, Flip-kun

Black Class Cur

Acting Alone

Killing Bryce

tombradley.org

www.ingramcontent.com/pod-product-compliance
Lightning Source LLC
Chambersburg PA
CBHW050312030726
47505CB00003B/678
* 9 7 8 1 9 0 7 1 3 3 7 1 8 *